*Emily's
Ghost*

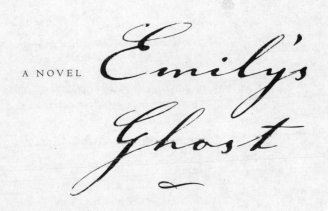

A NOVEL *Emily's Ghost*

DENISE GIARDINA

W. W. NORTON & COMPANY   NEW YORK   LONDON

For information about permission to reproduce selections from this book,
write to Permissions, W. W. Norton & Company, Inc.,
500 Fifth Avenue, New York, NY 10110

For information about special discounts for bulk purchases, please contact
W. W. Norton Special Sales at specialsales@wwnorton.com or 800-233-4830

Manufacturing by Courier Westford
Book design by Ellen Cipriano
Production manager: Anna Oler

Library of Congress Cataloging-in-Publication Data

Giardina, Denise, 1951–
Emily's ghost : a novel of the Brontë sisters / Denise Giardina. — 1st ed.
p. cm.
ISBN 978-0-393-06915-0
I. Brontë, Emily, 1818–1848—Fiction. 2. Brontë family—Fiction. I. Title.
PS3557.I136E45 2009
813'.54—dc22

2009010722

ISBN 978-0-393-33848-5 pbk.

W. W. Norton & Company, Inc.
500 Fifth Avenue, New York, N.Y. 10110
www.wwnorton.com

W. W. Norton & Company Ltd.
Castle House, 75/76 Wells Street, London W1T 3QT

1 2 3 4 5 6 7 8 9 0

*For Phyllis and my other walking companion*

I have read many Brontë biographies over the years. But I especially appreciated Juliet Barker's *The Brontës*, and Barker's willingness to meet with me and answer my questions. Thanks as well to the wonderful Brontë Parsonage Museum; to David Evans at Aitches Bed and Breakfast in Haworth for his hospitality and advice on walking the moors; to Michael Book and the West Virginia Raptor Rehabilitation Center; to Carolyn Sturgeon and the Brontë discussion group at the Kanawha County (West Virginia) Public Library, as well as the research librarians there; as always, to my agent, Jane Gelfman; to my editor, Jill Bialosky; to Colleen Anderson, Julie Pratt, Faith Holsaert, and Arla Ralston for writers' group advice; to West Virginia State University; and in memory of Arline Thorn and John Richards.

The lines from *Antigone* used in chapter 6 are translated by Don Taylor from Sophocles: *The Theban Plays*, Methuen Publishing Ltd., London, 1986; 1991 (reprinted by permission of Methuen Publishing Ltd.).

*No coward soul is mine*
*No trembler in the world's storm-troubled sphere*
*I see Heaven's glories shine*
*And Faith shines equal arming me from fear*

—EMILY JANE BRONTË

# PROLOGUE

Emily Brontë got on with her life as before, except she caught cold more easily. One moment in chains, coughing and struggling for breath, but going about her daily tasks as best she could. Then in an instant Emily would fly, as unfettered as Nero. Free.

But she must warn her father. Dear Papa. She decided upon an afternoon when a light snow dusted the ground so that Haworth, poor, mean Haworth, looked like a sugar-powdered confection. Branwell, her brother, near gone with drink and laudanum, slumped upon the sofa with a book, though he dozed more often than he read. The chores were done, the sisters returned from their midday walk, and Charlotte and Anne had sat down to their notebooks. Emily picked up a sheaf of papers and went with her dog Keeper across the hall to her father's study. Patrick laid down his Bible, which he had been perusing as he studied the lessons he would preach upon that Sunday. Keeper stretched out before the fire with a grunt and fell asleep.

"Papa," Emily said, "I want to speak to you about something very important, but difficult."

Patrick nodded and waited, his hands in front of him on the desk, his fingers touching. Out the window at his back, a pale drifting of snowflakes swirled around the church.

"I don't know how to say it except plainly. And I am sorry for the pain I must give you. But I believe I am dying."

Patrick sat still. His face was grave, but he did not seem surprised. Then he stood, took Emily's hand, and led her to the small settee in the corner, where he drew her close.

"I have thought you looked ill," he said. "You are thinner than ever you were. But how can you be sure you are dying?"

"I don't mean I shall die tomorrow, or next week, or even next year," Emily replied. "I get along, I do my chores and I take my walks. I write." She hesitated and then met his eyes, the right one clear thanks to the removal of a cataract, and the left whose pupil remained milky. "But I am certain I have consumption. I am short of breath. I have coughing spells."

"But should not Mr. Wheelhouse—"

"No," Emily said. Then she added, "Now and then I spit up blood. A diagnosis from Mr. Wheelhouse could be no more clear than that."

Patrick looked at his daughter and was silent.

"I tell you now because I want your promise. I want to live my life as normally as possible. I do not want to be coddled, or protected, as you know Charlotte and Anne will wish to do. I want my freedom. It is my most precious possession, Papa, and I don't want to lose it."

Patrick bent his head suddenly, covered his face with one hand, and began to sob. Emily put her arm around him and leaned her cheek against the top of his head.

"I want you to know something else, Papa. I have written a book. A novel."

"A—a novel?"

"Yes." Emily longed to tell him that his other daughters had written novels as well, but she dared not do so, not until they were ready to tell him themselves. "I call it *Wuthering Heights*. It is in London, Papa, ready to be published. I am nervous to have it so far away, as though I have sent a child off to school." It was not a happy comparison, she realized as soon as the words were out of her mouth. "But I copied a few of my favorite scenes before I sent it off, and I have one of them here." She indicated the sheaf of papers in her hand. "May I read it to you?"

"Yes," Patrick said. He wiped his eyes and sought to compose himself.

Emily began to read the words of her character Catherine as she faced death. "'The thing that irks me most is this shattered prison, after all. I'm tired of being enclosed here. I'm wearying to escape into that glorious world, and to be always there: not seeing it dimly through tears, and yearning for it through the walls of an aching heart; but really with it, and in it. Nelly'"—and here Emily stopped and explained, "Nelly is another of my characters, Papa"—"'you think you are better and more fortunate than I; in full health and strength: you are sorry for me—very soon that will be altered. I shall be sorry for you.'"

Emily stopped and folded the paper. She ducked her head in a fit of shyness.

Tears welled in Patrick's eyes. "Should death be so welcomed, child?"

"Oh, not if one expects a long life, Papa. But if one knows death is imminent, then should it not? And think, Papa. Think who I shall see." She took one of her father's hands, the skin dry and parched, between hers.

"But let us pray," Patrick said, "that the time comes no sooner than it must."

"Oh, no," Emily said. "Besides, I have another book to write."

*Part
One*

I

t night, the door to other worlds opened wide. Emily waited
as darkness fell, so ecstatic she shivered and wrapped her arms tight
about her chest. She was allowed her ablutions first because at age six,
she was the youngest. Though the water in the basin was no longer
frozen as it was in the morning, it was still so cold she blanched when
she splashed her face. She finished quickly, assured that Miss Evans
would excuse her for spilling a few drops on the floor. She was much
more careful when Miss Andrews, who was not so kind, supervised the
proceedings.

Emily was first in bed, which was cold. At home, Aunt Branwell
made certain a warming pan rested between the children's sheets while
they said their evening prayers. No one at the Clergy Daughters' School
tended to such niceties. Though Miss Evans might have, if she had
been allowed. But the Reverend William Carus Wilson dictated what
must be done, not Miss Evans. And he did not allow his charges, as he
called them, to be coddled. His students must submit to the discipline
of God Almighty in order to judge whether they were worthy to enter
the Kingdom. Mr. Wilson's certainty on this point increased in proportion to his absences.

Emily thought nothing of the Reverend William Carus Wilson,

for she had not met him. She did not even wonder about him, so he was not real.

She waited in bed for her sisters. Charlotte arrived to share her bed, wrap her arms around Emily against the cold, twine her legs with her younger sister's, and shiver. Emily breathed on Charlotte's fingers, close to her face, to warm them. They drew the single blanket as close about them as they could. At last their older sisters Maria and Elizabeth clambered onto the cot beside them, likewise clinging to one another for affection and warmth.

As Charlotte's body warmed her, Emily's mind began to wander. The rush candles on the tables cast their shadows upon the walls. The flames wavered, and light danced across the rough stone with each icy draft that blew through the cracks in the old latticed windows. Emily watched and was lost in the movement of light and shadow across glass and stone. When all the girls were settled, the candles were blown out. But often there was enough of a moon to keep the shadows alive.

Then the ghosts came and told the stories.

Emily did not consider their names. She simply knew them. *You*, and *you*, and *you*. *You* lived here so many hundreds of years ago. Before this school. In a cottage on this very spot. And *you* and *you* loved one another, and *you* (in her mind she pointed her finger) were jealous.

The story repeated itself night after night until at last, at their precious half hour of recreation just after tea, she told Maria. It was snowing outside, and dark, so no one went out to play. The girls huddled in groups, glad for a time to talk and even dare to laugh in the schoolroom without adults chastising them. Miss Andrews would be off, in one of her usual foul tempers, to oversee the punishment of some poor unfortunate girl who would suffer most of all from losing this morsel of freedom. Tonight, that girl was their sister Elizabeth. Elizabeth had not been feeling well, she had stumbled over her lessons as she often did and been accused of not paying attention. She was slow, Emily thought, through no fault of her own. But Elizabeth sat in the cold hallway try-

ing to recite French verbs while Miss Andrews stroked her long nose
between thumb and forefinger.

Emily once, after carefully observing this characteristic habit
of Miss Andrews, had asked the teacher if her nose was not so long
because she pulled upon it. Miss Andrews's anger rendered her temporarily speechless but Miss Evans, overhearing, could not help but laugh
aloud.

"Our little Em!" Miss Evans declared. "She is an imp, is she not?"
But at the look on the face of the other woman, she fell silent.

Emily, unnoticed by anyone except Miss Andrews, suddenly narrowed her eyes as if to challenge the teacher. Miss Andrews slammed
shut the book she had just opened and walked out of Emily's hearing,
careful to maintain her dignity. Then she turned and said, barely able
to maintain her composure, "There is something about that child that
is not quite right."

Miss Evans was startled. "Whatever do you mean?"

"I don't care if she is a clergyman's daughter." Miss Andrews glared
in the direction of the child, who had returned to her piece of embroidery. "There is something"—Miss Andrews lowered her voice—
"something possessed about her."

Miss Evans was alarmed for the child's sake, and said no more.
She was careful then to divert the attention of Miss Andrews away
from Emily as much as possible. But one could not change the fact
that Emily, the youngest, was the nursery darling of the older girls.
When Emily was shy, they thought it endearing; when she was over-
come with an irrepressible mischievousness despite her reserve, they
were delighted. And as Emily became more accustomed to the Clergy
Daughters' School, though she could not say she was happy, she became
more outgoing. Especially when she had made her new friends.

At last she told Maria about them. They sat upon the floor, cross-
legged, cradling the small cups of coffee that were their treat for that
time of day. Nothing more would be forthcoming save a small oatcake

just before bedtime. But at least they were warm, the fire in the great hearth banked against the cold. Maria made the Clergy Daughters' School bearable; since Emily could hardly remember her dead mother, Maria stood in her place. Though she missed Papa, she did not mind quite so much being away from home, for there she had missed Maria. Emily sipped her coffee and settled into her story. The white drifts outside kept calling her gaze toward the window, but she never interrupted her account.

"This school was built where their cottages once stood, you see. And their graves are not far from here. But they come back to the cottages because they were happy. Or, some of them were."

"What are their names?" Maria asked.

Emily knew it would have to come to that. She thought, whispering to her friends, What *are* you called? Then she gave a small nod and said, "Henry. And Mary. They loved one another. But Edward was jealous. And one day Henry and Edward were swimming in the pond and Henry began to drown. Edward didn't go for help. He let Henry die." Emily paused to consider the terrible scene, and then said, "Edward wanted to marry Mary when they grew up but she said, Never. And then one night when the moon was full, the devil came for Edward. He rode a black horse up and down past Edward's cottage, and at last Edward was so frightened he ran outside and fell into the pond and drowned just like Henry. And the next day Mary found a rose blooming on Henry's grave, though it was winter and snow was on the ground. She heard Henry's voice saying he was waiting for her. Then she died holding the rose but she is happy because now she is with Henry."

Charlotte had come close and was also listening. She gave a shudder. "I don't know if I like that story. I don't like stories about the devil."

"But it's like Papa's Irish stories," Maria said. "You know how the devil is always showing up."

"I don't like those Irish stories," Charlotte said, looking around at her friends. "Emily is the only one who likes Papa's Irish stories."

"I do like them," Emily agreed stubbornly. "Anyway, the people in my story aren't Irish. They live here."

"They're dead!" Charlotte pointed out. "They don't live anywhere." She shivered again, but more because she was secretly thrilled by the story, and also cold—her seat a bit further from the fireplace than her sisters'—than because she was frightened. Her best friend, Mary Taylor, overheard this last exclamation and came to see what had caused it.

"Emily has told a story," Charlotte said, generously, she thought. "But it is the sort of story you would expect from a child."

Several of the girls were gathering round. Charlotte was glad to see they were all her friends.

Mary Taylor looked closely at Emily. "Your sister Charlotte already tells stories," she said.

"I know," Emily replied. "She makes hers up."

Mary Taylor said with a bit more of a scoff than she intended, for she was at heart a kind girl, "Of course you do too."

Emily started to reply that her friends came to her at night and told her the stories. But she sensed no one should be told such a thing. Not here, not at the Clergy Daughters' School. She was very young, but she must learn to keep secrets that were hers, and hers alone.

Still, to make up for what she feared was rudeness, Mary Taylor asked Emily to repeat her story. Emily complied, and as she began again, other girls joined them, listening intently. They sighed at the final denouement, and several applauded. Everyone agreed that not only was the story fine but that Emily—who also read "very prettily" as Miss Evans noted of her dramatic way with a text—told it with a great deal of presence. Even Charlotte was impressed, and gave her younger sister a pleased hug.

Emily would have gone to bed that night happier than she had ever been at the Clergy Daughters' School. Except that Maria, in the next bed, could not seem to stop coughing.

⋈

The Reverend William Carus Wilson returned the next evening for a residence of several months. He had been away for some time, visiting various wealthy benefactors. Raising money for the school, Miss Andrews said admiringly. His lovely family would not accompany him this time, since they stayed on at the request of their latest host, a viscount. So Mr. Wilson would have more time to devote solely to his poor pupils.

Miss Andrews tried to raise everyone's spirits over the impending arrival. But Emily gathered that no one seemed to like the clergyman, or look forward to seeing him, except Miss Andrews. Even Miss Evans was coolly polite when she spoke of the visitation. She was also nervous.

"My friends all say he is a terror," Charlotte explained to Emily. "So make yourself even smaller than you are."

Emily nodded. Though she did want to see the headmaster. What would "a terror" look like? She would have preferred he arrive at a different time of day. All the girls were disappointed, for his carriage pulled into the drive just as they were to begin their evening recreational time. Instead they must line up to greet the arrival. Miss Andrews, who introduced Mr. Wilson, reminded the girls that here was the authority to which they must bow, the man who had undertaken their education with all its responsibilities, as if she had not mentioned this fact almost daily either in a prayer or an admonition. The girls stood in ranks, oldest to youngest, for inspection. Emily was at the end, the shortest and most restive, though she tried to stand still. The Reverend Mr. Wilson was a tall man of fair complexion, wrapped from head to toe in the furs that had kept him warm on his journey. When he walked, he kept his hands clasped behind him, and peered down from his great height to study the girls. Now and then he put a monocle to his eye to aid his sight, and pointed to some imperfection—a collar folded under or a stray curl peeking from beneath a cap. He seemed to hate and even fear hair, so much did he wish to ensure the girls tamed their own. Emily thought he looked terribly silly, a great bear with a protruding glass eye.

But she froze when he reached the end of the line, leaned down peering through his monocle, and Miss Andrews appeared suddenly at his side. "This is our youngest, Miss Emily Brontë. I believe, sir, that you should speak with her as soon as possible. I shall inform you of the reason after you rest and have a bite to eat."

The Reverend Wilson raised an eyebrow and straightened. "Very well," he said with a parting glance at Emily.

The others sensed Emily was in danger. Miss Evans kept the child's arm in a protective grip all the way to the dormitory that night, and some of the other girls came up to her and hugged her, or patted her upon the back, as she made ready for bed. All three sisters gathered round. Maria and Elizabeth, who had been there longest, already knew about the Reverend William Carus Wilson. But though Elizabeth felt somewhat better, Maria was so ill that the sisters only kissed Emily, climbed onto their cot, and fell into their mutual embrace. Charlotte hugged Emily until she thought the younger girl fell asleep, and then she drifted off. But Emily only waited, and sought guidance from her ghosts. They were mostly silent, but then Henry said, "We don't know what he wants. He is an intruder here. But if he asks about us, just tell him."

Emily nodded, Charlotte's arm around her neck, and fell asleep as well.

❧❦

The next morning Miss Evans was so concerned about Maria that she sent for Mr. Hawthorne, the local physician. Mr. Hawthorne diagnosed inflammation of the lungs and applied a blister to Maria's chest, a burning hot poultice designed to draw out the poison. Maria cringed at the painful application to her chest but then lay still, crying silently.

"She should remain in bed for a few days," Mr. Hawthorne counseled, and left.

But Miss Evans, busy with the welfare of forty other girls, failed to tell Miss Andrews. She also did not notice that Emily slipped back upstairs after breakfast with a scrap of bread she had scrounged from the kitchen when Cook turned her back. Emily considered that she was stealing, but as she left the kitchen with her prize, she was passed by another servant, a large girl with a blotched face named Nancy, carrying a tray with a covered dish. Emily followed down the hall and saw Nancy draw up before a closed door that Miss Andrews had always referred to as "Mr. Wilson's study," though no one ever studied there as far as Emily could tell.

"Nancy," Emily said.

The serving girl turned, startled.

"What do you have there?" Emily asked.

"The headmaster's breakfast," said Nancy, who was in a foul mood because she now had extra work. "And you nearly made me drop it, you did."

"What is it?" Emily asked, eyeing the elegant silver cover she had never seen before.

"Eggs and toast and a rasher of bacon," Nancy replied.

Emily's eyes watered with longing, even though she had just eaten her smidgen of porridge. She considered the crust of bread in her pocket, scurried on up the stairs, and thought no more about theft.

Maria ate her bounty gratefully, but because Emily lingered she was late for Bible study. And because Emily was late, she was caught at once when Miss Andrews, who taught the older girls, came to inquire why Maria was tardy. So Emily watched in horror as Miss Andrews caught Maria by the arm and dragged her from bed, despite her cough and fever and the hot blister that burned her skin. Maria cried out in agony. And Emily reacted as any spirited six-year-old might do upon seeing an older sister so abused. She threw herself upon Miss Andrews's leg and bit her upon one bony calf.

A few minutes later Miss Evans, who had missed her youngest charge when she began the Old Testament lesson for the younger girls, ran up the stairs to look for Emily. She met the party upon the stairs— Maria now dressed though her face was drawn and pale, and Emily, who had been crying and whose cheek bore a vivid red mark. Miss Andrews, in the middle, had a tight grip on each girl's arm.

"Take Maria to my group," Miss Andrews said, her eyes glittering unnaturally. "Tell them to wait for me. I shall be there as soon as I deliver this—" Miss Andrews started to use a pejorative term, but instead only shook Emily's arm sharply. "I shall take this one to the Reverend Wilson's study, and then return to my pupils."

Miss Evans put her arm around Maria's waist for support and watched, her hand pressed to her mouth, as Miss Andrews disappeared down the stairs and into the gloom of the hallway, dragging Miss Evans's "dear little Em" behind her.

⁂

The Reverend William Carus Wilson was finishing his breakfast. He scraped his plate with a piece of toast that soaked up the last of the egg yolk. Then he cut the remains of the bacon into pieces with his knife and fork. Emily watched carefully, her mouth watering. She knew little of money but she did not think that her father, a clergyman like Mr. Wilson, could afford bacon. Mr. Wilson pressed a napkin to his mouth and seemed to notice for the first time the small child staring up at him from beyond the desk. (Though he must certainly have been aware of her presence, for Miss Andrews had made a dramatic entrance and Mr.

Wilson, while ignoring the child, had expressed fulsome appreciation to her. Miss Andrews had blushed as she left the room. Emily watched the pair through narrowed eyes and decided to cast them in a story as demon lovers.)

Mr. Wilson was disconcerted. The child stared up at him steadily, the irises of her eyes seeming to disappear beneath her upper lids, so that the whites predominated, like an epileptic in mid-fit. He paused in dabbing his lips and then let the cloth drop, and gave an involuntary shudder. He had at first thought Miss Andrews overdramatic, but he began to share her misgivings. "Why do you stare, child?" he demanded. "Keep your head down as a modest girl would do."

Emily continued to stare, though her gaze had focused beyond him. She was fascinated by the rank upon rank of books, in shelves from floor to ceiling, their dark bindings scored by gold titles. Emily sensed most had not been taken down from their places in a long time. She thought of books calling to be rescued and of fairies gathering to do the job, scurrying about and toting the heavy volumes upon their backs until none remained. Then the wee folk would leave the books at the foot of the beds of poor scholars.

She was shaken from this reverie by the voice of William Carus Wilson.

"You are Emily," he said in a deep voice. "Your father is a clergyman."

"Yes," Emily said brightly, turning to address him.

"You will speak when spoken to," Mr. Wilson said sharply.

"But you spoke to me," Emily said.

Mr. Wilson regarded her with what seemed to be grave disapproval. He stroked his chin. "Can it be," he said after a time, "that even in a clergyman's family, a servant of the devil may be found?"

Emily was so surprised she could not have answered back even if encouraged. She stared at her interrogator.

"Head down!" he said.

Emily ducked her head and studied the carpet, which was of a deep blue woven with pale pink roses. There was nothing so grand anywhere else in the school. She saw out of the corner of her eye that the headmaster had begun to leaf through a book at his elbow. Then he stopped.

"Emily Jane Brontë," he read. "I see here a notation from your teacher which says you 'read prettily.' Indeed. But do you read faithfully? Or do you vainly bask in your accomplishment, to the detriment of your soul? Do you seek to please God Almighty, or another master?"

Emily stared at the floor, glad now of the admonition to keep her eyes down.

"Answer me, child!"

"I—I don't know what you mean," Emily stammered. She concentrated upon one bloom that seemed to yearn toward a bee.

"I hear you have been telling stories."

The child brightened. "Oh yes," she said, looking up. "They're quite lovely stories."

"Lovely stories about ghosts and fairies and the devil?"

"Oh yes. The ghosts are ever so nice." Emily spoke quickly in her excitement. "Well, two of them are. One of them was quite bad once. But I think he is really very sorry now. And the fairies can be very wicked. But they don't think so. They think themselves ever so clever, and they don't do things the way people do, not at all. They have their very own way of—"

"Silence!" the Reverend William Carus Wilson roared, and smacked his hand flat on top of his desk so that Emily jumped. When he was certain he had silenced the girl, he leaned forward so that he could stare directly in her face. "You, child, are possessed by Satan."

Emily took a step back. "I'm not," she whispered. "I tell stories."

"Do you know what happens to little girls who are not saved?"

William Carus Wilson continued as though Emily had not spoken. "They go to Hell. Only those God chooses to have by his side go to Heaven. Those he casts away shall be cast away forever. I sense, Miss Emily, you are cast away."

A tear formed in the corner of her eye. She wanted her papa, wanted to sit upon his knee and listen to an Irish story. Papa told stories about the devil, and Papa was not going to Hell. Papa had never told Emily she was going to Hell. Papa said God loved Emily. She felt the tear lose its grip on the corner of her lashes and slip down her cheek, so she ducked her head to keep Mr. Wilson was seeing it.

She heard, rather than saw, the headmaster take down a book from the shelf behind him. Some of the books, at least, were not lonely. She waited.

"Here is a story I have written myself," the Reverend William Carus Wilson said in his sonorous voice. Emily heard him sit back in his chair. "My stories are published in this book. Do you know, Emily, how special it is to have a story published in a book?" He began to read the story of a young girl, only just older than Emily, who had sauced an elder, an old uncle who had reproached her for her outspokenness. When chastised for her behavior, the child, named Susan, laughed. But then Susan became ill.

"'She cried to God,'" the headmaster read, "'but God would not listen. Susan, you see, was not one of God's elect. Night after night as she rolled upon her sickbed, she begged for forgiveness. She acknowledged how terrible it was to speak harsh words to her devout uncle. But there was no answer, for God had turned his back upon the reprobate. As he always does. A child can be such a lost one, you see, as well as can grown men. So Susan died, and went to Hell. She cried out there, in agony, but no one cared.'"

Emily heard the book slam shut.

"So you see, Emily, God does not help those he has cast out. Tell me, have you been cast out?"

Emily watched the bee and the rose, which did not move. She fervently hoped she had not been cast out, but it all sounded terribly unfair. She decided to ask Maria. Maria would know.

"Answer me, child."

"I don't know," Emily whispered. "I haven't done anything to be cast out."

"Haven't you? You broke the rules. And you bit a teacher. You have done enough this morning to earn yourself a trip to Hell even if God had not already so determined."

Emily felt dreadfully cold.

"Do you fear you shall end like Susan in my story?" the headmaster continued, his voice thick with unctuous delight. "Or did my story not impress you?"

Emily looked up and met his gaze. In her eagerness to answer, she forgot to be afraid. "It wasn't a proper story at all!" she exclaimed.

It was the clergyman's turn to be astonished. "Not a proper—"

"That little girl Susan didn't tell you that story," Emily said.

"Of course she didn't!"

Emily was excited again. "Then it's not a proper story. It's just something you said. In a proper story the people come tell you everything. Then you just write it down. But no little girl would ever tell a story like yours. I don't believe Susan is real at all."

William Carus Wilson leaned back in his chair, both hands planted palm down on his desk. His face was red. Emily thought for a moment he would flee. Instead he stood abruptly, went to the study door and flung it open, and bellowed, "Miss Evans!"

He turned back toward Emily and folded his arms. When Miss Evans appeared in the doorway, a frightened look on her face, he said, "Dear Miss Evans. This wretched girl is your charge, I believe. Take her now and stand her on a stool in the schoolroom. Keep her in place for half an hour. And inform the other pupils that for the next week, they are to shun her. Explain to them further that their souls will be in danger if they listen to this—this little reprobate and her stories. They should take great care of her."

"But—but her sisters," Miss Evans said, "her sisters must not shun her? Must they?"

"They must. They are in more danger than anyone."

⁊⥙ᴄ

Emily endured her time on the stool. She pretended that because she could not see the other students, they were not there. She considered what it was to be so unusually tall. Someday I shall be tall for good, she thought. Perhaps I shall be so tall I shall be able to touch the ceiling. She decided to write a story about a giantess, the first woman on earth, even before Eve. The giantess said her name was Agatha, and the conversation began. So the time passed rather quickly.

When she was let down from the stool, her sisters Charlotte and Elizabeth sent yearning glances in her direction. Once, as they were putting away their French books and preparing to take up their arithmetic, in a moment when Miss Andrews had gone out of the room to consult with the headmaster, Emily saw Miss Evans draw Charlotte and Elizabeth to her. The teacher put an arm around each girl's waist and whispered in each ear, while looking at Emily. Then Miss Evans smiled, and her sisters smiled.

Emily learned that even Miss Andrews would say nothing if Charlotte and Elizabeth came to her and gave her a hug, as long as they did not speak. Since Emily fancied that she could tell what her sisters were thinking, she did not feel quite so alone. As for the silence imposed upon her, it certainly could not shut the mouths of her friends. The ghosts and the fairies and, yes, the devil were as noisy as ever.

But Emily missed Maria terribly. Maria remained sick in bed. Emily did not see her sister until that night. And very soon, terribly soon, she would not see her at all.

❧

Patrick Brontë was shocked to receive word from the Clergy Daughters' School that his oldest daughter Maria was ill, perhaps mortally ill, and he must come to retrieve her. He set out by coach, leaving his son Branwell and youngest, Anne, in the care of their Aunt Branwell.

"What have you done for her?" he asked Maria's teacher, a Miss Andrews, as he stood beside his daughter's bed looking down at the still, sleeping form.

"The doctor has been here every day," the woman said.

Patrick felt a tug on the hem of his coat. He looked down to see Emily clinging to his leg. "Papa, they haven't done anything," Emily said. "They haven't even given her broth. Or eggs, though Mr. Wilson eats eggs. And Miss Andrews pulled Maria out of bed by the arm and hurt her terribly."

"Why I never—" Miss Andrews sputtered.

"You did," Emily said. "It's why I bit you."

Miss Andrews, after a poisonous glance at Emily, turned on her heel and left. She did not return. Nor did Patrick lay eyes upon Mr. William Carus Wilson, who he was told was off to dinner at the house of the neighboring squire. But Patrick relaxed somewhat when another teacher, Miss Evans, came to tend to his daughters. She was a kind enough woman, and the children seemed to regard her with affection. He studied the girls. Emily had taken Miss Evans by the hand, and Charlotte looked well enough, though worry about Maria had drawn her expression. Elizabeth on the other hand appeared pale and tired. But Patrick put that down to concern about Maria.

In any event, Patrick had already spent more money than he could afford on coach fare, and there was the necessity to hire a conveyance for the return trip. He had enough to deal with to see Maria back to Haworth and to keep her as warm as possible against the February cold. So he kissed each of the others in turn, promised to write every day with news of their sister, and left them to the tender ministrations of the Clergy Daughters' School.

☙❧

For the next three months, the Brontë girls prayed in their bed at night after everyone had retired. They slept three to a bed, Emily wedged in between Charlotte and Elizabeth. She was no longer allowed to tell stories, not even to her sisters. Only to her invisible friends could she speak freely.

The news from home was not good. Their father walked a terrible line—he did not want to leave his daughters hopeless yet he dared not give them hope only to have it crushed. Maria was dying. The girls sensed it, even when Patrick shared with them how their sister included them in her prayers each night, how she asked every Sunday after the service what hymns had been sung, the way she listened when Branwell read to her, and little Anne snuggled with her in the bed to keep her warm. Elizabeth had once heard the school doctor, Mr. Hawthorne, pronounce the word "consumption" after one of his visits. She told this to Charlotte, though not to Emily, who she judged too young.

Then one afternoon the headmaster called the three sisters to his study. They stood on the carpet before the desk. Elizabeth, who had never been in the study and who was by nature the most timid, was terrified but kept her arms around her little sisters to protect them. William Carus Wilson studied them implacably for a moment, and then picked up an envelope that lay on the desk.

"I have a letter from your father," he said, his voice warm not with compassion, but with import. "Your sister Maria has died."

Charlotte cried out and Elizabeth began to tremble. Emily said nothing.

The headmaster waited and then added, "We have written to inform your father that you, Elizabeth, are often ill as well. We are recommending he send for you to return to Haworth." Then the Reverend William Carus Wilson stood and came around the desk. He leaned closer and said to Emily, "Do you understand, child? God has called your sister away. It is your fault. It is a warning to you. If you continue in the devil's ways, perhaps Elizabeth here shall be lost as well."

Elizabeth, who had begun to weep, clutched Emily more tightly.

"God is punishing you, Emily," the headmaster continued. "When you tell stories about the devil, and bite your teacher, you must be punished, must you not? You will have a taste of what Hell is like. If you are one of the lost, you may at least convince Elizabeth and Charlotte to follow in the paths of righteousness."

Emily stared at him. As she stared she called for Agatha the giantess. And then Agatha was leaning down, from very high up. She engulfed William Carus Wilson so that he withered and disappeared like a wisp of smoke. She looked down on Emily and smiled, her green robes flowing about her.

*Did you eat Mr. Wilson?* Emily wondered.

*Of course not,* the giantess said. *He is not real.*

Emily had the strength to look away then. As far as she was concerned, William Carus Wilson had once again ceased to exist.

2

hen Patrick brought the girls home to Haworth, Emily lingered outside Elizabeth's sickroom. Aunt Branwell bustled about the bed, or sat sewing, or nodding, while waiting for Elizabeth to beg to sit up and cough, or to ask for a sip of water. Though Patrick would have much preferred a physician, none resided in the vicinity of Haworth and so the family must make do with the occasional visits of the local surgeon, Mr. Wheelhouse. Emily thought he caused more misery than anything. The smells from the room where Elizabeth lay, the large corner room she shared with Aunt Branwell, were of camphor and blood. Emily noted that when Elizabeth coughed, the cloth Aunt pressed to the sick girl's mouth came away spotted bright red.

Then Elizabeth died. Baby Anne was not allowed into the bedroom where the corpse lay, but Emily was judged old enough for a brief visit. She was just tall enough to see over the edge of the bed. Elizabeth looked like a wax doll, an effigy of her former self. Her freckles had faded. The story people gathered close, whispering sadly among themselves, and then vanished as well.

No one could be bothered with Emily. Patrick Brontë was prostrate with grief and Aunt Branwell, who had been nursing night and day, was exhausted. Yet the adults must husband enough strength to order a coffin and arrange for a clergyman to conduct the service, since Patrick had no will to bury his own children. Branwell and Charlotte, who had always been close, went off to console themselves. And so Emily wandered away to the moors behind the house. The house dog, Grasper, followed her, so she was not alone. She crouched amid a stand of bracken and lay down on her back. The dog settled beside her. It was a glorious day in May, not at all the sort of day when someone should die. Emily smelt the fragrant air, listened to birdsong, and watched the clouds lumber like great elephants across the sky.

*Emily*, someone said, *it wasn't your fault.*

Emily turned her head. She recognized Maria's voice.

*Elizabeth is here*, Maria continued. *She told me what that horrible headmaster said. It wasn't your fault.*

"No, it wasn't," Emily said.

*God wasn't punishing you.*

"No. God wouldn't do that, would he?"

*Of course not. How very silly.*

Emily began to cry. "Maria, will you talk to me every day?"

*No. I've too much to do here. There's ever so much to explore. Elizabeth has already gone on, and so shall I. I wanted to tell you, that's all.*

"Where are you? Where are you going?"

*I met Shelley just now and I'm going to talk to him. After that we shall see. Elizabeth is with Mama so perhaps I shall visit them.*

Emily nodded. It did sound lovely. She would like to meet Shelley someday. She lay quiet for a time and heard voices swirling all round, though she could not make out what they said. Then she got up and went back home to the parsonage. She was hungry and it was time for tea.

Part
Two

William Weightman was afraid of Haworth; his friends in Bradford, for he thought of them as friends —though he knew there was more to it than camaraderie—had been ecstatic. *Perfect for the cause!* various ones had exclaimed. *You could not be better placed. Take a wager which will blow first, South Wales or West Yorkshire.*

After his experiences among the Tyneside coal pits he thought himself ready for an upheaval. But he had his call, one that scalded the soul, to add the white heat of religious conviction to the cause, like his hero William Wilberforce. He thought it propitious that he shared a first name and a set of initials with the great emancipator of slaves. He had not told these thoughts to his bishop, who suggested Haworth as his destination. Perhaps the bishop knew and was secretly sympathetic; perhaps the bishop was oblivious. But he was an instrument of God's call one way or the other.

When William Weightman made his way alley by alley, hovel by hovel, dodging septic effluent as best he could, he stopped to take the hand of a small girl who had wandered out into the air and to wish her good day, making the circuit from Gauger's Croft to Ginnel to West Lane and back to the Black Bull, where, shaking with both fear and a corrosive anger and drenched with sweat, he had another cider and steeled himself for his first meeting with the Reverend Patrick Brontë.

William Weightman was not alone in his anxiety. Patrick had awaited his new curate with apprehension. Several years earlier, after serving Haworth for his entire incumbency, after an unceasing round of baptisms, marriages, and funerals—especially funerals—he had given in to the pleading of his children and sent out a cry for help. He was sixty-two years old and suffered from failing eyesight. The work was more and more beyond him. With contributions from the Pastoral Aid Society (and a bit from his own meager income), Patrick scraped together enough to hire an assistant. The Reverend William Hodgson had proved less than satisfactory. He was a cold and formal man who kept his own company. It was rare to receive Mr. Hodgson for a visit to the parsonage, much less to hear from the poor of Haworth that he had come to call.

Even Patrick did not find much solace in his fellow clergyman. Though he stood as strongly as anyone in defense of the established Church and its privileges, he went for comfort himself, on a Sunday evening when his own duties were done, to the Methodist chapel in West Lane. He found he needed to rest, one of the congregation, and be ministered to. Now and then. He would sit quietly in the back, undisturbed by the preacher—who knew him well and respected him—and pray silently and watch while others sang and wept. The Methodists were not hateful and narrow as were some sectarians, Patrick observed. Besides, they were so close to the Anglicans, like cousins. Their existence, Patrick said more than once, was a reproach to those in the established Church who would turn their backs on the poor. His own dear late wife had been a Methodist before her marriage. Aunt Branwell, who had come to Haworth to tend to the children after her sister's death, had herself just transferred back from the followers of John Wesley.

When the Whig government passed a Poor Law Act, supported by the mill owners, Patrick joined his Methodist colleague in assailing it. According to the new law, the churches were no longer to provide charity—instead the poor, the sick, the elderly, must apply for aid at workhouses. After hours of tedious labor they would receive a daily ration of a potato, a lump of cheese, and a stringy morsel of shredded meat. The timing could not have been crueler, Patrick thought, since many in Haworth were laid off due to a downturn in the market for cloth. He opened his Sunday school building for a meeting, and the weavers and mill workers crowded in.

Patrick faced them and said, "As most of you know, I am a Tory. And this Poor Law has been forced upon us by the Whigs. But I do not stand before you to promote any party. I stand here as a representative of Jesus Christ, to plead for the poor. If hard times should come upon us, and people are deprived of relief, then rebellion may break out as it did in France, and that concerns me as a citizen. I believe this law is contrary to the constitution of England, and that concerns me as well. But most important this law is contrary to Scripture and the teaching of our Lord Jesus Christ."

They interrupted with applause on several occasions and stood at the end to acknowledge him. Other speakers followed, all of them radicals and Chartists. Strange bedfellows, Patrick thought. And Hodgson, his assistant curate, spoke briefly. Patrick had appreciated the gesture of support. He also knew that the man's heart wasn't in it, not really. The crowd listened politely. Patrick sensed from their reserve that they didn't really know the speaker. When Hodgson left two years later to take over his own church in Lancashire, hardly a ripple was felt in Haworth.

Patrick again tried to go it alone. He baptized and he married and he buried. Incessantly. He fell ill himself and took to his bed. When he was somewhat better, sitting up in a chair in his bedroom and looking out the window, Aunt Branwell entered with a bowl of bread and milk. His youngest daughter, Anne, slipped in quietly behind her aunt.

Patrick took the bowl from his sister-in-law and worked to corral a bit of bread with his spoon.

But Anne stepped forward and spoke. In her usual way, she hesitated before the words came, as though she had some difficulty forming them, and then rushed to get them all out.

"You must have an assistant," said Anne. "If my brother and sisters were not from home, they would stand beside me and say the same. Soon I shall be gone for a governess as well and only Aunt will be here to persuade you. Or to help you."

Patrick paused to consider his youngest daughter over his glasses. "And if an assistant is no more help than Mr. Hodgson?"

"You must try," Anne said, her voice warm with resolution. And so difficult it was for Anne to speak forcefully, he knew he must consider her plea.

Patrick despaired of finding a suitable candidate. Most of the clergy he encountered seemed called, as he complained to Aunt Branwell, "to comfort the comfortable and afflict the afflicted." He decided to consult the Bishop of Ripon for a recommendation. "Please," he begged, "suggest someone who might have some sympathy for the poor of Haworth. As for myself, I also could not bear a Calvinist, who would preach the unchristian (to me) doctrine that many people are born damned with no hope of salvation. We all of us here could use a man of hope."

To his astonishment the bishop wrote back at once. "Your letter seems providential, for a young man of my acquaintance is set to matriculate from Durham who would fit your needs quite adequately."

Quite adequately would be more than sufficient, a beleaguered Patrick decided. The spring and early summer had been unusually damp, promising to ruin the peat harvest and leaving Haworth to face a winter short on fuel.

As for Patrick, he was by then overwhelmed by family problems. His son Branwell had been in Bradford seeking a living as a portrait painter but had returned, his venture a failure. Branwell spent an inordinate amount of time drinking at the Black Bull. Charlotte had completed a temporary position as governess and seemed out of sorts and disinclined to seek another. Emily had attempted to teach at a nearby girls' school but fell ill and returned miserable to Haworth. Her father, who feared the ghost of past association with such schools, was not surprised. Only Anne was now gainfully employed at her new position of governess in a local gentleman's house, but she wrote heartrending letters about her unhappiness.

So Patrick waited anxiously in his study after receiving word the new curate would arrive that hot August day. When the knock came, he did not wait for anyone else to answer, but threw open the door himself.

⚜

To open a door to a stranger is to open the door to a new life. Both Patrick Brontë and William Weightman sensed it, though neither was aware of framing a thought. Weightman saw a man of advanced years—thin, gray, and slightly stooped though still tall—with the searching gaze of one whose sight is impaired. Patrick, despite his weak eyesight, could make out at close range a frank, open face, youthful and fresh with a pleasing English blush across the high cheekbones. Brown hair with a hint of auburn, brushed forward in the modern manner, registered in a brief moment. But what touched Patrick, what remained with him ever after, was the warmth of the hand that gripped his own, firm and welcoming. As though William Weightman ushered in Patrick Brontë, and not the other way around.

"You must be—" Patrick hesitated, surprised at his own shyness.

"William Weightman," the young man finished for him, and stopped inside as though he had arrived at the place he would rather be than any other.

And Patrick thought, Here is indeed hope. "Come in, come in," he said, and calling toward the kitchen, added, "Tabby, our visitor is here. We should like some tea, and bread and butter."

The servant Tabby Ackroyd appeared at the kitchen door, a sturdy woman with a smudge on her cheek, her cap askew and a small shovel in her hand, for she had been cleaning out the ashes in the stove when Weightman arrived.

William Weightman said at once, "May I help?" and indicated the shovel.

Tabby gaped at him, so surprised she was that a visitor should ask such a thing. Then she managed to say, "Nay, sir, I have just finished. But thank ye kindly."

Patrick put his hand on the young man's arm. "Come in my study," he said. "We shall talk, and have our tea."

"You are most kind," said Weightman. "It is early for tea. Will it be an imposition?"

"No, no. I expect you will be tired and hungry after your journey."

"I am indeed. Breakfast was far too long ago."

"We shall set that right," Patrick said. "Do you have a trunk?"

"It is just outside. I shall carry it in myself when we are finished."

"Good, good." Patrick indicated a straight-backed chair by the window and took his own seat at his desk.

Weightman made mental notes of the parsonage to judge his new situation. The entryway leading to the kitchen was bare save for several framed drawings on the wall. Patrick's study was also plain, the furniture utilitarian. The only luxury was a cottage piano that stood against the far wall.

"Do you play?" Weightman asked, and nodded at the instrument.

"Not I," Patrick said. "My daughter Emily. You shall meet her, and her sister Charlotte, when they return from their afternoon walk. I have another daughter, Anne, who is away serving as a governess, and the children's Aunt Branwell is gone for a few days as well, visiting a friend. Then there is my son Branwell." Patrick stopped a moment as though searching for words. "He is, um, about. He may be back in time to join us for supper. But most likely not."

"Ah," Weightman said. He waited while Patrick removed his spectacles, wiped them with his handkerchief, and returned them to his rather sharp nose.

"Well then," Patrick began. "The bishop has written to tell me something about you. You are from Appleby."

Weightman nodded. "Yes."

"A pleasant place, I have heard," Patrick continued. "I must confess I have not been to Westmorland."

"It is a quiet farm country," Weightman said, "and not in the way of drawing visitors save those with farm business."

"Is your father a farmer?"

"My father owns the largest brewery in Westmorland," Weightman answered, his eyes downcast. "He is well positioned because of his trade."

Something about the young man's demeanor gave Patrick pause. He made a canny guess. "Is the elder Mr. Weightman pleased with your choice of vocation?" he asked.

"He is not," Weightman said, still refusing to meet Patrick's eyes. "Nor am I reconciled to my father's vocation, which contributes to inebriation, and so a great deal of misery."

The older man tactfully changed the subject. "And you studied at the new college in Durham. I am curious why."

Patrick had indeed been curious at this piece of information from the bishop. He had himself been proud to study at Cambridge, a more welcoming place for evangelicals than Oxford. More welcoming as well for a poor scholar from Ireland, as he had been. His own impoverished background ensured that his curiosity about Weightman's choice of a school was not based on snobbery. But University College, Durham, was new, it was not Oxford or Cambridge, and he wondered what sort of young man might be drawn to it.

But before Weightman could answer, the sound of the back door being thrown open could be heard, followed by women talking and laughing, accompanied by the scrabbling of claws on the flagstone floor. A large dog burst into the study. The beast stopped dead at the sight of a stranger and let out a sharp bark, then seemed to determine that anyone allowed into the sanctum of the study to sit peacefully upon a chair must be a friend. A small ruckus ensued, the dog heading straight for Weightman to offer a greeting and Patrick crying "Emily!" A young woman rushed into the room calling with equal vehemence "Keeper!" She reached for the dog but the animal had already placed its front paws on the visitor's knees and raised himself up. The beast thus arrayed was as tall as the seated man. It offered a slurping kiss, which only partially missed its mark. Emily grabbed Keeper by the collar, but Weightman stopped her.

"It's all right," he said in his quiet, friendly way. "I like dogs."

And the excitement of the moment calmed most wonderfully. Even Keeper grew quieter as Weightman held the dog's head in both hands and tousled his ears. Then the animal dropped down and retreated to the corner where Emily followed him, his collar now held firmly in her hands.

"You shall find Emily to be a great animal lover," Patrick was saying more by way of explanation than apology. "Dogs, cats, birds. They are all in abundance here. Emily is their chief caretaker."

Weightman stood with a more formal greeting for Emily, and studied both animal and woman as he did so. The dog was a brown, short-haired creature of unknown provenance though perhaps with a touch of mastiff. Despite the size it had already achieved, Weightman guessed by its quick, clumsy movements that it was still young. But Emily had wrested the dog away with surprising strength. Now her face was turned to one side as she knelt and addressed the animal—not the people in the room—and though her voice was low, she spoke as intensely and at such a length that she seemed to assume Keeper's comprehension. Weightman could not take his eyes off her, in part because she seemed so immediately to have forgotten his own presence. She was unfashionably tall and thin, gawky as a young colt, and dressed in a plain dress of faded green muslin. Her face could not be called beautiful, nor was it plain. Interesting, he would have described it, with a straight nose, large expressive eyes, and a firm chin. Her hair was disheveled and fell across her face—she brushed it back with an impatient hand and tucked it behind her ear.

"This is my daughter Emily," Patrick was saying. "Emily," he said again to call her attention to the introduction.

She stood then and, with a quick stride toward Weightman, looked him in the eye, thrust out her hand, and shook his own with as firm a grasp as ever he had known in a man. Then just as abruptly she turned and knelt once more beside the dog.

Weightman barely had time to register all this when another young woman, this one short, trim, and rather more buxom, entered the room at a more sedate pace than the first.

"And my daughter Charlotte," Patrick added.

Charlotte's introductory approach was more traditional, a brief curtsy, a small hand extended palm down for him to take and to lean over. Her smile was pleasing but her face was plain, the skin rough, her eyes set at an odd angle so as to be somewhat piercing, and her brow a bit overwhelming. She wore a set of spectacles, which she removed at once as though self-conscious of them. But her warm manner was winning.

"You are Mr. Weightman," she said at once. "I hoped you would have arrived when we returned from our walk. Emily and I have been speculating about you as we took our turn upon the moors. We do so hope you will stay and help Papa."

Weightman bowed and said, "I intend to stay, Miss Brontë. What I know of the situation here inclined me to it even before I arrived."

"Indeed?" Charlotte gave him an inquisitive look. "It is strange that Haworth, of all places, should give such positive advance notice of itself."

It seemed to Weightman that Emily cast a reproving glance toward her sister from her corner. But it was Patrick who replied.

"Mr. Weightman and I are just becoming acquainted," he said, giving Charlotte a significant look.

Charlotte, picking up on his cue, said at once, "Then Emily and I will retire to the parlor."

Weightman, who prided himself on sensitivity, was certain that Emily stiffened in disapproval, though she still focused her attention on the dog.

"For that matter," Weightman said, "I would like to get to know all of you, as I have hopes that we shall be great friends. We shall have tea soon. Could we take it in the parlor?"

Just as he ushered himself into the house, Patrick thought, the new curate had taken charge of the situation. Patrick did not disapprove. And his response told Weightman much about the temper of the man he would assist, and the relationship between father and daughters. "There is more room in the parlor," Patrick said, "where all may sit together and get to know one another. It is indeed kind of you, Mr. Weightman, to suggest it."

So they crossed the hall, the four of them (and the dog, Weightman noted with amusement). Tabby brought a tray of bread and butter and a dish of preserves. And Emily asked, in a strong Yorkshire accent, "Will you have some bread and butter yourself, Tabby?"

The servant glanced at Weightman, then at Patrick, who nodded.

"Shall I slice it?" Tabby asked.

"I shall slice," Emily replied, taking up the knife with an air of some pride.

Patrick said, "Emily bakes all our bread. And yesterday was baking day, was it not, Emily? So this loaf shall be very fresh."

Emily smiled for answer but did not take her eyes from the loaf as she carefully sawed at it. First she removed the heel and set it aside, then cut again and handed a thick slab to Tabby. Extraordinary, Weightman thought, for young ladies of his acquaintance would have given him a carefully chosen first slice on a plate, and along with it a meaningful glance that would have said, See, here is an attainment of mine. He sensed that Emily Brontë wanted no comment from him, that Emily Brontë was more interested in whether Tabby approved of the bread. Charlotte, he also noted, was uneasy, glancing from Emily to Weightman. Then she said, "Emily, should you not see to our guest first?"

Emily seemed surprised. "Oh," she said, and glanced at Weightman. "He seems strong enough to wait."

William Weightman laughed aloud. "And so I am," he said, and when a chagrined Charlotte intervened and handed him a plate of bread and butter, he passed it on to Patrick. "Mr. Brontë, after you."

"Ah," Patrick said, seeing nothing unusual in what had transpired. He set about spreading his butter with great relish.

So the unconventional tea party commenced. The two young women settled upon the sofa—Keeper the dog leaning close against the legs of his mistress—and the gentlemen pulled up chairs. Tabby, after eating her slice of bread with a generous helping of plum preserve, excused herself to tend to the shepherd's pie, made from the scraps of Sunday's roast mutton, that would replace that night's usually meager supper. And Patrick said to his daughters, "I was just asking Mr. Weightman about Durham."

"Oh indeed." Charlotte sat forward on the edge of the sofa. "We are all ears."

Weightman smiled, in part because Emily was busy slipping buttered pieces of the bread's heel to Keeper. All ears indeed. But as he spoke he decided that Emily, despite her seeming inattention, was listening closely.

"You have noted," Weightman began, "that my home in Appleby is a market town in a quiet farming area. But it is not necessarily bucolic. There has been much suffering in the countryside as the common farm laborer finds more often there is no work."

Patrick nodded. "I have read reports in the Leeds papers. There are new machines, and a consolidation of farmlands as well."

"My choice of university may not be all that puzzles you," Weightman continued. "I am twenty-five years old and I have studied in Durham since I was twenty-three."

Charlotte followed where he led them. "We must wonder, then," she said, "where you were in the intervening years."

"Yes, that is my point. My parish priest, who has sent a letter of recommendation here to accompany the Bishop of Ripon's, will have told you, Mr. Brontë, that even as a schoolboy I had an interest in the Sunday school in Appleby, and through it I befriended a number of poor families in the district. I watched them disappear, one after another. As I grew older I learned to anticipate the signs of their leaving, and I learned their destinations before saying goodbye."

Weightman set down his empty teacup, which Charlotte refilled at once.

"I learned that many of our people were emigrating. Their destinations varied—North America, Australia, South Africa. But even more were not going so very far. They were traveling to the north and east, to the coal mining area around Durham and Newcastle. In many cases the fathers went first and then sent for their families. They tended to migrate to the same coal pits, where they would know one another and so have some support. I spoke with mothers, helped them to pack their meager belongings. I composed the letters they dictated—for most could not read or write—telling their men they were on their way. I also read to them the letters they received from Tyneside."

Weightman looked at the floor as he spoke, as though it now pained him to meet anyone's eye. Emily stared at him, her fingers stroking Keeper's ears.

"I gathered from my share in the correspondence that the work was difficult and dangerous, the living conditions horrific. Yet the women listened stoically as I read. I only saw a few quiet tears, even when a fellow miner wrote to say there was no use to come on, for someone's husband was already dead.

"And in nearly all cases, they left anyway. For there was no money, no food, no work, but there were sons to go where the fathers had gone before and perished. By the time I reached my majority, I was determined to go after them, to find where they had gone and reestablish the acquaintance with as many as I could, to see if I might offer some aid, some comfort."

Weightman stopped to sip his tea and chew his bread. He raised his slice and said to Emily, "It is delicious."

She nodded curtly and said, "Mine tastes like straw as you speak."

"I did not mean to put you off your tea," Weightman hurried to apologize.

"I do not chastise you," Emily said.

"So you went to the coal pits of Tyneside?" Patrick asked.

"I did," Weightman said. "Many Appleby families were going to Gravesend. So there I went after them."

"But whatever did you think to do?" Patrick asked. "You were not yet accepted for the Church."

"No," Weightman said, "nor was I even attached to a bishop. But the dissenting sects were there, and I wished to observe them, in particular the Methodists. We were wrong to let the Methodists go. The Established Church has betrayed our people by neglect, sir, I do not hesitate to say it."

"Nor will I contradict you," Patrick agreed. "I daresay you found little of the Established presence in Tyneside."

"None, sir, to our shame," Weightman said bluntly. "But once I had located many families I knew in Gravesend, I settled in. I found a position in a chapel school run by the Methodists, as a teacher. It paid enough to nourish myself and a bit to share. Many of the boys left for the pits and the girls to help their mothers or, when a bit older, to marry."

"As foolish as the weavers' daughters of Haworth if they married young!" Charlotte exclaimed.

Weightman looked at her and said in a gentle voice, "Necessity is a strong motivator. Besides, most do not stay married long."

Charlotte looked puzzled. But Patrick sensed the change in the young man's mood, a growing darkness at variance with the cheerful lad they had only just met. "You were how many years at Gravesend?" he asked.

"Four," Weightman said.

"And why did you leave?"

Patrick was curious what the answer would be, for he thought from his memories of reading the newspapers that he knew. But he sensed also it was more difficult for Weightman to speak.

When he did find his voice, the young man said, "I went to school myself then, in Durham. To be ordained." He looked around at them. "And here I am," he added, the cheer forced back into his voice.

"Well," said Patrick, and clapped his hands, "we are pleased you are here."

When tea was done, Charlotte suggested that she and Emily take the new curate on a walk around Haworth.

"But you have only just come from your own walk," Weightman said. "Are you not tired?"

"No indeed," Charlotte replied, "for our walk today was shorter than usual. Emily and I turned back early in anticipation of your arrival."

Emily raised her eyebrows but said nothing, leaving Weightman to suspect that she had herself been in no great hurry to meet the new man, and the excitement had been all her sister's. His suspicions were confirmed on the subsequent walk round the village. Charlotte often glanced at him and talked in animated fashion. She seemed pleased by the curious stares the trio received, the two Brontë sisters squired about town by a handsome young gentleman. So Weightman—who thought well enough of his own appeal—fancied. They made the steep descent of the high street down to the river where they studied the distant aspect of the textile mills with their chimneys arrayed like minarets.

On the strenuous return up the high street Charlotte walked slowly and clung to Weightman's arm for support, now and then catching his eye and offering a smile. She leaned in close when he spoke because of her myopia—she continued to do without her spectacles to make a better impression. Weightman took note of this, and of her position as the Reverend Brontë's oldest daughter, and reminded himself to exercise due caution, both for the sake of his own position and of Miss Brontë's feelings. He suspected that her feelings would be easily hurt. William Weightman, though he admitted to himself that he enjoyed, more than he should, the attentions of the female sex, had no desire to hurt anyone's feelings.

Emily walked apart. At river's edge she seemed absorbed by the flow of water and the flight of waterfowl. On the steep ascent, as Charlotte labored, or pretended to, Emily went on ahead and then stopped to wait. She said nothing while Charlotte chattered on. Then she caught Weightman by surprise.

They had reached St. Michael's once more, and paused to study the tombs of the cemetery that clustered close about the church and extended up the hill past the parsonage.

"All asleep," Charlotte said. "To wake someday—what do you think, Mr. Weightman? To Paradise? Or some to Perdition?"

Weightman considered. He could not guess the Miss Brontës' views on the subject of the soul's destination. He thought it best to be honest, for he disliked hiding his deepest convictions and he sensed the question was genuinely asked.

"I believe in divine punishment," Weightman said. "But I don't think that means eternal damnation. Hell is the absence of God and is experienced in this life. God is a loving God. If our faith is of any value at all, it is to tell us that. It is beyond my scope to imagine a loving God condemning his creatures to an eternity of torment. But in the end, I leave it to God, as we are bid to do."

Charlotte clapped her hands. "Well spoken, sir. However you are received in Haworth church, you shall be much appreciated by the Brontës."

He thought the expression on Emily's face could be interpreted as approval.

"And where, sir," Charlotte continued, "does the thirst for a punishing God come from? For it is widely expressed."

"Certainly there are passages in the Bible which speak of divine punishment," Weightman said carefully. "Taken literally and out of context, they arouse terror."

"Some people love the terror," Emily said.

Weightman could not be sure if it was what Emily said, or that she finally spoke at all, that he found so arresting. He turned to her and, rather than responding, waited for her to say more.

"People need the terror," Emily said. "It makes them feel alive and important even as they are so frightened. What could inspire more terror than the torments of Hell? And what greater sense of importance? So much personal attention! It is terror that gives lives meaning and makes it bearable for people to live in this world, drab as it is."

"Emily is fanciful," Charlotte said.

Emily looked a clear rebuke at her sister and didn't reply. For Weightman's part, he was so startled the sphinx had spoken that he felt a quick irritation at Charlotte.

"And you?" he asked Emily. "Do you feel that terror?"

Heedless, Charlotte spoke for her sister. "Emily," she said, "is not afraid of anything. Not on earth or in Heaven or Hell. So she claims. Now Anne, our youngest sister, believes as firmly as we do in universal salvation and yet frets for her own soul. As though God would save everyone but her. When you meet Anne, who is the dearest, sweetest creature imaginable, you shall understand the absurdity of her fears. But Emily—Emily fears nothing. Though sometimes she might."

Emily had walked on out of earshot, perhaps a good thing, Weightman thought, given Charlotte's last remark. But she stopped at the corner of the cemetery and waited for the others to catch up.

"Do you know, Mr. Weightman," she said, "the back garden was once full of graves and even the parsonage itself is built over bones. Have you decided not to lodge in the vicinity?"

"I believe," Weightman said, "I am to reside with the Widow Ogden at Cook Gate, where the previous assistant lodged."

Emily looked at him keenly, and then said, "Better for you, then. Your sleep will be much more sound."

She disappeared around the side of the house to free Keeper, who had been tied up at Charlotte's insistence to keep him from following them. They must give their undivided attention to Mr. Weightman on their walk, Charlotte had insisted, without the distraction of a dog.

Odd, Weightman thought. Charlotte had been distracting, and distracted. Emily, on the other hand, had never let him go.

❧

At supper Mr. Brontë mentioned his son Branwell only once, to speculate that he would not be home. After evening prayers in the study, Weightman saw Patrick draw his daughters aside. Weightman stepped into the hallway and pretended to study the assortment of framed drawings on the wall. He saw the names then—the Brontë children were responsible for each scene of moorland, estates, ruined cottages, and animals.

He heard Emily say, "I'll wait up. I don't mind. I want to write anyway."

Patrick's voice was too low for Weightman to understand, but he sensed the relief in it. Then the old man emerged from the study and said with forced cheer, "Well then. It seems Branwell is away, so you shall have his room to yourself. It is at the back of the house, and so it is quiet. Tomorrow we shall turn you over to the Widow Ogden."

Patrick led Weightman upstairs with a candle, saw him settled, and then left him. But sleep, for Weightman, did not come easily. He tossed and turned thinking of the eventful day, his impressions of the village, the church, and most of all of the man he would serve, and his family. He wondered what Emily was doing downstairs, alone, in darkness save for candlelight.

He drifted to sleep at last but a noise woke him. It came from outside—he had thrown his window open to catch the night air from the moor behind the house. Voices drifted up—a man's voice, then a woman's, followed by a low moan.

Weightman peeped out the window, his vision aided by ample moonlight. The woman stood with her back to him, but Weightman knew it was Emily Brontë. Before her stood a large man bearing up the slumping form of another.

"Inside," Emily said. "He'll not go in the house tonight, for we've a visitor in his room."

"The laundry, then?" the man said.

"The mat's in the corner," Emily said. "He's used it before."

The large man disappeared into an outbuilding, dragging the other with him. Emily waited. Finally the first man reappeared, alone.

"Thanks to you, John Brown," Emily said. "He's led us another jolly round?"

"'Deed he has," John Brown replied.

"Get you to bed, then."

Weightman watched as the man disappeared into the darkness. Emily went inside the house. Weightman lay back on his bed, pondering what he had just seen. The insensate man, inebriate, he guessed, was Branwell, whose bed he lay upon. The burden he had sensed whenever the name had come up in Haworth parsonage was now explained.

The door below opened once again. He sat up and looked out the window. Emily Brontë stood there, the dog Keeper with her. She wore a shawl against the night air. To Weightman's astonishment, she walked out the back path and disappeared like a ghost into the darkness of the moor.

Still awake and restless, he heard her return later, heard the door close behind her and her tread, no longer ghostlike, upon the stair.

2

harlotte Brontë was aware, painfully aware, she was not beautiful. When the sisters spoke amongst themselves, she was given to comments of self-disparagement. She lamented the roughness of her complexion and its lack of a pleasing bloom. She criticized her short stature and pointed out that her head seemed too large in proportion to her body. Charlotte was a talented artist and at one time entertained notions of making money with her drawings despite the fact that she was a woman. And yet on the rare occasions when she drew herself, the result was a hideous dwarf of exaggerated disproportion whose gigantic head seemed ready to topple off her body.

"You portray yourself as something monstrous," Anne once protested. "You are nothing of the sort." (Anne, who above all wanted everyone to think well of themselves and be happy.)

"I *am* something monstrous," Charlotte, in an especially foul mood, had retorted.

The longing for feminine beauty extended beyond herself. Once, while straightening their father's room, the girls came upon a drawing of their mother hidden in a drawer. Emily wanted to go to her father and ask him if enough time had passed to dull the pain of his wife's passing, so that they might display the picture. Charlotte would have none of it.

"It is not well done," she had declared. "The artist has no sense of proportion, and the portrait does not show our mother in a flattering light. I shall use it to draw another likeness. A more becoming aspect, as *I* remember she possessed."

And so Charlotte drew the same bonnet and dress, the same profile, on a more conventionally pretty, delicate face. When she was done, she presented the new version to her father, who looked bemused but consented that it should be hung. It was the occasion of one of those rare but titanic fights between sisters. Emily accused Charlotte of disfiguring their mother and hanging a stranger upon the wall, and Charlotte claimed Emily could not recall their mother's true form for she had been too young. Emily in turn wondered if Charlotte, given the chance, would like to perform some macabre surgery upon her sisters, something out of Mary Shelley's *Frankenstein,* to render them "beautiful." She spat the word "beautiful" as though it were a curse. Their fight ended with Charlotte in tears and Emily repentant. But not really repentant.

When the picture was hung, Emily refused to look at it. She placed the original in her father's chest and now and then took it out when she wanted to remember her mother. She also began to pay attention when Charlotte shared with her sisters the stories she wrote about her fantasy kingdom of Angria. In Charlotte's Angria, a hero based upon the Duke of Wellington reigned supreme. The heroines were fetching, the men unable to take their eyes off them. Emily knew it was what Charlotte longed for, an exotic England dominated by a Duke of Wellington who would fall in love with a Charlotte Brontë.

Charlotte loved men of a certain type, with what she called "dash," which she judged the duke to possess. Such a man would want a woman of great allure, and such a woman would draw troops of admirers amongst the opposite sex. Charlotte would have loved to be such a woman, to cut a swath through the eligible males in the neighborhood, high and low, to have dozens, scores trailing after her. She wished to be adored by those she deemed worthy and those she did not. She would taunt the latter with her charms, and then send them chastened away.

The former, who would naturally be very, very few in number, she would entertain. One alone, one worthy above all, she would submit to. Alas, it had no chance of occurring in reality, and Charlotte felt the want.

Still she tried. Emily could only love her sister for the effort. There was courage in it, a refusal to give up the unwinnable fight. In a battle-field warrior, it would be the *Chanson de Roland,* Charlotte raising the horn defiantly to her lips and refusing to retreat in the face of certain death.

If only the cause was worthy. Emily thought men did not merit such heroic effort. Like Charlotte, she wrote fantastic stories. But Emily, leading Anne, created the land of Gondal in the South Pacific. In Gondal, lovers tormented one another. The heroes were women, and they were defiant above all. Emily read the novels of her favorite, Sir Walter Scott, with their jousts and feuds and adventures. The men of Scott's novels were larger than life. Emily's women were as well. In her mind, Emily played the women, and she studied men, looking for one to fit the part of hero. But Emily did not know a man who was not small. Infinitely small.

Emily thought herself no more a beauty than Charlotte. She did not care. She rarely observed herself in a mirror, and she had no interest in fashionable clothes. When Charlotte was at home, Emily allowed her sister to arrange her hair. The tongs resting in the hearth were long and thin like a giant's knitting needles. Charlotte pulled them from the hot coals with a pot holder and wielded them awkwardly, crimping Emily's dark hair into curls that lasted only until the first damp. When Charlotte was away, Emily ignored her hair except now and then to take scissors and whack it off at her shoulders.

Emily did not understand the games men and women played. Flirt-ing was as incomprehensible as Mandarin. What was it for? she wondered. To win the companionship of a creature who was not half so interesting as the dog Keeper. No. Emily wore what was at hand, and comfortable. She said what she felt, and kept silent otherwise. The men whose companionship she craved existed inside her head.

So Emily watched with some bemusement as Charlotte fell into an obsessive infatuation with William Weightman.

"You barely know him," Emily pointed out.

"One can tell!" Charlotte said. "He comes with splendid recommendations from his bishop. And what a kind, genial manner. What a pleasant demeanor and friendly smile." She paused in thought a moment, then added, "One could not hope such a look might be bestowed upon oneself? Could one?"

Emily was tempted to say, No, one could not. She did not like to be hurtful, would only be so when she felt sorely pressed. So Emily kept her silence.

Charlotte marshaled her forces with all the command of her hero the Duke of Wellington. No sooner was Aunt Branwell returned home, scarcely had she set a welcoming cup of tea to her lips, than Charlotte told her of the new curate and begged for an invitation.

"In time, in time," Aunt Branwell murmured, and set the cup again to her lips.

"Soon, soon," Charlotte begged, matching her aunt repetition for repetition. "He is new, he is alone at the Widow Ogden's, and he shall want company. But you can be certain that as word of his arrival spreads, every lady in the district shall be clamoring for him and we shall not see him again."

Charlotte might have added "every young and eligible lady." That she skimped in her description of the ladies who might clamor for Mr. Weightman's attention was not lost on Aunt Branwell. But because it did seem proper to issue Patrick's new curate an invitation to tea, she offered no objection.

The guest list was entirely in Charlotte's hands. Emily was amused to see that it included a few trustees of the parish and their wives, John Brown the sexton and *his* wife, and several of the neighboring clergy and *their* wives (but only those who lacked unmarried daughters). In the entire list, not a single eligible young woman was included save Charlotte and Emily.

"Miss Sugden or Miss Dury?" Emily suggested (provocatively, she knew).

"No, no, no," Charlotte said in a breezy manner. "He shall be bored with them soon enough. Let him have mature company first."

The guests arrived at the parsonage on a Sunday when the last service was done. Mr. Weightman appeared late, claiming he had been held up on the way by stopping in to see how old Mrs. Dobbs was faring. Charlotte, who had been nervously passing round refreshments, melted with relief (though thinking very ill of old Mrs. Dobbs) and took charge of Mr. Weightman while Emily stood by the door and disappeared for long periods to the more congenial company of Tabby Ackroyd and Keeper in the kitchen.

But Emily was in earshot when Charlotte, seated next to Mr. Weightman on the sofa, posed the Question. It was the Question she had caught Charlotte practicing the night before, seated at the mirror in Aunt Branwell's bedroom. Charlotte had refused to be embarrassed or angry, and said mildly, "Wouldn't you like to know as well?"

"I don't care," Emily had said.

"You have normal human curiosity, don't you? Perhaps I am more honest, that's all." Charlotte studied her reflection in the mirror. "One must know where to begin."

"Or end," Emily replied, flopping full length on the bed. "I admit to some modest curiosity about why Mr. Weightman has chosen Haworth. Beyond that, I don't care."

"If the young man is engaged, or otherwise spoken for," Charlotte continued unabashed, "then one might go about being his friend." She turned and looked at Emily. "Without disappointment."

Emily relented, as she usually did. She went to her sister and began to brush her hair.

"Do not chide me for my dreams," Charlotte said softly to the mirror. "They are all that I have."

Emily, who spent so much time in her own fantasy world, had no heart to chide anyone for dreaming. She merely said, "Your dreams are too based in reality."

Charlotte began to laugh. "Sister!" she said. "Do you hear what you say? It makes no sense!"

Then Emily began to laugh as well.

But she did not laugh when Charlotte posed the Question. It was carefully placed, as Charlotte had planned, so it was not the first query posed to the new curate. And it was not an inquiry coming from thin air and thus drawing attention to itself. Rather she slipped it in, her voice admirably casual, when Mr. Weightman spoke of his home, as he was wont to do upon inquiry.

"Ah yes, Appleby," Charlotte said. "And tell us, Mr. Weightman, is there someone in Appleby of the fair sex who holds your affection, someone we might delight in meeting someday?"

William Weightman had the good grace to blush, and Charlotte had her answer. Emily sighed for her sister's sake. Weightman went on to say that, yes, there was a young woman in Appleby he held dear. The ladies in attendance tittered in anticipation while the men sat bored.

"Engaged?" Charlotte asked, nothing in her voice to signal the crashing of her hopes.

"Not exactly engaged," Weightman said. "I have not yet applied to her father, who is rather exacting in that regard. But Miss Walton and I have a mutual understanding."

Mrs. John Brown, the sexton's wife, who was a bit coarse and socially inept, said, "And why do you wait, sir?"

Weightman hesitated. Emily guessed he agonized over his choice of words, and she wondered why. When he did answer, she understood.

"I am very taken with Haworth," he said, "but I am not certain it would suit Miss Walton."

He went on, in answer to more questions, to explain Agnes Walton was the daughter of a landowner of some means. Her father's station was above his own father, who was a brewer, and yet the brewery was quite prosperous. And though their parents' equality in financial terms meant there might be no impediment, still—

William Weightman concluded with a shrug and changed the subject. Emily could picture the consternation in a certain landowning Westmorland family when their daughter's potential husband, despite his father's prosperity, first chose the Church and then took himself off to serve among the hovels of Haworth's weavers.

Charlotte guessed as well, though Weightman's admirable reticence allowed Mrs. Brown and the others to follow him without being offended. That night as she and Emily lay side by side in bed, she scoffed, "So. Gentle Agnes Walton is far too good to be seen in the muddy alleyways of Haworth. You see, Emily, I am not the only person who finds our clime unsuitable for genteel folk."

Emily turned on her side and refused to be drawn into an argument they'd had many times before. She preferred the company of rough folk, when she wanted company at all. The poor of Haworth did not care if she did not keep to a social calendar. Only the better sort, the mill owners and their families, had any expectations, and they had long been disappointed in Emily Brontë. The feeling was mutual, for Emily despised expectations.

She was relieved when Charlotte dealt with her disappointment (more acute than even Emily had realized) in the way she often employed. Charlotte left on a long trip.

༈

A few years after the disastrous early attempt at schooling that ended
in the deaths of his two oldest daughters, Patrick had tried once again.
His three remaining girls would need an employable skill someday,
since they had no money with which to attract a husband. Charlotte, he
thought, possessed a portion of feminine wiles, though it was difficult
for a father to judge. But she was no physical beauty. Some men might
find Emily and Anne attractive. Anne was sweet and quiet, with light
brown hair and a fine complexion. Emily was exotic, dark, lithe, and
mercurial. But both were painfully shy, Anne out of genuine humility,
and Emily obstinately so. Patrick feared none of his girls were likely to
marry. What would become of them when he was gone? A near-fatal
illness had decided him. The girls must make their own way in the
world. To do that, distasteful though it was given their earlier experience, they must be schooled.

Patrick found what he prayed would be a satisfactory place, Miss
Wooler's school at Roe Head. Alas, only Charlotte really took to it.
She studied hard, but just as important, she made friends whose continued interest in her was a point of pride. Charlotte saw a bit of the
world compared to her sisters, even though it might be a small bit. She
had been, to her way of thinking, adventurous. When Emily and Anne
lasted only a few months between them at Roe Head (Emily especially
upset by the confinement and memories of William Carus Wilson),
Charlotte had been pleased. Upon her return to the parsonage, she
taught her sisters some of what she had learned herself over the years at
Miss Wooler's. She never let them forget that she was, of all three, the
most accomplished and worldly.

Patrick might have pointed out that though Charlotte possessed the
most formal education, she had done little with it. She chafed under the
burden of being a governess, and left several positions after only a brief

attempt. Meanwhile Anne, quiet but plucky little Anne, had got herself a position with the family at Blake Hall and plugged away at her duties. She often wrote letters home about the difficulty of managing the rambunctious children in her care. None of the Brontës could imagine Anne enforcing discipline with much vehemence, so delicate was her constitution and so gentle her nature. But she did not leave her post.

Charlotte did not view this as strength. To take the initiative to do new things, to see new places—that was what was most admirable. When, swift upon the initial disappointment with William Weightman, Charlotte announced her intention to spend the autumn with her friends at the seaside, Patrick did not oppose her. The friends were wealthy and Charlotte would travel easily in their company, her expenses taken in hand as a matter of course. Perhaps the exposure might even throw her in the way of some eligible young man, a clergyman perhaps, possessing his own homely qualities and valuing a sharp mind and bold personality over physical beauty or wealth.

So Charlotte went to Bridlington, and Emily tried not to mind. She did not want to go herself. Not really. It would be fine to see the sea. But perhaps not so fine as what she imagined. She would not like to be away from Keeper or the other animals. Besides, at the seaside it would be more difficult to write. Emily carried the larger world in her head, but the doorway to that world opened most easily atop her familiar moors.

The world opened also when she made bread on Wednesdays. Tabby knew not to bother her, but took herself on her errands. Patrick would be in his study, Aunt Branwell at her sewing in the parlor and Charlotte beside her aunt, helping to mend. Branwell would be God knew where, though often upstairs in bed after a night out.

On this particular Wednesday, not long after Charlotte had gone to the seaside, Branwell was away as well, in Bradford with his artist friends. Emily kneaded dough in blessed silence. Her mind was so far away on the island of Gondal that she did not at first notice the knock

on the back door. It sounded again as she reluctantly withdrew her fists
from the mound of dough and grasped the handle with a towel.

William Weightman stood framed by the pale light of an overcast
September morning. But the disposition he brought into the room was
sunny enough.

"Good morning to you, Miss Emily," he said brightly.

Emily, wrenched from her fictional world, fought back a surge of
irritation. She nodded, said "Good day," and went back to kneading
her dough. She thought Weightman likeable enough as curates went,
and she had no wish to be rude. But if he left soon she might return to
the trials of Alexandrina Zenobia as she sought a way out of the prison
cell where she had been deserted and held captive. Emily was caught
between possible solutions. Should Alexandrina languish awhile and
suffer? Was there a way to attempt a spectacular escape? Or should she
beguile her guard with favors (in a way no clergyman would approve)
and then steal away?

Weightman was oblivious to the sufferings of Alexandrina Zenobia. He leaned against the doorframe studying Emily, who stood poised
on the doorstep of her Gondal prison and now stepped back into the
parsonage kitchen. She continued to knead the dough.

"So," Weightman said, "this is the day the wonderful parsonage
loaves are baked."

"Yes," Emily said. She could think of nothing to add, and preferred to ignore compliments, which she considered insincere. She continued to knead. But she wondered what Weightman would make of
her silence. She decided she didn't care, and waited for him to speak
again, or leave.

"Is your brother here?" Weightman asked.

Emily stopped kneading dough and looked up. She picked up a
cloth and wiped her hands. Then she said, "Branwell is not here. He's
in Bradford visiting"—she hesitated—"friends."

"You seem reluctant to name them friends."

Emily was used to being ignored, not questioned by one she considered a stranger. She took a moment to answer, and Weightman waited. Had he not, she would have dismissed him. She told him at last, "I have used a term incorrectly, for I think my brother's companions are no true friends."

Weightman's face was all attentive concern. "May I speak with you," he said, "without troubling your father?"

"It would be better to speak with Charlotte," Emily said. "But since she is away, and Aunt Branwell does not like to talk about her nephew just now, I must stand in."

"Good. It is you I would seek to speak to in any event." He took Emily's frozen astonishment as an opportunity to pick up the chair that stood in the corner and gesture for her to be seated.

"I am not ready to sit," she said, and went back to working her dough to cover her confusion.

So Weightman placed the chair opposite her and took it himself.

"I must tell you," he said, "what I saw on my first night in Haworth when I slept in your brother's room."

Emily's motion slowed. Weightman proceeded to recount what he had seen and heard outside the window that night.

When he was done, Emily said, "I had hoped that you were asleep and we might not be heard."

"I sleep ill in a strange bed," Weightman said.

"So our secret is out." Emily would not look at him as she worked the dough. "It is some relief. But you were right not to mention it to Father. He is at his wit's end with Branwell. He is also ashamed. So his daughters try to keep the worst from him."

"Your sister Anne is away," Weightman observed, "and now Charlotte as well. Your good aunt, I would guess, is not much help."

Emily met his eyes and was touched by the concern she saw there. At the same time, she was not used to it, and so discomfited. She shrugged, covered the pan of dough with a cloth, and set it on the cupboard shelf to rise. When she turned back, Weightman was still watching her with the same expression.

"How may I help?" he asked.

She wiped the table. How might a man help? She didn't know. She said, "I am going out back to feed the birds."

Without waiting for a reply, she picked up a sack with the stale remains of the previous week's bread and went outside. Weightman followed. The geese Emily called by the names Victoria and Adelaide toddled up, as did a bevy of chickens that appeared from behind the washhouse. Emily scattered pieces of dry bread amidst the squawking birds. After a time, she said, "My brother is a poet of modest talent, and a portrait painter, also of moderate ability. He does well enough to make his way precariously in the world with his pictures. But it galls him, you see, that Charlotte and Anne and I possess more talent than he does. It should gall *us* that because we are women *we* are deemed unfit to make our way as portrait painters or authors. For us it is teaching or nothing. But Branwell has the advantage of his sex. It is not enough. It is all our faults, perhaps; we have made over him too much as the only boy. He must paint like Sir Joshua Reynolds or compose poems to match Coleridge. And if he cannot compose to match Coleridge, then by God, he shall match him for sipping spirits in taverns and imbibing opium when he can get it."

"I see," Weightman said, impressed both by Branwell's situation and by Emily's propensity to talk. "And your father has been unable to impress his situation upon your brother?"

"My father is overwhelmed."

"Would you object if I spoke with Branwell?"

Emily looked away. "It would be most kind," she said at last, "if you could take him in hand."

"I have spoken with the Widow Ogden," Weightman said. "She is prepared to take on another boarder. I can keep Branwell under close watch for a time."

"But we shall have to find some way to pay the Widow Ogden," Emily said, doing mental calculations in her head. It was money the family did not have.

"It is arranged," Weightman said. He did not tell her that he had at his disposal a sum of funds sent each month by his father to use at his discretion.

Emily watched the fowl bobbing their heads up and down. Weightman followed her gaze.

"According to Descartes, they are mere machines, with no feeling," he said.

She stiffened, and an angry look crossed her face.

"Of course I do not agree," he hastened to add.

"Nor should you," Emily said. She went back inside the kitchen.

Weightman followed her, finding her change of mood so abrupt he would not have been surprised if she had closed the door behind her and shut him out. She did not, as though she assumed he would come in after her, but neither did she engage him in conversation. Instead she took a second batch of dough, already risen, from the cupboard and set about dividing it into portions for loaves. Without looking at him she said, "Would you stoke the coals in the oven please."

He did as he was asked, while she took out pans, greased them with shortening, and filled them. All was done in silence. Weightman did not know—could not guess—that two times were most precious for Emily to escape into her fictional world of Gondal. One was bread-baking time, which he had interrupted. The second he was now about to trespass upon with all the heedlessness of a child blundering into a spider's web.

"One more thing I was curious about," Weightman said, unaware he was about to squander much of the good will he had created with his solicitude regarding Branwell. "I also saw you leave that night, alone with your dog, and return much later. I wonder, and though I say nothing to judge you"—he held up his hands palm out to emphasize his point—"if it is wise for a young woman, the Reverend Brontë's daughter, to be out upon the moors at night alone. And I wonder, if your father because of his age did not retire so early, would he know and—"

Weightman was going to say "approve." But the word died in his throat. For Emily Brontë turned and regarded him with eyes which, if he tried to describe them for a novel, he would choose a word such as "smoldered" or "blazed" to accompany.

"I am grateful," Emily said in a still voice, "for your concern for my brother. But not even gratitude will allow you to encroach."

William Weightman saw that the interview was at an end. He left, giving the appearance, in his own mind at least, of a whipped puppy.

❧❦

Late that afternoon, Weightman stepped out the door of a hovel in the Haworth slum of Gauger's Croft to see the back of a tall woman accompanied by a large dog disappear around a corner. He knew her at once though he could not see her face.

"Was that not Mr. Brontë's daughter?" he asked old Widow Bland, who was passing by.

"Aye," said Widow Bland. "'Tis bread day."

"And what does that mean?"

"Miss Emily bakes the parsonage bread. They cannot spare much, but she bakes more loaves than they need. Then she goes to Old Dean and gives the loaves to him. And Old Dean knows who stands most in need."

"I did not know Miss Emily visited in the neighborhood," Weightman said.

"Oh, she wanders though she does not much talk," Widow Bland said. "Except to Old Dean. She and Old Dean get on famous." The Widow Bland thought a moment. "Old Dean's dog Robbie is a great friend of hers and that brute that follows her."

"Ah," said Weightman.

"Robbie's a border collie, you know," Widow Bland said. But Weightman's mind was elsewhere.

Several days passed before Branwell returned from Bradford. Weightman gave him time to settle back into his old habits. Then one evening, he left the Sunday school building, where he had been working on his sermon, and walked around the church to the Black Bull.

The inn sat a stone's throw from the parsonage and St. Michael's, at the point where the high street dropped in its sharp descent. Village legend had it that drunkards tottered out of the inn, lost their footing, and rolled downhill, breaking their necks. No one had witnessed this. But mothers used the story to frighten sons who had begun to imbibe too frequently.

The room was hazy with smoke when Weightman entered, but it was not crowded. Weightman ordered hard cider and settled at the bar to study the merry group in the corner that included Branwell Brontë. Branwell, alone among the children of Patrick Brontë, had a large number of friends and loved to be with them. He belonged to the local Masonic lodge and the Conservative political society. Two of his current companions Weightman knew to belong to one of the town's leading mill-owning families, the Merralls. A third was John Brown, the chairman of the Three Graces Masonic lodge and the sexton of St. Michael's Church. Brown sat facing the bar and nodded in acknowledgment when Weightman met his eye. For though John Brown often drank with Branwell Brontë, he also knew, and approved, what William Weightman intended to do.

As for Branwell, Weightman was struck by the contrast with his sisters. If he were to label the women with a single word, he would have named Emily difficult, and Charlotte hungry. He wondered for a moment how he would classify Anne, the youngest, when he met her. In any event, if she was anything like her sisters, there could not be a greater contrast than with Branwell.

The object of Weightman's attention was a smallish young man with a lively expression. His hair was bright red, the most obvious example of their Irish heritage to be found among the Brontës. (Though Weightman guessed that Patrick, now white-headed, might have once possessed the same coloring.) Branwell had a sharp nose, upon which perched a pair of spectacles, thin side-whiskers, and a pointed chin. His face was flushed—Weightman was not sure if from his natural complexion or from spirits. He was laughing loudly at one of his companion's jibes.

Weightman wiped his own mouth, picked up his mug of cider, and walked to the convivial table.

John Brown sprang to his feet on cue.

"Branwell," Brown exclaimed, "have you met your father's new curate?"

They shook hands all round. One of Branwell's friends, Hartley Merrall, said, "So, do the Established clergy drink with dissenters like my brother Stephen here?" Then he poked Branwell in the side. "Branwell does, of course. But then, he is practically a pagan."

"Not so! Not so!" Branwell protested. "I am almost as tolerable a heretic as a Baptist."

The two Merralls laughed uproariously. Weightman could see they were drunk, yet glancing at Branwell, he guessed young Brontë was much farther gone, though the evening was young. The Merralls, who were businessmen, would soon go back home and rise to work on the morrow, not much worse for the wear. Branwell, he guessed, would stay longer at the Black Bull.

Weightman met Brown's eyes and nodded.

The sexton said, "I would think the three of you might calm yourselves enough to pay heed to the Reverend Weightman."

"We shall!" cried Hartley Merrall. "Unlike my brother here, I have stayed in the Reverend Brontë's church, though my attendance is infrequent. The Established Church is, after all"—he searched for the proper word, then gave up—"Established. So, Reverend curate, what have you to say for yourself?"

"In fact," said Weightman, and took a sip of his cider, "I have something very important to say to Branwell, though not until I may speak with him in private." He pushed his tankard away. "By the way, friends call me Willie. And so you should call me."

Branwell, who was easily and inordinately pleased when inebriated, put his arm about his new friend and proclaimed, his voice ever more slurred, "Willie Weightman. An alliterative name. Worthy of a poem. Worthy Willie Weightman. Shall I write a poem about you?"

Weightman smiled. "You may."

"And what would you be in his poem?" Stephen Merrall interrupted. "A romantic hero? Or a highwayman, perhaps?"

"I would be sad, I think," said Weightman. "Tragical even."

Branwell sat back and looked askance. "You? Tragical? No, no, no! Your eye is too bright, your cheek too rosy for tragical."

He waggled only a finger, but the effort nearly caused him to tip over. Weightman realized if Branwell was so far gone, he must act.

"Indeed I am too farcical for tragedy," he said. "That is why I must speak to you, Branwell. Now, if possible. And alone."

"What, now!" Branwell protested. "And alone! But I have room for more gin, as do these fellows, I'm sure."

"These good fellows are leaving." Weightman rose as he spoke. "They have employment on the morrow. And I am in a bit of a rush."

John Brown had risen as well and grasped Branwell by the left arm, while Weightman gently placed his hand under Branwell's right elbow and lifted. When Branwell staggered to his feet, still astonished, Weightman leaned close to his ear and said, "I am in a great deal of trouble. I need your help."

The three men made their wobbly way to the door. There John Brown left them while Weightman guided Branwell out into the crisp night air.

They went for a time in silence, Branwell walking willingly enough but with the air of one who is in a trance. After a time he stopped and protested, "But I shall have lost it, you know. The edge. The knife's point upon which I balance. I shall fall off and be sad."

"I shall let you down gently."

"Where are we going?" Branwell looked around, puzzled, for they were heading along West Lane.

"We're going to my lodgings. But first we shall take the night air and I shall tell you my troubles."

"The night air shall clear my head," Branwell said grumpily, "and therein lies the problem." But still he allowed himself to be led.

Just beyond the village they came to a stile, where Weightman sat and pulled the other man down beside him. Branwell leaned his head back against the stone and turned his head to stare at Weightman. "I can't see your face," he mumbled. "It is in shadow. Can we not find a hearth? And a companionable glass?"

"I told you," Weightman said. "I am in deep trouble and I need your help. It took all my strength tonight to enter the Black Bull and go to you."

"Well then?"

"It is drink. I must resist. That bit of cider tonight called to me, and very nearly did me in."

Branwell began to giggle. "Cider! Good God, man! You are a baby."

"I am," Weightman said. "Weaker than a baby. I need your help." He shook Branwell by the shoulders. "You love your father, do you not?"

Branwell grew quiet. "Of course I love my father."

"Then help me. I am his assistant, and he needs me. But he needs me sober as a judge. Come live with me at the Widow Ogden's. You shall watch out for me, and keep me on the straight and narrow."

"Yes, but—but—" Branwell sputtered, and then lapsed into silence. Weightman waited for him and let him think. At last Branwell said, "What about—what about me?"

"Will you come with me tonight?" Weightman put his hand on Branwell's elbow. "Tomorrow we'll talk and you can decide."

They rose, Branwell swaying but more steady, longing for a drink and yet sentient of the cry for help from his father's curate. They made their way back to Haworth, to the Widow Ogden's off Lord Lane.

3

*I*n December, Anne Brontë came home in disgrace, at least in her own eyes. Her employers at Blake Hall, the Inghams, had asked her not to return after her Christmas holiday.

"I was not strong enough," was all she said. Anne would elaborate no further, but took to her bed. Her fever was high, her cough insistent. The result of overwork and an unusually blustery December, Charlotte assured Anne. But Emily dreaded worse; she feared that Anne suffered from consumption. She took turns with Charlotte and Aunt Branwell at Anne's bedside, until at last her sister began to improve.

The letters Emily had received from Anne over the past months had already given her an idea of her sister's tribulations. Her charges were young children of six and five, a boy and girl, but their tender age belied their capacity for mayhem. "At such an age," Anne had written, "one could expect an eagerness to please. And yet these two will not even sit still long enough to consider *how* to please. Worse, they strike out with feet and fists when crossed in the least."

Now Anne explained as she lay back exhausted from her bout with illness, her blond hair fanned across the pillow, "They would do nothing I asked them to do. Their mother and father stood aside and would not compel them. The children would not sit, they would not listen, they refused to do their lessons and threw paper and pen back in my face. They even ruined a frock by flinging the inkpot at me. My legs were black and blue from their kicks. If I threatened to call their mother, they laughed. When I did speak to their mother, *she* laughed in turn and said the children were *lively*." Anne rose up in agitation but then lay back on her pillow and closed her eyes, while Emily and Charlotte sat at her side with their needlework and heaved sighs of commiseration.

"One day they stole my portable writing desk," Anne said. Her eyes filled with tears, for as her sisters knew, the desk had been a parting gift from their father, and dearly purchased. "I had in its drawer a poem I composed for my own enjoyment. Cunliffe saw me with it and disdained it, so he and Mary grabbed the desk and threw it out the open window."

"Good heavens!" Charlotte exclaimed. "Whatever possessed them?"

Anne shook her head. "Meanness and high spirits. Cunliffe wished to show me how far he could toss my desk, his mother said, since I would not pay proper attention to him. The desk shattered upon the pavement. It was raining. The poem and a letter I was writing to you were ruined as well." She paused to wipe a tear from her cheek. "It was my lowest point, I think. But rather than my tears causing the children to repent, they ran outside in high spirits, got soaked themselves, and their father chastised me for letting them get wet. They would have their deaths of cold because of me, he said."

Charlotte was indignant. "It is appalling. You should have given notice, then and there. The Inghams have failed, not you."

"I lasted two months beyond," Anne said, "by sheer perseverance. Now Mrs. Ingham has the satisfaction of being the one to take action. She says I taught the children nothing, and I cannot manage them. Soon the next child in age was to have been given over to my care. Then I would have three to look out for. It needs someone more capable, Mrs. Ingham said."

"More capable!" Charlotte jabbed her needle into her embroidery ring. "It sounds to me the Inghams need a jailer."

Emily said, "It is a good thing that I have not offered myself for such a post. In your place, I would have tied the little savages to a chair. But it is not fair that the youngest and gentlest of us should be so put upon. You and I, Charlotte, have not offered ourselves out."

"The life of a governess is appalling," Charlotte protested.

"It is indeed," Anne said. "In some ways. And yet it has its satisfactions."

"Enlighten us," Charlotte said.

"In the proper situation," Anne began, "one could have great influence. So many young people have no proper models."

"Especially spoiled rich young people," Emily noted. "And they are the ones whose parents can afford governesses."

"The family needs the money from my employment," Anne said.

Emily set down her sewing and pressed Anne's hand. "We can do without your money," she said. "We can, and we will."

"But," Anne said, "I would not quit so easily. I want to teach, I do. I want a useful occupation, and I want to do some good. Perhaps with older children, who listen to reason, I might do better. Surely a young lady of fourteen would not throw my writing desk out the window."

"And yet," said Emily, "a young lady of fourteen will wish to spend her time catching the eye of a young gentleman, rather than studying Shakespeare and Milton. She may consider knowledge itself as an impediment to her quest. That is what I see in the young ladies of this district. You must consider, Anne, that any family which can afford a governess is likely to produce such silliness."

"Perhaps I should teach at a school," Anne said.

"We should start our own school," Charlotte said with a clap of her hands. "We would be in charge, and set our own hours, and we would only teach girls like ourselves, who loved to learn and who wanted to do something useful with their lives."

They were lost in thought for a time, considering how that might be, and thinking very well of the idea. Though Emily did not wish to leave the moors. She loved knowing every square inch of a place. She loved the way the wind roiled the grasses upon the heights, the company of birds and other wild creatures, the glimpses of fairies out of the corner of her eye. Emily could imagine herself nowhere else, no more than amputating a limb.

Anne said, "Wherever would we find the money to start a school in the first place?"

So that was that. They turned to other topics, in fact, to the topic that most often arose when Charlotte was present—the Reverend William Weightman. Or Willie, as he was now known to Patrick, Branwell, and Charlotte.

Aunt Branwell was from a more formal generation. She could not call a clergyman by his Christian name, much less a nickname, even when he had requested it. Though she admired the young curate very much.

Anne had not yet been introduced to Weightman and so would not give herself permission to think of him as Willie. As for Emily, she held herself aloof. Though she was forced to admit that she rather liked the young curate, she was not yet ready to acknowledge that sentiment to Weightman himself. Liking, it seemed to Emily, must be earned. Once earned, it must be maintained. And while Emily might acknowledge that she approved of William Weightman, and might begin to judge that even an acquaintance with his shortcomings was unlikely to lower him in her esteem to any great degree, she was far from convinced that he might admire *her* in return. Without such mutual esteem there would be an imbalance.

Emily thought well enough of herself. But she was prescient enough to notice, and honest enough to admit, that many others did not. The educated classes in the neighborhood were antipathetic toward her—

the feeling was mutual for she hated their superficiality, their frivol-
ity, and made her dislike plain on the rare occasions she was forced
into their company. Emily assumed the Reverend William Weightman
found her odd as well. That being the case, she thought she would
never call him Willie.

Charlotte, on the other hand, used Willie's nickname at every
opportunity, to prove that she was on familiar terms with a young
and eligible gentleman of great charm. She returned from her time
at the seaside determined to maintain her distance from her father's
curate. But not long after, she learned two things from Emily. One was
that William Weightman rarely mentioned the name of Agnes Walton.
The second was that William Weightman had become a great friend of
her brother Branwell's, and under the curate's guidance Branwell spent
far more time sober than drunk.

"It is a marvel, even a miracle," Charlotte gushed, pleased the conversation had turned onto so congenial a subject. Anne listened and
Emily sewed. "He is a wonder-worker, is Willie. Our wayward brother
is enamored of him."

And so are you, Emily thought.

"But how did he accomplish it?" Anne asked.

Charlotte recounted the story she had told several times before
to those friends she wished to impress with the qualities of the new
curate.

"It is as though he understood our brother even before he began,"
she said. "Branwell is easily led, and enthusiastic, and Willie played to
those qualities."

"Branwell is also kind," Emily pointed out. "And Mr. Weightman
was drawn to that as well."

"However did Mr. Weightman make such judgments," Anne wondered, "when he did not know our brother?"

"His method was brilliant," Charlotte continued. "Branwell does love a cause, and a campaign, and now he sees ushering Mr. Weightman into Haworth society as his cause. He introduces Willie to everyone, accompanies him as faithfully as his hunting dog."

"I think," Emily said, "Mr. Weightman actually enjoys Branwell's company."

Anne said, "Indeed, when he is sober, Branwell is as good a companion as anyone."

Charlotte only half heard. "They are mismatched. No one would say that our brother is a leader of men. Not of any sort. But William Weightman—ah, there is another matter."

"And yet," Emily said, "he is a flirt."

Charlotte waxed indignant. "Why do you accuse him in that way?" she said. "He is high-spirited."

"He is a flirt," Emily repeated.

"On what evidence do you charge him?"

"I first noticed while you were gone," Emily said, "and you should have noted yourself upon your return, except that you are so enamored of him."

"I? Enamored?"

"Yes, enamored. Otherwise you might see how every eligible young lady in the parish puts herself in his way after church."

"That is not his fault."

"It is not," Emily agreed, "except that he encourages it. He lingers with them, leans over their hands which he clutches at length, stares them in the eye with that smile of his, asks after them."

"He is friendly," Charlotte protested.

"He is. And serially friendly. Just when Caroline Dury is all aflutter in Keighley and sure he is set upon her, he will spend his time, and take his tea, with the Sugdens. And by the time the Sugden girls have calmed down, he can be found in a parlor full of young women in Oxenhope sipping tea."

"How do you know all this?"

"I listen to Branwell," Emily replied. "He laughs about it."

"Branwell!" Charlotte laughed in turn. "A reliable source."

"He is now, for he is a great friend of William Weightman, as you note yourself, and he is sober."

Anne had been listening, her head turning to follow first one, and then the other.

Emily clasped Anne's hands and added, "I only wish to warn our youngest sister. You must enlarge no notions, Anne, about the Reverend William Weightman. I speak no ill of him for he is in many ways admirable, a great help to both our father and our brother, and so to us. But I believe he would be dangerous to fall in love with." She glanced at Charlotte as she spoke.

"There is no need to warn Anne," Charlotte said grumpily. "He would have no interest in her, for she is a child."

Emily resisted the temptation to roll her eyes by ducking her head to attend to her embroidery. It was her decided opinion that if, indeed, William Weightman showed an interest in any of the Brontës, Anne would be his victim (for so Emily termed it). Anne was quiet and gentle, she was kind, and she seemed the very essence of the vulnerability that called men to protect. As well she had blue eyes, fine blond hair, and pale skin. Emily could well imagine William Weightman holding out a protective arm to encircle her sister. And it would not be a bad thing if he were sincere. But if he was not, Emily Brontë would most certainly rake out his eyeballs.

The sisters talked until Anne nodded and Emily called Charlotte away. They retired to the parlor, where they sat before the peat fire. Although the window was closed against the cold, sharp sounds from the graveyard could be heard. A shovel chipped at the hard earth; a chisel bit at a blank of headstone. Charlotte went to the window in a state of nervous irritation and stared out. Then she turned and said, "It is our front lawn. The graveyard. We step outside and we are in it. We close our windows against the sound of its maintenance, yet it invades the house."

Emily said nothing.

Charlotte returned to the hearth and sank once more onto her chair. "The house itself is a tombstone. Do you not see it, Emily?"

"I do not," Emily said. She was used to the graveyard in front, as well as the other, more ancient, upon which the house sat. When she walked upon the moors at the back of the house, she felt people with her, striding ahead, lagging behind, catching the crook of her arm with invisible hands, and whispering. The folk who had left their mortal bodies in Haworth churchyard were no more dead than she was. But Emily would not say this to anyone.

Charlotte stood abruptly and began to pace. "I fear Anne has consumption. Do you not think so?"

"I don't," Emily lied. If her younger sister was so afflicted, there was nothing anyone could do. Emily could have pointed out that her father or his curate performed a number of funerals a week, and that the digging of graves carried on incessantly. No one should expect the Brontës to be exempt. Maria and Elizabeth had not been.

Emily only added, "Very few in Haworth live to age thirty. It is not Haworth's fault."

Charlotte pounded her right fist into the palm of her left hand. "Why does Father keep us here?"

Emily continued to stitch. "Being away did not help our older sisters," she said. "Besides, no one cares for Haworth. If they did, something might be done."

"Oh bosh! What could anyone do about this filthy place?"

"Much," Emily said. "If anyone cared."

Charlotte added a block of peat to the fire. Then she said, "It is past time we had Mr. Weightman to the parsonage again. I pray he might keep the chill away."

❧

That Christmas season the Reverend William Weightman was a regular and diverting addition to the Brontë Sunday afternoons. He dined with them after the early afternoon service and then accompanied them for walks upon the moors. Charlotte counted it a great achievement, and a hopeful sign, that Weightman so gladly joined them despite both the material and feminine attractions found among the families of the local gentry. She had hoped the Brontës possessed one advantage in attracting the curate's company—the proximity of the parsonage to the church. After a long morning and two services, Weightman would be glad for rest and refreshment, and the parsonage was next door. It would take a far greater effort to visit, say, the Sugdens or Merralls.

The Brontës had another, greater advantage, though Charlotte did not stop to consider it. William Weightman was inordinately pleased to be invited to the parsonage because he found the conversation stimulating. Branwell's company had been interesting enough, though Weightman found the young man immature; the sisters were infinitely more fascinating. The other families in the district offered an hour or two of tedious pleasantries, embellished with complaints about ungrateful mill workers or descents into local gossip. The Brontës talked of politics, of literature, of theology, and save for frail Anne, they traipsed the moors in all weather.

Weightman noted that while in most families the women retired to another room, not to be seen again, that was not the state of affairs at the parsonage. Patrick, far from the overbearing paterfamilias, was often the most quiet of all. Clearly the old man admired his children and their intellect, and wished to allow them their scope.

Charlotte needed no encouragement to speak out. It was what Weightman admired most about her. He remained aware that she was attracted to him, and she fooled him not a whit by pretending to be coy.

But feminine guile required her silence, accompanied by smiling nods of assent when Weightman spoke. Charlotte, despite her infatuation, would be heard. Nor would she tailor her opinions to suit his. She was at heart a conservative who, even when she recognized injustice, saw no need to address it beyond basic charity. She had little sympathy for the travails of the weavers of Haworth unless, as she put it, they sought to "raise themselves to a level of nobility that only suffering can obtain." Weightman dropped hints that he disagreed; Charlotte did not care.

Weightman was drawn to Anne. She was shy and quiet, and yet he sensed strength beneath her frail exterior that Charlotte and Branwell did not possess. In a different time and place she would have been the humble Christian maid who stepped calmly into a Roman arena filled with wild animals. She awakened in Weightman a great protectiveness. His feelings for her were entirely fraternal.

And then Emily. Strange to think that he, a self-confident, intelligent, and bold young man, might be afraid of a woman. And yet Weightman thought he was. Emily possessed an undercurrent of passion he found unsettling. He doubted her reserve grew from shyness. Emily was feline in her watchfulness, and perhaps as dangerous. Like Anne, she was at first quiet in his presence. That changed, and she entered into seemingly reluctant conversation. He took it for a compliment. Emily weighed him in some personal balance, and then decided he was somewhat worthy of her notice. Though she rarely addressed him directly. When she had something to say, she directed her words to the entire group, not to Weightman in particular.

He decided it was because Emily Brontë did not expect his, or anyone else's, agreement, for her observations were often extreme. Whether the subject at hand was the interpretation of Holy Writ, the foibles of local society, or the plight of the workers of Haworth, Emily invariable staked a claim to the most radical position.

Weightman recalled a particular ramble on the moor above Sladen

Beck when he accompanied three of the younger Brontës and the dog Keeper. Frail Anne remained at home, as she often did when the fierce January cold was at its worst. The party had not even passed beyond Penisrone Hill before an argument commenced.

A number of topics arose and had been dispensed with, including the current issue of *Blackwood's* magazine, and Mr. Dickens's latest novel, *Oliver Twist*, with its depictions of London's unfortunate class. The latter book had formed all the Brontës' recent reading, as it had just become available from the circulating library at Keighley. The general subject thus established, Charlotte asked, "And have you followed, Mr. Weightman, the latest Chartist riots in Monmouthshire?" She glanced, as she spoke, not at Weightman but at Emily, as though anticipating a rise. The entire family did seem to enjoy the sparks that flew when political topics were discussed.

"What a mess!" Branwell added before Weightman could respond. "Were I in the government, I would recommend sending in the troops and giving the rioters a dose of lead."

"Why?" Emily demanded. "For standing up as free men?"

Weightman glanced at her. Her cheeks were red, but whether from the cold east wind or her emotions he could not tell.

"And what do you think, Mr. Weightman?" Charlotte turned their attention back to the curate.

Weightman considered his words, not wishing to be forthcoming, and yet feeling compelled to offer some support to Emily. Truth be told, his position was closer to her own than she knew.

"I think we must remember compassion," he said at last.

"Of course, compassion," Branwell scoffed. "You are a member of the clergy, after all, and a kind fellow. You must show compassion. But someone else must apply discipline."

"Discipline!" Emily cried. "Is that what you call it, to turn loose the most powerful army in the world on poor miners and factory workers as you suggest?"

"Emily," Charlotte reproved, "Mr. Weightman should have a chance to respond to our brother."

Weightman was careful to keep his eyes down, pretending to consider his steps upon the uneven ground.

"Very well," Emily said. "Proceed, Mr. Weightman. Tell us how compassion may be applied in this situation. Would you offer everyone involved a bowl of soup?"

"Indeed I would," he answered cautiously. "And I would hope things might be reasoned out."

"Vain hope," Emily said, "without justice."

"And if you ask Emily what she means by justice," Branwell said, "she will give you some claptrap about men of property being forced to part with their hard-earned bounty and turn it over to the ignorant."

"Have you noted," Emily said hotly, "the peat harvest is off again this winter, and old and young in Haworth are shivering in their hovels as we speak. Obedience will not keep them warm when their masters think of them not at all. Nor will Mr. Weightman's bowl of soup help for more than a few minutes."

"It will keep them working as they should do," Branwell said.

They had come to the headwaters of the beck. A narrow footbridge crossed the frozen water and the path continued steeply up the other side to higher ground. It was their usual stopping point on the shorter rambles they were inclined to in the cold, and they turned to go back the way they had come. But Emily stopped and said abruptly, "I feel like going on." She turned and continued across the bridge.

It was clear from the way she set out that she not only did not expect their further company, she did not desire it. They stood and watched her retreating form as she clambered up the steep hill, Keeper at her side. Unlike her sisters and the other women Weightman knew, she did not wear full petticoats, and her skirt clung to her slender form. He could not take his eyes off her.

"Will she be all right?" he wondered.

"She will go all the way to Ponden Kirk," Branwell said. "She is in one of those moods."

"She will be fine so long as Keeper is with her," Charlotte said. "To urge her to return would only mean she would determine to walk all the way to Lancashire."

"She has a strong will," Weightman observed, somewhat superfluously, he realized.

"Something you must understand about Emily," Charlotte said, linking one arm through Branwell's and the other through Weightman's. "She is a great theorist. She can dream you any sort of philosophy and apply it to a utopia. Practical, she is not. Nevertheless, she will defend her position, untenable though it be."

❧

A few days later Weightman was again invited to the parsonage, this time for a festive supper. Branwell, who at Weightman's urging had been applying for teaching positions, had received a job offer in the Lake District.

"Tutor to a wealthy family," Branwell explained. "And I owe it all to you."

"Of course not," Weightman demurred. "You only needed to apply yourself."

"Yet you inspired him," Charlotte said as she slid an especially thick slice of roast beef onto Weightman's plate. It was a sign of Brontë joy at this upturn of Branwell's fortunes that they served roast beef instead of mutton.

Patrick Brontë looked at his curate over his glasses. "Indeed we all appreciate your good influence."

"Amen," Aunt Branwell seconded. She had grown especially fond of the young curate, who always paid her small kindnesses.

"And you must come for a visit," Branwell insisted. "We shall have some lovely rambles among the lakes."

"You might meet Wordsworth," Anne suggested.

"Indeed I expect some inspiration from the environs myself," Branwell said. "The lakes shall call forth my own poetry far better than Haworth can."

Emily said, "Fine poetry may be written in Haworth."

"I'll have none of your parochialism tonight," Branwell retorted. "I shall see the world even if you do not wish to."

"I do not need to," Emily agreed amiably enough.

After supper they retired to the parlor where Emily was persuaded to sit at the cottage piano and play for them. She was not so technically proficient as Caroline Dury, the daughter of the curate of Keighley, who hit all the most difficult runs with aplomb. Emily sometimes skipped notes, or paused in the midst of a progression, though she covered for herself admirably well. But she also played with a passion Weightman had not heard before in a parlor and only rarely in a concert hall. As she worked her way through a piano arrangement of Beethoven's Fifth Symphony, he found himself leaning forward as though the music were an invisible rope drawing him toward her. Emily, that gangly young woman severe of aspect, seemed to melt, her features transfixed with sheer joy as her fingers coaxed beauty from the piano keys.

Afterward Weightman carried his teacup into the kitchen. Emily, who had disappeared upon finishing her performance, stood stacking dishes in the sink she had just filled with hot water from the hearth.

"You still have chores?" he said with surprise.

"Tabby has gone to bed early with a cold," she answered. "I'll just set these to soak and I'll do them in the morning when the light is better."

She took the cup from Weightman's hand and set it in the tub.

"You play with great emotion," Weightman said.

Emily turned, took up a towel, and wiped her hands. "The world breaks Beethoven's heart," she said. "As it does mine. And so I can play him. Not all composers are so open to me."

"Ah," Weightman said. He was considering a response when Charlotte entered and said, "Come, Mr. Weightman, Emily. We are going to have a game of charades."

And so Weightman and Emily nodded to one another and went to join the others in the warm glow of the parlor.

4

anuary was bitter, for the peat harvest failed and people fast ran out of fuel. Patrick Brontë and William Weightman joined with the clergy of the dissenting chapels to organize what relief they could. But one by one the chimneys lost their plumes of smoke. Families huddled together for warmth, and saved bits of fuel to use every few days to boil potatoes. Otherwise they ate their plain fare, even the oats, cold and raw. They lacked strength to work and yet labor out of doors was preferable to staying in, for at least it set the blood to flowing.

The Widow Bland noted on her journeys to the pump to fetch water that the chimney of Old Dean, who lived around the corner, had been without smoke for several days, as had many others in Gauger's Croft. But she had not noted the old man about on his walks, and the door was shut tight. Nor was his dog Robbie to be seen. A knock on the door roused a sharp barking inside, and scratching at the door. Mary Bland hesitated a moment, then tried the latch. The door swung open with a creak. Robbie bounded out and ran straightway to lift his leg against the side of a wall. The length of his piss told Mary that it had been desperately needed. The dog turned then, ran back inside, and began to bark.

It took a moment for her eyes to adjust to the darkened hovel, but the figure sprawled before the hearth gradually came clear. Old

Dean lay upon his back, one arm stretched across a brick of peat he had been carrying to the cold hearth. Mary could not see his face, but she doubted not what she would find. She was poorly in her knees and no longer able to walk far. So she hobbled home and dispatched her grandchildren, Susan and Samuel, one to fetch the surgeon, Mr. Wheelhouse, the other to the parsonage.

Little Susan Bland did not quite reach the parsonage for she first encountered William Weightman walking to the Sunday school. He kept his books and writing materials in a cubbyhole off the main class-room, and there he prepared his sermons and the lessons he taught the children. His mind was on John Donne, for he had an idea to teach the Holy Sonnets to the older pupils. But the cries of Susan Bland inter-rupted his reverie, and he altered his route, the child's small cold hand in his large one, to Gauger's Croft.

It took only a cursory examination to tell Weightman the old man was dead. He had already prayed with Mary and Susan Bland when Samuel arrived with Mr. Wheelhouse. The surgeon must make his own examination while Robbie paced back and forth before the cot on which they laid the corpse. The dog paused to watch suspiciously as Mr. Wheelhouse poked and prodded the still form of his master. He gave a low anxious whine. Suddenly he turned, barked a high joy-ful yelp, and ran to the door where two figures stood blocking out the light. One was a large dog, which came forward at once to greet Robbie. The other was a woman, her silhouette black against the sun-lit doorway. When she stepped forward into the room, Weightman recognized Emily Brontë.

She held a basket which she dropped as she entered the room. It was full of bread and the loaves tumbled across to the hearth. She ignored Robbie, who was joyful at her approach and ran frantically between the woman and her dog as though imploring them for help. Mr. Wheelhouse, just finishing his examination, nodded to her and said, "Miss Emily."

Emily leaned closer in the gloom and stared at Old Dean, then stifled a sudden sob and turned away, her hand pressed to her mouth.

"Either his heart stopped or he suffered a hemorrhage in his brain," Wheelhouse was saying. "It makes no difference which, I suppose." He glanced at the corpse. "He was a hard old man, and I daresay he lived longer than many of us shall."

Emily gave another sob and then mastered herself. She turned to Mr. Wheelhouse and said, "I'm glad he died before you got here."

Her tone of voice was not malicious, merely matter-of-fact. But Wheelhouse took clear offense. "Why is that?" he said sharply.

"Because you would have bled him," she said, her voice flat. "And it would have done no good."

"Please, Miss Emily, do not criticize me for doing the best that can be done. I cannot help Haworth has no physician."

Emily stood, her arms folded and her face turned away. "I do not criticize you," she said. "A physician would do no more good than you do. I simply do not want any of you around if I am taken ill."

Mr. Wheelhouse acted as though he wished to respond and then thought better of it. He picked up his surgeon's bag, put on his hat, gave a nod to Weightman, and left.

Young Susan Bland, a thin, sickly child, commenced to cry. Her brother stood looking down, his hands in his pockets. Weightman bent and picked up the brick of peat that lay where Old Dean had dropped it. He handed it to Samuel.

"Take this home with you," he said. "It's likely the last divot of peat in Haworth. I know Old Dean would want you to have it for this last act of kindness."

The Blands thanked him and the Widow asked what should be done.

"I shall see to the burying," Weightman replied. "It shall be tomorrow and we will post the time at the church."

"He will have his mourners," Mary Bland said. "He was much

loved in this neighborhood." She turned to Emily. "And thank you, Miss, for the bread he brought round."

Emily nodded and did not reply. She had grown so quiet and withdrawn that the shadows seemed to have devoured her. But when the Blands had taken their leave, she spoke. "You said a prayer?"

Weightman answered, "I did." Then he thought he should offer more comfort. "I'm sorry. I didn't know you were close to him."

"Do you know it now?" she said. "I can't say that I was. Only he told me stories of the moors, and I remembered them. That is all."

"You wept for him," Weightman pointed out.

Emily said, "I shall not weep again in front of others. I shed tears when I am alone. But to weep before others is terrible."

Weightman could not think what to say. Hers might have been an acceptable answer from a man. From a woman it was decidedly odd. And yet he was touched as she took up the lone blanket in the room and spread it over the old man, covering his face, and went on to gather up the loaves of bread scattered across the floor.

"If you like," Weightman offered, "I shall take Old Dean's place with your bread. I too know who stands in great need."

He expected her to reject him, but instead she handed him the replenished basket and said, "I shall hold you to that promise, Mr. Weightman."

Weightman felt as though he had passed some test. He accepted the basket. He was about to suggest that Emily return home while he saw to the arrangement of coffin and gravedigging. But she went to kneel beside the collie dog and wrapped her arms around his neck.

"What shall become of Robbie?" she cried. "Poor, poor Robbie."

Weightman set down the bread basket, knelt beside her, and stroked the dog's head. "Will he leave the corpse, do you think?"

"He will not."

"He will be hungry."

"Oh, he will be. I shall go home at once and bring him something to eat." Emily turned to Weightman. "He must go to the burial. He must."

"He shall," Weightman agreed. "And then?"

Emily joined Weightman in stroking the dog. "Perhaps we can keep him at the parsonage. Perhaps he will stay with us."

"He knows Gauger's Croft," Weightman said thoughtfully. "How old would you reckon him?"

"Old," she replied. "You see how he hobbles about. Old Dean told me once that Robbie was eleven, and that was more than a year ago."

Weightman thought quickly. Then he said, "The Widow Ogden has said I might have a dog about. I am often in Gauger's Croft, and Robbie could join me on my rounds and see people he knows. He could rest at my feet at the Sunday school or wander the churchyard if he wanted to visit his master's grave. Then he could come in safety with me to Cook Gate."

Emily leaned back. "It would be so kind of you," she said with more feeling than Weightman had ever heard from her. "And we could help at the parsonage as well. Old Dean would not want Robbie put down early, or to wander friendless."

"Very well, then," Weightman said with a smile. "I shall leave you to tend Robbie now, and I shall take him in hand tomorrow after the burial."

He stood to leave. As he reached the door, Emily called, "Mr. Weightman. Thank you."

He paused. Then he nodded and said, "Miss Emily," and went out into the sunlight.

❧

On the morning of Old Dean's burial, the skies opened over Haworth, a cold relentless rain on the verge of freezing. A crowd of mourners trudged up the hill from Gauger's Croft to the church, where Old Dean's body rested in the nave.

William Weightman had seen the old man stretched out and coffined the night before. At Emily's insistence, Robbie had been witness as well. The dog watched with a worried expression in his eyes, alarmed border collie eyes that surveyed all with their whites showing, his head resting on his front paws, as the body was enclosed and the coffin nailed shut. Robbie rose once, when the lid was closed, to sniff the wood up and down along its roughly closed joints.

"It is the rudest coffin I have seen," Emily observed. "They have taken no care with it at all. The lid does not fit properly."

"I know," Weightman said. "The wood itself is thin enough for a man to break with his bare hands. But there was not enough money for a better coffin, and the alternative was a winding sheet. I thought—" He did not finish. For fear, he considered, of her tongue-lashing. The coffin makers at the top of the high street were busy, and had no interest in a poor man from Gauger's Croft. So they had shoved their cheapest product at him, and he had thought the money saved might best be used elsewhere.

"If the coffin required money, who paid for this one?" Emily asked. When Weightman did not answer, it dawned on her. She tried to atone for her previous comment and said, "Old Dean deserves the dignity of a coffin. He would be honored by it."

"He does," Weightman agreed. "He was the oldest man, I don't doubt, in Haworth."

Emily nodded and leaned over Robbie to fix a rope to his collar, and to hide her own emotions. Old Dean had passed most of his life on the moors, and had ended his days in Haworth when it became harder for him to walk great distances. He moved to the village to live with a daughter who was employed in the Bridgehouse Mill. The daughter and her husband and children were all dead, carried away by hard work and the waves of fever that swept through the poor precincts of Haworth. Old Dean had survived them all. He had turned to Emily, the two of them drawn together by the dog Robbie and held fast by the store of tales Old Dean accumulated over the years.

Emily stood, and Robbie stood with her, as the two men who brought the coffin and wielded the hammer and nails to fasten it, raised the wood box upon their shoulders. They went in procession to the church, Mr. Weightman taking up the rear.

Robbie, barely visible in the waning light of early evening, surveyed the placement of the coffin in the nave.

"Let me keep Robbie tonight," Emily begged Weightman. "He will want to stay close to Old Dean until he sees him in the ground."

Weightman agreed, and left for his own lodgings with the Widow Ogden. Emily went on to the parsonage where Aunt Branwell grumbled at having not one but two dogs in the house. But Robbie, who was glad to see Keeper, settled his tired old bones before the hearth fire and slept away the evening and the night.

The next day Emily had not the heart to make Robbie wait in the pouring rain, so she slipped him inside the church. Patrick Brontë was away in Bradford, trying to rouse his superiors to take some action for poor relief in the district. It was a blessing to have a curate like Weightman to handle pastoral duties such as funerals while Patrick was away. Emily was glad as well. Her father would not have allowed the dog in the church. But Weightman glanced at Robbie lying at the end of the Brontë pew, a smile on his face, and then opened his Book of Common Prayer as if to say, There may be a dog present, but I certainly have not seen it.

Whatever William Weightman did after, Emily would be his champion. Robbie settled with a deep sigh by the pew and kept a close eye upon the proceedings. Emily wondered what Robbie might make of the smell, for certainly he was close enough, and the coffin thin enough, to catch a whiff. Though it was winter, there would be enough change for a dog to note. And just as surely, Robbie would register the difference. His master, and yet not his master. Emily could see the confusion in the dog's eyes.

When the service was done, Emily waited with Robbie in the pew as people roused themselves and filed toward the back of the church. But William Weightman threw open the door and then called them up short.

"Dear friends," he cried, his hand raised, "it is cold and the rain continues, and you are going to homes without hearth fires. I do not think that brother Dean would wish you to linger in the downpour to watch his burial. It was good of you to come, but I suggest that you leave the interment to the sexton, John Brown, the gravediggers, and myself. Go home and warm yourselves as best you can, and leave to us the disposal of Old Dean's bones."

After a moment's hesitation, all seemed to agree and, bundling themselves and their children as best they could, ventured out into the downpour to run for their cold, but dry, hearths. Emily remained, the dog leashed in her hands. She walked to the back of the church.

"Miss Emily," said William Weightman. "I have an umbrella. May John or I escort you to the parsonage?"

"Robbie and I intend to see to the burial," Emily said. Even as she spoke, the dog pulled the rope from her grasp and headed to the coffin where he set to sniffing.

"Then I insist upon you standing under the umbrella with me," Weightman said. "I don't want you catching your death."

They waited in the vestibule until a squad of four men, under the supervision of John Brown, carried the coffin to the open grave and lowered it into the hole with ropes. Then the men retreated into the shelter of the church until the curate could say the final words and the burial commence.

Weightman opened the umbrella and, turning, offered Emily the crook of his arm. She took it with her left hand and clutched Robbie's rope with her right. They proceeded to the grave. Because space in the churchyard was at a premium, and the death rate steep in Haworth, Old Dean's grave had once belonged to others. Every few years, some of the graves were opened, the bones burned, and the spot made available for a new occupant. But Old Dean would at least rest until flesh and coffin could rot. Probably, Emily thought, he would not be moved in her lifetime. Though the old man could not afford a headstone, Emily would know the spot, and would be able to lay a flower whenever she liked. Perhaps he might talk to her.

She walked beside Weightman, trying to keep dry but not wanting to cling too tightly. She would not be like Charlotte, who would take advantage of William Weightman's proximity to remind him of her own. Still she must admit the sensation of his closeness, the hardness of his arm through the cloth of his coat, the smell of his dampened hair so near to her face, were quite pleasant.

When they reached the edge of the grave, Weightman relinquished Emily's arm and said, "Here. You hold the umbrella and I shall be free to use my prayer book."

Emily took the umbrella handle and held it with Robbie's rope, careful to shield Weightman as best she could. The dog, who could not be so protected, shook himself and settled beside the grave with a ponderous groan, his head resting upon his paws.

Weightman read, "'I am the resurrection and the life, saith the Lord: he that believeth in me, though he were dead, yet shall he live: and whosoever liveth and believeth in me shall never die.'"

He picked up a muddy clod that lay beside the grave, ready to cast it ceremoniously on top of the coffin as he pronounced, "'Forasmuch as it hath pleased Almighty God of his great mercy to take unto himself the soul of our dear brother here departed, we therefore commit his body to the ground; earth to earth, ashes to ashes, dust to dust—'"

What he did not anticipate as he stepped close to fling his divot was that the careless excavators of the grave had undercut the top. The sodden soil at the edge, thus unsupported, gave way beneath Weightman even as he cast his morsel of earth. Emily felt the ground collapse and stepped back, clutching the umbrella. Robbie leaped back as well and began to bark even as William Weightman dropped into the grave feetfirst. Emily heard the sound of splintering wood.

She approached the open grave and peered over. Weightman stood, his shoulders and head visible above ground level. One of his booted feet rested on the edge of the coffin, the other had broken through the thin wood of the lid and plunged inside.

Weightman looked down and wondered what part of Old Dean he trod upon. He closed his eyes, gave a deep sigh, and looked up.

The pallbearers, roused by the sudden disappearance of the curate, approached, expressions of horror on their faces. Robbie was pleased. He barked excitedly, his tail wagging.

Emily gazed solemnly at Weightman, and he looked back. She saw a strange light in his eye, more devilish than clerical. Then he said, "One foot in the grave."

She burst out laughing, though she tried to suppress it, and then lapsed into giggles. Weightman laughed as well. He leaned his face against his upraised arm, his chest heaving. Robbie was beside himself with barking.

Laughter in such a circumstance struck the pallbearers momentarily dumb. Then John Brown cried, "Come out of there, Mr. Weightman, come out! There'll be no good luck in that."

His plea did not chasten Weightman, who sobbed with laughter. The curate stretched forth his arm to be hauled up. It was awkward work, and Weightman muddied the legs of his trousers against the wall of the grave as the men pulled him out. When he had righted himself, he turned to Emily. She had stopped laughing, but pressed her hand against her mouth, her eyes alight with mirth.

Weightman took out a handkerchief and began to wipe the mud and rainwater from his face. He tried to sound severe. "You, Miss Emily, possess an odd turn of humor."

"Indeed," John Brown interrupted, "you'll be lucky if you do not curse yourselves."

"Oh bother," Emily retorted. "If we cannot laugh at death, what can we laugh at?"

John Brown stared at her. "Miss, I would have said the opposite," he muttered.

"And I would say the power of death is defeated when we laugh," said Weightman, calmer now but in a lighthearted mood. "Or rather, death has been defeated, and our laughter acknowledges it."

"Certainly Old Dean will not mind," Emily said. "He is laughing as well. Besides, the worms will have more ready access to him. They will appreciate the convenience."

John Brown shuddered at such irreverent talk. He went to pick up a shovel, but as he raised it, he cried, "Egad, Mr. Weightman, you've left your prayer book down there!" He nodded at the open grave.

"Well," said Weightman, "I certainly will not go back in after it. Let Old Dean have its use, I have another at home." He stepped back beneath the umbrella, though he was drenched to the bone. "Now I shall escort Miss Emily back to the parsonage."

❧

The sudden appearance of William Weightman, wet and stained with mud, in the parsonage hallway caused a commotion. Charlotte emerged from the parlor, where she had been reading. Anne, feeling better day by day, came downstairs. Even Aunt Branwell emerged from the back of the house where she had been attending to the washerwomen who came once a week to do the heavy laundry. Emily, who had only just recovered from her fit of laughing, began all over again at the expressions on their faces.

Aunt Branwell was at her best when confronted with a domestic crisis (which explained why she so quickly came to the rescue of her dead sister's children all those years ago). She was also blunt with Emily, the most unconventional of the sisters. Emily took her aunt's objections in good-natured stride. She accepted that she and the older woman were opposites, and thought there was no reason to judge either. She also enjoyed her aunt's odd turns of phrase. Aunt Branwell was perhaps the most out-of-place resident of Haworth, as though a palm tree had been planted upon the brow of Penistone Hill. She was the well-off daughter of Cornish merchants, and yet in her way as eccentric as Emily. Thus the following exchange: "Law, child"—from Aunt Branwell—"have you been dragging Mr. Weightman through the mud?"

"I beat him first, then I dragged him." Emily, who despite the umbrella was a bit sodden herself, fell into her third fit of laughter. Weightman, wholly unused to a hysterically jolly Emily, was carried along with her.

"Where on earth have the two of you been?" Aunt Branwell continued, seeing nothing humorous in the situation.

"A funeral," Emily said.

This answer was enough to send Emily and Weightman into fresh paroxysms of glee, to the confounding of their audience.

"But, but—" Aunt Branwell lapsed into confused silence. She knew her niece's oddities, but this was beyond her comprehension.

Anne, the first to catch a glimpse of their true mood, asked, "Who died? Dogberry?"

Emily and Weightman shouted with glee at this mention of Shakespeare's moronic constable.

Finally Charlotte, who had never, if truth were told, been fond of comical theatrics, pointed out, "While all stand making great fools of yourselves, Mr. Weightman is dripping all over our clean floor and will likely be dying of a cold in the morning."

Weightman managed a calmer demeanor then, and said as he wiped the water from the end of his nose with his sodden handkerchief, "Miss Brontë, you are the second person after John Brown to claim my adventure of this morning will send me to an early grave."

Charlotte failed to detect the teasing tone that underlay his remark and colored slightly. "Of course I would not think such a terrible thing," she said. "But someone must take you in hand and get you out of those wet clothes." She turned to Emily. "Sister, how have you got Mr. Weightman into such an uproar when he has just come from a funeral, as he says?"

"Oh," Weightman reminded her, "Miss Emily was at the funeral as well. And my predicament was none of her doing."

Charlotte, who had not comprehended that her sister might know someone in the village well enough to mourn, looked astonished. "Emily? Who has died that was close to her?"

Emily had gone serious and silent, the drawbridge pulled up, the shutters closed. She looked down at her feet.

"The old man I sometimes carried bread to has died. That is all."

"It was Old Dean," Anne added helpfully since she knew her sister better than anyone, then lapsed into silence when she saw Emily wanted no explanations.

Weightman was as surprised at Emily's reaction as he had been at her outbursts of laughter. He would have assumed that her entire household knew Emily's devotion to Old Dean. He began to observe the sisters more carefully. Charlotte was watching Emily just as intently, and then shrugged and said, "You chose an inclement day to show your respect."

Emily said in a matter-of-fact voice, "He chose an inclement time to die."

This might have roused Charlotte to a further rebuke but, practiced in this dance, she chose to maintain silence. She turned instead and said to Weightman, "Our aunt is most familiar with Papa's clothes, as she tends to their cleaning regularly. You are taller than he is, but you might fit into one of his suits."

"Indeed," said Aunt Branwell. "And if you leave your wet things, tomorrow Tabby can tend to them. They will need to dry overnight in

any event. Then a stout brush and some water and vinegar should do
the trick on those stains."

Aunt Branwell led Weightman upstairs to Patrick's room and gave
him a pair of pants and jacket. Afterward Weightman and Emily huddled in the kitchen before the fire, the only one in the parsonage, since
Patrick thought it unseemly to heat the entire house when the village
suffered. They drank a fortifying cup of tea. Robbie, who followed
them into the hall and stood to the side, was led into the kitchen to lie
beside Keeper. Emily was quiet and seemed to barely notice Weightman's presence. No flattery, he thought, no flirting or coyness. But
Weightman sensed Emily prized an inner circle, a small one whose
only occupants had been Patrick and Anne Brontë, Tabby Ackroyd,
Keeper, and Old Dean and Robbie. Now William Weightman had
gained entrance.

atrick Brontë wrote from Bradford that a load of coal purchased by devout Christian merchants would soon arrive for the poor of Haworth. When the carts were unloaded, William Weightman spoke to the villagers who stood with their buckets, waiting to receive the black lumps of fuel.

"Remember from whence this fuel came," Weightman said, "and thank those who went belowground at great peril to bring it to you."

Charlotte, who stood watching the distribution with her sisters, said, "How odd. He did not even mention the men who paid for the coal, or God. I hope Papa shall not be upset with him."

✣

Charlotte had "lost her heart," as she termed it, to Weightman, even as she thought herself more familiar with his flaws. All men had faults that must be endured. But she was also alarmed, for she feared Anne was growing enamored of the young curate. Charlotte judged her youngest sister to be fragile and innocent. She might herself love patiently and without much hope, but there was no possibility Anne could endure a man so fickle. (As Weightman continued to be. The most recent rumor divined from Branwell's correspondence was that Weightman had met a young lady in Bradford, where he lately had been spending time on his day off.) Charlotte saw no possibility Weightman could sincerely grow to love dear little Anne, so kind and yet so painfully shy. Yet he might raise her hopes in a most cruel manner.

And there they were, Anne and the curate, lingering behind Charlotte and Emily as all four skirted the brow of Penistone Hill. Charlotte glanced back. Weightman had offered the crook of his arm, and Anne had taken it. They were deep in conversation.

Charlotte turned to Emily, who was striding along beside her, and said, "We are going too fast for the other two."

Emily obliged, and slowed a little. But when she otherwise said nothing, Charlotte added, "Does it not concern you? They are arm in arm, and only have eyes for one another. Mr. Weightman is along as our chaperone, and yet he needs watching himself."

Emily glanced back. She said, "I only see Mr. Weightman and Anne enjoying their conversation. As for being arm in arm, he has often escorted you in the same manner." Emily did not wonder that Weightman had not done the same for her since Old Dean's funeral. She had no desire to be escorted and assumed Weightman knew it.

"But it does not affect me as it does Anne," Charlotte said. "Look at her face."

Emily did as she was told, then said, "It looks no more radiant than yours when you are escorted by Mr. Weightman."

"Oh bother!" Charlotte slapped at her sister's arm and started to walk again.

Then Emily seemed to think better of her reaction. She took Charlotte's arm in hers, in the same way Weightman squired Anne, and said, "Mr. Weightman is simply being charming Mr. Weightman. But perhaps Anne needs a reminder."

"Then you will speak to her?" Charlotte said gratefully. Both assumed that Emily, not Charlotte, must approach Anne. The younger sisters had always been a pair, the closest of confidantes. Charlotte on the other hand had been Branwell's partner until her brother grew up and began to disgrace himself. Charlotte took his behavior as a personal repudiation. Because of that, and because like Branwell she harbored ambitions outside Haworth, Charlotte felt both allied by necessity to her family and at the same time, in a way she could not describe, estranged. And so frequently did Charlotte expect Emily to disagree that she now threw her arms about her sister in gratitude.

"A détente?" Mr. Weightman called.

He and Anne were still some yards behind. As they drew closer, Anne said, "We were just remarking that Charlotte and Emily must be arguing, the two of you were so intent upon your conversation and your expressions so serious."

"We do not always argue when we are serious," Charlotte protested. "Only sometimes when Emily is obstinate."

Emily grabbed Charlotte's arm. "Charlotte thinks me obstinate because she thinks me radical. And yet we are sisters, for all that. Who can long separate sisters?"

"None can separate the Brontës, of that I am sure," Weightman said as he approached. He smiled down at Anne as he spoke. Charlotte glanced at Emily to see that she had taken notice.

Picking up her cue to interfere, Emily said, "Tell us, Mr. Weightman, how is your young lady at home in Appleby?"

"If you refer to Miss Walton, she does well," he replied. "I receive a letter from her every week." His face grew more morose. "Though our prospects are worse than ever."

Charlotte could not refrain from the conversation after all. "And do you consider other possibilities?"

"Perhaps," Weightman said.

"I understand," Charlotte said, "that you have met someone in Bradford."

Weightman laughed. "Where did you hear that?"

"A letter from Branwell. I must warn you, Mr. Weightman, do not tell anything to our brother that you wish kept from others. Branwell has no judgment about what to share and what not."

"Well," Weightman said, "I have met a young woman in Bradford. Her father is a merchant who has taken the lead your father established in organizing fuel relief for the poor of West Yorkshire. Mr. Stafford is a fine Christian gentleman."

"You did not thank Mr. Stafford for the coal when you oversaw the most recent distribution in Haworth," Charlotte pointed out.

"I thanked those who dug the coal," Weightman said, his voice neutral, "and Mr. Stafford did not perform that work." Emily glanced at Weightman, for his response interested her. But then he continued. "The need is ongoing and your father asked if I would take over the visits to Bradford since his age discourages him from traveling. Mr. Stafford has since invited me home to dinner and I made Miss Margaret Stafford's acquaintance."

Anne had been listening with her eyes down. Now she said—with what to Emily's practiced ear seemed disappointment but determination—"I'm sure Miss Stafford felt honored to make yours."

Weightman shook his head. "My situation is no more appealing to Miss Stafford than to Miss Walton."

"So, Mr. Weightman, you are in a quandary," Emily said. "You are acquainted with two young ladies who no doubt find you charming, and yet do not approve your 'situation.' By that I assume they do not approve of Haworth. How then does a young man proceed?"

"Proceed?"

"You must choose," Emily asserted. "One of the young ladies, or your situation."

"Why do you assume they find me charming?" Weightman asked.

"Because," Emily replied, "when you speak of your regard for either one, you are inordinately pleased with *yourself*. And I beg you," she added, "do not change the subject. You are avoiding my question."

"You watch me closely, Miss Emily," Weightman teased. "Do you make me the object of your study?"

Emily replied, "Only for the purpose of studying you scientifically."

Weightman threw back his head and laughed. "It is a relief, Miss Emily, to learn your purpose so clearly. It is not, if I may venture to be so bold, in keeping with your character to ask such questions otherwise. It would sound as if you were flirting."

Emily was shocked and offended. "Good God no!" she exclaimed. "I would not know where to begin. I am honest, and flirting is dishonesty."

"Ah," Weightman said.

Charlotte was chagrined for her sister's sake. But she merely said, though her voice gave away some of her feeling, "You must not heed Emily, Mr. Weightman, when she is in one of her moods."

Emily rolled her eyes and said nothing further. Anne had dropped Weightman's arm and taken Emily's, as though in defense. The party reached the head of the beck, and Anne was tiring. The dogs watched to catch a signal and retrace their steps. Emily whistled for Keeper. Charlotte quailed at this unladylike display. Mr. Weightman, she assumed, would long since have noted the oddness of Emily Brontë, and Charlotte hoped no blame would be assigned to her. But Emily, it seemed, was not done with pursuing Mr. Weightman's attention.

"You have still not answered my question," she said. "How shall you choose between Haworth and the young ladies, or even between the young ladies themselves? February approaches. Shall you send a valentine to both Miss Walton and your new young lady in Bradford?"

"Miss Walton or Miss Stafford? You raise an interesting point." Charlotte thought Weightman spoke as though she and Anne were not present. "I might send a valentine to each of them. Neither would be the wiser, for they do not know of one another's existence. And yet, I think not. It does not seem right, or sincere."

"That is commendable," Anne said timidly, "for it would also be unkind."

"It would be," Weightman agreed. "And since I cannot be what either wishes me to be, a valentine cannot mean what they would hope. In that case, I shall send one to neither young lady. Perhaps it has happened that one of you has received a valentine that raised your hopes needlessly. If so, you will know what I mean."

"Oh," said Emily, "none of us has received a valentine."

Charlotte would have preferred Weightman to believe that the Brontë sisters, Charlotte especially, had been inundated with valentines. But she bit her tongue.

"It seems to me," Emily was saying, "that you are fond of your young ladies, but not in love with either of them. Although perhaps you do not yet know Miss Stafford well enough to tell how strong the attachment might be. Perhaps the lack of passion is on your young ladies' side as well. You doubt their commitment to follow you here. That, I do not understand. Were I in love, I would move heaven and earth to be with that man."

"I believe you would," said Weightman.

"I wonder," Charlotte ventured, hoping to divert the conversation, "if you are not a bit stubborn, Mr. Weightman. It does your cause no good to reside here. If you mean to remain in Haworth for some reason, you should set your sights in the neighborhood if you are to have any hopes at all." Though do not set your sights upon Anne, she thought.

"Do not be surprised, Miss Brontë, at my resolve to stay," Weightman replied. "Do you not believe in a call?"

"A call?" Charlotte looked puzzled for a moment, and then said, "Do you mean a religious call?"

"I do. I believe God brought me to Haworth, and God intends me to stay until he deems otherwise. And if God wishes, he shall provide me with a wife."

"It is a most admirable attitude," Anne said.

Charlotte sighed. Anne was truly taken in. She gave Emily's arm a shake to make certain she noticed, but Emily seemed lost in thought. Charlotte knew her sister well enough to realize this could mean either Emily paid the closest attention, or Emily was lost in her imaginary world and was not paying attention at all.

Then Emily said, "Robbie is tiring. The cold affects his bones, I think, and we have come a long way."

The dog was indeed lagging behind, plodding doggedly, Charlotte thought (and forgave herself the pun), along the frozen moor path, his tongue hanging out despite the cold. Still it was frustrating to think that Emily's attention was on neither Mr. Weightman nor her writing, but an animal.

Weightman stopped and waited for Robbie to catch up. Then he stooped, scooped up the dog, and began to carry him. Robbie rested his head gratefully against Weightman's arm.

"We have half a mile to go," Charlotte observed. "Is he not too heavy?"

"I daresay he weighs less than three stone," Weightman responded. "If I tire I shall set him down again."

Charlotte was left grumpy to find she envied a dog. Perhaps if I sprained my ankle, she thought.

"Concerning our previous conversation, Mr. Weightman," she interjected, determined to maintain her presence verbally if not otherwise, "I wonder if you must only do good by causing a hardship for your young ladies and burying yourself in this godforsaken place? Could you not relinquish your scheme of living here as a sort of missionary and do just as well for the poor by residing elsewhere?"

Weightman did not answer. Charlotte continued, for she saw such advocacy as serving her own cause. If Weightman could be convinced to look elsewhere, he would be happier, and if she were so fortunate as to attach herself to him, she would be fortunate as well.

"Suppose you were the incumbent of a large church in Bradford or

Halifax, or even further south," she continued. "London perhaps. You could use your considerable influence to awaken people to the suffering here, and cause them to contribute great sums with which to do good."

"I think not," Weightman said.

"Do you disagree with my premise entirely?" Charlotte protested. "It is practicable. And sensible."

Weightman paused to shift Robbie more comfortably in his arms.

"It may be practicable for many clergymen. They are valuable. But my call is different."

"And it is an absolutely clear one?" Charlotte said.

"It is clear to me."

Charlotte was at a loss. She said little the rest of the way home. At the parsonage they all took a sustaining cup of tea before the kitchen hearth. Then Weightman left to cross the lane to the Sunday school building. Anne retired upstairs for a nap, and Charlotte and Emily picked up books with which to pass the remains of the afternoon.

But Emily kept an eye to the window, to judge the waning of the light. When she guessed it close to the time when Weightman would be forced to abandon his desk, she put down her book, murmured something about going to feed the chickens and geese, threw on her cloak, and went outside with Keeper.

To her relief Weightman had not yet left his desk. The dog Robbie was stretched across the floor before the cold hearth. He raised his head when Emily and Keeper entered, thumped his tail three times on the floor, and rose painfully to greet his fellow dog. Weightman looked up, surprised.

"Miss Emily," he said.

"Do I come at an awkward time?" she said. "Are you in the middle of a thought?"

"No, no," he said, putting down his quill. "I have finished my sermon and was looking it over for any last changes. A writer, you may guess, cannot catch everything on one draft."

Emily smiled, for she did indeed know, but merely said, "Would I delay you if we spoke? You are not off to visit some ill parishioner?"

"I finished all my parish visits before we took our walk," Weightman replied. He stood and drew up a chair. "I fear you shall shock your sister if she learns you have paid me a visit alone."

Emily knew that he meant Charlotte, not Anne. "Oh bother," she said, and sat down.

Weightman laughed. He took his own chair, leaned back, and regarded her with interest. "It is a convention you judge useless," he observed, no hint of criticism in his voice, "much like walking the moors in the middle of the night."

"It is," she said. "I will not trim my sails for convention."

He nodded. "At least not when you see no reason."

"But there is a reason to confront you," Emily said. "You have not been straightforward with us, Mr. Weightman."

The smile left his face and he looked both surprised and puzzled. "Oh," he said. "But how? I pride myself on honesty, Miss Emily, and wonder how I have offended."

"I did not say you were dishonest," Emily replied. "I mean you have not been forthcoming."

"About—?"

"About why you are here. And what happened before you came here."

"Before I came here?"

"You spoke of it the first time you met the family, in the parlor. You talked of living among the miners of Tyneside and teaching their children. Only you did not say why you left there, and you quickly changed the subject. Nor have you ever returned to it."

"Ah."

Emily watched his face a moment to judge how he responded. It was not easy to tell. He had a countenance that seemed open enough, and yet she thought him quite capable of hiding his emotions. She also thought that just as she searched his face, he studied hers.

She asked, "What is your text for this Sunday?"

He paused a moment as though trying to decide whether to follow this new direction of hers. Then he picked up the Bible that lay atop his desk and turned to the place he had marked.

"Paul's first letter to the Corinthians," Weightman said. He read, "'But if there be no resurrection of the dead, then is Christ not risen; And if Christ be not risen, then is our preaching vain, and your faith is also vain. For if the dead rise not, then is Christ not raised; And if Christ be not raised, your faith is vain.'"

"And is he raised?" Emily said.

Weightman closed the volume and leaned back, relaxing once again. "Yes," he said. "The first fruit, as Scripture says. I would not be a clergyman else."

"Then," Emily said, "given your certainty in that matter, what will you not speak about?"

For a long time he sat watching her and did not answer. The shadows in the room fell partly across his face. Then he said, "You remember that I taught the children of Tyneside. What you may not realize is that many of the children, the boys, also went into the mines. They had to, if their families were to survive. There was an explosion at Wallsend Colliery. Eighteen June, 1835. I shall not forget the date as long as I live. One hundred and two miners were killed." Weightman stopped and took a deep breath, and then continued. "Seventy-five of them were boys. Most of them my boys, who sat to me to learn their letters and sums after a long shift underground. The youngest was eight years old."

"Dear God," Emily said. "What could so young a boy do in a mine?"

"He was a trapper. He opened and closed the trapdoor, so the mine could be ventilated and so the mule carts could pass through." Weightman paused. "Robbie Roseby. Poor child, I think of him every time I say this dog's name. Only the night before, he had mastered his 'sixes' in the multiplication table."

Weightman stood as though he felt the need to pace. "I lost every boy in my school," he said. "I should have stayed for the sake of the girls, I suppose. I did for a time, to minister to them best I could. They had lost their fathers and brothers, after all. But I didn't have the strength. I went to Durham, to study for ordination. And then I came here." He pulled his chair closer to Emily, sat down, and leaned forward, clasping his hands. "Do you see? I lose them here as well. Just last week one of my best young Sunday school scholars died. I held her hand, and prayed with her mother and father, and when she passed on, I closed her eyes, and then I buried her. But I haven't lost them all. Not all at once. For some of them there is time."

"Time for what?" Emily wondered.

"Proper sanitation, for a start," Weightman said. "I keep writing to London, urging someone to come look into our situation. The water supply is contaminated. Not just in Gauger's Croft or Ginnel, but yours and mine as well. Look at the privies, and look where the wells stand. They are close. Then there is the question of better medical care. Our surgeon, Mr. Wheelhouse, is overworked, and we have no physician. The mill workers are unemployed half the time, and they starve and freeze. Good God! What couldn't be done to better their lot?"

"But one man cannot do it," Emily said.

"Of course not."

"There must be a movement to set things right!" Emily had heard her father speak of such matters, though he was naturally cautious. Charlotte showed no interest; Anne expressed sadness but wondered what to do. Emily wondered as well. But she also took note when voices were raised in protest. She was partial to revolutionaries, an especial admirer of the Americans of George Washington's generation. Some of her most vehement arguments with Charlotte and Branwell had been over the activities of the Chartists, and their father's unlikely alliance with them in their childhood.

But her thoughts on the matter were interrupted. For Weightman said, "Now I have a question for you. Why are you studying me scientifically?"

"Why—"

Emily was taken by surprise. She watched Weightman as closely as he did her, and then decided. She said, "I write, and I wish to know more about men. I do not know many men, to ask them how they think. Only my father. And Branwell, but he is often" she paused—"useless."

Weightman nodded and said nothing.

Emily waited in the quiet, and then added, "I write poetry. And stories. I do not speak of my writing, except to Anne."

"Then I shall keep your secret," he said.

"I shall never mention it again," Emily added, unnerved at having confided so much. She thought she could have been no more vulnerable if she had stripped naked.

Weightman nodded again and said nothing. The light was fading fast. Emily stood to hide a fit of trembling. "I must go," she said, and disappeared before the words were out of her mouth. She left so suddenly that even Keeper was taken by surprise, and lumbered to his feet to follow.

Emily was so unsettled she went off to walk with Keeper, despite the earlier ramble of the day. She was angry with herself. Her confession had been out of character. Perhaps it was a pastor's gift, she reflected, to counsel people in distress and coax—perhaps even trick—them into revealing the depths of their souls in order to bring solace. As quickly as her anger flared, it dissipated. But her mind played over a nightmare fantasy—William Weightman in someone's parlor, the Sugdens' perhaps, a saucer of tea upon his knee, proclaiming, Do you know the oddest thing: the vicar's gangly daughter, the middle one, the odd one, composes verse and some sort of stories she will not talk about. Is that not priceless?

She shook her head to dispel the scene. She trusted her own judgment, and she had judged William Weightman worthy. He would not betray her.

Emily went home. Her father's door was shut. Charlotte was preparing to climb into bed with Aunt Branwell.

"Where have you been?" she asked through the open door.

"Walking," Emily replied, and went into her own small room. Anne was already in bed, but raised her head as Emily threw off her dress and pulled on her nightgown. Emily's room was not much more than a cubbyhole at the front of the house, wedged between the bedrooms of her father and aunt. There was no fireplace. The sisters snuggled together in the narrow bed for warmth.

Emily had planned to tell Anne about her visit to Weightman's study, and about the clergyman's terrible experience on Tyneside. She was used to confiding in Anne as with no one else, not even her father. But even as she opened her mouth to speak, she changed her mind. She should be no more forthcoming about Weightman than he would be about her. So she sighed, squeezed Anne around the waist, and fell asleep.

❊

On Valentine's Day, Patrick Brontë returned from his daily stroll to the post office in possession of a mystery. In addition to the usual clutch of circulars and church correspondence, he brought with him three letters of identical pink paper folded and stamped with red sealing wax, each addressed to one of his daughters. He handed them over, a puzzled look on his face.

"I would not have been surprised someday to find one of my girls had a secret admirer on Valentine's Day," he said. "But all three at once?"

The sisters wondered who the sender might be, and enjoyed prolonging the suspense by delaying to break the seals. Aunt Branwell came downstairs to learn about the commotion, and Tabby appeared from the kitchen, swiping her soapy hands against her apron, to examine the pink stationery and declare, "Valentines, are they? And who from, do ye think?" Then she answered her own question after clapping a wet hand over her open mouth. "Mr. Weightman, I'll warrant!"

Anne and Emily shrieked and, giggling, wrapped their arms around one another. Charlotte stood to one side, her face red, and smoothed away a wet patch on the pink where Tabby's fingers had touched it. "Do you think?" she said. "The postmark is Bradford."

"Mr. Weightman goes to Bradford," Emily said.

Anne was the first to open her valentine. She looked up. "There's no signature," she said. "But there is a poem."

"Read it," Charlotte demanded.

Anne read:

> "Soul divine
> A purer soul I do not know
> You'd make the hardest heart to glow.
> A gentler soul could not exist
> Nor kinder one by nature kissed.
>
> Your sweetness melts the heart that attends
> Your kindness warms the heart just so
> Your innocence cries for all to be
> As constant, warm, and kind as thee."

"He has captured you!" Emily exclaimed.

Anne held her fist to her mouth, trying not to laugh. "In very bad verse," she said, "and yet very kind."

"The meter is terrible," Emily agreed, "and yet the sentiment to be greatly valued." She opened her own and read:

> *"Brave soul,*
> *You fear nothing, that I see*
> *Of all things that is clear to me.*
> *Were I in trouble or facing battle's woe*
> *Your companionship would see me through.*
>
> *In times of sorrow and despair*
> *I'd want no more than your courage there.*
> *And should I face e'en death's dark sea*
> *I know you would my champion be."*

She grew quiet a moment, and then she looked up from the card and smiled at Anne. "It is a high compliment," she said.

Anne linked her arm through her sister's. "He sees you as extraordinary, as do we all."

"Strange," Charlotte said. "It is almost as if he were writing to a man."

Anne turned to Charlotte. "Now yours," she urged.

Charlotte opened her valentine slowly, her face flushed.

"'Away fond love,'" she read, and looked up as though reluctant to continue. "How he does speak," she murmured. Then she continued:

> *"Though you do long to leave this place*
> *I urge you, turn to its embrace.*
> *For though you wish to go away*
> *Those who love you wish you would stay.*
>
> *Don't go away, whate'er you do*
> *For I must fain recover you.*

*Your strength and honesty are dear*
*Your love, devotion required here."*

She folded the valentine carefully. Patrick Brontë had taken the poems from Anne and Emily and read them over, but Charlotte thrust hers in her pocket before he could ask for it. He looked over his glasses. "Indeed," he said, "this is Mr. Weightman's handwriting; it is familiar and he does not trouble to disguise it." He clapped his hands. "Well, he has certainly made this Valentine's a memorable one. No doubt now you shall have him for dinner again and feed him royally."

"Oh, we shall," Emily agreed. She noted Charlotte had drifted into the parlor, and followed her sister. "Are you displeased?" she asked.

"No, no," Charlotte said, though Emily thought her manner odd. Charlotte had taken the valentine out of her pocket and was reading it over again. She shook her head back and forth, "The verse is indeed quite bad," she said as though speaking to herself, "but surely he must be forgiven that. It was a great effort on his part."

"It was," said Anne, who had come in the room, "and most thoughtful. He must have had it in mind ever since Emily let slip that we'd none of us had a valentine."

"I wonder," Charlotte said. "Each one was addressed so succinctly. Anne, he appreciates your qualities, as he should. And Emily he admires, as also he should. Why, he would even take you into battle with him, sister. I think we must give you a martial nickname. But my valentine—" She hesitated as though unsure whether to confide what she was thinking. But Charlotte, being Charlotte, could not help herself. "Do you notice? It is the only one to use the word 'love.'"

Emily opened her mouth as though to offer a scornful retort, but Anne stepped close and trod on her foot. Emily closed her mouth at once. "We had not noticed," Anne said.

"He says he loves me," Charlotte continued, looking down at the card. "And he says if he lost me, he must recover me."

"I think," Emily said, "if he meant to express intimate sentiments to one of us, he would not have sent all three of us a card."

"But he is kind, as you say," Charlotte said. "And he knows we are close. He would not hurt two of us by only writing to a third."

Again Anne sent Emily a warning look. Emily heeded it. And later, in the kitchen, where Anne and Emily stood peeling potatoes, Emily said, "I have long known Charlotte was in love. But this time she is delusional."

Anne sighed. "There is nothing to do except let her learn for herself where things stand. I hate to see her hurt. But you know she will not listen to us, so best not provoke her." After a moment, she said, "Perhaps we should warn Mr. Weightman."

"I think," Emily said, "Mr. Weightman will judge the situation without us."

That evening Charlotte proposed the three of them write Weightman an answer. "He will guess we are onto him," she said, "and if we do not reply he will be hurt. But it would also be best if we responded together."

Emily and Anne were so relieved at the sensibleness of Charlotte's response that they agreed at once. After the supper dishes had been put away and Aunt Branwell and their father gone off to bed, they sat around the parlor table with their heads together.

Charlotte insisted on copying the poem. "Our response must project fondness, nothing else," she insisted, and proceeded to compose most of the verse herself. Emily and Anne, happy to humor her, offered the occasional suggestion.

They finally agreed on the following verse:

> *"We cannot write or talk like you;*
> *We're plain folks every one.*
> *You've played a clever trick on us,*
> *We thank you for the fun."*

"What a joke!" Emily hooted. "We all of us can write better verse than he can!"

"But he must be flattered," Charlotte said. "He is a man." She continued to read aloud:

> *"Believe us when we frankly say*
> *(Our words, though blunt are true),*
> *At home, abroad, by night or day,*
> *We all wish well to you.*
>
> *And never may a cloud come o'er*
> *The sunshine of your mind;*
> *Kind friends, warm hearts, and happy hours,*
> *Through life we trust you'll find.*
>
> *Where'er you go, however far*
> *In future years you stray,*
> *There shall not want our earnest prayer*
> *To speed you on your way."*

"But it sounds as though he were leaving," Anne pointed out.

"Of course he shall," Charlotte said.

"I don't know," Emily mused. "He speaks as though he plans to be in Haworth for many years to come."

"He is dedicated," Charlotte replied. "But how long, in reality, can he stay in such a place?" She signed the poem with a large "Charlotte B." and handed the quill to Emily. "He is good as a good curate should be. But he shall come to his senses, find a prosperous living, and take a wife."

When they had all signed, Charlotte folded the letter and took a wafer from the drawer to seal it. She studied it a moment first, lost in thought. "If only one could write more," she murmured. "But it would not do. He must be allowed to decide."

"Young men are like the Lord," Emily said dryly. "You cannot dictate to them."

Anne, who knew the tone of her sister's voice, kicked her beneath the table. Emily smiled and said nothing further. Charlotte, oblivious to any teasing, sealed the letter and set it upon the hall table to be mailed the next morning.

# 6

Patrick Brontë watched the growing friendship between his daughters and his curate with pleasure, and yet some trepidation as he considered Charlotte's feelings. The objects of her affection had once been the sons of local gentry, young men of wealth and standing, entirely unobtainable. Charlotte turned down two marriage proposals from men who did not interest her. One was the brother of a school friend, a clergyman who made it clear that he was not in love but wanted a wife to run the school he had founded. The other was also a clergyman, a Mr. Pryce, who proposed to Charlotte in tears only the day after meeting her while visiting Haworth with friends. Charlotte rejected him, not able to convince herself he was serious. Six months later, the young man, rather fragile in health (as well as in mind, Patrick guessed), was dead.

Patrick believed in both cases Charlotte acted sensibly. She would not marry for the sake of being married, though the first proposal would have left her secure for life and many women would have been tempted by it. Charlotte considered love, a novel notion in some quarters, to be a requirement.

Patrick was nevertheless taken aback by his daughter's obsession with Weightman. When turning down the previous clerical applicants, Charlotte revealed an attitude Patrick had not realized she possessed—

contempt for the clergy, especially curates. She regarded them as a dull and dunderheaded bunch, their scope not suitably heroic, especially those who labored in the vineyards of provincial places like Yorkshire.

Her father was hurt. Patrick realized at his advanced age that he would never leave Haworth, nor progress past the perpetual curacy that tied him in a subordinate role to the vicar of Bradford. So be it. He was where the Lord had placed him. So, he suspected, was William Weightman. Patrick dared hope when he could no longer serve his charge at Haworth, Weightman would step into his place and carry on.

That could not please Charlotte, who wanted the world. And yet here she was, moping around the parsonage, staring out the window at the Sunday school building where Weightman kept his study, talking of nothing but the curate and his future.

Patrick sighed. It had a great deal to do, he suspected, with Weightman's looks. An attractive boy if somewhat disheveled, with a clear eye, a firm chin, and a straight back. Patrick was aware that a number of young ladies in the district had lost their hearts to Weightman, and when it was the young man's turn to fill the pulpit, the quantity of bonnets in the pews increased and the faces of their wearers were upturned with expectation. But he thought Charlotte would finally see reason, and he hoped the fall would be no more hard than necessary.

Anne was taken with Weightman as well. But unlike Charlotte, who was an incorrigible romantic, Anne possessed a core of good sense. Finally recovered from her illness, Anne studied advertisements and sent out notices for positions. She knew the chances of a Brontë sister marrying, with no money and modest looks, were slim. She would need to make her own way in the world. Anne would not let attraction to Weightman trump reality.

But it was Emily who astonished. Patrick felt closer to Emily than her sisters. Part of this was selfish. Emily was not inclined to pursue young men. Her lack of interest was not due to a rejection of the male sex but grew from an intensity of character that could not be matched by those she encountered in a general way. Emily would not lower her standards. And so her expectations would not be met.

As Patrick Brontë declined into old age, with all its deficiencies, Emily would be the daughter who stayed home. He would lean upon her. He did already, as Aunt Branwell grew more decrepit.

But beyond such practical considerations, Patrick admired Emily's attributes. She was outspoken—at home, at least. Of all his children, Patrick enjoyed talking with Emily about items in the newspaper, or speculating over problems in the parish. In public Emily said not two words to anyone. And yet Patrick would have termed her bold. As he looked the other way while Emily wandered on her own unescorted, and went out on the moors at night (he had heard her, and upon chastising her in the morning, realized his words had not the least effect), Patrick thought of her as a sort of son.

He agreed, when Emily asked, to teach her to shoot the pistol he kept in a drawer beside his bed. The gun was a habit he had acquired upon his arrival in Haworth, when the district had been especially lawless. Patrick had carried the pistol for a time upon his pastoral rounds; as he grew more familiar with West Riding folk, he stowed it away, but took it out now and then to keep it in firing order. Emily alone of his children noticed. She became a proficient shot. He admired to watch her stand in the back garden—her hair loose and her tall figure dappled by the play of sun and shade—and extend her arm to take aim at a target. She would have done well, Patrick thought, in the American backwoods.

William Weightman was a sort of son as well. Patrick had begun to call the young man by his nickname. Willie. A boy's name. His boy now, for Weightman was estranged from his own father. The elder Weightman thought his son had thrown his life away by burying himself among the poor of Haworth. He threatened to cut off Willie's allowance.

Patrick sat down with Willie to plan parish affairs for the coming March. When the work was done and Tabby carried in a tray of tea and Emily's good bread and butter, Patrick said, "I wish to thank you, Willie, for the valentines you sent. My girls were most pleased to receive them."

"How did you know——" Weightman began.

Patrick raised his hand. "We were onto you quickly. You need not have walked all the distance to Bradford to post them. Your mark was all over."

Weightman looked sheepish. "I'm glad that all was taken as I meant."

"Indeed," Patrick said. "And you will receive an answer." He had decided not to mention Charlotte's infatuation. It would exist without the valentines, after all.

"They are fine young women," Weightman said. "I enjoy their company more than I can say."

Patrick considered how to put his question. Finally he said, "I must ask. Why do you take such an interest?"

"Do you find it inappropriate?"

"I do not. I find it unusual."

"Ah." Weightman thought. Then he said, "I enjoy the company of women. They are in many ways more admirable than men. They have fine minds, which they have not been allowed to develop. Yet women feel deeply. They possess a quiet compassion. I understand why, when our Lord rose, he appeared at the tomb first to women. They would not scoff or turn away from him as men would. They would worry over him." He paused a moment and smiled. "I have a fancy that they first asked Jesus if he would like something to eat. The writers of the Gospels, being men, didn't bother to mention it."

"I see," Patrick said. It was the sort of response he was coming to expect from his curate. "Well, your friendship has been a great boon. I am especially pleased for the sake of Emily and Anne. They are ignored when the society of the vicinity is gathered, because they are so quiet. And because——"

"Because they do not fit," Weightman supplied.

"I suppose that is one way to put it," Patrick acknowledged.

"It is a compliment, rather than the reverse."

Patrick was grateful. "Emily and Anne are rarely invited to anyone's parlor," he said. "Not that Emily minds in the least. Anne feels the want." He paused. "Emily dislikes to sit and sip tea in drawing rooms, and so she is not invited. She would rather traipse the moors and engage in her daydreams. You will understand that it does my heart good to see how she has warmed to you."

"Emily is quiet," Weightman said, although as he spoke, he remembered the challenge in his study. "Yet I think her fearless. I daresay sipping tea in a drawing room seems tame to her."

Patrick nodded, pleased. "But society, as you know, does not countenance that in a woman. Emily has no place to apply her gifts, so she turns inward. This village, these moors, and her own soul, are her field of inquiry. And being narrow, her purview is intense." Patrick sighed. "I suppose I am criticized in polite circles because I do not rein her in. But it would break my heart to see."

Weightman thought it might be well nigh impossible to rein in Emily Brontë. But he said nothing. The two men sat companionably for a time. Then Weightman said, "May I change the subject? I understand you once had Chartists speak in Haworth. Emily told me."

Patrick felt an instant of shock. "Oh yes," he admitted. "It was over the Poor Law. It did little good," he added.

"It always does some good," Weightman said.

Patrick sipped his tea and regarded his curate over the brim of his saucer. "Why do you remind me of this?"

Weightman leaned forward, his hand clasped between his knees. "I posted my valentines in Bradford for a reason that has nothing to do with secrecy. I go there on my day off. I helped raise the coal relief, as you asked. And as Charlotte may have mentioned"—here he allowed himself a smile—"I met a young lady I called upon once or twice. That is not why I keep going. I have long been in contact with Chartists in Bradford. They are some of the most active in the north of England. And I will admit to you that I am in some sympathy with their cause."

Patrick felt the ground give way beneath his feet. And yet the sensation was not unpleasant. "Do you know," he said after a time, "how a poor Irish boy was able to go to Cambridge? William Wilberforce was my sponsor. He not only helped free the slaves, he pursued many another worthy cause as well. I was one of them. I felt obligated to come to Yorkshire afterward, to serve in Wilberforce's home county."

"I did not know that," Weightman said. "It only adds to my admiration, for Wilberforce was my boyhood hero."

"He had a great deal of sympathy for the poor people of England," Patrick continued. "He called for relief, and provided it at his own estate. But he had no sympathy for agitation. He witnessed the bloodshed in France, you know."

"I would be the last to condone violence," Weightman said. "I am as good a Christian, I hope, as I have the strength for. But Wilberforce was of an older generation, your father's generation. And though he faced with open eyes the terrible condition of the African slaves, he had not yet seen the horror of what our English workers now face. Poor they were, in his day, but with the means to tend crops and animals and gather fuel. Even in these textile districts, the handloom was in the cottage with them. Now they are herded into factories and chained to power looms. Those who keep home looms do so in horrible conditions. We raise relief, fuel and blankets and oats, and next year we shall do it again. And the year after. They die out of hand all the while."

Patrick feared Weightman's direction.

"Not just men," Weightman continued. "Women. Children. Working fourteen hours in a mill, six days a week. They lose fingers and limbs to the power looms. They breathe poisonous fumes that destroy their lungs. Eat nothing but oatcakes day after day. My God, a potato is a treat. Their drinking water is tainted. They die because no one cares."

Patrick stirred. "Have you an answer to your latest letter to London about sanitary conditions?"

"I have not. I shall write again. I shall write again and again until someone comes to examine our situation. Or until the outcry is too great to ignore." Weightman leaned forward. "But in the meantime, you and I bury them. Every day. It is the same with the dissenting pastors. And no one of the stature of Wilberforce speaks for our people in Parliament. If Wilberforce were a young man today, he would support the Chartists."

"I think," Patrick said, "it is unwise to speak for the dead. Yet I am not opposed to what you say, though I have thought the Chartists bold."

"You have no objection if I continue to talk to them?"

Patrick studied the shining face of the boy who leaned toward him. His love overwhelmed him.

"No," Patrick said. "I trust you."

Weightman reached out and grasped the older man's hands, the skin papery-thin. "Thank you," he said. "I shall not trouble you again."

❦

William Weightman was invited, upon the suggestion of Patrick Brontë, to lecture at the Keighley Mechanics Institute. His subject was to be the classics, his primary field of study after theology, at Durham.

When he told the sisters over tea one day after a ramble on the moors, Charlotte cried, "Oh, I should love to hear your lecture! I know so little of the classics."

"I should like it as well," Anne added.

Emily sat silent and studied her teacup. Of course she wished to go, but she would not admit how much.

"It is unfair," Charlotte continued, "that women are not thought to be suited for classical studies. That portion of our education is neglected." She turned to Weightman. "You could supply our ignorance."

"I think it would be splendid if you came to my lecture," Weightman replied.

"What?" said Aunt Branwell, who had just entered the parlor. "What lecture?"

Charlotte said, "Mr. Weightman is giving a lecture on the classics next week at the Keighley Mechanics Institute. We would like to attend."

"Of course you cannot," Aunt Branwell said.

"But Aunt," Charlotte cried, "we are quite used to walking that far!"

"Your father is no longer well enough to escort you there and back in a day."

Emily was unable to keep silent, forced by the absurdity of the situation. "Father lectured in Keighley last month."

"And because of his health and his years, a carriage was sent for him," Aunt Branwell pointed out. "They will do no such thing for a strapping young man like Mr. Weightman."

"We can walk with him," Charlotte said. "He already escorts us on the moors."

"He escorts you in the daytime," Aunt Branwell said, "and that is quite controversial enough for me, even though your father allows it. It is something else to be out in the countryside late at night with a young man. Think of the scandal in the church if it were known. The parson's daughters, caught out with the curate."

Weightman burst out laughing. "Indeed, Miss Branwell, I should have my hands full with the lot of them."

Emily laughed and Aunt Branwell looked scandalized. But she also harbored a soft spot for the young man, who never failed, when he saw her, to take her hand and bow over it. He was also inclined, at more informal moments in the parsonage, to tease her in a flirtatious manner, which caused her to giggle. So she simply said, "It is, I am afraid, impossible, Mr. Weightman. I hope the size of your audience will be adequate without my nieces."

"It is not the size of his audience," Emily cried. "It is the loss to us!"

Anne said, "You shall have to teach us in absentia, Mr. Weightman. Perhaps you could be kind enough to share your lecture notes. What shall your subject be?"

"I plan to speak about the plays of Sophocles," he replied. "Particularly *Antigone.*"

"Was Antigone not a woman?" Emily asked.

"Indeed. A strong one."

"I should like to hear that lecture," she said, her voice tinged with regret.

"I would as well," Charlotte said, casting a reproving look at her aunt. "Perhaps Papa will allow it."

"He will not," Aunt Branwell said. She was confident she would carry the day. She had long ago judged, by now and then threatening to return to Cornwall, when Patrick Brontë would give in and humor her for the sake of her oversight of his household. "Not without sufficient escort."

Weightman looked thoughtful but said nothing more, and the subject was dropped.

⁂

Three days later an invitation arrived at the parsonage. Mr. Theodore Dury, the married curate of Keighley, wished the Brontë sisters to join his family for tea before the lecture by Mr. William Weightman at the Keighley Mechanics Institute. After the lecture, he proposed to escort the party back to Haworth. Due to the lateness of the hour, he hoped he might spend the night at the parsonage.

Patrick Brontë, who had seconded his sister-in-law's objection to the visit to Keighley, emerged from his study to find his daughters dancing around the hallway while Aunt Branwell stood by, looking suitably perturbed.

"Oh, can we, can we, can we?" Charlotte, Emily, and Anne cried all together.

"Well," Aunt Branwell said. She looked helplessly at Patrick. Then she threw up her hands. "Why on earth young women should wish to spend an afternoon and evening walking four miles and back in order to hear about some ancient heathen or the other, I shall never understand. But there is no objection now. Only"—she cast an aggrieved look at Patrick—"it shall be a late night waiting up."

Patrick removed his spectacles and wiped them on his sleeve. "I think, Aunt, that Mr. Weightman has in this case provided what is needed. With Mr. Dury in tow, no one need wait up."

"Still," Aunt Branwell said, "there is hospitality to be provided."

"I shall make all the arrangements beforehand," Emily said. "We shall put Mr. Dury in Branwell's room, and no one need wait up. Oh, please, Papa, please."

"I have no objection," Patrick replied. "I daresay my curate has proven himself as intrepid in arranging this endeavor as anything he has accomplished."

"Oh, he is a blessing to you!" Charlotte cried. "And to Haworth. Soon, Keighley shall know his worth!" Then she clapped her hand over her mouth. "Dear Lord! Caroline Dury shall be present!"

Emily folded her arms across her chest and said, "Caroline Dury does exist, sister. The question is, shall you be there?"

Charlotte gave her usual swat to Emily's arm. "Oh bother! Of course I shall be."

Since Haworth sat high on the brow above Keighley, the walk down would be easy, but the return strenuous. The Brontë sisters ate a hearty early dinner and packed sandwiches for the way back, enough for Mr. Dury. They dressed for the February cold. Anne in particular was forced to assure her aunt that she would keep her scarf close about her neck and her bonnet tight upon her head. William Weightman assured Aunt Branwell he would offer Anne his arm for support. Charlotte was disappointed. But she put on a brave face and hoped William Weightman noticed her unselfishness.

The party set out in high spirits just after two in the afternoon. They cut across fields to avoid the mud of the roadway, picking their way past islands of brittle old snow and wandering sheep. Weightman carried a leather pack over his shoulder with the papers containing his talk and their sandwiches. Otherwise they were unencumbered. The conversation was much as it was on their walks upon the moors, discussions of books and politics and theology. Charlotte saw the landscape in a blur. She had been careful to pack her spectacles, but equally careful not to let Weightman see her in them. So she stumbled now and then, and caught his arm for assurance. That put her in a fine frame of mind.

"Tell us about your lecture," she begged. "What are your major points, so that we shall be ahead of everyone else."

"No, no, no," Emily cried, "don't make him repeat himself, sister! You shall double his effort. Let us hear his talk, and ask questions upon the return."

Charlotte agreed and they continued on, pausing now and then to let Anne rest. But the Brontës grew more quiet and circumspect as Keighley parsonage came into view. It was of the same brown stone stained black with soot as the other buildings in the district, but larger and more imposing than their own home. Not unfamiliar, for they had been there with their father. Still their demeanor changed. Even as Weightman pounded upon the front door, they ducked their heads and gathered their cloaks about them. In the hallway they hesitated, for cries and laughter had greeted Weightman's appearance. Two young women, Caroline Dury and her friend Sarah Sugden, the daughter of the wealthiest man in the district, descended upon Weightman. They dragged him into the parlor before he had time to speak. The Brontë sisters waited for a morsel of attention. It fell to Mrs. Dury to greet them and usher them into the parlor.

Caroline Dury and Sarah Sugden established William Weightman in the center of the sofa, and themselves upon either side. He glanced at the Brontës as they entered, a momentary sheepish—but also pleased—expression upon his face as if to say, What can I expect? Then he turned his attention back to the young women pelting him with questions from either side. Mrs. Dury took the Brontës' cloaks and bonnets and led the sisters to chairs near the window. Anne and Charlotte settled at once, and remained silent. Charlotte looked particularly forlorn. She was careful to meet no one's eye and directed all her attention to the smoothing of her skirt. Emily drew her chair as far back as she could, to a spot where she had a full view of the sofa without calling attention to herself. She observed the scene with amusement. Intelligent and free conversation in the open air was one thing. The silliness of a parlor was another.

The elder Durys were embarrassed that their daughter and her friend had forgotten the presence of other guests besides Weightman. But like many indulgent parents, they were unable to determine how to respond. Mrs. Dury thought her husband should take control of the conversation, but that good gentleman was somewhat of a daydreamer and lax in social situations. At last Mrs. Dury cleared her throat and announced, "Caroline, your other guests want refreshment." This persuaded Caroline to recall her duties and pour tea for the Brontës, careful to show herself to the best advantage as she did so. But she was soon back beside Mr. Weightman and offering a tray of tea cakes. The tray was not passed to the Brontës until Weightman himself made a point of standing and offering it to each of the sisters and the elder Durys.

Caroline Dury was a pretty girl, small and dark with fine brown eyes. A sweet girl and enamored with eligible young men. As indeed she should be, for since her family was not possessed with much more wealth than the Brontës, she would have to rely upon her beauty and charm to catch a husband. Caroline had no expectations of a moneyed catch—a clergyman like her father would be acceptable. But Weightman held an especial attraction. Not only was he charming and good-looking, his family was well-off. Though he seemed to have no interest in his father's money, he would assuredly inherit it someday. Caroline Dury sensed William Weightman to be the greatest catch she might aspire to in the West Riding.

There was a time when Caroline would not have invited Sarah Sugden to the parsonage when Weightman was visiting. Sarah, blond, buxom, and gregarious, was one of the great beauties of the district. Her father was a mill owner with a prominent rented pew in the church at Keighley. Under other conditions, she would not have considered the less well-endowed Caroline Dury as a friend. But neither girl possessed a close sister to confide in. Both were enamored of William Weightman, and so when they wished to speak of him, which was often, they found one another to be congenial company. Of course they knew they were competitors. But each thought the presence of the other would show off her own qualities to better advantage. And so their bond was strong, at least temporarily. It was the comradeship of gladiators.

Caroline Dury knew herself to be at a disadvantage, yet she was possessed of talents that stood her in good stead. Caroline was the better pianist and had as well a pleasant voice. Sarah Sugden possessed good looks and a well-rounded figure, but Caroline knew her way around a parsonage. Sarah had a considerable fortune. Still, Weightman would not lack resources of his own someday. He would be well settled, and had no need to grub for money when pursuing a wife. And his position in Haworth bespoke humility. Caroline knew herself to be humble. Sarah, on the other hand, assumed that her own wealth allowed her a certain hauteur. She would insult even her friends, from time to time, without realizing it. Caroline valued Sarah's company particularly because her friend provided this contrast to Caroline's own modesty.

Such a contrast was on display in the parlor of Keighley parsonage, for Sarah's conversation, as usual, varied between insipid and conceited. Caroline hoped Weightman might note it. The only notice either took of the Brontë sisters, once they were handed their tea, was to lament the long walk from Haworth and to cast sidelong glances at the spattered state of the hems of the Brontë skirts. How extraordinary to make so long a journey by foot at this time of year.

"Did you not know the way would be muddy?" Sarah Sugden wondered aloud. The answer, of course, held little interest, and so when it was slow and spare in coming, was ignored.

Then Sarah used the topic to turn the focus back upon William Weightman.

"Mr. Weightman," she ventured, "does not your father, since he has some means, retain horses and a carriage?" How flattering for a man, she thought as she spoke, to be made the center of attention.

"He has a four-in-hand," Weightman replied.

Sarah did not notice that he spoke somewhat reluctantly. She clapped her hands. "Of course he would! Perhaps, if you come in great demand in Keighley as a result of your lecture, he shall supply you as well. Then you can make the journey with more ease."

"I think not," Weightman said politely. "Mr. Brontë and Mr. Dury do not have an equipage, nor does any clergyman in the district I am aware of."

Sarah looked puzzled for a moment, but recovered her composure. Caroline sipped her tea and waited for her friend to hang herself.

Sarah plowed on, oblivious. "I understand why you wouldn't want something as ostentatious as a Clarence. But why not a gig or a curricle for pastoral visits?" She clapped her hands in excitement. "Or even a phaeton once you are wed?"

Weightman was long in answering. Then, before he could form a polite response, Caroline Dury said in a low voice, "Perhaps he does not want to put on airs."

"Put on airs!" Sarah exclaimed. "Why is an equipage 'putting on airs' if it can be afforded? What an example to the district, what a thing to aspire to! Think of the excitement it would give the poorer children, to see it! Why not at least a horse, Mr. Weightman? Think how much more easily you might visit your far-flung parishioners. Some of them are quite extended and difficult to reach. The mill owners are building their homes further and further from Haworth these days."

"Indeed they are," Weightman observed.

The conversation died then, and Caroline was congratulating herself on her wisdom in keeping silent. Even Sarah had the sense to blush and return to her tea, to cover her surprise at the brevity of the curate's response. Weightman took a sip from his own cup, a solemn expression on his face. But as he sipped, he raised his eyes and met the gaze of Emily Brontë. She had upon her face the look of one wandering in a zoo and watching the antics of some exotic species.

Weightman could not resist. He winked at her. Nor could Emily stifle her response. She laughed.

No one but Emily had seen the wink, and everyone stared at Emily except Weightman, who suddenly took a great deal of interest in another tea cake. Emily had come to know him well enough to read the twitch that tugged at the corner of his mouth.

Sarah Sugden felt discomfited by this sudden outburst of laughter, as though she sensed a personal affront. What a strange response, and what an odd duck Emily Brontë was. Sarah was suddenly determined to point this out.

"Miss Emily," she said with more than a hint of sarcasm, "I did not think you could laugh."

"Miss Sugden," Emily retorted at once in her strongest broad Yorkshire accent, "I did not know you could think."

The scene was as frozen as a painting. Then the Reverend Dury, who was most certainly paying attention now, began to cough, and then urged his daughter to the piano to play for the guests. Caroline was gratified to show off her talents, especially in a way that contrasted so clearly with both Sarah's faux pas and the extraordinary rudeness of Emily Brontë. Good Lord, Caroline thought, just before launching into a difficult piece by Mozart, Emily had sounded as coarse and rude as a Haworth weaver. How embarrassed her family must be.

The Mozart was a triumph of technical proficiency. Caroline considered she had won the right to be escorted to the lecture hall upon the arm of William Weightman. A petulant Sarah Sugden walked beside but had little to say on the way to the Keighley Mechanics Institute. She was so cross that she had begun to think a man who refused to keep a phaeton was not worth pursuing, no matter how attractive otherwise.

❧❦

Charlotte Brontë, who lagged behind with her sisters, was in an equally foul mood. When at last she did speak, she was forced to keep her voice low, for the elder Durys were close behind.

"Whatever were you thinking," she whispered crossly to Emily, "to speak so to Sarah Sugden?"

"She was rude," Emily replied.

"Is it a reason to be rude back?"

"An eye for an eye," Emily said. "In some cases. I think no harm was done. Sarah Sugden is impervious to insults from the likes of me."

Anne said, "I thought Emily was funny, though I dared not laugh."

"And what," Charlotte demanded, "must Mr. Weightman have thought?"

"He would have laughed as well," Emily maintained, "although he also did not dare."

Charlotte shook her head in despair. "No, no. Look at him." She nodded ahead to Weightman, who was engaged in animated conversation with Caroline Dury. "We have been entertained in her house; she has been the gracious hostess while we sat like lumps, or"—she glanced at Emily—"not. Then there was the piano. Is there a more accomplished pianist in the district than Caroline Dury?"

"I find she can make any piece boring," Emily said.

"Bah," Charlotte said. "She never misses a note, even on the most difficult runs. And she has a full piano to play upon, not just a cottage piano. However her father affords it, I do not know. As for me, I cannot play at all. I cannot see the notes unless my nose is right up against a sheet of music."

"You have other talents," Anne said.

Charlotte would not be placated. "No, no, it is hopeless. I do not doubt they will be married by the end of this summer. I must give up Mr. Weightman."

Emily wanted to say, How can you give up what you never had in the first place? But of course she did not say it. Instead she grabbed Charlotte's arm, and Anne's as she strode between them, and pulled them closer. Despite Charlotte's silliness over the curate, she saw the difference between her sisters and the others. That was how she thought of the Durys and Sarah Sugden. The others. She found it amazing that Weightman could be so patient with drawing room conversation, and move so easily between one world and the other.

At the Mechanics Institute, Weightman escorted Caroline and Sarah to a place of honor on the front row. The Brontës followed and were grateful when Weightman motioned for them to sit at the front as well. Even Charlotte put aside the disappointments of the afternoon to hear what Weightman had to say, and to see his face as well as she could in her nearsighted way. Charlotte wanted knowledge more than she wanted a man, as did her sisters.

Nor did Weightman disappoint. Upon his introduction, he launched into a spirited discussion of Sophocles and the play *Antigone*. Weightman explained to his audience, many of whom had no knowledge of the subject, the workings of Greek theater and the gifts it had bestowed upon dramatic productions down to the present day. Because there remained a whiff of the disreputable surrounding the stage, an added frisson attended the subject addressed by a handsome young man in clerical garb. The ladies, in particular, were enthralled.

As the lecture continued, it was also apparent that some of the gentlemen were scandalized. Though the Mechanics Institute was a progressive organization providing educational courses for the workingmen of the district, the audiences for the evening lectures drew from the most prosperous levels of the town, including mill owners. The subject matter of *Antigone*, as Weightman presented it, was a young woman who rebelled against recognized authority by breaking the law. Nor, it seemed, as one prosperous burgher whispered to another, was she ashamed of it. Quite the opposite.

Weightman read several scenes from the play. A discussion with Patrick Brontë before the lecture had convinced him it would not be a good idea to solicit female help in reading the parts. There was not a father in the district who would be pleased to see his daughter standing upon a stage with an unmarried man and reading lines from a play in full view of her neighbors. Patrick had shaken his head in private at Weightman's even suggesting it. That boy, he thought, shall get himself in trouble yet. But he thought it fondly, and with a smile upon his face.

So Weightman read the parts of both Creon and Antigone, careful to let his audience know who was speaking. But the message could not be clearer.

"'You dared to disobey the law?'" Weightman recited as Creon.

And he answered with Antigone's defiant response: "'Yes, I did. Because it's your law, not the law of God. You are merely a man, mortal, like me, and laws that you enact cannot overturn ancient moralities or common human decency. I would rather suffer the disapproval and punishment of men, than dishonor such ancient truths.'"

Weightman spoke with such passionate intensity that some of the ladies of more delicate constitution let out tiny gasps. Emily Brontë sat up straight and took a deep breath. Such sentiments were similar to the ones expressed by the heroes and, yes, heroines she wrote about when she and Anne created stories set in their fictional land of Gondal. At that moment, she felt herself inspired to storm some great height.

When Weightman was done, the lecture hall filled with thunderous applause and an undercurrent of talk. Women who stood and nervously posed inquiries about one point or the other dominated the question-and-answer session that followed. Now and then a skeptical gentleman would rise and challenge the speaker. One such inquiry came from a prosperous-looking man Emily recognized as the owner of the Bridgehouse Mill.

"This play seems to approve of sedition against the government. Would you agree?"

Weightman looked not at all flustered. "I would," he said.

The gentleman was not done. "Would you further explain," he demanded, growing a bit red in the face. "Does *the play* approve of sedition? Or do *you* agree with sedition?"

Weightman did not turn a hair. "I agree that the play approves of sedition." He continued, still in a calm and pleasant tone of voice, "I believe, however, the play only approves when governmental authority tramples on human decencies."

There was a pattering of gloved female applause.

A bit later, Mr. Dury rose to ask, in a friendly way, "Mr. Weightman, do you think Sophocles a talented playwright in his depiction of women? Does there in reality exist a woman, save for a common harridan, who would speak so to a man in authority?"

Weightman's eyes met Emily's. She felt a sudden clutching in the pit of her stomach. Then Weightman said, "Yes. I have known fine women capable of this."

"Extraordinary!" Charlotte whispered. "Where on earth could he have met such a woman? Do you think he means Agnes Walton back home in Appleby?"

Anne reached out and gave Emily's arm a quick squeeze. Of course Anne knew.

As they waited for Weightman, who upon the dismissal of the crowd was mobbed by a group of well-wishers, mostly women whose reluctant husbands dragged behind, Caroline and Sarah discussed the lecture.

Sarah was in a sulky mood. "I thought the sister Ismene was far more admirable than Antigone. She was sensible."

"I would prefer to have Ismene for a friend than Antigone," Caroline Dury agreed. "But the play is about Antigone, after all. Plays are about singular people, not normal, likeable people."

"That is true," Sarah agreed.

The Brontës stood aside and listened, Emily with her arms folded, eyes downcast and a smile upon her face. The wait required patience, for Weightman had been waylaid by a line of women. But at last Mr. Dury dragged him away by pointing out that a long and difficult walk lay ahead of the Haworth party. Caroline and Sarah were deposited with Mrs. Dury back at the parsonage, where they would speculate on the strangeness of the journey Mr. Dury and Mr. Weightman must endure. Then the two clergymen began the trek back up to Haworth with their charges.

The night was cold but bright with moonlight, so it was easy enough to find the way. Except for Charlotte, who still refused to rely upon her spectacles. Fortunately, even as the party descended the front steps of the Keighley parsonage, Emily stood close and spoke in Weightman's ear.

"Why don't you escort Charlotte?" Emily whispered. "She would so enjoy your company. And between us, Mr. Dury and I can carry Anne along quite well."

That was the way they proceeded. Charlotte, who knew nothing of the plot, accepted Weightman's arm with joy. Whither thou goest, I will go, she thought, keeping her eyeglasses firmly in her pocket. And Anne, with a companion on either side, scarcely felt the stress of the steep ascent. At first the way was smooth, broad, and level. As the party left the outskirts of Keighley, the road began to rise precipitously. Houses were fewer and farther between, and then rare. But the roadway was still wide and even enough for a cart or coach. The party could walk five abreast with ease, concentrating more on conversation than on their footing.

The journey was an astonishing one for the Reverend Theodore Dury. In his years in the district, he had only known the Brontës of the parlor, the painfully shy young women who scarcely opened their mouths. On this walk, he became acquainted with a different species of Brontë. Dury liked Patrick Brontë; in fact, he did not mind the trip to Haworth because it would give him a chance to breakfast with Patrick on the morrow and discuss business of the vicarage. He knew Patrick to be fond of his daughters, as any father should be. But he had never understood what seemed to him the inordinate pride Brontë took in his girls. Such drab little mice, Theodore Dury would have said, rather dull than accomplished.

But the Brontë sisters on the walk home were so far the opposite of that picture that he was shocked for a different reason. Scarcely was the town left behind when the Brontës began pelting Weightman with such pointed questions about his lecture that they caused Dury's head to spin. Nor did the sisters seem content to simply listen to and accept Weightman's answers. They challenged him.

Certainly Ismene was weak, Anne declared. And yet was not Antigone cruel to her? Indeed, agreed Charlotte, though Antigone was brave, was she not also too proud? Was that part of her downfall? And yet, Emily chimed in, would pride not be necessary when one takes such a great risk? How else sustain oneself in the face of certain death, if not with pride?

Weightman joined in as easily, Dury thought, as if he were talking with a group of clerics. Which surprised the Reverend Dury and made him uneasy. It would be more appropriate if Weightman maintained a paternal air with the young women. The Reverend Dury should be the center of the conversation, the young women retiring. But the roles were reversed, the Brontës carrying on a vigorous conversation with Weightman while Dury trudged along in shy silence.

"Did not Sophocles write other plays?" Charlotte asked.

And to Dury's astonishment, Weightman began to explain the story of how Oedipus was told by an oracle that he would kill his father and marry his mother.

"Mr. Weightman," Dury admonished, "do you think that a fitting topic for young ladies?"

"*Oedipus Rex* was one of the key texts in my studies in classical drama at Durham," Weightman replied.

"But these innocent young ladies are not at Durham," Dury reminded.

"They should be," Weightman said. Dury was taken aback. This was not the polite and charming young curate of the drawing room, but an oddly rebellious one. He decided to mention this to Patrick Brontë when they spoke in the morning.

And to his continuing amazement, Emily Brontë proclaimed, "I should like to read some more of those plays. Perhaps I could try to read them in the original Greek. I have already done some Latin translations on my own, Horace and Virgil. It is difficult with no instruction, but I make progress."

"I have a Greek lexicon. You may borrow it if you like," Weightman offered.

"Father has one as well," Emily said. "Though I never paid proper attention to it. Now I shall. But may I borrow a play from you? And which play do you recommend?"

"The Greeks have given us more strong women figures besides Antigone, which you might enjoy," Weightman said. He considered a moment, and then said, "For tragedy, I recommend Euripides. *Medea* perhaps."

Emily said, "Horace mentions *Medea* in his *Ars Poetica*."

"But—" Dury sputtered. "But—" He could not bring himself to finish his protest, to inform Emily Brontë that *Medea* was about a woman who killed her own children.

Weightman went on as if he hadn't heard Dury. "But you might want to start with a comedy by Aristophanes. I think you would like *Lysistrata* very much."

When he sensed Emily was about to speak, Dury said, "Do not ask what it is about," before she could in fact ask. Dury felt his face turning red with embarrassment as he remembered that *Lysistrata* featured a group of women who agreed to deny their husbands the pleasures of the bed until they stopped fighting a war. "Really, Mr. Weightman," he said, "I question the appropriateness of a young woman translating that play."

"I suspect, then, that I shall do it," Emily said at once.

Dury was speechless. Charlotte, sensing his discomfort, said, "You must never mind Emily, Mr. Dury. She will always take an unlikely course."

Finding his voice at last, Dury said, "Mr. Weightman, how do you propose to address my concern?"

"Of course, I shall mention it to her father," Weightman said.

Emily did not reply. She resented being spoken about as though she were not present, but knew that Patrick Brontë had never denied his daughters reading material.

The conversation took other directions, all pleasant ones to the Brontë sisters. Silver moonlight showed the undulating swells of moorland, here and there broken by jumbled boulders or jagged white streaks of unmelted snow. The outline of Haworth loomed above them, not an impoverished mill town but a castle astride a promontory. Emily imagined her Gondal heroine, Alexandrina Zenobia, slipping past the castle guard to meet her lover on the moors. They passed the dark hulk of the Ebor textile mill with its distant hissing of steam and running water. *The dungeon where Alexandrina Zenobia was held before she made her escape.*

Anne asked Mr. Dury the question that had become a secret code as the sisters sorted out the good clergy, in their view, from the bad.

"What do you think," Anne asked, "of the possibility of universal salvation?"

"Universal—what? Universal salvation? You mean that everyone would go to Heaven?"

"Yes," Anne said.

"Preposterous!" Dury cried. "Why bother to be a good Christian?"

"Is that the reason one is a good Christian?" asked Emily. "To get to heaven? But is that not selfish?"

Dury continued as if he hadn't heard her. "Murderers and lechers and pagans in Heaven? I think not! I have my doubts if Catholics shall be there!"

"Heaven would be too crowded," Charlotte said.

Dury missed the mockery in her voice. "Precisely," he said. "And how would it be Heaven if one were cheek to jowl with riffraff?"

Charlotte coughed, said "How indeed?" and added Dury to her list of ridiculous curates.

Emily glanced at Weightman. She could not see his face in the dark, but she fancied she knew him well enough to think his silence meant he was biting his tongue. Emily took a deep breath of the night air. She was exhilarated by the way words rang loud as hammer blows in the cold air.

"I don't want to go to Heaven at all!" she cried. "I want to come back here. To the moors."

"Come back?" Dury was shocked again.

"Yes," she said. If not for her support of Anne, Emily would have turned in a circle waving her arms over her head, crying, Here! Here! Here! and then run off into the dark. She was forced to imagine doing it. "It sounds so terribly boring, Heaven. Only the good people there, and sitting around all eternity contemplating their tedious goodness. I think they should soon be cross-eyed from the effort."

"Dear Miss Emily," Dury said carefully. "Do you wish to sound a Hindoo? You are a good English clergyman's daughter."

"Ah yes!" Emily cried. She felt herself drunk with energy. "But I am Irish, you see. And so I am wild."

"Hush!" It was Charlotte's turn to grow alarmed. "Our mother was English and our father—"

"Is Irish," Emily finished, refusing to be cowed.

"He does not speak of it often," Charlotte said. She glanced at Weightman. She considered her Irishness, like her spectacles, something not to be pointed out.

"Papa speaks of it to me," Emily said. "He is not ashamed of it."

Weightman broke his silence. "Perhaps, Miss Emily, there is something Irish about your idea of Heaven. The Celtic church fathers thought Heaven was close as earth, and only a thin border between."

Emily nearly stopped walking. She forced herself to continue for Anne's sake. "Indeed?"

"Indeed. And the highest spots, like mountaintops, are where Heaven and earth meet. Your moors could be such places."

"They are," Emily said. "Heaven shall be what we need. That is all. Of one thing I am most certain—I require moors for my Heaven. And animals."

The Reverend Theodore Dury said not another word on the way to the parsonage. He had heard enough heresy on the walk to Haworth to fire several pyres in the old days. Two points he resolved. One was to speak to Patrick Brontë on the morrow, to ask whether he ought to more closely monitor the ideas his daughters were exposed to. The other was to sit his own daughter Caroline down in their Keighley parlor and urge her to set her sights elsewhere than the Reverend William Weightman.

## 7

*E*harlotte considered the occasion of William Weightman's lecture in Keighley to be a disaster. The walk to town had been pleasant enough. But the adoration of a large portion of the female audience at the lecture reminded her of the hopelessness of her own situation; the ease with which Weightman fell in with Caroline Dury and Sarah Sugden in the parsonage parlor, while barely saying two words to Charlotte, had been particularly wounding. She was cross for days afterward, and Emily and Anne knew enough to leave her alone. Charlotte felt herself at a crossroads. She decided she would make one more effort. If that did not work, she would once and for all give up the idea of William Weightman (who, she had begun to suspect, did not deserve her loyalty, being incapable of loyalty himself).

Caroline Dury's musical display had been especially galling. But Charlotte possessed her own gifts. The greatest, she considered, was her ability to draw. Although Branwell had gone so far as to study portraiture with a teacher in an attempt to make a living with his art, Charlotte knew she possessed more natural ability than her brother. She would paint William Weightman's portrait.

Charlotte made the suggestion as though Weightman would be doing her a favor—she wanted the practice, she said, in a tone of voice she hoped he would consider modest. Weightman agreed at once. Her offer was a touch of genius, Charlotte considered, for it assured that Weightman would be a regular visitor to the parsonage. He would be in close proximity, a captive for conversation. And since Charlotte proposed that the portrait be done as a gift for Agnes Walton, the Appleby sweetheart, she had the means to monitor his attachment to that young woman, and a natural way to inquire, now and then, if another might take pride of place in the curate's affections. If the report was good or ill, Charlotte would have it first.

She suggested as lengthy a process as possible, a pencil drawing, then pending Weightman's approval she would move on to oil.

"Must I sit totally still?" Weightman asked.

"Reasonably so," Charlotte said.

"But may I talk?"

"Of course you may," Charlotte assented, secretly pleased. "And you may choose your pose. Although I would suggest a profile, since you have a good strong nose and chin. I would also suggest you pose in your academic gown from Durham, for you look well in it."

Weightman nodded, and the natural blush of his cheeks deepened. "Miss Brontë," he said, "you would make a fine advertisement for me."

"I think," Charlotte said dryly, "you need no help from me, Mr. Weightman. But we shall capture you for posterity."

She set about the task that would occupy her for much of the spring. She had Weightman to herself. Anne had managed to obtain a new position as governess near York, one she would take up in May. Much time was given to preparation, to sewing the items of apparel she would need, and brushing up on her studies, since her pupils this time would be older girls. And Charlotte timed the session with Weightman when Emily was most likely to be occupied with helping Tabby in the kitchen or tending to the animals. When Tabby groused that Charlotte might help more with chores herself, Charlotte answered that the capture of Mr. Weightman on canvas in the full bloom of his youth was fully as important as dressing a dead chicken. Emily, who was stirring a batter for pudding, kept her head down. But as Charlotte went out the door, Emily said in the strong Yorkshire accent she enjoyed for poking fun, "Sister, perhaps you should paint the dead chicken and dress Mr. Weightman."

Tabby let out a great whoop and Charlotte froze. She decided not to dignify Emily's jibe with a response. Emily knew that the blow had been well struck. But Charlotte would not have her nose put out of joint for long, for the sessions with Weightman pleased her immensely. She sat him beside the window and kept a pile of books to set at his shoulder for a backdrop, she fussed with the arrangement of his hair (what a particular joy!), combing it carefully forward and arranging it in delicate feathers around his face. She commented upon the academic stoles he draped over his gown, asking him to remind her which award he had received for one or the other. She had opportunity to learn about the joys of a university education (and to covet it), to discuss points of Scripture or other areas of study as a way to show off her own erudition.

At night, when talking to her sisters, Charlotte passed on what she and Weightman had discussed, as though it was almost as satisfying as experiencing it the first time. She had taken to calling the clergyman "Miss Celia Amelia." It was an old habit Charlotte picked up at boarding school, where the girls would give feminine names to men who intrigued them so they might talk about them without being reproached by their teachers.

She judged the time did not pass in a burdensome way for Weightman. The only area of discord was her lack of understanding about what Weightman saw as the stringent nature of his religious calling. She tried to be sympathetic, even as she attempted to argue him into a more comfortable notion of what it might mean to be an Anglican clergyman. Upon reflection, on her bed at night, she admitted that what appealed was not William Weightman of Haworth, but the *idea* of William Weightman ensconced in a well-endowed seat, say, at Cambridge. She dropped broad hints about her father's stories of the joys of that town and suggested how the curate's gifts might be employed there. Weightman seemed interested, and yet he did not. At some point he mentioned that his hopes for Agnes Walton were at low ebb. Charlotte sighed, was encouraged, and continued the pleasant task of staring at the profile of William Weightman and re-creating it on canvas.

The weeks passed, the portrait took shape, and the time was coming when the trajectory of all the family's lives in connection with William Weightman would be changed, and set in the pattern that would continue as long as everyone drew breath. When Emily Brontë looked back upon that spring, her memories were tied up with the church, a kaleidoscope of scenes from Easter to Whitsuntide. She saw Weightman standing before the congregation in his black gown singing in his strong voice, "Christ our Lord is risen today, A-lleluia," and then sitting with his chin in his hand and listening to her father's Easter sermon, delivered as usual without notes. At one point, Patrick said, "An especially joyous Easter, this one, the first with my new curate, Mr. Weightman, among us. Already he is beloved in Haworth. And does not the new life of the season have more meaning when one so vital and dedicated is among us?"

Weightman had smiled, nodded modestly, and blushed. Charlotte, who held Emily's hand in the Brontë pew, pressed it tightly as she shivered with excitement.

A few Sundays later, Emily sat with Anne in the same pew, after everyone else had departed. Anne would leave the next day for her new post as governess to the Robinsons of Thorpe Green. She wanted to linger and pray, but instead began to weep. Emily sat with her arms around her sister, tears coursing down her own cheeks. She anticipated the emptiness of her bed without Anne, the loss of conversation—the most intimate conversation she knew. Then there was her guilt as her sister went out into the world while she stayed contented at Haworth. When she spoke of this, Anne said at once, "No, no. It would be terrible for you to leave. You have tried it before and it kills a part of you, you know it does. And although I am sad, there is also a part of me that wants to go. I want to teach young women to lead useful lives. I want to see how others live, and to meet new people, and to test myself." Then the tears welled up in her eyes. "But still I shall miss you and I grieve."

William Weightman stood outside the church along with Patrick, shaking the hands of departing parishioners. When all had dispersed, Patrick took the brief walk through the graveyard to his parsonage dinner. Weightman turned to close the church door. Then he heard sobbing and went inside to investigate. The sisters sat with heads bowed, arms around one another, their heads bathed with light from the opaque windows. Weightman, who knew Anne's situation, went to sit in the pew beside them. He thought they might ask him to leave, but they did not.

Emily was astonished that Weightman only sat, without inquiring about their distress, or offering advice or consolation. Once Anne realized the curate had no intention of interfering with her grief, she gave herself the freedom to sob while Emily held her. At last Anne was spent and grew quiet. Weightman sat close, his arm across the back of the pew like a protecting angel.

When Anne had regained her self-control she turned to Weightman. "Thank you," she said. "It is a comfort you are here."

He nodded and said, "You leave tomorrow?"

"I do," Anne replied, her voice now calm. "Although I weep, Mr. Weightman, I do not want you to think I despair. It will be a great adventure."

"I know what you mean," he said. "When I left my family in Appleby to go to Tyneside, I wept as well. And yet I knew I took the path God led me upon. So there was sadness but also anticipation."

Anne smiled so brilliantly that Emily squeezed her shoulder in response. "You are right," Anne said. "I have such anticipation of how

I might mold the two young women I shall teach. They are older girls and of such an impressionable age." She thought a moment, and then added, "I shall be a month at Thorpe Green, and then what do you suppose? The entire family shall go to Scarborough by the sea for the summer. And I shall accompany them. I have never seen the sea, Mr. Weightman. I do look forward to it!"

"Do you know what?" he replied with equal enthusiasm. "I have a friend from my time at school in Durham who is curate at St. Mary's Scarborough, serving under the vicar Mr. Millar. His name is George Easton. I shall write to him at once and tell him to look for you."

"Oh, Mr. Weightman," Anne said. "It would be so kind."

Emily sat silent the whole time and watched, and listened. Weightman glanced at her as if to see how she judged his counsel, but did not press her to speak. When they all stood to leave, she simply said, "Thank you, Mr. Weightman. You are our best friend." He bowed, and they exited the church.

❧

The portrait was finished; Charlotte planned to present it to Weightman at a family dinner in late May after church. Anne was gone to Thorpe Green by then, and had written back to say that though she was homesick, her new situation looked to be far more satisfactory than the last. Her charges were vain and shallow, but sweet and pliable, their father a distant man who did not interfere, their mother a silly woman but easy to contend with. Anne was content, she said, and looking forward to her time at the seashore.

Patrick shared Anne's letter at the Brontë dinner table, the veiled portrait standing in a place of honor beside the front window. Charlotte picked at her food. When the great moment came, Tabby was called in from the kitchen as a witness. Charlotte stood and unveiled the picture with a flourish. Everyone applauded.

"It is the precise image!" Aunt Branwell exclaimed. "And how distinguished you look, Mr. Weightman."

"It is a fine painting," Weightman said. "Even if the subject is not worthy of so much effort from a talented artist," he added with a nod toward Charlotte.

Charlotte blushed. "I am glad it gives you pleasure," she murmured.

She was suddenly too shy to ask what he was going to do with it, afraid that the answer would center on Agnes Walton. But of course Emily blundered right in and said, "Shall you give it to your young woman when you go to Appleby? Father has given you time off to travel this summer, has he not?"

"He has," Weightman said. "But I am not certain when I shall go to Appleby. I would also like to visit South Wales." When he sensed some explanation was expected, he glanced at Patrick. "There is a young lady whose acquaintance I made while she was visiting relatives in Bradford. So I hope to go to Wales to meet her family."

"Ah," Patrick said, "I thought I had often seen a postmark from Wales on your letters when I collected them from the postmaster."

Weightman nodded. "We have been corresponding a great deal of late."

He did not notice, but Emily did, that Charlotte had gone pale and cast down her eyes. Nor did she look up or speak a word for the remainder of the meal, or put another morsel of food in her mouth. When a short interval had passed, she stood and said, "I feel ill. Excuse me," and rushed out. Weightman stood but Emily said, "Never mind, Mr. Weightman, her stomach has been troubling her lately."

"Has it indeed?" said Aunt Branwell, ever obtuse. "I did not know anything of it, and I share a bed with her."

"You know Charlotte does not like to complain," Emily said, and was glad that her aunt said nothing further.

Patrick Brontë invited Weightman to his study to smoke a pipe and talk over parish business. Emily waited until Weightman and her father retired and closed the door behind them. Then she went upstairs. She found that, rather than go to the room she shared with Aunt Branwell, Charlotte had retreated to Emily's small chamber. She lay stretched across the bed, her face buried in her arms. Emily sat beside her sister and began to rub her back. At last Charlotte turned her head. Emily saw her face was wet with tears.

"I am such a fool," Charlotte said. "As usual. Why should I think he would love me?"

"Some of us do love you," Emily said.

"You are not a young man!" Charlotte said sharply.

"There was that young curate who visited a while back," Emily ventured.

"He was mad!" Charlotte cried, and turned her head away. She breathed heavily for a time, then sat up and pounded the pillow. "What angers me—and mind you, it is myself I am angry at—what angers me is that he is not worth it. Whyever did I think he was? He is vain and will flirt with anyone who wears a skirt. Nor will he care a fig whose feelings he hurts."

"I think," Emily said, "you should not blame your judgment. It is easy to see how a woman might admire Mr. Weightman too much."

"Not a woman of intelligence once she sees how shallow he is!" Charlotte declared. "He is as vain as that ridiculous Sarah Sugden. Miss Celia Amelia. I named him well, did I not? I shall continue to call him so. That way I can laugh at him and he shall not even know it."

Emily wanted to point out that the silliness seemed all Charlotte's just then. At last she said, "Sister, he has his good points, which you shall become reacquainted with in time, when you have got over your hurt."

Charlotte picked up the pillow and tossed it in a disgusted manner. "I hope not. I hope he will not be here that long. He has no business being a clergyman. A man of the cloth should be holy, and sober, and high-minded. Mr. Weightman is nothing of the sort. He is easily pleased and so he thinks everyone else is easily pleased as well. He wants novelty of all sorts, he wants things stirred up. He should never have been a parson, he should not have been."

Emily bit her tongue. She continued to stay silent when Charlotte cut Weightman on several occasions after, walking away without shaking his hand or speaking after church, even standing up and leaving the kitchen table once when he came in the back door with the dog Robbie in tow. On that occasion Weightman stood awkwardly in the doorway, and then looked at Emily, his cheeks flushed with embarrassment.

"I was going to suggest a walk upon the moors," he said. "But I think not. Your sister is upset with me."

Emily saw no sense in pretending the situation was otherwise. "She is," Emily said. "But it is not for anything you have done, Mr. Weightman."

"I am glad to hear that," he said. "I would not give offense to my friends. But even if it is inadvertent, I am sorry for it." He hesitated. "If I may ask, has it something to do with what I disclosed at dinner on Sunday? About Wales?"

"It does," Emily acknowledged.

"Ah," he said. And after a moment, "Perhaps I was remiss in sitting for the portrait. I fear your sister took the time spent as something more than I meant."

"Do not blame yourself," Emily said. "It is a tendency of Charlotte's. She will recover." Then she sighed. "I am sad enough myself. Keeper and I would enjoy a walk on the moors with you and Robbie. But if Charlotte did not go as well, my aunt would have a conniption."

Weightman smiled. "Yes," he said. "Well . . ."

After a moment or two of pleasantries, he left to walk on his own. Emily sat, struck so forcefully by her loss that she felt ill. For a moment she thought she might hate Charlotte for what she had ruined in a manner that seemed to Emily casual and selfish. The loss was intensified a few days later when word came from the Widow Ogden that Mr. Weightman was ill.

Patrick Brontë paid a call, and upon his return Emily read the seriousness of the situation. "It is something in the bowels. Pray God it is not cholera," was all her father said. Cholera had once been known only in Asia, but ten years earlier an epidemic in England and Wales had killed thousands. No one knew what caused the ailment, but it seemed to strike the poor, who were thought to have brought their sufferings upon themselves with their filthy habits. For its capriciousness and sudden onset, there was now no disease more feared.

When Emily mentioned Weightman's illness to Charlotte, her sister said, "And why does Miss Celia Amelia insist on spending so much time in the poor precincts?" She caught a glimpse of Emily's face in the mirror, set down the iron with which she had been curling her hair, and said, "I'm sorry. That was unkind. I pray Mr. Weightman will recover."

"As do I," Emily said, unable to hide her anger.

"But dear God," Charlotte added, "why does he want to stay here? Why does Father stay?" She lay back on the bed. "Oh, Emily, I want away."

The next day, Emily heard from her father that Weightman improved, that he might be up and about by the end of the week.

"Mr. Wheelhouse cannot identify the illness," Patrick said as he bent and rubbed Keeper's head. "A miasma of the place, but not the worst, thank God."

"Mr. Wheelhouse knows nothing," Emily replied. She kept a sharp eye out for Weightman as the week progressed and was pleased on the Friday to glimpse him, looking pale and disheveled, as he disappeared into the Sunday school building with Robbie in tow.

❦

By Whitsunday Weightman had regained enough strength to take charge of the Sunday school activities. He convinced Patrick a special celebration for the children was in order, as was done in other parts of Yorkshire and Lancashire. There would be church, then on the holiday Monday a parade through the town, with singing and banners, and sweet buns and beer.

At the Sunday service the church was packed with a cacophony of children, whispering, talking out loud, some tired from work in the mills, others boisterous at the change of venue. Some older children who could read were in charge of the lessons. Then Weightman preached, and his sermon was brief.

"Today is Whitsunday," he said, "the day of Pentecost when the apostles gathered and tongues of fire danced upon their heads, and the Holy Ghost stirred them all. What a party that must have been! You will have heard, children, that you should fear God. Some of our churches will preach that, yes, and that you should fear hellfire. But why should you fear?"

He paused and Emily guessed what he thought. Why should these small ones fear Hell when they lived in it already?

"A friend once forced me to talk about some of the sad things I have seen in this world." He glanced at Emily and her stomach felt as though someone had grabbed hold of it and squeezed. "It hurt to think about those things. Man can do great wrong to man, it is true," Weightman continued. "But beloved, do not fear that God will do so as well. A God who would give away all his power and become a weak and vulnerable man is not a God to be afraid of. He is a God to be loved."

Because she was the daughter of Patrick Brontë and was expected to, Emily walked in the Whit-Monday procession the next day. Charlotte went along as well because she taught in the Sunday school. Her face bore a cynical expression as she watched the children crowd around Weightman, vying to walk as close to him as they could, the littlest ones taking turns holding his hands. Charlotte leaned close and whispered in Emily's ear, "What a scene this would make in a book. Celia Amelia in her element."

But Emily had some investment in the day and was pained by Charlotte's sneering. She had baked the buns the children consumed because Weightman had begged her help, along with Tabby and the wives of the postmaster and John Brown the sexton. The exotic ingredients, sacks of nuts and currants and sugar and flour, had mysteriously appeared at the back door of the parsonage. Paid for by Weightman, Emily suspected, though he never said so. She and Tabby spent two days in the kitchen loading the stove in shifts while the family was condemned to eat cold meat sandwiches. In the end Emily stood against the wall of the washhouse watching children who had never in their lives seen a nut or a currant cram their faces with buns and then cavort in the uneven pasture behind the parsonage.

Weightman had insisted upon a maypole. A pagan thing, a few of the dissenters of Haworth grumbled, and made sure their unfortunate children kept well away. Weightman had the pole decorated with ribbons of every color, more ribbons than children. The Haworth Brass Band was importuned to play, and produced a great deal of loud and boisterous music. The children chose streamers of their favorite colors and danced round and round. In the end they were allowed to cut off the ribbons and take them home, bits of bright color to gaze upon before they faced their twelve hours at the power looms, before they might lose their fingers or limbs or lives.

Emily wondered at the irony of bringing pleasure to factory children by giving them ribbons made by some other child in a factory. But what could one do? She studied the throng. One child, Susan Bland, stood aside clutching her grandmother's hand, looking like a small skeleton. Because of Anne's situation, Emily had become a student of consumption. She guessed the child was in the last stages and in a short time would be dead. And yet Susan Bland stared at the dancers and the ribbons with yearning.

Then William Weightman noticed the child and her longing, and picked up Susan Bland, placed her upon his shoulder, and joined the dance. He asked the child's favorite color. Emily could not hear the child's answer, but Weightman reached out and handed her a pink ribbon. The child clutched the ribbon with both hands, a look of sheer joy on her face while William Weightman danced around the maypole to the tunes of the Haworth Brass Band, twisting and turning with Susan Bland upon his back.

Emily Brontë watched, and knew she loved him. Unlike Charlotte, she loved him without hope, but with a passion beyond speech. She would tell no one. Not her father, though she told him much. Not even Anne, whom she told everything.

She would confide in Keeper. And she would write.

8

harlotte dealt with her hurt feelings in her typical manner, by going off to visit her school friends. Emily had no doubt the name of William Weightman would be bandied about among the friends with great contempt. She did not care as long as she did not have to hear it.

Emily only saw Weightman from a distance, in church or going to and from the Sunday school building beside the parsonage. She spent most of her time alone, since her father was caught up in as many pastoral duties as his health would permit, and both her sisters were away. Emily and Tabby and the two old people decided they would eat more simply. So there was less to do in the kitchen. When her household chores were done Emily escaped with a book or a notebook and pen for poetry or drawing to the dining room when the weather was inclement, or to the moors when it was good. With supper over and devotions done, and everyone else in bed, Emily read in her father's study with Keeper for company.

One day, as she and Tabby cleaned up after the midday meal, a knock came at the back door and William Weightman entered.

"Miss Emily," he said. "Tabby."

Tabby rubbed her hands on her apron and said, "There is a sad look on your face, Mr. Weightman."

"I am sad," he said. "I think a time has come." He looked at Emily. "Robbie's time. You know he has moved more slowly of late?"

"I have noticed it," Emily agreed. She paid close attention to the animals of her acquaintance.

"He is in the kitchen at the Widow Ogden's. He would not come with me to the Sunday school. He only lays and looks at me. He is in pain. Every breath is a kind of whine. Now and then he thumps his tail on the floor, but that is it. He rarely raises his head. His eyes follow me, those border collie whites with the stare that fixes you."

"He is telling you, Mr. Weightman," Emily said. "Poor Robbie."

"Yes," Weightman said.

"It was good of you to give him this last bit of time after Old Dean."

Weightman nodded. He did not move, as though reluctant to set in the motion what must come next. Keeper lay in a corner of the kitchen waiting for Emily and their afternoon walk. When Weightman had appeared, he stood and wagged and greeted the curate with a bump of his nose against Weightman's thigh. Then he sat back down and watched from the woman to the man and back again.

Weightman glanced at Tabby and understood that Emily and Tabby were as one, and that whatever he suggested would cause no scandal in that quarter.

"I'm going to take him up on Penistone Hill," he said. "Will you and Keeper come as well?"

"We will," Emily said. "How could we not?"

"Shall I fetch Robbie and meet you on the hill at back of the parsonage? At the last stile?"

"Yes," she said.

❦

Emily arrived first and saw him from a distance. He carried Robbie in his arms, and had a shotgun with a strap slung over his shoulder. When Branwell had been in Haworth he had gone grouse hunting with Weightman. Emily supposed it was the same weapon.

As they approached, Robbie raised his head and then dropped it again as though even that effort at greeting wore him out. Emily went to the dog, put a hand on either side of his head resting upon Weightman's arm, and looked into his deep brown eyes.

"Oh, Robbie," she said, "you're going to see Old Dean. Won't you be happy?"

The tail thumped once at the mention of Old Dean, and then fell limp. The party, two people and two dogs, trudged up the lane toward the crest of Penistone Hill. The manicured pastures with their cropped grass, neat stone fences, and flocks of chickens and sheep were soon left behind. The lane narrowed to a path that wandered through stands of heather, bracken, and moor grasses, alternating bands of deep green, brown, and white. Like waves upon the ocean, Weightman thought. Emily had no such frame of reference and so only saw her unending moors.

They came to the place where the way bent downward toward the path along Sladen Beck the Brontë sisters favored on their walks, which followed the beck to its source in a fall of water down a narrow cleft in the hill. But Weightman turned and said, "There are farmsteads that way. Let's go up."

Emily followed him back toward Haworth but on a path that climbed upward, until they were at the crest of Penistone Hill and could see most all the world Emily knew.

"Here," Weightman said. "Not as many people come here, do you think?"

"No," Emily said. She did not tell Weightman that Old Dean would have approved. He had explained that clans of fairies met at the highest point of their territory. *The crown of Penistone Hill,* he had said. *'Tis where the fairies of Sladen Beck and Haworth hold their court.*

Weightman tramped down a bed of grass with his boots, then stooped and gently laid the dog in the depression. Robbie thumped his tail three times and lay still, looking away as though he had begun to forget the two people already and to scout out where he would go next. Keeper approached and sniffed Robbie's rump, then his muzzle. He walked away and sat beside Emily.

"You may want to walk back, Miss Emily," Weightman said. "You can wait for me just out of sight there."

"No," Emily said. "I want to stay here." She desperately did not want Weightman to think her a coward. Still she added, "I think, though, that I will not look. If you don't mind."

She turned and knelt beside Keeper, covering his ears with her hands. She shut her eyes. She heard Weightman unsling the gun, heard a click as he primed it.

"That'll do, Robbie," he said.

The blast cracked the air and caromed from one side of the moors to the other like a live thing dying itself. Keeper shrieked and skittered away before stopping to wait, his tail between his legs. Emily put the back of her hand to her mouth.

Weightman stood beside Emily, shouldering his shotgun. "It's done," he said.

Then she began to cry. Weightman stepped close and put his arm around her. She leaned against him, burying her face against his shoulder. They stood for an eternal second, and then both seemed to wake from a kind of sleep and stepped back at the same time.

They walked away. Keeper paused to see why Robbie did not follow. Weightman was lost in thought. He did not measure his gait to allow Emily to keep up—she was nearly as tall as he was and kept up easily.

But she stopped. "Wait," she said. She pointed.

Weightman heard the sharp cries of a bird, and saw a flapping movement. Emily dropped to her knees and Weightman knelt beside her. A small bird with a dark brown back, not quite old enough to fly, lurched awkwardly as it tried to escape them.

"A hawk," Weightman said. "A merlin. Is its nest about?"

"No," Emily said. "It's been abandoned and has floundered its way here. Looking for something to eat, no doubt."

"Its parents may have been shot," Weightman agreed. "Or perhaps a larger bird of prey took them."

Emily picked up the hawk and ran a finger gently along the back of its head. It stopped struggling but its breast heaved.

"I suppose," Weightman said, "we should leave it to its fate."

"What is its fate?" Emily said. "We are its fate."

"Emily, do you have any idea how to keep a hawk?" Weightman did not notice, nor did she, that he had not called her "Miss Emily."

"I can try," she said. When he looked doubtful, she repeated, "I can. Besides, we were meant to find it. It is somehow connected to Robbie."

"To Robbie?" Weightman stared at her, puzzled. "How can there be a connection?"

"Everything is connected," Emily said. She took off her shawl. "I'll carry it in this."

Weightman studied her and then said, "All right." He took the merlin and held it while Emily folded the shawl and clasped the bird to her breast. The hawk breathed and fluttered beneath the shawl like a second heart beating. They walked toward Haworth.

"Where will you keep it?" Weightman asked.

"I'll put it in a cage," Emily said. "In the washroom. I don't suppose Aunt will let me have it in the house."

Weightman smiled to think of the scene that would occur when Emily introduced Aunt Branwell to the merlin.

"You should make a nest of some sort in the cage, out of old rags," Weightman pointed out. "To keep it warm."

"When it grows larger I shall let it out and see if it can fly around the washroom. And after that, I'll let it go."

"People do keep hawks and use them for falconry," Weightman pointed out. "They have done for hundreds of years. It could be as much a pet as anything."

Emily stopped. "I wonder what merlins eat?"

"You need to learn how to catch sparrows," he teased. "Or mice perhaps, or voles."

"Oh," Emily said. She began to walk with a worried expression.

Weightman said, "It might just as well eat some other sorts of raw meat. If you asked the butcher, he might keep by some offal."

Emily smiled. "Mr. Pearson will do that for me. I deal with him regularly." She glanced at the bundle she carried. "And I shall find something for it at home. I suppose it is starved to death."

"You must keep your cat away from it," Weightman added.

They talked of the bird until they reached the place where the path to the village dropped over the hill. There they stopped. Neither spoke, nor did they discuss what the reaction in the town might be if the curate and Mr. Brontë's odd daughter were seen returning from a ramble on the moors. Emily dropped her head and said, "Goodbye, Mr. Weightman. And thank you for Robbie's sake. Dear Robbie."

She turned and took the pasture lane back to the parsonage, the bird clutched to her chest.

~⚜~

Branwell Brontë returned to Haworth in July, in disgrace. He had been let go from his position as tutor in the Lake District. Haworth gossip had it that Branwell had got a young girl pregnant and been asked to leave. Pastor Brontë, it was whispered in the village, cannot control his own family.

Weightman found Branwell where he expected, drinking in the

Black Bull with his old friend Hartley Merrall. Branwell fell silent at Weightman's approach and looked sheepish.

"Good old friend," Branwell said. "How have you been?"

"Well enough," Weightman said. He did not return Branwell's smile. "I had thought to visit the Lake District during the time I have coming in August, to see you. No need now."

Merrall, who was just finishing his pint, sensed the curate's mood. He clapped Branwell on the shoulder and stood.

"I'm off," he said. "The good curate plans to turn your drinking bench into a confessional."

Branwell waved for another pint, a resigned look on his face.

"I had thought," he said to Weightman, "you might want companionship."

"I might someday," Weightman said. "But your father is distraught, and your aunt and sisters"—for Charlotte had returned—"are angry. Or so I hear from Tabby."

"I wondered who was the source of your gossip. That old crone."

"Watch how you speak," Weightman warned, staring at Branwell over the brim of his glass. "I love Tabby, and she and I get along like a house afire."

"Do you indeed," Branwell said grumpily. But he had caught a glint of mischief in Weightman's eye, and a lack of clerical approbation, despite Merrall's pronouncement. "I am the cause of the upset in the parsonage. Now you want to know the reason. I think you are a gossip."

"There is a fine line between being a gossip and a pastor," Weightman acknowledged.

"You say that with a great deal of smugness," Branwell complained.

Weightman ignored him. "Was it drink?"

"It was not!" Branwell said indignantly. "I raised a glass from time to time, of course. But not every day. I did my duty. I taught the bloody little sod as well as anyone could teach a boy with porridge for brains."

Weightman waited. He knew that whatever had got Branwell in trouble, he was a bit proud of it. Still a boy.

Branwell needed only a few more sips of his pint. "I got a girl pregnant. What do you think of that?"

Weightman considered. "I think," he said, "it has been done too often to be a great accomplishment."

"Hah!" Branwell exclaimed.

"Who was she?"

"My landlord's daughter. Margaret Fish. My God, Willie, she practically climbed in bed with me one night after her parents were asleep. Several nights, actually. They lodged me in the garret and all she had to do was sneak up the stairs."

"Did you offer to marry her?"

"I did. But only after it was certain they would say no. Should I be mad enough to tie myself to as silly a creature as I ever met? After all, they aren't certain the child is mine. I am only one of the finalists, and not even the one they most fancied. Nevertheless, my employer felt I was not a good example for his son. So I've got the sack." He took a deep drink from his glass. "My sisters are furious. Charlotte called me a reprobate, and Emily said not a word but looks at me like I'm some specimen of worm. If Anne were here I'm sure it would be three." He sighed. "You understand, don't you? My God, you're a man. You've been with a woman?"

"Yes," Weightman said.

"Yes!" Branwell began to feel comradely. "Tell me about it."

"No," Weightman said. Then he added, "That is one difference between being a cad and not being a cad."

Branwell looked sheepish. "I haven't been telling the entire village," he said. "I only talk about it among friends. Besides, no one here knows Margaret Fish. But everyone in the village gossips about it because my father is clergy. It must be like that for you as well. You could not be involved with a woman unless you were courting to marry. So what do you do?"

"Do?"

Branwell slapped the table. "My God, man. You've got desires."

"Ah," Weightman said. "To quote St. Paul, I burn."

"You burn?"

"Quite hotly. But there is nothing I can do, as you say."

"What of your Agnes Walton in Appleby?"

"I will see her next month," Weightman said. "Her father has invited me to go hunting. I think he has in mind to entice me with the combination of his daughter and a more comfortable living."

"You'll take it, of course!"

"Not of course. It is doubtful."

"You, my friend, are mad."

"Perhaps I am," Weightman acknowledged. "And perhaps I shall change my mind. I want to talk with Agnes again."

"I'll warn my father to be on the lookout for a new curate," Branwell said. "By the way, why is Charlotte now angry at you?"

"I'm afraid I disappointed Charlotte greatly," Weightman said.

"You see," Branwell said. "And you didn't even have to get her pregnant to do it."

# 9

*B*ranwell Brontë fancied himself a poet, an unappreciated poet. But he decided to change course. He admired the captains of industry emerging in Britain. In particular he was enthralled by the railroads thrusting their way into the isolated fastness of the West Yorkshire moors. A new line, the Leeds and Manchester, was excavating a massive tunnel beneath Blackstone Edge. A tremendous engineering feat, Branwell exclaimed over the newspapers he commandeered each morning before anyone else could read them. Here is the future! he was fond of proclaiming. (There is a fool, Charlotte added under her breath.)

Branwell decided to seek employment with the railroad. He set about the task with what Patrick called "admirable determination," and landed a post as assistant clerk for the Leeds and Manchester line.

Once again a celebration was in order. It would be a small and subdued affair. Anne was away at her post as governess at Thorpe Green. Worse, as far as Branwell was concerned, William Weightman had not returned from his leave of absence.

"I'd like Willie here," he complained at the celebration supper.

He did not notice the expression on Charlotte's face.

"I thought he'd be back by now," Branwell continued. "I've had a letter. It sounds as though the wooing of dear Agnes does not go well. Her father remains unhappy that Willie resides in Haworth and she begins to look elsewhere. In any event, Willie finds Agnes a bit of a bore as well. At least, that is how I read it."

"Willie has gone on to South Wales," Patrick ventured.

"To see his inamorata!" Charlotte cried. "Whom he has been corresponding with for months. So much for Mr. Weightman's faithfulness to Miss Walton. I do not know why Father keeps him on. I think it is disgraceful in a clergyman."

"Another woman?" Branwell exclaimed. "He made no mention of her to me."

"Of course not," Charlotte said. "He is too ashamed."

Patrick cleared his throat. "There is, I believe, a young woman Mr. Weightman has been writing in South Wales. He has been open about the correspondence. I would be out of place, Charlotte, if I dictated affairs of the heart to my curate. It is none of my business."

Charlotte fell to dissecting a slice of roast beef, and Emily remained silent, thinking.

❧❧

Charlotte turned again to the idea of the sisters starting their own school. Emily expected the scheme would come to naught. The Brontë education was too incomplete, especially in the classics and the teaching of foreign languages, to attract students. Especially not to a place like Haworth.

Then there was the question of money. The purchase of property would require a significant amount of capital. No one the girls knew had that sort of money. Except, Charlotte pointed out, Aunt Branwell. Their aunt had inherited a goodly amount from her family in Cornwall. But she was very close with it, since she considered that she held it in trust on behalf of her dead sisters, and there were other nieces.

Charlotte decided to approach Aunt Branwell, whose immediate answer was "No."

"But I ask no more than the portion you mean to leave us," Charlotte pleaded.

Aunt Branwell was glad to provide for the future of her nieces. But she did not like to be reminded that she would one day die. Had the request come first from Anne, by far her favorite—sweet, docile Anne she had raised from infancy—Aunt Branwell might have considered it. But she often felt Charlotte at odds with the rest of the family. As though she were ashamed of us, Aunt Branwell thought. And she sensed Emily was not keen on the school plan. Aunt Branwell valued Emily's help around the house. She did not want her going off to start a school.

The scheme languished. Charlotte had resisted seeking employment because she did not want to be away from William Weightman. But that was no longer an impediment. Now Haworth was unbearable. Charlotte wished to find a position so she would never have to look upon Weightman's cheerful, false face again. She began to scan the advertisements. Perhaps she might be lucky, like Anne, and find a family who would take her to the seashore in the summertime.

Emily was absorbed in her writing and her animals, including the young falcon ensconced in its cage in the washroom despite Aunt Branwell's protests. (And despite the qualms of John Brown's wife, who came each week to help with the laundry. She was so afraid that "yon vulture will peck my een out" that Emily was obliged to carry the cage outside each Thursday before Mrs. Brown came to supervise the tubs.) Emily continued to help Tabby in the kitchen and walked upon the moors with Charlotte. The arrival of autumn brought the heather to full bloom, carpeting the hills a brilliant purple. The royal season, Emily thought it, her favorite time of the year.

In addition to the poems she showed no one, Emily wrote stories about her fantasy island of Gondal. These she sent to Anne, who replied with a fillip of her own. In one of her letters, Anne noted in a teasing manner, "Your tales of Gondal are more and more, shall we say, passionate. Alexandrina Zenobia's latest encounter with her lover had me quite limp at the end of reading it. Needless to say, we could never share that with someone else."

Emily knew why her writing had taken this turn. At night she lay on her bed, alone since Anne was away, and dreamed of William Weightman. She remembered the brief moment on Penistone Hill when she had leaned against him and rested her head against his shoulder. She recalled his smell. She wondered what his mouth would taste like. She wondered what he would look like if he stood before her as naked as a Greek statue. She shivered, and shook herself and thrashed on her lonely cot. Next day, she would write.

And then, although William Weightman had not yet returned from his time off, he enlivened life at the parsonage. Even at a distance, Emily thought, he gives us a frisson.

❧❦

A special delivery post wagon arrived with a crate for the parsonage. Weightman was in Appleby after his return from Wales, and invited to hunt with the father of Agnes Walton. A farewell engagement, Weightman explained in the letter that accompanied the crate. "We part on good terms. He respects me even as he has given me up as a future son-in-law."

The crate stood encased in ice, which the driver assured had been replenished at regular intervals. A brace of wild birds—grouse, duck, and partridges, all still in their feathers—lay spread upon the frozen shards. Beneath the ice was a large salmon. All shot or taken by his own hand in the past day, Weightman assured them.

"Law!" Tabby cried, her hand to her breast, "how busy our lad has been!"

"Mr. Weightman is a veritable slaughterhouse," Charlotte said before she turned away.

Emily began to laugh. "Are you ready to pluck, Tabby? And should we serve the fish tonight before it goes off?"

The rest of the day was spent preserving the fowl in confit—it was already determined that Weightman's homecoming would be celebrated with the very ducks he had provided.

But next day a man in a black suit and tall black hat banged upon the parsonage door. When Emily opened it she disliked him at once for his small eyes which darted here and there, sizing up everything he saw, both Emily and the interior of the hallway. Although she usually stood back and threw open the door, assuming the visitor wished to see her father and was in some need, she stood firm.

"Constable Massey with the Metropolitan Police," the man said. "I must speak with the Reverend Patrick Brontë."

"Is anything wrong?" Emily asked. She wondered if Branwell was in trouble at his new job.

The man looked Emily up and down with a bold eye that seemed to undress her and then dismiss her. He said, "When did a chit like you start asking the questions? Now go and tell your master I haven't got all day."

Emily realized that the man—taking in her loose shift, her untidy hair, and the smudges upon her hands and face from cleaning the parlor fireplace—assumed he was talking to a servant. She took her time answering.

"The Reverend Brontë," she said in her strongest Yorkshire accent, "is working on his sermon. I hope you will not disturb him."

"Sermons can wait until Sundays," the man said.

"Excuse me," Emily said, and shut the door in his face.

She went at once to her father and explained the situation. They knew the sermon must be interrupted and the man dealt with, so Patrick put down his pen and fixed upon his nose the spectacles that aided his failing sight.

The man had begun to pound once more on the door. When Emily opened it, he said, "Careful lass," an edge to his voice, "or I shall have you sacked," and gave her a poisonous look as he passed. She was careful to pull the parlor door only partially closed. Patrick had grown hard not only of sight but of hearing; Emily hoped that would force the visitor to speak up. She sat on the bottom stair to listen.

"You are a long way from London," she heard her father say.

"On business from Sir Robert Peel's government," the man said. "I need say no more about its importance."

Her father's reply was inaudible. The man's voice dropped as well but rose after Patrick interrupted to say, "Speak up, please. I am not so young as I was."

"I said," the man repeated more loudly, "I have it on good authority that you are a true son of the Church, a good Tory, and a patriotic Briton."

"I hope I am all three," Patrick agreed.

The constable continued, "You have a curate here. One William Weightman."

Emily froze.

"Yes," Patrick said. "A fine young man."

"Surely he has some faults?"

Emily hoped the nature of the question angered her father as it did her.

Patrick's voice was careful. "His sermons when he first came were above the heads of our more uneducated parishioners. I spoke to him and he has since made great improvement."

Emily could imagine the glazed expression on the face of the impatient visitor.

"Mr. Brontë, are any of these names familiar to you? William Lovett? Henry Vincent? John Cleave?"

Emily assumed her father had shaken his head.

"You are familiar with the Chartists?" Constable Massey said.

Caution, caution, Emily silently counseled Patrick, remembering the time Chartists had shared a platform with her father. She squeezed her hands into fists and prayed he would not mention it.

"I read about them in the newspapers," Patrick said.

"Mr. Peel's government abhors their aims. They want a greater voice for the lower orders. All men over the age of twenty-one should vote, they claim. A secret ballot, most devious. No property ownership would be required, so a layabout in the London gutter or an agitator in a Leeds factory would stand equal to a lord."

"That would be a great change," Patrick said.

"The Chartists are agitating in London," Massey continued, "in Leeds and Bradford and Manchester, and in South Wales. We expect to have several leaders in hand any day now. At a meeting two days ago attended by some thousands, one of them spoke against the Metropolitan Police. The blackguard called us 'evil,' and charged we were 'an unconstitutional force.' I expect that fellow will be serving a year in jail for libel soon enough."

Silence in the study.

Massey said, "We have reason to believe your curate is in touch with Chartists in Bradford and in South Wales, in Swansea, Cardiff, and Monmouthshire."

Emily closed her eyes and whispered, Please, Papa, take care.

"How do you know all this about my curate?" Patrick asked.

"We have our means," Massey said.

Emily could have strangled him for the unctuousness of his voice alone. Oh, that I were a man, she thought. I would kill him and leave him on the moors to be picked apart by carrion crow. She was shocked at the violence of the thought, and then she was not. She thought herself capable of it, in will if not in physical strength, and she did not care.

"What I know of my curate," Patrick said in a careful, measured voice, "is that he is a fine clergyman. He often goes to Bradford on his day off. And he has been in Wales, yes, to see a young lady."

"I don't know about young ladies," Massey said. "But he has been spending his time in the company of coal miners." When Patrick did not respond, Massey continued, "We think he has been a sort of courier, a go-between for the radicals in Bradford and Wales. Saying to their faces what they do not care to put on paper, or delivering letters they do not wish to post."

"Do you charge him with something?" Patrick said sharply.

"We do not. Not yet. We are content to watch him. You should consider whether you wish to continue on with such a man as your assistant. Given your own admirably patriotic views, which are evident to all who speak of you, it would seem like an odd match."

Patrick said, "I will take that into consideration."

"However," Massey continued, "we think it wise you keep Weightman on for a time. That way we can keep an eye on him, and see if he leads us in any interesting directions. Are you aware of any correspondence he has received? An abundance of letters, perhaps, from unlikely sources or locations like Wales?"

"No," Patrick lied.

"We will peruse his mail," Massey said. "We shall intercept and read anything that comes from South Wales or Bradford or other industrialized areas before sending it on. But if you notice anything that alarms you, please let us know."

"Of course," Patrick said.

"If, after a few months have passed, you want to let this fellow go, that will be understandable. Assuming he is not in custody."

"Thank you."

It had gone on long enough, Emily decided. She went to the door, knocked, and looked in.

"Sir, your dinner will be cold soon," she said to Patrick, careful not to call him Papa. She looked at the constable. "I am sorry, we do not have enough to offer you anything."

Massey looked put out and his neck turned a telltale red. "I am not here to socialize," he said. "I have said all I have to say." He turned to Patrick. "I am in Bradford at the Savoy Hotel if you would like to make inquiries. I may stop in again when your Mr. Weightman has returned. Just to have a look about. If you see me, I would ask that you not seem to recognize me."

Then the constable left, stuffing his hat on his head as he went out the door.

Emily sat in the chair Massey had vacated.

"Dear God," Patrick said, "did you hear that?"

"I did. I was sitting on the stair."

"You know I do not approve, Emily!"

"I also know you are glad I did it this time." She took her father's hand. "Are you going to turn on him?"

"Turn on Willie?" Patrick reached for the pipe on his desk but did nothing with it, only stared. "Did you hear what he called me? A patriotic Briton. But what does that mean? I would have thought it meant one upheld ancient moralities and individual virtue and common decency. It does not mean that one sets a police force to spy on a young man because he cares for the poor."

Emily went to her father and flung her arms around his neck. "Please, Papa, what will you do?"

"What any Christian would. As soon as I see Willie, I will warn him so that he may avoid the trap they have set."

"Is he really involved with the Chartists?"

"He is. He told me as much. He's kept nothing from me except the Welsh correspondence. The young lady does not exist, I suspect. I shall rebuke him for that dishonesty."

"I expect he wanted to spare you worry."

"I expect so. But it was wrong of him."

"But was it also not wise? When they throw men in jail for speaking their minds? For standing up for common humanity? Dear God, I am so proud of Mr. Weightman."

It was an old cry of Emily's. To calm her, Patrick said, "Daughter, did you not call me to dinner?"

"Yes," she said, "but only to get rid of that horrid man. It is too early."

"That was inhospitable." Patrick smiled and squeezed her arm. "And I thank you for it."

That night as they waited for their father to emerge from his study and lead them in their nightly devotions, Charlotte perused the *Leeds Intelligencer*.

"I see the Duke of Wellington is urging Mr. Peel to crack down on those awful Chartists," she said. "The dear old duke. What should we do without him?"

Patrick had entered the parlor, carrying his prayer book. He shot a look at Emily that stopped her before she spoke. So she bit her tongue.

☙❧

William Weightman returned from six weeks away to a chorus of "halloos" in the high street as one after another welcomed him home. A gaggle of children ran to him; a coin apiece to two older boys guaranteed that his trunk would be carried to the Widow Ogden's. Then Weightman headed for the parsonage. Emily saw him from her upstairs window as she sat reading. She heard the knock on the front door, and her father's voice crying "Good to see you, my boy," and the closing of the study door. She went into the parlor and sat on the sofa with her book so she might hear when Weightman emerged. When he did, he did not look about him but only straight ahead, his face grim, as he went back out the front door. Emily ran across the hall.

183

"What happened?" she asked her father.

Patrick was not surprised to see her. He took off his spectacles and rubbed his eyes. "We talked first of his dishonesty. He admitted it at once and was repentant. Embarrassed, I would say. Then I told him how I learned about it, and warned him he must look out for himself. He was sobered, and thanked me so for telling him that I thought he might burst into tears." Patrick set his glasses back on his nose. "It was a bit like breaking a young horse, and gave me no pleasure at all," he said. "Especially when he was in such high spirits when he came in. I sent him away chastened, and with much to fret about. Poor boy."

More would ruin Weightman's return to Haworth. He duly attended his homecoming dinner at the parsonage and remarked on Emily's excellent duck confit. But Branwell and Anne were absent, and Charlotte remote to the point of rudeness. Weightman sat quiet, even morose. Charlotte assumed with satisfaction that he must find his return to Haworth a comedown after traveling in more civilized locales. Given the dashing of her own hopes, she had taken a perverse delight in Weightman's loss of Agnes Walton. Let him languish on the bed he has made, and may his Welsh love prove fickle as well.

Emily sensed Weightman's unhappiness but could not think how to respond without giving away her own feelings. It took Patrick, the pastor, to get at the heart of the matter. As Weightman was leaving, Patrick touched his arm and said, "You seem not yourself tonight. I hope you are not unwell."

"Oh," Weightman said, "it is just that I came straight from the bedside of little Susan Bland, who is dying. She is a particular favorite of mine. I will go back now; she won't live through the night."

They all had been standing by to wish Weightman good night, Charlotte reluctantly. When he had gone, she seemed chastened. "Well," she said, "I suppose there is some good in him after all."

Emily said nothing. She knew Susan Bland was dying. She had stood at the kitchen door that morning and ladled broth into a dish for the child's grandmother. Thank ye, she had been told, for a mite that would barely fill five spoons. But with the wine and the jar of fruit preserves provided by Mr. Weightman, the child's last hours would pass as well as they might.

Emily did not want to sit beside a deathbed; she wanted instead to defy death by ignoring it. Were Death a person, she would spit in his face. But she was glad Weightman was different, for the child's sake. He would get no sleep but would be up the next day, going about the work of a curate.

Emily lay awake that night as though joined in Weightman's vigil. Long after the others slept, she called Keeper, crept down the stairs, and slipped out onto the moors in back of the parsonage. There she lay on her back in the grass and watched the stars, felt the movement of the earth as it careered through space and eternity. She picked out a star for little Susan Bland to fly to. Not until the dawn birds sang did she return to her room for a few hours' sleep.

⁂

The child died and was interred in a tiny grave at the far edge of the cemetery. Weightman buried her, consoled her grieving family, and then life went on as before. A few mornings after, Emily met Charlotte rushing up the stairs as she was going down.

"I am going to my room to sew," Charlotte said as she brushed past. "Celia Amelia is in the kitchen."

Charlotte seemed to expect that her sister would join her, but Emily continued on. There she found Weightman sitting companionably at the table with Tabby and sipping a cup of tea.

"Miss Emily," Weightman said as he stood, "do come join us. Tabby has just been telling me about the fairies."

Emily smiled. "Indeed, Tabby knows more about the fairies than anyone in Haworth. Only Old Dean was her match."

"Whoosht," Tabby said, and made a movement with both hands as if to push away compliments.

"Tabby was just saying that when she was a child—" Weightman prompted as Emily drew up a chair and poured herself a cup of tea.

"When I was a little 'un fairies lived on the moors and in the dells, I was saying. Yon crest of Penistone Hill was one place they met, as Old Dean has told Emily. But I was raised beyond, below Ponden Kirk. Where the great rock is, Mr. Weightman. Have you been there?"

"I have on some of my walks," Weightman said. "Branwell and I have hunted down below."

"In the shelter of the great rock at Ponden Kirk, that is where I saw the fairies when I was young. Saw them with my own een."

Emily had heard the tale many times but enjoyed it again, and the company.

"I spent the night with my father's sheep, for we sheltered 'neath the rock during a storm and it grew too dark to move about for fear of losing the way and falling into a bog. I saw their lights then, I did, though it were raining too heavy for fires, one would think. Yet these burnt on despite. Next day there were the black marks upon the ground where they had been. They could burn through the rain, fairy fires, and the little people themselves stay dry round them. I thought it might ha' been a wedding, for there were little garlands strewn about."

"I wish I could see fairies," Emily said. "When I go out at night and watch the stars, I wonder if they have fled somewhere there, to the Pleiades or beyond."

"They have fled," Tabby agreed. "Sometime after I was grown. It were the factories as had driven them away."

"Indeed they did, Tabby," Weightman said. "Indeed they did. And a great much else besides."

They fell silent, as if the fairies had laid a spell upon them. Then Weightman finished his tea and turned to Emily. "I brought something

186 *Denise Giardina*

for you from Appleby," he said, and produced a leather pouch he had placed on the floor beside his chair. "A present from the gamekeeper at Mr. Walton's estate. Tabby tells me you still have the hawk."

"I do," Emily said, and dropped her eyes. "Though I think now it might have been wrong, Mr. Weightman, even if it would be dead if we had not rescued it. For it is still in its cage and is a sad prisoner. I would not be a jailer. But I fear what would happen if I let it go. As you predicted, it is much attached."

"Here is a remedy," Weightman said, and, opening the pouch, he removed several lengths of leather, a large glove, and a small handbell. He held up several short strips of leather. "Jesses and bracelets," he said. "The bracelet goes on each leg and the jess is attached to it. And here is a collar of little bells to go around the neck while you're training. So you can hear where the bird is when you can't see it." Next he unrolled two long leather leashes, one around ten feet long, the other fifty feet. "These are creances. You attach them to a jess on one leg. Use the short one at first when you are training until the hawk learns to come to you at the sound of this." He picked up the bell and rang it a few times. Keeper, who was sleeping in the corner, raised his head and pricked his ears. "When you reach the point where you want to fly the bird out in the wild, you switch to the longer creance. You should have trained the bird to come to your fist. That is why you wear the gauntlet. And someday, if all goes well, the hawk will fly out and hunt and return to you all on its own."

Emily had been looking from one object to the other, her eyes wide. "Oh, Mr. Weightman," she whispered. "Oh, Mr. Weightman." Suddenly her eyes filled with tears and she was so ashamed for him to see that she fled into the parlor and shut the door. After a few moments of standing in the middle of the parlor clenching and unclenching her fists and wiping her eyes, she regained her composure. Weightman was still at the kitchen table with Tabby. He showed no surprise at her sudden flight, or equally abrupt return.

"Will you show me how?" she asked, not looking at him but kneeling beside Keeper to scratch behind the dog's ears.

Weightman smiled. "When I finish my tea."

"Lord," Tabby said, "a good thing 'tis not wash day!"

❧

Emily and Weightman went to the shed with the leather pouch and a parcel of offal from the butcher's. When they pushed open the door to the washroom, the bird squawked in greeting. Emily said, "This is Nero, Mr. Weightman."

"Good Lord! A bloodthirsty name!"

"Hawks are bloodthirsty creatures, are they not?" Emily replied.

The bird regarded the intruder with a beady eye. Weightman examined the merlin. The bird's back was a dark bluish gray. When he opened his mouth to squawk, Weightman saw the tongue was a matching blue.

"A male," he said. "Take him out of the cage and hold him, since he is used to you."

Emily did as she was told and held Nero to her chest. Weightman took out a bracelet and showed Emily how to fix it to the bird's right leg. Then he instructed her to hand Nero over while she attached the second bracelet to his left leg. They repeated the process with each jess.

"He seems not to mind my holding him," Weightman observed.

"No," Emily said. "He has lost his fear of humans."

Weightman showed Emily how to attach the shorter creance. "Are you right- or left-handed?" he asked.

"Left-handed."

"Then put the glove on your right, so the left will be free." He handed her the gauntlet, then the end of the creance. "Now let him go," he commanded.

She did so, and the bird made at once for the rafters, where he hopped about for a time, shocked to find himself elsewhere than his cage or Emily's embrace. He shook himself with excitement.

"Oh!" Emily said. She was too moved for words.

Suddenly Nero launched out and landed on the edge of a washtub. Emily was forced to let the creance go as it tangled in the rafters, lest the bird be caught up. But Weightman stood on tiptoe and managed to retrieve and untangle it. He handed it back to Emily, and gave her the bell. He took a strip of raw meat from the pouch and hid it in his hand.

"Now," he said, "we must time this." He stood close beside her and took the creance. "Hold up your fist. Then ring the bell."

Emily rang the bell as Weightman held up the meat next to her glove and tugged on the creance; the bird sensed the meat and the upraised fist and flew toward them, but veered and headed for a far corner of the rafters. He squawked at Weightman as though lecturing him.

"I think," Weightman said, "he wants me away. Perhaps he is jealous. Never mind, Nero, you must put up with me for a time."

He urged Emily to stand next to the bird, and then used the creance to force Nero to step on her fist while she rang the bell. Weightman thrust meat into the bird's mouth.

They repeated the experiment. Sometimes the bird stepped cautiously onto Emily's upraised fist from an adjacent post; other times Weightman must use more force to guide it to the glove while Nero protested. When they moved, the bird veered away.

But on the final attempt, Nero flew in from a distance of about five feet. The merlin settled upon the glove even as Weightman guided the meat into its open craw with two fingers. Then the hawk flapped his wings once and settled onto Emily's upraised fist. She could feel the grip of its claws through the leather.

For a second no one moved. Then Emily and Weightman reacted

together, he crying, "It worked!" and she simply, "Oh! Oh!" Their cries startled Nero so that he flew back up into the rafters once more. He was so adamant in his refusal to return that Weightman was forced to mount a footstool and bring the bird down himself, even as Nero flapped his wings and verbally abused the man most vigorously.

Weightman handed the merlin back to Emily and said, "That's enough. The gamekeeper said the training sessions should be short, especially at first. And I think I have tried Nero's patience so he will not want to see me again for a while."

Emily gave Nero a hug and put him back inside his cage, where he settled upon his perch and glared at the two humans.

"I wish you had four hands," Weightman said. "It will be harder for you to manage by yourself."

"When he is more consistent about gaining my fist," Emily considered, "I can hold the bell, meat, and creance all in one hand, with the creance wrapped around my wrist in case I drop it. Later I can keep the meat close and grab it quickly after he lands."

"Soon you will not need the creance at all as long as you stay inside. But when you decide you are ready to try outdoors, I will help you with the longer leash."

"Mr. Weightman, I don't know how to thank you."

"Would you consider your friendship to be sufficient?"

Emily studied Weightman and was surprised to see he was sincere. And as she judged his sincerity at that moment, another thought, equally astonishing, occurred to her—that William Weightman, gregarious and flirtatious William Weightman who was loved by many throughout Haworth, adored by women in Keighley, and esteemed as well in Appleby and beyond, was, at some other level, deeply lonely.

An idea came to her that, even as she blurted it, she feared he would think absurd. "May I share with you a poem I wrote, as you once offered yourself in a valentine? I have shared my poems with no one except Anne. If you look for a token of my friendship, I can think of nothing that would cost me more."

To her relief he said, "I would be honored."

Emily ducked her head, unable to look at him. Then she said, "The verse is about this hawk. I hope you will not think it trivial." She closed her eyes and recited:

> *"And like myself lone wholly lone*
> *It sees the day's long sunshine glow*
> *And like myself it makes its moan*
> *In unexhausted woe*
>
> *Give we the hills our equal prayer*
> *Earth's breezy hills and heaven's blue sea*
> *We ask for nothing further here*
> *But our own hearts and liberty*
>
> *Ah could my hand unlock its chain*
> *How gladly would I watch it soar*
> *And ne'er regret and ne'er complain*
> *To see its shining eyes no more*
>
> *But let me think that if today*
> *It pines in cold captivity*
> *Tomorrow both shall soar away*
> *Eternally entirely Free"*

Emily dared open her eyes. Weightman was looking at her intently. "That was lovely," he said. "Thank you."

Emily nodded.

"You speak of eternity as though it is not to be feared, but longed for."

"Yes," she said. "I sense it will be larger."

"And not far away but close at hand," he mused. Then, "You spoke of yourself as well as the falcon. Do you feel so alone, even with your family here?"

She thought he required honesty, and so did she. "Yes," she said. "Are you not lone as well, Mr. Weightman?"

He didn't answer. Then he smiled. "Might we not call one another by our Christian names?" he said.

She considered. "You may call me Emily. Although not when the family is about, especially Charlotte. I do not know that I could call you Willie. Perhaps it will come more naturally someday."

Weightman laughed. "Very well. I have one more request and then I shall go. I wonder if I might have a copy of that poem? I should like very much to look at it again."

"You will be my first reader," Emily said solemnly.

She went to her room as soon as he had gone and copied out the poem in her best script on a precious sheet of paper. When she saw him leave the Sunday school building, she slipped across the lane and into the room. She laid the poem in the middle of the desk, with his Book of Common Prayer at one corner for a paperweight.

ᴐᴉᴄ

Emily had another gift to offer later that week. She went with Keeper to the Sunday school building and found Weightman at his desk. The curate stood, offered her a chair, and sat back in his own seat as though not at all surprised at her presence. But he noted, "When you appear unannounced, I expect a challenge."

"And any thoroughgoing Christian should welcome a challenge," she answered.

Weightman laughed and said, "Please let me hear it."

"You no longer go to Bradford on your day off?"

"Not for a time," Weightman said. "I had been visiting a young woman but I no longer—"

"Mr. Weightman," Emily interrupted. "I most certainly will not call you Willie if you continue your deception. I overheard the policeman talking to my father about you and the Chartists."

"You overheard?"

"I eavesdropped," Emily said. "A particular sin of mine. I know a great deal about the goings-on in Haworth and the district, Mr. Weightman, but very little of it is told to me directly."

"I see," said Weightman.

"I am aware the Metropolitan Police watch your mail. It is difficult now to be in touch with your Bradford friends."

Weightman studied Emily Brontë. "It is," he said. "The mill workers here depend upon me for their news. I have not yet figured out how to continue to help them."

"I do not know how to restore your South Wales correspondence," Emily said, "and I suppose your friends there will find other means. But I should be glad to receive any mail from Bradford."

She expected he would laugh at her. Instead he narrowed his eyes and gave another of those searching looks that seemed to scour her soul. "Events are moving toward some sort of action in the next year," he said. "Not violent, of course, or I would not be party to it. But a stoppage of work. Would you wish to support that?"

"I would. I have long had sympathy for the workers."

"And how would you explain the letters to your family?" he said.

"Aunt Branwell will not notice. She is more and more frail, and spends most of her time upstairs in her room. Anne and Branwell are away. Charlotte—" Emily thought a moment. "I hide much from Charlotte. My writing, especially. She is always urging me to publish my poetry, when I deny I am even composing it. I love my sister, but I will not jump through hoops for her like a circus animal. I shall hide the correspondence before I pass it on to you, but if she notices, I can pretend it is related to my poetry, and put her off by claiming privacy. Besides, she may not be in Haworth long. She has received an offer of a position as governess and is likely to take it after the New Year."

"And your father? He has already chastised me for subterfuge."

"As have I," Emily said. "So you may choose between us."

When Weightman shook his head as though he could not believe what he was hearing, Emily hastened to add, "I know how my father esteems you. He loves you like a son, especially as his own has been such a disappointment. Besides, I see no need to worry him about something so trivial as letters. And as he has declined in age, he has delegated the task of fetching the mail to me."

"And what of gossip in the village about any letters you might receive?" Weightman said. "I notice that my own romantic attachments turn up quite often as a conversation piece among our good neighbors."

"Would it not be entertaining," Emily said, "to wonder who might be writing Mr. Brontë's odd daughter? But if you think that would call attention, why not have me correspond with another woman?"

"I shall consider it," was all Weightman said.

A week later, when she went into the kitchen to help Tabby with breakfast, Emily found a sealed letter waiting on the sideboard. The address, written in Weightman's hand, was

*Mrs. Margaret Bishop*
*5 Vicar Lane*
*Bradford*

"Mr. Weightman has been here," Tabby said without turning from the pot of porridge she was stirring. "He said I am to give that letter to you, and t'say nothing about it otherwise. 'Aye,' I told him, 'I can keep a secret well as t'next.'" Then she turned and cocked her head at Emily. "'Give this to Emily.' That's what he said. Not 'Miss Emily.'"

Emily went to Tabby and gave her a hug. "He is my friend, Tabby, nothing more. But perhaps the best friend I have ever had. Except for you, of course."

"And what manner of mischief are you and your friend up to?"

She was tempted to tell Tabby, but knew she must not. Instead she put her mouth to Tabby's ear and whispered, "We're helping the fairies return to Penistone Hill."

Tabby reached around and gave Emily a swat on the backside.

Emily took the letter to the post after breakfast. Three days later she received a response addressed to "Miss Emily Brontë," which she tucked into her pocket before delivering the rest of the parsonage mail to her father in his study. She crossed the lane and handed the letter to William Weightman at his desk, along with a basket of the bread she had baked earlier, for distribution in the village.

"Emily," he said as she turned to leave, "since I no longer go to Bradford on my day off, I can often be found upon the moors on Tuesdays. Perhaps I might see you there from time to time."

"Why, Mr. Weightman," Emily said, "it would be improper, would it not, for an unmarried clergyman to walk unescorted on the moors with an unmarried woman. Especially a woman who goes abroad at night alone with her dog."

He had the decency to look abashed. "You recall," he said, "how I chastised you when first we met."

"I do."

"Perhaps I have decided," he said, "that women are no more to be confined to a cage than is a merlin. The moors are very large as well, and very empty."

"They are," Emily said. "And people do meet upon them from time to time." She left him with that, and closed the door behind her.

10

ew Year of 1841 slipped in almost entirely without notice. Anne had not come home since her employers, the Robinsons, judged she had not been with them long enough to warrant a holiday. Her heartbroken letter informing Emily of this fact caused her sister to weep, but there was nothing to be done.

Charlotte accepted the position as governess to the White family at Upperwood House and would also be gone after the new year. It could not be too soon, she thought. The situation between Bradford and Leeds was close to several of her old school chums. She talked of little else as Emily helped her pack. She had hopes, she told Emily. She would be in society, even if only as an employee at Upperwood House. On her days off, when she would visit her friends, she would be among people of education and refinement.

"Mary Taylor's family is a bit unconventional for my taste," Charlotte said. "Her father is very nearly a radical in many of his opinions, and the sons are wild as well. But refined people, nonetheless, educated people I can talk with on a level of equality." Then she touched Emily's arm in apology. "Not that I cannot talk with you in such a manner, and Anne when she is here. But she is not here, and you are all I have. There, I will meet new people. Perhaps a young man. There are a number of clergy in that district who are also acquainted with

Papa. Perhaps one might be in want of a wife. It is the surest hope for a clergyman's daughter with attainments though not beauty or wealth. Perhaps I might be fortunate enough to meet a cleric who takes his situation far more seriously than himself."

Unlike Miss Celia Amelia, she need not add. Emily ignored her and continued to sort out stockings for mending. Charlotte watched and sighed. "Poor sister," she said. "Leaving is all I want, and you are forced to stay. I am so sad for that."

"You are sad that I must stay here," Emily replied. "And Anne is sad because she cannot *be* here. So I must either feel sorry for myself, or guilty at my good fortune. I think I will be reconciled to my situation and make the best of it."

Charlotte gave her a hug. "You are such a simple soul!" she exclaimed. "I am glad you are here for Papa. With Aunt so much an invalid now, you are especially valuable to him."

Then Charlotte was gone, and Emily was once again left alone in the parsonage with only the two old people and Tabby.

❦

Not long after Charlotte's departure, a doleful ancient ritual was observed in the cemetery. The churchyard was full; Haworth parish suffered a multitude of deaths. John Brown the sexton and his grave-diggers designated an area every few years to be excavated and cleared, so the grave sites might be available for the new dead. A bonfire was lit in the field beyond the churchyard, the oldest graves emptied and the contents carried off in carts to be burned. No one could recall when the practice began. Surely in the last few centuries, Patrick said. Much earlier, Emily thought. She could see in her mind's eye the graves beneath the house, and the unmarked graves behind, and knew they too had been disturbed. She fancied the hillside had long ago held an ancient funeral pyre where the dead were burned, until a Christian missionary converted the pagans, called for burial, and established a church on the site. But then the old burning ways returned every few years, to remind that this had always been a place reserved for the dead, who were ash, dust, bone.

She went outside to watch. Patrick and William Weightman were both present to supervise the proceedings, offering prayers for the dead and for the living men who disturbed the bones with their shovels, ensuring an atmosphere of decorum was maintained. (In earlier times, legend had it, the gravediggers would be drunk, would sing at their work to scare away ghosts and the devil, and play football with skulls they found. A strict evangelical parson in the late eighteenth century had put a stop to all that.)

Patrick did not feel well and went inside as soon as the prayers were done, after assuring himself that Weightman would remain for the duration. The younger man stood morosely by, holding a burning torch in one hand and his prayer book in the other, while John Brown and his gravediggers toiled. The coffins they dug up had long ago collapsed into a mixture of sawdust and earth; the bodies dissolved as well so that only a jumble of bone fragments remained mixed in with the meal of earth. Now and then a white shard appeared in the torchlight, and then disappeared in a shower of dirt onto the back of a cart. The distant bonfire, already at a roar, would be difficult to maintain, for the material was more of a nature to damp down the flames than fuel them. In truth, the fire would consume little of what it received, and purification of the remains would be more symbolic than literal. Those who found themselves walking through the far pasture would avoid the spot for years to come.

Emily walked to Weightman's side and stood. He glanced at her but he did not say, as John Brown had muttered when he had seen her earlier, that it was no place for a woman.

"The worms have done their job," Weightman said.

"The worms think it common work," she replied. "But we cannot bring ourselves to do it in the daylight."

Weightman took a deep breath and said, "Though I deal with death every day, and have done for years, I have not seen this before. How old do you judge this part of the graveyard to be?"

"I believe most of the headstones go back to the late 1600s and the turn of the last century," Emily said. "They will disturb none who have been here less than a hundred years."

They stood for a long time watching the flash of shovel and soil and bone in the torchlight.

"What does it matter," Weightman said, breaking the silence, his voice so intense that Emily started. "Life is elsewhere. It must be."

He turned to her, his face hidden in darkness, as was hers.

"Mr. Weightman," John Brown called, "we have the last of the bones out, and waiting to be carted off. A final prayer at the bonfire, if you please."

Weightman stirred, clutched the prayer book to his chest as though for protection, and trudged away into the dark. But not before he had reached out and brushed Emily Brontë's cheek, ever so gently, with his fingertips. As though to assure himself, Emily thought, that she was warm flesh.

❧

Winter passed into spring. Weightman again sent valentines to the Brontë sisters, now in their scattered locations. They shared their responses by letter. Anne and Emily laughed over the verse, as badly written as the previous year. Charlotte noted to Emily that she had received her valentine at Upperwood House. "I consider it to have the same worth as its sender," she wrote, and Emily could almost hear her sister sniff with disdain as she penned the words. "It might have been written to anyone."

*But it wasn't,* Emily thought. *He was kind enough to write it to you.* She determined to say not a word in Weightman's defense. If Charlotte wished to turn her back on friendship, that was her decision.

Emily went out each afternoon after dinner with the hawk Nero. They had progressed to the long creance on the moors above the parsonage, and Emily knew it was time to try the merlin on his own. But she hesitated. First she decided she must wait for warmer weather, so if the bird did become lost, she might stay for hours if necessary and look for him. But as the snows thawed and the earliest spring flowers began to appear, she was forced to admit she had become attached to the hawk. He had shown himself to possess a personality and an intelligence that surprised her. Nero tolerated Keeper, and sometimes, to Emily's amusement, perched on the dog's broad back and dug its claws into his thick fur. Keeper would twist his head back left and right to try to see what had hold of him, and then stand still as a statue until the bird lifted off in a slow leisurely flight.

But fifty feet was its scope. As the spring air quickened the hawk's blood and made him more and more agitated so that he even began to peck at himself with his sharp beak, Emily decided it was time. But she wanted William Weightman to be present.

ༀ

Tuesday afternoons with Weightman became a habit that winter. Weightman had noticed the regularity of the parsonage schedule: breakfast at nine, followed by the post and newspapers, then chores, dinner at two, an afternoon walk for the younger family members, tea at six. Then came a time Weightman knew nothing about, when the sisters wrote or read or talked together in the parlor. If the mood called for music, Emily sat at the cottage piano and played. At half past eight the family gathered for prayers. Patrick and Aunt Branwell went to bed, and the sisters continued for several more hours.

Weightman supposed that Emily would be alone on the moors sometime between three and six. He knew just as well the Brontës' favorite haunts, having accompanied them himself from time to time.

On a cold February afternoon Emily arrived with Keeper at the last stile on the path that led up Penistone Hill to find Weightman leaning against the stone wall. Neither asked permission; they simply fell in together.

On a subsequent Tuesday when the weather turned and a rare sunny day promised spring warmth, the curate stopped early by the parsonage, as Emily was peeling potatoes for Tabby, and suggested they carry books to the waterfall at the head of Sladen Beck.

"We could sit upon the rocks and read," Weightman suggested.

"Why do you not take dinner with us first, Mr. Weightman?" Tabby asked. "I have a fine roast chicken, and Emily has made pudding." And so began a second habit, for Weightman had until then packed a sandwich and a wedge of cheese for his dinner on his day off, to be eaten cold and alone. With Charlotte not around to disapprove, Patrick and Aunt Branwell also looked forward to the cheerful young man's presence at Tuesday dinner. Were they so distracted afterward, one by pastoral duties, the other by the need for a nap, that they did not question if Weightman and Emily went off together? Or did they not notice, because Weightman always set off first, and went to the stile, while Emily followed soon after to meet him. Emily thought it an odd situation; she and Weightman had not so much as held hands, and yet some people would think their actions scandalous. For the sake of Weightman's career, she worried. But when she mentioned it to him, he said, "There is nothing wrong if I happen to run into Mr. Brontë's daughter on my walk. Besides, I think my position in Haworth is established enough to risk the gossip." Charlotte would have made great fun of his self-assurance had she been there to hear him.

Emily especially remembered the "book day," as she thought of it. She brought her copy of Sir Walter Scott's *Rob Roy*, which she was rereading for the fourth time. She had nothing new. The Brontës, too poor to purchase many new books, depended upon the lending library at Keighley. Branwell used to accompany the sisters to the town but he was long away, and Patrick no longer able to walk the distance. There were times when the sisters would slip off together, so desperate were they for books. But now Emily was stranded, for if she went alone she was sure to be noticed. On occasion she heard of someone making the trip, John Brown, or a local tradesman, and begged for a copy of anything new. But this resulted as often as not in a disappointing read, something trivial and sensational rather than satisfying, and then there was the problem of returning the material before a fine might be levied.

On that clear March day when she settled upon the turf with her back to a gray boulder and Keeper beside her, and pulled out her book, Weightman asked what it was.

"Sir Walter Scott, my favorite novelist," she replied. *"Rob Roy."*

"Oh yes. Have you not yet read it?"

She ducked her head. "Many times."

Weightman seemed surprised. "You must like it then." He opened his own book. Emily could not help but stare. The book was new, its cover shiny with lack of use and half of its pages uncut.

"What do you have?" she asked timidly.

"I am behind," Weightman said. "This is Balzac, *Le Père Goriot.* It has been out several years now, but I have only just sent for it."

"You sent for it?" Emily said. "Not from Keighley library?"

"Oh." Weightman sat up, suddenly realizing what she had assumed. "No. I mean I ordered it from London."

"You—you bought it?"

Weightman chided himself for his insensitivity, and for his continued reliance on the allowance his father posted.

"I'm over halfway through," he said in an embarrassed rush. "When I'm done, I'll give it to you."

"No," Emily said at once, and felt near tears. "I would only borrow it."

Weightman shut the book. "Emily, I'm sorry. I hadn't thought."

"I cannot even get to Keighley," she said.

Weightman said, "I have two shelves of books in my room and you are welcome to them. Here is what I shall do. Tonight I will list everything I have and bring it to you. Then you may choose whatever you like and I will share it."

Emily closed *Rob Roy* and looked out over the fall of water. "Thank you," she said.

"It must be very hard for you," Weightman added. "You have lost the companionship of your sisters, and you are forced to read books you already know well. Do you have trouble filling your time?"

"I write," Emily said. She quailed inwardly as she said it, and yet she also longed to speak again about her work, as she had not done since Anne and Charlotte left.

"You wrote the wonderful poem about Nero," Weightman said, his voice gentle. He picked up a pebble and tossed it into the beck, which ran fast because of the time of year. "What else do you write?"

She considered how much to tell him. Her prose was devoted to tales of the fantasy island of Gondal she had shared with Anne for many years. She sensed Anne was not so keen as she had once been, though Emily still found it a comfort to follow the exploits of Alexandrina Zenobia, an adventuress who went where Emily had never been able to go. But Emily thought it a betrayal, even though Anne wrote less and less, to talk about their work with anyone else.

She could, however, talk about her own hopes. "I long to write a novel," she said at last. "I have not written a word as yet, but I think about it often."

"A novel? How splendid!" Weightman leaned forward. "Can you speak about it?"

She shook her head. "Very little. I could only truly know it as I wrote it, you see. So how can I speak about it now? It may be some years yet before I start. But it looms."

"But can you say anything at all? Where would it be set?"

Emily stared into space as she tried to shape her thoughts. "I would set it here. My fellow feeling with Sir Walter Scott, you see, is that he writes of wild and desolate places with peaks and valleys and heath. Not civilized places, not flat green cultivated places with pretty gardens where people take tea on benches. I want places where the landscape torments people, and people torment one another."

She loved the openness of Weightman's face, the way, when he thought deeply about something, one could almost track the changeableness of his feelings as he moved from one idea to the other. At last he said, "No Jane Austen then?"

"I have not read Jane Austen. I have heard of her, of course."

"She writes of love in an entertaining manner."

"But is love an entertainment? And where does she set her scenes of love?"

Weightman considered the question. "I suppose most of her scenes are set in parlors or drawing rooms."

"Then I question her," Emily declared. "Love should not be confined to a parlor, no more than this merlin should be confined to his cage. Love must span eternity if it is worthy of the name, otherwise it is only affection." Emily was seized by a spasm of passion. "The hero and heroine I am considering for my novel would wreak havoc on one of Miss Austen's parlors. They would be more at home in Hell than in a country house."

Weightman raised his eyebrows and Emily's shyness returned. She was certain he must be appalled, and she cursed herself for sharing with him.

Weightman was indeed reserved and thoughtful on the way back. They had reached the place where they must part so they would not be seen returning to the village together—Weightman to follow the road to West Lane, Emily to climb to the pasture behind the parsonage. She assumed he was happy to put the discussion of her writing behind him. *Who would wish to read such a horrible book?* she imagined him thinking. *And by a woman? How monstrous!*

Instead, William Weightman said his goodbye and then added, "I shall expect to read that book someday. And to be disquieted by it, and moved as well."

And he said it, Emily thought as she lay on her bed that night, without a hint of condemnation, or of condescension, and not with mere politeness, but with warmth. The next morning when she came to the kitchen for breakfast, she found Weightman had been there and departed. Tabby pointed to a slip of paper on the cupboard, a list in the curate's clear hand of some thirty volumes he possessed. Weightman's taste was catholic. Some of his books were favorites she would like to reread, but most were new to her. She chose Dickens's *Pickwick Papers,* Charles Darwin's *Journals and Remarks,* the naturalist's just-published account of his recent trip aboard the HMS *Beagle,* and another new volume, the complete works of the poet Shelley, with notes by his widow Mary. She left the list on Weightman's desk while he was out on his pastoral rounds. The next morning he appeared at the parsonage for his meeting to discuss parish affairs with Patrick Brontë. He carried the three volumes under one arm.

"An offering for Emily," he told Patrick.

"Oh my," Patrick said, putting on his spectacles to study the titles. "She will be pleased."

And Emily, who had heard the front door open and her name called from the kitchen, was pleased indeed. She touched the collected Shelley with an especially reverent hand. If Sir Walter Scott was her favorite novelist, Shelley was her most beloved poet. She had been four years old when he died, but she dreamed she had known and loved him. She kept the Shelley long after she had finished with the other two volumes, and returned it only reluctantly.

The Tuesday afternoons continued, and Emily broached the subject of the merlin. Weightman agreed it was time, and added, "When you spoke of his plight in his cage, I knew you were set on this course."

He asked where she intended to try. Emily had been debating this point, and decided to carry the bird several miles to the wild area around the rock at Ponden Kirk. Falcons seemed to thrive there, and if Nero became lost, he might have the best chance for survival.

Because of the distance, they would need the entire day. Tabby agreed to manage dinner preparations by herself, and Emily packed a bag of sandwiches for the journey. Then she went to tell her father she would be taking a longer walk. Patrick looked up from his desk and stared at his daughter over the top of his glasses.

"Gone all day? Where are you going?"

"To Ponden Kirk." Emily tried to keep her voice casual. "You know I have made the trek before."

"Yes, with your brother and sisters. But alone?"

Emily's heart sank. *Please, don't forbid me, please,* she thought.

"Keeper will be with me. I want to see if Nero will fly on his own. I may release him there."

Patrick was drawn to the edge of desperation in his daughter's voice. He had not heard that note before in Emily. Something was drawing her beyond herself, and only her writing, he had assumed, could do that.

He had also observed her friendship with William Weightman. He began to think that Emily, for once in her life, was in love.

Patrick knew Ponden Kirk. He passed by on pastoral visits to the manor house at Ponden Hall but rarely stopped. The place was well known in the district, a massive rock formation high above one of the most isolated moors. Why was it called a "kirk," an old word for church? No one knew, but more educated people in the West Riding speculated the name reflected antecedents of pagan worship. An opening cleft the bottom of the pile of rock. It must be crawled through, and only by one person at a time. Some claimed that a maid who went through the rock cleft would either be married before a year was out, or remain unwed for the rest of her life. Another tale, more ominous, held that if a couple went through the opening one after another, they would die if they did not marry in a year. Or, if they married other people, they would kill themselves and haunt the moors forever.

Emily knew the stories. Weightman might not, Patrick suspected, since he was not from the district. He had already guessed that his curate, whose day off was Tuesday, would accompany his daughter to Ponden Kirk. Should he forbid it?

He studied Emily's face as she stood before him. He was moved by her loneliness as well as the intensity and, yes, the purity of her passion. And Weightman? He thought of the young man who spent his days going from hovel to hovel in the poor districts of Ginnel and Gauger's Croft, offering Scripture and prayer and food and solace.

Patrick said, "If Tabby says she does not need you, then go ahead. Take care of bogs on the way."

Emily ran to him and gave him a hug and then bounded out, a wild thing, with Keeper at her heels.

They set out separately as usual. They had come over time to hate the subterfuge, but feared to end it. So Emily walked with Keeper and the merlin past farmsteads to the waterfall on Sladen Beck, where Weightman waited. They took turns carrying Nero, though Emily bore most of the burden, for the bird was unsettled when Weightman had the gauntlet and craned his neck backward to glare at the man. They stopped several times to let the falcon fly on the long creance. He soared out, but settled back and took his mouthful of offal from the Haworth butcher.

"My fear," Emily said, "is that he would starve."

"But has he not taken small animals even on the creance?"

"He has. And he catches mice in the washhouse. So he knows something of what he must do."

The dell narrowed, the path forced them up onto a ridgeline and the moors took them in so that they forgot to talk, both of them absorbed in their thoughts. At last the mass of Ponden Kirk loomed and the valleys fell away all round its height. They stopped to eat, Nero's creance tied to Emily's wrist. The bird settled on a rock and scanned the expanse below as though he forgot for a time the presence of the man and woman. Emily watched the merlin, and Weightman watched her watching him.

"I wonder if he will return to the bell?" Emily mused.

"If he returns," Weightman said, "that is what he wants. And if he does not return, that is also what he wants."

Emily looked at Weightman. "I know," she said.

They talked of other matters as they ate. Emily said, "Since I help deliver your letters, may I ask what is happening with the Chartists? I know I must tell no one, but I should like to be kept informed."

"I think that is reasonable. The plans continue. It will take time to bring all the many mills together for some joint action. But here is what will happen. You understand the factories are powered by great steam boilers?"

"Yes."

"The boilers hold the water, and they have plugs so they may be drained if need be. At a certain hour, when all is ready, the plugs will be removed and the water drained."

Emily clapped her hands in delight. "It is brilliant! The looms will stop?"

"And not start again until the plugs are replaced. All over the north of England, can you imagine? And the threat of a similar stoppage will remain as long as people are in those mills, until the demands of the workers are met."

Emily heard a note of hesitation in Weightman's voice. "What could go wrong?" she asked.

He turned to his sandwich and chewed, then stopped. "The timing must be right. The market is depressed, so a work stoppage will drive up the price of cloth. That would please the mill owners rather than harm them. Besides, there is a split among the Chartists. Some advocate violence. They say it is the only way to achieve our goals."

"And you disagree?"

"Of course. I am a clergyman. I preach the gospel of loving one's enemy, of turning the other cheek."

"I must say," said Emily, "when I consider what is being done to the poor people of Haworth, I want to pick up a gun myself and storm the barricades."

She read the shock on Weightman's face, and ducked her head. She was used to writing about violent revolution in the stories of her fantasy land of Gondal, and had to warn herself that others did not live in her world.

"It would be a disaster for the Chartist movement," Weightman said, "if it turned violent."

Emily said, "I have read about revolutions. George Washington was one of my childhood heroes. We could bear a whiff of revolution in England."

"I think not," Weightman said. "Not for myself, for I would have to turn away. And not for the British people, who would turn on us."

They fell silent for a time. Keeper, sprawled on his belly, worked his way close for a handout of scraps. Nero trod back and forth on a nearby rock and tugged at Emily's wrist. She sensed Weightman's eyes upon her, probing in a way she was unused to.

Then he said, "Would you approve if the workers turned to violence?"

Emily picked apart a sandwich she did not want and fed the pieces to Keeper. "Some things are worth dying for," she said, her head down.

"But worth killing for?"

Emily looked up then. "I don't know."

"If the Chartists turned to violence, your father, as a Tory and a leader of the established Church, might be a target."

"The people of Haworth know Papa is their friend," Emily objected. "They know as well that nothing in the district will change unless they force it. Why should the mill owners sleep peacefully in their beds when they help people to die?"

Weightman shook his head. "When the genie of violent revolt is out of the bottle, it will not be forced back in until innocent people have been killed." He added, "I must tell you, this is not the sort of conversation one has with a woman."

Emily's cheeks flushed with anger. Much of it was at herself—she should not have been so forthcoming—but at Weightman as well, for drawing her into conversation and then offering what she saw as abrupt criticism. Go back to Sarah Sugden, she thought sullenly, who will talk of any silly thing you want. Nero saw something just then, something no one else could see or imagine, and began to squawk and flap his wings. Emily welcomed the distraction.

"It is time." She stood and brushed her hands upon her skirt. She was glad at the sudden change in atmosphere, for it forced her to deal with the merlin once and for all. She put on her glove and called Nero to it with her bell. Weightman stood as well. He knew Emily was upset. He had not meant to offend, more to think out loud. Emily was a mercurial young woman, and one with talons to match the bird's. Weightman pursed his lips and watched her fumble with the creance where it attached to the jess, then stop and look back at him.

"When I unloose it, he will fly?"

"He will," Weightman said. "And be free."

The word seemed to steel Emily's resolve. Free. Nothing was so valuable, not wealth, not fame. Not love. Freedom.

She let Nero go before she could change her mind. The bird

exploded from her fist as he was used to on the long creance. But he did not stop. With nothing to fetter him, he rose, higher and higher, first in a tight circle, then a widening one, farther and farther until he was a black speck in the blue sky.

Emily forgot herself and began to run. She did not notice Weightman followed, staying close behind her with his longer legs but surprised at how she covered the rough ground. She ran until she was out of breath, a stitch in her side, then the bird wheeled and headed back in the direction of the great rock of Ponden Kirk, where he settled on a ledge, fluffed his wings, and looked down on the human pair as imperiously as his namesake.

Emily stopped, gasping for breath, and clapped her hands over her mouth to keep from crying out for pure joy. Nero shrieked and set out again. He led them beyond the kirk, Emily running again and Weightman following, unable to take his eyes off her. He thought Emily, arms flailing and skirts billowing to her thighs so that her chemise and stockings showed, might take off and be lost to the earth.

Then she fell. Her toe caught on a rock and she tumbled. Weightman dove after her, to break her fall. They crashed into a stand of heath and came to rest in a jumble of arms and legs, the breath knocked out of them.

Emily was first to move. Her gasps became a low moan. She rolled onto her back, turned her head, and stared straight into Weightman's eyes. He looked back unblinking. Then Emily saw his face change and grow tense. His stare hardened, he pressed his lips together. He turned onto his side, away from Emily.

Suddenly she knew, as she watched him breathe, his hand clenched in a fist and pressed against the side of his head. Emily Brontë had no direct experience with male desire, though she was well acquainted with her own. She had heard Branwell, passionate and indiscreet Branwell, speak of it. She was in its presence, and knew that Weightman turned away from her, not toward her, because he fought it.

She wanted nothing more in that clear moment than for Weightman to turn and roll atop her. She sensed how close he was, felt the heat rise from the back of his shirt. But she also knew Weightman was a clergyman. Either he would give up Emily Brontë after leading her along the path of what he would consider a terrible error, or he would give up the ministry. She could not bear either outcome. She knew as well—she forced herself to think so as to calm herself, as she sensed he did—that if he were willing to give up his calling for her, she would love him less. And if he found the strength to relinquish her, she would love him more. They were doomed, either way. The realization brought her to tears. She squeezed her eyes shut. When she opened them, Weightman sat, his head cradled in his arms resting upon bent knees. He turned his head. They conversed without words.

Weightman pushed himself into a standing position, leaned over, and offered Emily his right hand. She took it, felt its warmth and strength, and allowed him to pull her to her feet. They walked toward the gray mass of Ponden Kirk. Weightman stopped and put his hand on Emily's arm.

"Try to call the merlin," he said.

To her chagrin Emily had forgotten Nero. Glancing about, she could not spy him. She fumbled in her pocket for the bell, suddenly awkward. She rang it. The sky remained empty. She rang it again, waving her arm as hard as she could.

"Look!" Weightman called, and pointed.

The hawk was coming, a speck emerging from the shadow of the rock. He grew larger and larger, circling as Emily sounded the bell, then swooped down and settled on her outstretched glove in so precipitous a manner that she almost toppled over. Weightman caught her and they stood frozen, astonished that the bird had come back. As Weightman made sure Emily had righted herself, his arms about her, he reached round and fixed the end of the creance, which Emily had forgotten, to the bird's jess.

They stood motionless for a moment, until Nero calmed himself on the glove. Then they began to walk back toward Ponden Kirk. Keeper brushed against Emily's thigh and sent her bumping into Weightman. The man and woman moved farther apart. When they reached the kirk, Weightman stopped.

"Someone in the village told me it is a great tradition to crawl though that cleft in the rock," he said. "I have never done it. Have you?"

"No," Emily said.

Weightman said, "John Brown told me people have been going through the cleft since the beginning of time." He smiled. "Perhaps we should before we leave."

Emily brushed her hair back from her forehead. Twigs of heather and gorse were caught in her hair and her dress. Weightman was similarly disheveled. "Perhaps you will not want that connection with me, Mr. Weightman, since I fear I have more in common with the fairies than with convention." She began to fiddle with Nero's jess, too shy to look at him.

"Who better to be paired with at Ponden Kirk," he replied, "than a fairy?" He reached out and pried Nero from the glove. "You go first and I'll hold Nero, then we can switch. That way, whatever we do and wherever we go in the future, we can declare a bond because of Ponden Kirk."

Emily nodded. She went to the opening, got down on her hands and knees, and crawled through, the ground pricking and scratching her palms and knees. When she was out the other side and came back to Weightman, he was grinning. "A good thing you have more in common with the fairies," he said. "I daresay I shall never see the backside of a lady disappearing beneath Ponden Kirk."

Emily blushed and slapped his arm, as she was used to teasing with her sisters. Then she held Nero and watched as Weightman followed her lead. She wandered round to meet him as he emerged on the other side. He said nothing at first, only resumed walking, Emily at his side. But then he said, "One can feel how old it is in there, can't one?"

"Yes," Emily agreed. "One can imagine people wearing animal skins as they crawl through."

They covered half the distance back to Haworth before either spoke again. It was something else they had in common, the ability to be together and yet alone at the same time. Then Weightman said, careful not to look at his companion, "Emily, would you ever consider marrying a clergyman?"

The question nearly took Emily's breath, and she was a long time answering. She knew the import of her response, knew how she loved him, and knew what would be lost.

And yet I must be honest, she thought. Even if it breaks my heart and his.

"I could not do that to any clergyman," she said, her voice so low he had to lean closer to hear her. "Especially if I loved him."

After a moment, he asked, "What do you mean?"

"Can I be other than I am?" she asked. "And being what I am, what could I bring to that marriage except scandal for my husband, and misery for me."

"But you live in a parsonage," Weightman protested. "You already know the life."

"I do," she said. "In the kitchen. But in the parlor, you may note, I am often absent. Because I am helping Tabby, or because I am on the moors, or because I cannot bear the silliness of the conversation. It is allowed in a daughter, but a wife who absented herself in that way would be the object of gossip or worse. And her husband would suffer among his parishioners." When he fell silent, she added, "What clergyman could bear a wife who wandered the moors without detriment to his career? And what of my writing? How could I pursue it?"

"The writing could not be put aside?" But even as he spoke he shook his head and said, "No, forgive me that I even suggested it. But"—he tried to keep his voice neutral—"would scandal ensue even here? In a poor place like Haworth?"

Emily did not answer at once. She was too near tears to make a reply. Finally she said, her voice again fallen to nearly a whisper, "You know as well as I, even here. You know as well as any the way I am seen in the village. And there is more. Suppose I were to produce a child. I imagine I would love it well, but how might I mother it unless I strapped it to my back and traipsed the moors with it like an American Indian and her papoose? And how would *that* be received? But how deal otherwise with the confinement, for I believe the 'confinement' of motherhood lasts far longer than simply bearing the child." She paused to regain her composure, and then said, "I am so forthcoming only because *if* such a situation were to arise"—she emphasized the speculation—"I would refuse only out of love. Please understand that."

"I do understand," he said, looking straight ahead.

They fell silent again. At last they came to the foot of Penistone Hill where the path climbed the hill and left the low road to West Lane. They were both weary, their hair tangled and clothes stained and covered with bits of twig and leaf. It would take little more than seeing the two together, Weightman realized, to create the scandal Emily feared.

"Emily," he said, "I enjoyed today more I can say. But I also"—he paused to search for words—"I must walk in the wilderness for a time. Only until I resolve something in my mind. So you may not see me at close hand for a while. It will have nothing to do with my respect and affection for you."

"No," she said, her head bowed, a dull ache in the pit of her stomach.

He turned to leave, and she stood and watched him go. Perhaps it was only desire he felt, she thought. The proximity of a woman, the beauty of the setting, the excitement of the bird's flight. He will get over that soon enough and feel nothing for me. Except pity, perhaps.

At last, when he was out of sight, she made her own forlorn way home, in the company of her dog and the merlin.

II

*E*mily saw William Weightman only after Sunday services, when she shook his hand upon exiting the church. He continued to look her in the eye, and what she read in his face was a warning, though one couched with affection. She felt proud she was capable of meeting his clear look with one of her own.

Then he was gone, to Appleby again on a spring holiday. Emily learned in a letter from Branwell that Weightman's hope of Agnes Walton was rekindled.

"Willie is reconsidering how ensconced he is at Haworth," Branwell wrote his sister. "Agnes is a patient girl, he writes, and still holds him in great esteem. Perhaps he will yet pry himself away from us and go on to better things."

Better things. Of course Weightman deserved more. Emily would wish him well, and then forget him. At least, she would try.

But then he was back again in May and greeting her at the church door with much of his old exuberance.

"Miss Emily," he said as he took her hand, "I have a surprise for the Sunday school children, and for you as well, if you will accept it."

"Whatever can you mean?" she wondered.

"Willie has a secret he has been hiding from everyone," said Patrick, who stood beside his curate. "Something will be delivered here on the back of a cart. But he will not say what."

"It is not more dead birds for me to pluck?"

"You will find out soon enough," Weightman said. "And I hope that will entice you to invite me to dine with you tomorrow."

"Of course," Patrick agreed. "Aunt was just saying the other day how she missed having you to the house."

Next day the cart arrived in Church Lane bearing a cottage piano similar to the one in Patrick's study.

"For the Sunday school," Weightman explained. "I found it in Bradford on my way back from Appleby. It is old. One or two keys stick, I'm afraid. But the children will not care. They will love to have some music, don't you think?"

Emily ran her fingers lightly over the instrument as he spoke. The sound was tinny and the ivories were stained and chipped, but except for a low G, the keys could be struck easily enough. "And who shall play it?" she asked, as if she had not guessed who Weightman had in mind.

"Ah," Weightman said, "I did hope that you would, in fact, play for us."

"Did you?"

Weightman would not be put off. "You do not teach in the Sunday school as your sisters have done," he pointed out. "But you help in other ways, and seem happy to do it. I thought this, as well, might be something to your liking."

"I see." Emily folded her arms. "I would only have to play? I would not have to teach? I cannot discipline children, Mr. Weightman, I learned as much when I once tried to teach at a school. If I like the mischief that is being made, I will join it. And if I do not like it, I would rather go off and spend time with some upstanding dog or other."

Weightman pulled a solemn face. "I shall see to the discipline. We cannot have the pianist standing in the corner for mischief-making, or running out in search of dogs. So, you will play?"

Emily stuck out her hand. "Agreed."

Weightman shook her hand and said, "Accepted." He turned to Patrick. "You have no objection if we add music?"

"How could I," Patrick said, "when it is presented to me as such a fait accompli? Though my predecessor, Mr. Grimshaw, may be rolling in his grave."

"I will provide him with a musical accompaniment," Emily said.

So she came to sit among a group of boisterous children, banging out the hymn "All Hail the Power of Jesus' Name." They loved the song and particularly the line "And crown him LORD—OF—ALL" (this last shouted more than sang, as vehement as any Wesleyan, poor children partaking in royalty). The jangling of the old piano strings boomeranged from one stone wall to the other, adding to the ruckus.

Weightman shared Bible stories, and Emily noticed the curate had a fondness for those like Joshua at Jericho, or David and Goliath, where the hero faced great odds. The lessons he drew from his text were nothing like those she remembered from her own scant school days, when the Reverend William Carus Wilson enjoyed telling stories about children who burned in Hell for all eternity.

Weightman invited Emily to comment on the Bible lessons, a backhanded way, she suspected, to get her to teach, so she declined. But when the subject turned to Adam and Eve, she agreed to speak and told the children, "The first people were titans, as tall as trees. Eve is our mother of the earth. All the stars sprang from her, and the rivers and trees and moors as well. When you look upon the moors, still today, you see the shape of her body. When you hear the birds sing, you hear Eve's voice. The clouds are the decorations about her head." Emily glanced at Weightman and saw he had turned pale. "That first woman brought forth life," Emily concluded quickly, to bring the story round to something more conventional, "and from her descendants our Lord was born."

The children took it all in with as much equanimity as they accepted any stories of talking snakes or enchanted trees. Weightman did not chastise Emily, though she noted with relief that he did not ask her to comment on a biblical passage again.

When the children had hurried out into the warm spring morning, Emily said to Weightman, "I have never heard the story of Jesus overturning the tables of the money changers in the temple told with quite such zest. You will have them ready to turn over some tables of their own."

Weightman winked. "That is the idea," he said.

Emily raised her eyebrows, then gathered her hymnal and sheet music and laid them in a neat stack.

"And how is Nero?" Weightman asked. He was himself busy sorting notes and putting away books.

"I let him off the creance regularly," Emily said, "up on Penistone Hill where we found him. I am prepared for him to fly off and leave me, but he always comes to the bell." She hesitated. It took a great deal of effort to inquire in a neutral voice, "And how is Agnes Walton? Branwell writes that you may be engaged to her."

Weightman stopped and looked at the ceiling, then turned to Emily and gave her a crooked smile. "I did propose to her."

"You love her then?" Emily said, still trying to sound casual. *Our friendship surely allows me to be a bit inquisitive,* she thought.

"I bear her a great deal of affection," Weightman said. "And I need a wife. A clergyman's life is difficult without one."

Emily said, her voice sounding more disapproving than she wished, "Is that sufficient reason to wed?"

Weightman's naturally rosy cheeks turned a deeper red. "For most people, it is enough," he said, and resumed his tidying up. "Agnes said yes, provided I leave Haworth. I agreed. I thought it likely that I would someday."

Emily's heart sank. She hugged her hymnal close and said nothing.

"Her father declared my departure must be imminent if I wished to wed his daughter." Weightman shrugged. "I said it could not be, and asked for a year or two here with Agnes as my wife, to see if she might like it well enough for a longer stay. Both father and daughter declined. They think me a hopeless case, you see."

Emily let out a sigh of relief. "I'm sorry," she said, not at all sincerely. She wondered if Weightman could tell. Still she could not help but add, "I think you are disappointed, but not dying for love."

He regarded her keenly a moment, then pursed his lips and said, "No."

She held his gaze and added, "And what did you do to heal your hurt feelings, Mr. Weightman?"

He smiled. "I went out and bought a piano," he said.

⋈

In June Charlotte and Anne came home to Haworth on holiday. Patrick wished to offer a roast goose in celebration. But Emily would not hear of wringing the neck of either Victoria or Adelaide. So her father agreed to the expense of purchasing a fowl from the butcher's shop. "Once Emily names an animal," Patrick told Aunt Branwell, "you should not expect to find it upon your plate."

"Why do we keep geese?" Aunt Branwell replied grumpily. "Shall they live out their days in this marvelous goose hotel? How splendid for them!"

Still, the dinner was fine enough. The poor anonymous goose, though small, was basted to a golden turn by Tabby, and Emily produced parsley potatoes, parsnips, and a summer pudding.

She prepared to endure insults about William Weightman from Charlotte, and to bite her tongue. But the curate was ignored. Emily sensed that her sister's interest was elsewhere. Charlotte's employer, Mr. White, was most congenial, she declared, though his wife was not. Charlotte spent an inordinate amount of time talking about the virtues of Mr. White.

Though Charlotte sometimes irritated her, Emily was glad to have her sisters again. She watched Anne closely to gauge her health. Her younger sister was still fragile, but her cough seemed to have been tamed. Perhaps the time spent by the seaside had indeed helped, and Anne was looking forward once again to a summer spent at Scarborough.

While Charlotte read a book, Emily took Anne outside to feed the parsonage birds. "Did you meet Mr. Easton when you were in Scarborough last summer?" she asked. "Mr. Weightman's friend?"

"I did," Anne said. "Mr. Easton is a fine man, devoted to his duties as curate. He drew me into helping with his pastoral visits, for he tends to many who have gone to the seaside for their health. But Mr. Easton is sad, I think."

"How so?"

"Since Mr. Weightman knew him, he has married," Anne said. "I fear it is a mismatch. His wife criticizes him, even in front of other people."

"That is terrible! Why would his wife treat him so?"

"She is ambitious," Anne explained, "and he is not. Mrs. Easton says her husband will not promote his own interests. She urges him on against Mr. Millar, his vicar, and she wants Mr. Easton to apply to the bishop for another position. Her ambition is the cathedral in York."

Emily scattered feed with such force that the chickens fled, squawking their protest. "I wonder," she said, "what women think when they marry? Do they have no judgment about the men with whom they exchange vows? Is that why they wish to remake them?"

"Surely some women exercise judgment," Anne said. "And love their husbands enough as they are."

"Too many young women are made to feel desperate at the need of marriage," Emily said. "So they marry even when there is no passion and are immediately dissatisfied. I cannot understand it."

Anne studied her sister and wondered at the color that burned Emily's cheeks and heightened the tenor of her voice. But she knew better than to inquire.

That night Aunt Branwell retired to sleep alone in Emily's narrow chamber so the three sisters could share their aunt's larger bed. They stayed awake luxuriating in one another's presence and sharing their separate adventures of the preceding months. Emily, listening, had a moment of self-doubt. "It is selfish of me," she said, "to remain at home and refuse to share in your travails."

"Nonsense," Anne said at once. "It is not as though we suffer. Here, I am the little sister, but at Thorpe Green, I am the older sister. The Robinson girls are fond of me, and I provide them with moral instruction which their mother does not offer. I believe I have a great deal of influence upon them. Besides that, I do look forward to going to Scarborough again. But Emily, you are every bit as useful here. Who else would look after the old people and the house if you did not?"

"I'm glad as well that you are here," Charlotte agreed, and gave Emily's arm a squeeze. "Although I am not so happy as Anne, I want my freedom, and if you will not claim yours, I will take your share."

"But I do have freedom," Emily protested. "That is why I feel it unfair that you do not."

"It is a different sort of freedom," Charlotte said. "Mine is an ordered freedom that allows opportunity and advancement. Yours is pure liberty, which is to your liking, but not to mine, for it does not allow one to go about in society." They lay quiet and then Charlotte added, "I enjoy the neighborhood where I have landed. My school friends are close, and they have taken me on jaunts about the countryside. There are interesting places around Rawdon and Birstall. One day, we went to visit an old country house. Our host showed us a tower room where a previous owner was rumored to keep his mad wife imprisoned. Would that not make a story?"

"You should incorporate it into Angria," Emily said, referring to the imaginary kingdom where Charlotte and Branwell set their tales of fantasy.

"No, no," Charlotte said, "I am done with Angria. That was childish, and I have put away childish things."

Emily said, "Is it really Angria you tire of? Or is it Branwell?"

"I plead guilty," Charlotte admitted. "Between that scandal in the Lake District and the way he takes too much drink, I have little patience. Certainly I have no desire to share anything so intimate as my writing." She sighed. "I envy you two. You have each other, while I have lost the great friend of my childhood."

"You have your school friends," Anne pointed out.

"Yes," Charlotte agreed. "Though one of them, Mary Taylor, is going abroad."

"Indeed?" Anne said.

"To Brussels. At least it will be fun to hear from her, and to enjoy the place vicariously, if nothing else."

Emily had no interest in Brussels. If given the chance to go abroad, she would choose the American frontier, perhaps the mountains of Virginia or the Carolinas.

Charlotte broke into her thoughts. "Emily, have you ever thought of writing a novel? Not set in Gondal, but here."

Emily considered how much to share. Finally she said, "Yes. I have thought of it."

"What sort of story?" Anne wondered.

"A love story. But a tortured one. More I cannot say."

"I should like to write a novel," Anne said. "I have seen so much of society these last few years. It is enough for several novels."

"Shall we pledge?" Charlotte said. "Someday we shall each of us write a novel, a love story."

Anne said, "But can we write of love when we have not known it?"

Emily started to speak, but thought better of it.

Anne continued, "Sometimes at night when I pray, I ask God why he ordered the world as he has. Why does what looks like such wonderful design in nature not continue with humanity?"

"What do you mean?" Charlotte asked.

"I speak of marriage," Anne replied. "There are few men, it seems to me, to whom a woman would want to give over her entire life. Or rather, some women might require one sort of man, and some another. How many women meet a man they could love with their whole hearts? Or perhaps they believe they have found such a man, but upon closer inspection, he proves rather different." She shifted restlessly. She did not tell her sisters that when she lay too long in one position, the congestion in her chest caused great discomfort. "Or perhaps a woman meets a sympathetic man, but he is spoken for."

"Do you mean," Charlotte ventured, "Mr. Easton?"

"I do," Anne said with a sigh. "I hope I do not think too well of myself if I say I would have been a more congenial companion than his wife. I have no ambitions that would conflict with his present situation, and he did like to call upon me for help summer last. I have a letter from him, welcoming me back in a few weeks, so I know he thinks well of me, and remembers me. I ask, why does God not order things so that we meet the men we are likely to be contented by—and to make content—when it is most propitious?"

"Perhaps," Emily said, "God prefers tormented love. It is more interesting than contentment."

They were interrupted by a loud shriek from the room next door. They heard their aunt cry, "Emily! Emily!"

"Yes, Aunt!" Emily jumped out of bed, for fortunately she lay on the edge closest to the door. She rushed to her own room to find nothing more alarming than a large yellow cat prowling back and forth over her aunt's prone body.

"What is it?" Patrick called from behind his own door.

"It's only Tiger." Emily scooped up the cat with one hand. "He was looking for me," she assured her aunt.

"How did he get in the house?" Aunt Branwell demanded.

"I let him in," Emily admitted. "He likes to sleep on the warm coals in the kitchen after the fires have died down in the hearth. Then he comes up and snuggles with me."

"I'll not have him in my bed!" Aunt Branwell cried.

"He expected to find me," Emily said, "and will be as glad to escape as you are to be rid of him. Here, I will close your door."

Back in the larger bedroom, Emily lay down on her back. The cat, who had found his accustomed bedfellow, settled on her stomach with a loud purr and began to knead.

"Now here," Emily said contentedly, "is a man."

⁓

Charlotte and Anne returned to their far-flung posts. One Saturday morning Emily went to her father's study to carry away his breakfast things, for Patrick always took a bowl of porridge and pot of tea at his desk, when William Weightman entered in a state of excitement.

"I've had a letter from Branwell," he said. "The Halifax Choral Society will perform Beethoven's last symphony, his Ninth, with a touring orchestra from the Continent. Branwell has procured two tickets through his railway employers and has asked me to meet him."

"Splendid," Patrick said. "I heard Liszt in Halifax and I have never forgotten the experience."

Weightman said, "But it is twelve miles, and the concert is next Friday evening. I shall have to walk all day on Friday and return the next day. I would need to change my day off, and take an extra day as well."

"You have given advance warning," Patrick said.

Emily stood. The two men looked at her inquiringly. She clenched and unclenched her fists and glanced at her cottage piano, as though seeking support.

"I should like to go," she said. "I have never heard a symphony, not with an orchestra. I have read about the Ninth. They say it is divine."

"But how on earth could you go?" Patrick asked.

"I shall write to Branwell. Perhaps he can procure another ticket. I'll do washing or take in mending to pay for it."

Weightman's surprise gave way to an understanding of Emily's longing. But he was at a loss for an answer.

"Emily," he said, "I will walk the entire twelve miles, and back again the next day. No one else would be with us."

Emily wanted to cry, *You and I walked six miles to Ponden Kirk and back again, and we were alone!* Yet she dared not betray their secret.

But Patrick said in a calm voice, "Do not think, Emily, to use Ponden Kirk for your argument. This is different."

Weightman turned to Patrick, his face stricken.

Emily recovered quickly. "I know the way to Halifax. The school where I taught at Law Hill was close by. I have walked twelve miles many times."

"But only once with my curate," Patrick replied.

Weightman stood. "S-sir," he stammered, a schoolboy caught in mischief, "We wished to take the falcon—"

Patrick raised his hand. "I have not chastised you," he said. "Because I trust you. That does not mean I approve." He turned to Emily. "Do not think, Emily, I would allow a trip to Halifax, even if a ticket were available."

Emily's eyes filled with tears, and she looked from one man to another. "But I desire nothing in the world so much. Oh, Papa! Only to hear Beethoven's symphony, the greatest, everyone says—"

Weightman clasped his hands between his knees and forced himself to forget his shock at Patrick's revelation. "Your brother and I will stay in common lodgings, and share a bed. We will meet Branwell's friends in a public house. There will be no ladies for your company. It is impossible."

Emily picked up the tray of dirty dishes and rushed out.

Weightman leaned back. "Dear God. I thought Emily would be excited by my news." Then he recalled Patrick's revelation. "You knew we went to Ponden Kirk?"

Patrick fiddled with the inkwell on his desk. He said, "You must consider me a most indulgent father."

"I do," Weightman said. "But also a generous one. A less wise man would be the ruination of a girl like Emily."

"You judge her extraordinary," Patrick said, pride in his voice.

"I do," Weightman said. "As strong-willed as any man." He shook his head. "Every young lady I have met wants a husband and children, and that is her scope. Emily has no desire to go beyond the West Riding, and yet she wants the world. One wonders whether to indulge or protect her, and whether it is possible to protect her without getting one's eyes scratched. But just when I am expecting such an assault, she will smile in a way that makes it worth the risk."

Patrick peered at his curate, and Weightman guessed it was not just because of his failing eyesight.

"Most men would not consider Emily one way or the other," Patrick said. "Most might even dismiss her as mad."

Weightman flushed. "I would defend her against such charges," he said.

"At times," Patrick pressed on, "I have thought you loved her."

Weightman met Patrick's eyes, and then looked out the window. A light drizzle fell among the tombstones and a ghostly fog obscured the church. "I have a great deal of affection for Emily," he said. "I asked her at Ponden Kirk if she could link her fate to that of a clergyman. She said it would be unfair to that clergyman. She spoke honestly. People would do more than raise their eyes to find their pastor with such a wife."

Patrick sighed. "At least as things stand now," he said. "I tell you, I don't know what will happen to Emily. Charlotte and Anne will make their way as governesses, unhappy though they may be. I cannot see Emily acceptable anywhere as a teacher or governess. When I am gone, Emily will be destitute. Her only hope will be if one of her sisters is in a position to take her in. Or Branwell, perhaps, if he settles down and marries."

Weightman sat up straight. "I promise you," he said, "whatever my circumstances, I shall ensure Emily is not destitute."

"You do not know what the future holds for you," Patrick said. "Though I thank you for your concern. But I also am considering some options. Charlotte has written often lately on the subject of establishing a school. She has learned that her post with the White family will not be permanent, as the children will be sent away to boarding school the next term. So Charlotte looks to the future once more. She has talked of a school in the past, one that my three girls might run on their own, but there are severe hurdles to be faced. One is the money needed to start such a school. My sister-in-law possesses some funds, but she has refused them before. She is waiting until after her death for the money to be distributed, and some of it will go to family in Cornwall. Charlotte wishes Aunt could be convinced to part with the Brontë share now. I wonder if I myself might sway Aunt Branwell with such a plea. I must convince Aunt that Charlotte longs for her money, but not her immediate demise. Or better still, leave Charlotte's name out of it all together, for they do not always get on."

Weightman nodded. He said a bit hesitantly, "I suppose such a school would have to be located in a more congenial place?"

"That is at an impasse as well. Anne suggests Scarborough, beside the sea, for she has grown to love it there. It would indeed be a congenial and healthy location for young girls. But Emily insists that an attempt should be made here first."

"It is unlikely that would succeed," Weightman said, though he was crestfallen at the idea of Emily going so far away as Scarborough.

"No wealthy parent would send a child here," Patrick said. "And what family would wish Emily to encourage their daughters to roam freely and say whatever is on their minds? Emily is aware of that, of course. But she insists she would be more suited to a school for poor girls. How on earth she thinks it would be funded I do not know."

Weightman smiled ruefully at the image. Poor Haworth girls in a school, he thought, when we cannot even keep them alive. And yet the idea gave him food for thought.

"Another hurdle is foremost in Charlotte's mind," Patrick was saying. "She believes all three of my girls need more proficiency in languages, especially French, as well as exposure to advanced teaching methods."

"That would not be needed at a school for poor children," Weightman said.

"Unlike Emily," Patrick said, "Charlotte plans for the more likely reality. Her friend Mary Taylor writes from Brussels about a school there, the Pensionnat Heger, which would accept older students from England who wished to train for teachers. Charlotte could not go alone so she proposes, since Anne cannot afford to leave her post at present, that she and Emily go to Brussels for a term to study."

Weightman rubbed his chin thoughtfully. "I doubt Emily would agree to it."

"I thought you might encourage her."

"Me?"

"Come, Willie. You know you are the only person besides myself whose advice she takes into account. She pays you a great compliment, by the way."

"She might indeed benefit if she were to study abroad for a time," Weightman agreed. "You see how she longs to hear a symphony. She would be in a city with great cultural amenities, she would be at close quarters with others." A hopeful look crossed his face. "It might be just the thing to modify her solitary nature, and teach her the patience to at least endure some social obligations."

"Is that what it would take to make her a clergyman's wife?" Patrick said gently.

William Weightman leaned back in his chair. "I suppose," he said. "Although if the clergyman was somewhat unorthodox, perhaps the wife might be also."

"And what, Willie, would you hope to result from the change?"

"Sir, I hope the change would not be too great. I would miss the Emily I know and love."

Patrick placed his glasses on his nose and looked over them at his curate. "I doubt you need worry about that," he said. "You will help convince Emily to go?"

"Yes," said Weightman. "I shall encourage Aunt Branwell to entertain your proposal as well, if you like. I believe, if I may say so, that I have a way with her."

Patrick laughed. "Not even Tabby has escaped your spell. Indeed, I should have locked up every female in the house when you first came through the door."

⸎

Emily had been thinking frantically as she raced through her chores. She ran upstairs to clear Aunt Branwell's tray, helped Tabby finish up the breakfast dishes and start the fire in the hearth that would cook their dinner. Then she went to her room and stared in the mirror.

The face that looked back at her was thin, and serious, with large eyes, framed with a tousle of dark brown hair held up at the back by a fan-shaped comb. Emily wore her hair up when she was about her chores. On the moors she let down her hair and tucked it behind her ears or let it fall in her face, shook her head and flung it back. The heroines of Gondal would wear their hair just that way—as a sign of their strength and freedom.

Emily took out the comb and let her hair fall about her shoulders. She sat on the edge of her bed, staring into the mirror, until she saw Weightman trudge across Church Lane and disappear into the Sunday school building. She opened the drawer of the narrow nightstand that stood beneath the mirror, and took out a pair of scissors. Then, gathering her hair in her left hand and pulling it up behind her head, she paused a moment to again study her reflection. I *will* carry this off, she thought.

She raised the scissors and cut off her hair to the bottom of her ears.

Keeper, who had stood a close watch, rose as she headed for Branwell's old room. There she put on a pair of her brother's trousers, a shirt and jacket. The trousers were a bit short, for Emily was taller than Branwell. She found an old hat at the back of the wardrobe and placed it on her head. No one saw her leave the house and cross Church Lane. Emily burst into Weightman's study, Keeper at her heels.

Weightman looked up, and then started so badly he dropped his pen and nearly upset his inkwell.

"May I go to Halifax?" Emily demanded. "I look a boy, don't I?"

He continued to stare at her, speechless.

"I won't expect to go with you to the tavern with Branwell and his friends. I'll stay to myself somewhere, in your room at the inn perhaps. I'll take a book to read. I can sleep in my clothes, on the floor." She spoke more and more quickly, at first out of hope but more and more out of desperation for she sensed this was not going well, it was not going well at all. Weightman had not been touched by her extravagant gesture; in fact the look on his face had only grown more horrified.

"Please," she whispered, "can't I go now?"

"No," he said.

Emily stood frozen. She cried out, "Don't look at me that way!

Don't! I can't bear it." She was hurt, and embarrassed, and angry she could not hear Beethoven, that she had acted so rashly, that Weightman was obstinate, angry that he must now think less of her, angry that she cared what he thought. "Oh, I hate being a woman!" she cried.

"Emily," Weightman said, and stood. "I'm sorry—"

That small bit of condolence was enough to send her flying out the door, along the lane behind the parsonage and on up the hill, Keeper at her heels. She stopped once and looked back, her hand pressing her side for she unaccountably had a painful stitch there, and saw that Weightman was following her. That was unbearable. She turned and ran on, but he caught up to her. He reached for her arm, and as he did he said, "You might as well stop! I can run faster than you."

She pulled her arm away, rounded on him, and screamed, "I know you *can* run faster, Willie, but does that mean you *must*?"

She glared at him, and then turned and began to run again. This time he did not follow her. She looked back, just before she disappeared over the brow of the hill, and saw him standing still, looking after her.

As for Weightman, he turned away after she disappeared, and realized with sadness that she had finally called him by his Christian name, and it had taken disappointment and anger to draw it out of her.

❧❦❧

On Sunday Emily remained in bed for she had no will to get up. Not even the prospect of a walk with Keeper on the moors was enough to encourage her to leave her room. Aunt Branwell had already expressed her dismay at her niece's short hair, and even Tabby shook her head at the sight of it and said, "At least that will mend." Patrick said nothing, though his face had registered his shock. Emily suspected Weightman had explained the circumstances. On Sunday evening, her father came upstairs and sat on the edge of her bed before retiring for the night.

He said, "It was wrong of you, Emily."

Emily felt her throat tighten. It was rare for her father to chastise her. She turned her head to stare at the ceiling.

"Willie is worried about you, because you weren't in church."

"I couldn't face him," she said to the ceiling.

"Because you're angry with him, or because you are embarrassed at what you did?"

"Both."

"I think Willie is a bit angry as well. Or at least I think he has a right to be. You blame him for something that is none of his doing."

"But it isn't fair," Emily said.

"No, it isn't. But blaming Willie for the conventions of society is also not fair. Is it?"

After a moment, she said, "No."

"I think an apology is in order. Then you will both feel better."

She turned her head and looked at her father. "He won't want to see me," she said. "He must think what everyone else thinks of me. Mr. Brontë's strange daughter, someone to laugh about when she is noticed at all."

"No, he doesn't think that."

She sat up then. "But *I* think so sometimes. Why can't I be like everyone else? Why can't I make social calls and engage in parlor gossip and flirt and long for pretty clothes as other young women do?"

"But Emily, I've never known you to *want* to be like that. You don't really, do you?"

She fell back on her pillow and stared at him. "No," she said. "Only—" She fell silent and looked away again.

"Only—what?"

She could not tell her father. What she really wanted was for Willie to carry her away to the moors and make love to her.

"Nothing," she said. "I cannot face Willie yet. But I will write him a note of apology and put it on his desk."

That was what she did, although she waited until the day before he was to go to Halifax. "I am feeling well enough to play piano for the children next Sunday," she wrote. "And I wish to beg pardon for my behavior. I did not mean to hurt your feelings and I think perhaps I did. That is what I am sorry for, because you are kind and do not deserve to be hurt. I suppose I should be sorry for much else, and perhaps someday I shall be. Yours truly, Emily Brontë."

She made sure he was away from his desk before she left the note, and she did not see him the next morning when he set off for Halifax. That night, when she knew Weightman and Branwell would be sitting rapt in the presence of an orchestra and chorus listening to Beethoven, she slipped out onto the moors with Keeper and cried herself to sleep beneath a blanket of stars.

❧

On Sunday morning, Weightman was back at his post, greeting the children as they made their noisy way into the Sunday school building. Emily entered without looking at Weightman and went straight to the cottage piano. A sheaf of sheet music was already on the stand. She picked it up and saw the word BEETHOVEN on the front.

It was a piano arrangement of the Ninth Symphony.

Emily turned to Weightman. He smiled and came over to her. "It was on sale in the hall Friday night. I knew you must have it."

"Thank you," she whispered.

The children continued to mill around, oblivious to the two adults, so Emily asked, "How was it?"

"It was the most glorious thing I have ever heard," Weightman said. "And all the way through, all I could think of was that you were not there to hear it, and that I wished so terribly you could have been."

"I went out on the moors and lay beneath the stars and tried to imagine it. Keeper and I heard only night birds. But I was grateful for that music." She looked down at the sheet music. "I shall begin to practice it at once. It will be a while before I have mastered it."

"When you do, I hope I may come to tea and hear it afterward."

"Of course you must."

"And I offer you a promise. Someday, I shall arrange for you to attend a symphony. I hope Charlotte and Anne will be able to come as well. We shall make a party of it, as we did in Keighley, and all shall be done properly."

Emily nodded, and brushed back the hair that escaped from its place behind her ears and fell into her face.

"Nothing to be done about the short hair, I fear," Weightman said in an awkward attempt at humor.

"I think I like it," Emily responded defensively. "Perhaps I shall keep it."

Weightman shook his head and walked away.

"George Sand wears hers short," Emily called after him. "And Liszt does not care."

Weightman rolled his eyes in mock exasperation. Then he clapped his hands. "Children, let us begin. Let's sing 'There Is a Land of Pure Delight' and then we shall learn a new song."

The children settled down on the stone floor and sang with the uninhibited vigor of the very young, some out of tune, about the wonderful pleasures that would await them when they died. Emily remarked on the despair of their situation as she and Weightman gathered up their things afterward and the curate pulled on his robe for the Sunday service.

"*They* cannot hear Beethoven either," Emily added.

"No," Weightman said. "Nor can they read the words they are singing. But do you know what I have been thinking? I have been envisioning a school for poor children."

"In Haworth?"

He set down his Bible and prayer book and folded his arms. "In Haworth."

"I have long advocated for that," Emily said, her eyes narrowed. "But how would it be funded?"

"Some sort of campaign must be organized," Weightman said, "and subscriptions raised."

"Haworth can barely afford the subscription to pay your meager salary," Emily pointed out.

"True. But I have written to the bishop, to see if he has any suggestions. Perhaps wealthy individuals elsewhere might be enlisted."

"The wealthy to help the poor?"

"Some rich people are altruistic."

Emily set down her music and folded her own arms. "And who might run this school, Mr. Weightman?"

He grinned. "I have some ideas. Perhaps we might discuss them during a walk upon the moors on my day off."

"You have stopped walking with me."

"I have asked your father's permission to begin again. And he has given his consent. All that is left is to invite me to dinner beforehand." Then Weightman picked up his prayer book, bowed, and went out the door.

12

utumn began with the September blooming of the heather on the moors into brilliant swatches of purple. Most afternoons when her housekeeping chores were done, Emily rambled with Keeper and Nero in tow. Again on Tuesdays, William Weightman accompanied her. They remained cautious. Neither spoke of their friendship; Weightman was careful not to touch Emily, and to keep a respectful distance. She longed to throw her arms about his neck and pull him down atop her in the tall moor grasses. But that would have been the end of it, and so she walked on and wondered if Weightman daydreamed about the same thing.

Nero distracted them. When Weightman asked if he could wear the glove and call the bird, she readily assented. It took a number of tries, for Nero remained skittish and kept trying to return to Emily. But at last he landed on Weightman's fist as reliably as Emily's, though he grumbled and fixed the man with an impertinent stare before settling down.

One Tuesday in October when the purple had disappeared from the hillsides and they climbed the moor beyond the falls of Sladen Beck, Weightman remarked, "I would like to try one more thing with Nero, with your permission. I wonder if he will come to me when you are nowhere in sight. We should find a place where you could hide, so if he does not come, you could retrieve him."

"Why?" Emily asked. "Do you want to take him hunting when I am not around?"

Weightman trudged on, his lips pursed and eyes cast down. "Charlotte and your father have been corresponding of late."

"Charlotte?" Emily burst out laughing. "What does she have to do with anything? Do you want to take Charlotte to hunt with Nero? She would as soon you were the prey."

Weightman smiled. "I am well aware," he said, "your sister does not love me. I wish I knew a way to make her my friend."

"The best you can hope for is polite tolerance. Charlotte is convinced yours is the most callow soul in Yorkshire, and when Charlotte becomes convinced of something, she will not be disabused."

Weightman said, "Nevertheless, your father shared Charlotte's ideas with me. And some of them are quite good."

"Oh," Emily said, "Charlotte is dear, despite her infatuations. And valuable. Were it not for Charlotte, the Brontë family would not try anything new under the sun."

"That," Weightman said, "is precisely it. You three sisters have talked about starting a school."

"Of course I have mentioned it to you. I want a school for factory children. Charlotte will only hear of a school elsewhere, where we would attract boarders of a certain social class. Then there is Anne, who has her heart set upon the seaside. So there you are, an imaginary school pulled in three directions. All three are at best abstract eventualities."

"Perhaps," Weightman said, "you might wish to be prepared for all three."

Emily stopped walking and stared at him. "I know that tone of voice. It is the same you used when you talked me into playing the piano for the Sunday School."

"Is it?"

"And the same you use when you urge Branwell to consider that he has had too much to drink."

"Indeed?"

"Which means you are about to deal me a spoonful of medicine," she said. "Whether for good or ill, I suppose I shall find out."

"I hope," Weightman said, "I should never offer you any medicine for ill, or force you to drink it."

"What then?"

"Let me take Nero," Weightman said. "You must be tired of carrying him."

"What *then*?" Emily repeated, and stamped her foot so the bird squawked and flapped his wings. Keeper barked in sympathy.

"Your father asked me to speak to your aunt about providing the initial funding for a school. I have done so, and she has agreed. So we are no longer talking about an abstract eventuality."

Emily stared at him. "A school here? For the poor?"

"That is not settled," he said. "The sort of school you wish for would need a more stable source of income, since its pupils would have no money. But Charlotte believes, and we all think she is correct, that the possibility of students of a more well-to-do background must not be dismissed out of hand. My scheme may fail; Charlotte's is necessary to your survival. And if such a school is to be undertaken, then the three of you need more training. Your aunt has agreed to pay."

"More training? No, no. I see where this conversation leads." Emily began to walk faster, her cheeks red with anger. When Weightman followed, she said, "No, Willie, I will not discuss it. I know enough to teach the children I wish to teach. I need no further training."

"But suppose I am not successful in raising money for a school for the poor?" he repeated. "Have you considered how you shall make your way when your father dies?"

"No!" She clapped her hands over her ears. "I won't listen to talk of Papa dying. I shall deal with that when it comes. Besides, I would not teach at all if it meant I had no time for my writing. I would rather be a washerwoman."

Weightman had grown practiced at handling Emily Brontë's moods. He changed the subject. But he knew she would continue to think about what he had said.

Weightman had an unwitting ally in Charlotte, who wrote Emily with the news that Aunt Branwell would pay to send her nieces to Brussels to learn French. She explained what she knew about the school.

> I cannot go alone; it is not done. Anne cannot go, since she is employed. That leaves you, dear sister. I know you were miserable at school before, but now you are grown. Think how proficient in French we would become. And there is the adventure of living in a city.

The letter went on for several pages. Emily read with a sense of dread that settled into the pit of her stomach. She did not want to answer the letter. But at last she sent out a brief reply.

> Are you certain Anne could not go? She might like to leave her post, and I am needed here.

On her bed she prayed, Please God, don't let it happen, please, please God.

❧

Weightman waited until Emily was captive in the parsonage kitchen on bread-baking day. He came when Emily shuttled dough back and forth from board to pan to oven, and was up to her elbows in flour.

"You are early," Emily said, giving him barely a glance as she removed hot pans from the oven with a heavy cloth.

Weightman set about putting more pans in the oven to take the place of those she emptied.

"I have news," he said as he worked.

"Do you?"

Weightman, unaware of Charlotte's letter, replied, "The family of your sister's friend, now in Belgium, has identified a school in Brussels to take older students like Charlotte who wish to improve their French."

"Have they?"

"She cannot go alone."

Emily banged pans against the counter to empty the finished loaves. "Can't she?"

Weightman closed the oven door on the fresh loaves he had deposited. "Might you think about the possibility? Of gaining another attainment, I mean?"

Emily shoved aside the loaves and resumed kneading the pile of dough on the counter.

"If you went to such a school," Weightman continued, "you would be forced to speak French from morn to evening. When you returned to England, you would be proficient in the language, or at least as much as you need be to teach in English schools."

"Do you think I don't know this?" Emily said. "I have had a letter from Charlotte, you know." She pounded the dough.

"Oh," Weightman said. "Then you think well of the idea?"

Emily slapped the mound of dough, plopped it over, and began to punch it. "I do not. I hope Anne will go instead."

"Anne has a post—" Weightman began.

Emily rounded on him and cried, "Why do you try to make me leave? Why do you want rid of me? If it is uncomfortable for you to walk on the moors with me, then let us stop as we did before. But must you send me away?"

"Emily," he said, "I do not try to send you away. If you went to Brussels I would miss you terribly. But it would do you good."

"Good? What good can there be? I could study French here. I can—" Emily was so upset she could not continue.

Weightman waited. Emily returned to the dough, which did not need more kneading, but received it anyway.

"There are practical reasons that keep me from going," she said at last, not looking at him.

"Such as—"

"What about my animals?"

"Tabby will feed the cat and the fowl. Your father will feed Keeper, and I will take him with me on my walks, as I did Robbie. As for Nero, why do you think I wanted to teach him to come to my glove?"

Emily considered. Then she said, "What of the Chartist letters I have been passing on to you? Shall I miss the plugs being pulled from the boilers?"

"It will be summer before anything happens. The market for cloth continues against us. As for the letters, I will think of something else."

Emily grew angry. "You have been planning this. Why are you conspiring against me?"

"It *has* been something of a conspiracy," Weightman admitted. "But your father and I think it best."

Emily picked up the dough and slammed it down against the table. "Papa is in on this, is he?"

"He wants what's best for you."

She shook her head. "You cannot tell me why this is best."

"Think how you would grow," Weightman said.

"Grow?" she replied. "Who wants me to grow?"

"I do," he said.

*"You?"* She turned and faced him. "Am I not good enough as I am? If not, I don't care!"

Weightman faltered, and then said in a rush, "I want you to experience something of the larger world. I want you to walk through a museum and look at the paintings."

*"You* want! What about what I want?"

"I want you to sit in a concert hall. As you know you long to do. The school in Brussels will take you to concerts, Emily. They will encourage you to play upon a full piano."

She stood still, listening despite her resolve not to.

"You have said to me that if you were a man, you would go to America, to the frontier, or on a voyage to the South Pacific. But if you know you have the courage for that, can you not do this, as a woman? The strong woman I know you to be?"

Emily leaned against the table. "Charlotte described the school," she whispered. 'We would share a dormitory with young girls. The school is enclosed on four sides, with a garden in the middle. It is in the heart of the old city, surrounded by other buildings. There will be no moors. Only buildings on four sides, and more buildings beyond. I fear I will die for a breath of air." She looked at Weightman. "I would be in prison."

Weightman stood beside her. "You told me on one of our walks about a story you were writing," he said, "about someone named Alexandrina. Is that right?"

"Yes," Emily whispered.

"Alexandrina was imprisoned in a dungeon because of her part in the cause she fought for. But she remained strong. And so will you."

"How do you know?"

"Because," Weightman said, and reaching out, he touched Emily's forehead with the tips of two fingers, "you will be free here. In your mind."

She gave him one of those piercing looks that never failed to melt his heart and break it all at once. Then she was in his arms. She felt the rough stubble of his chin pressed against her cheek.

"Six months," he said. "They will pass in no time. You will be back in August, in time to see the heather bloom."

Even as Weightman spoke, they heard the kitchen door open. Tabby entered, her shopping basket laden with purchases, and then stared at them as they sprang apart. Weightman flushed a deep red and turned round and round as though searching for something. "Tabby!" he said, more jovial than necessary, "Emily was saying she is out of pans, and I wonder where there are more?"

Tabby set down her basket and raised an eyebrow. "In t'oven, I daresay," she answered. "But first, Mr. Weightman, take care of your back. 'Tis dusted with flour."

He twisted his head, trying in vain to look over his own shoulder. Emily saw her floury handprints in several places. "Oh!" she cried, but could do nothing for when she raised her hands to brush off the prints, they were dusted liberally with flour. Weightman stood helpless, and then began to laugh.

"Emily," he said, "we are caught white-handed."

Tabby cackled with glee. "Aye, Mr. Weightman, and if you don't want all Haworth to see, you mun let me take a brush to't."

Emily rummaged in a drawer and, locating a brush, handed it to Tabby, who began pummeling Weightman's back. When she was done, the flour had been reduced to a light dusting. As the curate prepared to leave, Emily said as she gathered up a bunch of loaves, "Here, Willie, take these with you."

"I have a nice piece of mutton for later," added Tabby, who often as not offered the dinner invitations to Weightman, so sure she was that all in the house would welcome him.

⚜

In November, sleet and a sharp east wind punished Haworth for its exposed position on the brow of the moor. Winter promised to be more difficult than the year before. And William Weightman's father, piqued that another year passed without his son searching for a more beneficent living elsewhere, cut off his son's allowance.

Patrick shook his head over supper. "An appalling way for a father to behave. May I never do such a thing to any child of mine," he said, glancing around the table in his nearsighted way before continuing to eat his bit of cheese and bread. Only Emily was there to hear.

"Will Willie have enough to live on?" she asked.

"Willie has always lived simply, and must continue to do so," Patrick said. "Now he has no margin of comfort. And no one knows, except myself, how much he has given of his own money to poor people here. Scraps of meat have found their way into cooking pots, many a poor dying soul has been comforted with a dram of spirit, thanks to Willie. If his father means to punish him in as cruel a way as possible, this is it. But if I know Willie, the effect will be the opposite of what his father intends."

No more new books would be ordered from London. Weightman apologized for the loss on one of their Tuesday outings.

"It is no matter," Emily assured him.

"I shall walk to Keighley," he promised, "and bring you what you want from the circulating library."

She studied him as he walked beside her, his head down and his hands clasped behind his back. Curiosity overwhelmed her inclination not to probe. "Why do you stay," she asked, "when your father so hates your position here?"

Weightman would not look at her. He said, "I told you once I believe God has placed me here."

"Many people," Emily said, "would convince themselves God

could use them someplace else. For most, calls from God include convenience."

Weightman shook his head. "Even if I might be useful elsewhere, I would not give my father the satisfaction."

"Oh," Emily said.

"He is a bully," Weightman continued. "He dictates to my mother, and my brother and sister. But I have withstood him before and I shall continue. Besides, I am content here. I cannot say happy. Haworth is too difficult for anyone's happiness." He stopped and looked at Emily. "But one is so alive here. Every exertion, every breath precious, and sustaining."

But by December Weightman appeared not sustained, but haggard. Late one darkening afternoon when Emily sat drinking a cup of tea with Tabby, Weightman knocked once at the back door and then pushed it open. But instead of his usual cheery greeting, he sat at the table without removing his coat. He did not look at either Emily or Tabby.

Tabby set a cup of tea beside him and said, "There, lad, you look done for."

He nodded his thanks, but did not touch the cup. "I've just come from a funeral," he said. "My second today. I buried three people yesterday, one the day before, and two on Monday. Not one of them was above the age of thirty. Now I'm on my way to look in on a four-year-old boy who is dying." He glanced at Emily and said, "Matthew Moore from the Sunday school."

"The little boy with curly red hair," Emily said.

Weightman nodded. "I suppose I shall have to bury him—"

He stopped and continued to look down at the cup of tea in front of him. He was pale, and Emily noticed how thin he had grown. Then he closed his eyes and she was stunned to see a tear course down his cheek. For a moment she didn't know what to do. She had never seen a man cry, though she supposed her father must have shed tears in private. Then Tabby was waving at her, urging her to go to Weightman. Emily did so, standing behind him and wrapping her arms about his neck. He grabbed her arm with one hand like a man clutching a life preserver that held his head above water. Emily felt him heave with silent sobs as she pressed against his back. She laid her cheek against the top of his head. Tabby came close as well, sitting in Emily's chair and grasping his other hand between her two rough ones.

Weightman cried himself out like a small child, and then with a great shuddering sigh gave both their hands a squeeze and said in a broken voice, "Sit down, please, sit down."

Emily did so, drawing her chair close and continuing to hold his hand. He said, "I'm sorry. One can only see so much—" He took another deep breath and stared up at the ceiling, his eyes still wet with tears.

"You don't look well," Emily said. "Couldn't you take a rest?"

"If I don't tend to people, your father must," Weightman said. "And at his age, he can only do so much."

"But so can you only do so much. And it will do no one any good if you make yourself sick," Emily answered. "If only I could help."

"Unless you can convince the government to come to Haworth and study why people die right and left—"

"I know what they would say," Emily replied bitterly, "for I read it in the newspapers. They will say poor people do not care if they live in squalor, and so they sicken and die."

Weightman balled his hands into fists and pressed them against his mouth. "So they will say," he agreed. Then he stirred himself as though forcing himself to be cheerful and said, "Tabby, forgive me, I have let your cup of good tea grow cold."

"I'll get you another," Tabby said, going to the settle. "You should drink something warm before you go see that poor dying child. Or eat a bite, some cheese and bread perhaps?"

"No," Weightman said, "I should get along to Ginnel and look in on the little fellow."

He stood and went shakily to the door, leaning on Emily as he did so. Then he took his arm away from her and left without a word.

"Law," Tabby said, her hand pressed to her throat. "I have never seen that lad in such a state."

"No," Emily agreed. She went at once to her father, who was working on his sermon in his study, and told him what had happened.

"Willie must have a rest," Patrick said, taking off his spectacles.

"I doubt you will get him to leave Matthew Moore's bedside," she said. "That boy is one of his favorites."

"I shall speak with him tomorrow then," Patrick said.

No one was surprised when Weightman took to his bed with a high fever and congestion, not long after burying Matthew Moore. Mr. Wheelwright feared the congestion might settle into pneumonia. But the fever broke, drenching Weightman's bedclothes with sweat, and he was back out on the streets of Haworth a few days later. Patrick urged him to take a break from services and preaching for a week, and invited him to sit in the Brontë pew that Sunday as a member of the congregation.

Charlotte was home preparing for the move to Brussels. Anne was back at the parsonage as well, on Christmas holiday. Weightman found the three sisters in the pew on Sunday morning.

"Look who has returned!" he exclaimed, a smile lighting his face. "Your father has invited me to join you," he added a bit tentatively, for he was wary of Charlotte.

Emily gave up her seat next to Anne at once and moved to Charlotte's side of the box pew. Weightman settled beside Anne, his arm across the back of the pew.

"Miss Brontë," he said to Charlotte, "welcome home."

Charlotte nodded and merely said, "Mr. Weightman."

Weightman turned with relief to Anne, who was beaming a welcome. He leaned close and said, "Miss Anne, you are looking well."

"My asthma has not bothered me for months," Anne replied. "But I hear you have been ill, Mr. Weightman."

"I am on the mend," he said. He smiled at Charlotte again, but she was careful not to meet his eyes. He glanced at Emily and she saw the color mount a bit in his cheeks. Then Patrick entered the church to begin the service. Weightman picked up a prayer book, found the place, and shared his book with Anne. Charlotte cast a number of baleful glances at the two of them.

When the service was done, Charlotte caught Emily by the arm and led her out of the church, while Weightman lingered at the pew, talking to Anne.

"It is disgraceful," Charlotte began when they were outside. "Do you see how he is flirting with her?"

"Flirting with Anne?" Emily said. "Mr. Weightman?"

"Who do you think I mean? I feared as much last year. It is bad enough when he raises the hopes of an Agnes Walton or Caroline Dury. But it is unacceptable that he should toy with poor Anne's feelings."

"I think he likes Anne quite a lot," Emily protested. "He wishes to hear about her experiences these past months."

Charlotte ignored Emily's response. "Did you not see how familiar he was? He practically had his arm around her, and was most anxious to share his prayer book with her. And the way he kept watching her out of the corner of his eye, as though to see what impression he made upon her. At least she was modest and kept her eyes down."

"You, on the other hand, had no hesitancy about staring."

Charlotte swatted Emily's arm in her usual manner. "Someone must look out for our little sister," she said. "You have your head in the clouds too often to be bothered. But that fickle young man must be made to understand that Anne is not a plaything. Today shall be the only Sunday we see him in our pew, I hope. I shall speak to Papa this very afternoon."

"Very well," Emily said. "But you must wait until after dinner, because Mr. Weightman is invited."

⅍

Branwell came home for the holiday and the party was complete. Emily might have looked back upon it as one of the happiest times of her life, had not the prospect of Belgium loomed. She had reluctantly agreed to accompany Charlotte. Even Anne had urged her to it. I cannot oppose them all, Emily thought wearily. So she had resigned herself.

Weightman approved her decision after pushing her toward it, and yet once it was made, he too seemed subdued. He was outwardly cheerful, but displayed an underlying air of melancholy that seemed more than just the lingering effects of his illness. Only Patrick knew his curate's thoughts on the matter. Weightman had spoken to him after one of their meetings in Patrick's study, when Emily left the room after bringing a pot of tea and cups on a tray.

"She doesn't want to go," Weightman said as soon as the door closed behind her.

"No," Patrick agreed. He poured the tea and handed a cup to the younger man. "But she is resigned to it."

"Well, so am I." Weightman tried to sound resolute. "It shall do her good, surely. But I must confess one of my greatest fears. I have hoped time in Brussels might soften Emily and make her more amenable to social situations. But the more I consider, I fear the opposite. I fear instead it will confirm her in her isolation."

"You may well be right," Patrick agreed. "I remind you, Willie, we have agreed we must leave this matter in God's hands."

"Of course, of course," Weightman muttered.

"Your friendship with my daughter may not lead where convention dictates. But I think it still must be of great value to you both, for love is never in vain."

Weightman nodded and said nothing further on the subject.

❧

On Christmas Eve, the Haworth band made its rounds, ending at the parsonage where furniture was shoved aside and dancing, spiced by Tabby's good mulled ale, ensued. Branwell escorted Emily; Weightman shuttled between Anne and Tabby, and once even enticed Aunt Branwell to take a turn about the parlor. Charlotte declined, except for a single outing with her father. It was time to develop an air of sophistication before traveling to a city like Brussels, and rude country dances did not fit her idea of refinement. Then there was the unwelcome presence of William Weightman. But she must tolerate him, since the rest of the family had seen fit to include him. Charlotte decided to use his presence as a test of her ability to encounter new and inconvenient circumstances. She was traveling to a country with different mores from those in England, a Catholic nation whose very religious institutions would include elements of corruption. Weightman would suffice for practice. Charlotte forced herself to converse with him, though she could not resist poking him with a needle of sarcasm.

"Mr. Weightman, how does Agnes Walton?" she asked when he stood near her filling his cup with punch.

He bowed and said, "I have not heard, Miss Brontë. We do not correspond regularly as before. I believe she may be engaged to a gentleman from London."

"Indeed? You have let her get away from you?"

"I have," he answered, and turned back to the punch bowl.

"And your family? Are they well?"

"I believe so."

"Surely you know?"

"I would have heard if they were not," Weightman said stiffly, and moved away to sit beside Anne.

Charlotte felt a pang of guilt. She already knew from Brontë family conversations that Weightman's kin had distanced themselves. It was cruel, she supposed, to remind him of it on Christmas Eve. Still, she considered, he *should* be reminded of it. He had no business throwing away family connections, as well as a fiancée, for a place like Haworth. Let him go someplace where he might have more competition. Then we would see how William Weightman fared.

❈

Christmas passed; Anne and Branwell returned to their positions. Patrick determined to accompany his daughters to their foreign destination. Charlotte drew up a list of French phrases for the trip (*"S'il vous plait montrez moi le priver"*—*Please show me the toilet*) and a list of preparations (*repair tears and hems, sew handkerchiefs, nightgowns, petticoats, add pockets*). She took the liberty of remonstrating with Emily (*Sister, you must obtain new petticoats. The ones you have hang as limp upon you as a dishrag.*) She received a poisonous look in return.

On the last Sunday in Haworth, Emily sat in the family pew, riveted on Weightman. She watched every movement as he moved from pulpit to table to altar rail, trying to memorize him. At home, while Aunt and her father took their naps and Charlotte made an inventory of their belongings, Emily sketched a drawing of Weightman in the pulpit, clad in his black gown and white bands, scanning the congregation. She placed it in the bottom of her trunk, along with sketches of Keeper and Nero, careful to cover them with clothes so that Charlotte wouldn't see.

Then came the morning when the trio of Brontës were to set out on their journey. Patrick had hired a gig to take them to the railway station in Leeds; from there, they would travel to Euston Station for three days in London, then on to Brussels by boat. Charlotte's trunk stood in the hallway and she watched impatiently out the parlor window for a sign of the rented conveyance. Emily was in the kitchen; she said her good-byes to the geese and Nero and the cat Tiger, and then sat on the floor with her arms disconsolately around Keeper, who now and then licked her face. Tabby, as distressed as anyone to lose Emily, stood at the sink ferociously attacking the skillet she had used to fry the breakfast eggs.

Keeper roused himself at a rapping on the kitchen door, and then Weightman entered carrying a book. He looked at Tabby and said, "May I say a quick goodbye? Alone?"

Tabby went into the hall without a word and pulled the door shut behind her. Emily sensed she remained on the other side standing guard, and wondered if she and Weightman had conspired over the moment. The curate held out the volume he carried. The poems of Shelley.

"I want you to have this," he said.

Emily took the book and said, "To borrow, you mean."

"I want you to *have* it," he repeated. "To remember me by."

She ducked her head. "It is very kind," she said, and began to leaf through the volume. She stopped when she saw an inscription on the title page, in Weightman's strong hand.

> *For Emily*
> *With much love*
> *W*

Her eyes filled with tears. The hair she had tucked behind her ear fell across her face. Weightman reached out and brushed it back. He leaned close and whispered, "When you return, I hope we will have much to say to one another."

Emily looked up and their eyes met, for what seemed an eternity. She thought she could not breathe. He leaned close and his lips gently brushed her forehead.

From the hallway, Charlotte called, "Emily, the coach is here. You must fetch your trunk." Her voice came closer. Then, "Tabby, why on earth are you standing here?"

Weightman pressed Emily's hand, and then he was gone.

⊰⊱

He rejoined them as the gig prepared to depart, as though he had been working at his desk and sauntered across the lane to bid them farewell. Aunt Branwell was saying goodbye to each in turn. Emily hugged the old woman, who clung with a sudden ferocity.

"I pray," Aunt Branwell said, "I was not unwise to use my money in this fashion."

Emily could say nothing in return but "We are in God's hands, Aunt."

Aunt Branwell dabbed at her eyes with her handkerchief.

"Willie," Patrick said, "I know I leave the church in good hands. I will see you in a few weeks. He shook his curate's hand.

Charlotte was so pleased to be away that she was friendly to Weightman. "Goodbye," she said, offering her hand. "We are off on our great adventure."

Then she followed her father as they saw to the lashing of the trunks to the back of the vehicle.

Emily turned to Weightman and said in a low voice, "I put the book in my trunk. I don't want Charlotte to know I have it. But if she does find it, how shall I explain the inscription?"

"Tell her it is from Mr. Wheelhouse," Weightman said.

Emily could not help the yelp of laughter that escaped her. Then she stood still. "I will miss you," she whispered.

"I'll write."

"I don't want Charlotte to see your letters. Otherwise she will say terrible things about you and I can't bear it. I shall not be in a foreign country with the one person I must cling to for support, and hear her say such things."

"I'll write through your father. And don't worry, I shall take good care of Keeper and Nero."

She nodded.

"Emily," Charlotte called, "are you coming?"

Emily turned and saw that her sister was already in the gig, and her father waited, holding the door for her. The expression on Patrick's face was apologetic. She turned toward Weightman, a look of panic on her face as though she might fling herself upon him and refuse to go.

Weightman took her hand. "Miss Emily," he said, "you shall take Brussels by storm." With that, he handed her to her father.

As the gig rolled down Church Lane, Emily stole a glance back. Weightman stood beside Aunt Branwell, his arm around her for support. He waved. Then the gig turned the corner into Ginnel and he was gone.

13

*E*mily's time in Brussels passed like a prison sentence. She kept a running tally on a piece of paper, numbers from one hundred eighty-four to zero. Each night before she went to bed, she held the sheet up in the flickering light of a candle and marked through the highest number. She circled the zero and placed a star beside it—the day to go home.

She had been entranced by her three days in London. The dome of St. Paul's Cathedral loomed over the Brontë lodging in Paternoster Row. Emily loved to stand beneath that dome inside the venerable church, and stare upward. A miniature of heaven, the light altered, suffused with the divine. She took in the paintings at the National Gallery and communed with the kings and queens of Westminster Abbey (alive, she knew, for she sensed their presence as clearly as the anonymous spirits of Haworth).

London taught her that she could bear the press of people for short periods of time, and even study them with fascination. She resolved that once she returned home, she and Anne should go together to towns, Manchester, or York, or Liverpool. They could even go to Edinburgh and on to the highlands of Sir Walter Scott, if Branwell might be persuaded to escort them. Or perhaps—but her mind drew back from the thought of William Weightman's company on such a journey. The likely disappointment of those hopes was too painful to contemplate.

The little party crossed the Channel, and the immensity of the expanse of water, the roughness of the waves, awed Emily and appealed to her romantic nature. But she felt physically pummeled by her first sight of the Belgian countryside. It was flat. Entirely flat. How on earth could people go from place to place? How keep from becoming utterly lost, with no winding streams, no heights and moors in distinctive shapes to guide them or force their path in any direction? Then she began to wonder how people decided where to place their towns, their houses, their barns. Any one site would do as well as another, and would the array of choices not be maddening? And how become so attached to a place that one's soul became a bondsman to it, so that one would die for that patch of earth? Flat land demanded no allegiance. Emily pitied the Belgians.

Brussels swallowed her. She found the Pensionnat Heger imprisoning as she had feared, but she was also oddly relieved to be within its confines. One would not become quite so disoriented, since here were garden footpaths and four closed walls, and a schedule that must be followed. She now understood how Nero had adapted to his cage in the Brontë washhouse. It was not the hawk's birthright. But it was a fixed point to keep him from utter annihilation. Emily thought of herself as the merlin's sister.

Although the Brontës lodged in one of the dormitories, a long room lined with cots, Madame Heger had put up a curtain at one end. Behind it, the Brontës found two cots and two dressers, as well as their own washbasin. Charlotte sank onto her bed with a murmured "Thank God for privacy."

The other pupils, young girls, stared at Emily with her tall, lanky body, her carelessly tossed hair, and plain, unfashionable clothes. She gathered from Charlotte, who was far more adept in the language, that they thought her clothes ugly, and her aspect glum and off-putting.

Charlotte was the strange foreigner; Emily the monster who accompanied her.

"You really should smile more," Charlotte offered. "You scare them. And I said you should get new petticoats. See how full they wear them here; they are stiffer even than mine."

"I don't care what they think about me," Emily answered. "Nor will I spend what little money I have on new petticoats. These girls look ridiculous—if you pushed them over, they would roll like balls."

Emily was not inclined to do anyone's bidding at the Pensionnat Heger, least of all Charlotte's, the author of her misery. The price of Emily's company was Charlotte's acceptance of her sister's independence.

Monsieur Heger, who would tutor the two Englishwomen, was short, sturdy, and dark with piercing eyes and a pockmarked face. When he met with the Brontës in his study, he made clear what he expected.

"I will assign passages of great French writers," he said, while Charlotte translated for Emily. "You will write essays on subjects I assign, and you will try to write in the style of French of those writers. That way you will be forced to pay close attention not only to what they say, but how they say it."

Emily objected. "I write in my own style," she said, "not someone else's."

Monsieur Heger, upon receiving this impertinent objection in Charlotte's hesitant translation, said, "But my dear mademoiselle, your style is in English. How do you know what it is in French?"

Charlotte translated and looked at Emily with an expression that pleaded for good behavior.

"I don't care what it is in French," Emily said.

Charlotte shut her eyes and sighed, then offered her answer in a tentative voice. Emily guessed that her sister did not translate exactly. Even so, Monsieur Heger gave Emily a sharp look.

"We will start with something simple," said Monsieur. "Each of you will give me an essay you will title 'The Cat.' Two pages in French, please, so I may judge where we stand."

Emily received these instructions with relief, for what better did she know than animals? But what took her a few minutes in English took hours to translate into French. She wrote:

I like cats. The cat is more like humans than any other creature. Dogs are too good to be compared to humans. Cats, on the other hand, are cruel, ungracious, and hypocritical. They pretend to love and then kill, and think nothing of it. This is like humans. We call this politeness.

Compare how a cat plays with a mouse to the way men torture a fox and then throw it to the dogs. I have seen small children act in the same fashion. They kill butterflies and smile. Imagine your lovely little angel as a cat, with the half-swallowed tail of a mouse dangling from his mouth as he beams at you.

Monsieur Heger, when he met to discuss their work, told Emily, "Your written French is simple but adequate, though you have trouble with the spoken language. I would ask you not to rely upon your sister as we speak. Mademoiselle," he said, with a nod to Charlotte, "I ask you to wait outside."

Charlotte retreated reluctantly and closed the door.

"Your content—" Monsieur Heger hesitated, and then said to Emily, speaking slowly so that she might more easily comprehend, "mademoiselle, I have not encountered such a thing. Not even in a boy."

Emily would not be bullied. "You see why copying someone else would not come naturally to me," she said in awkward French.

Monsieur studied her. Then he said, "Let me make myself clear. Mimicking the style of French writers can help you gain an under-standing of the language. I do not mean to stifle your originality. Even

260 Denise Giardina

if I think what you say inappropriate. You are," he added, "a misanthrope, mademoiselle, to compare people, especially children, to cats
in this manner."

Emily considered, and then said, "But a misanthrope does not like
people. I do compare people to cats, but as I say in my first sentence, I
like cats. I sleep with one at home."

Monsieur Heger gave a sudden loud laugh so that Charlotte, listening in the anteroom, grew alarmed. What, she wondered, had Emily
done to embarrass them? She was relieved, when her sister emerged
from the study, to see Monsieur seemed pleased.

When they were walking back to their quarters, Emily said, with
grudging respect, "He is difficult. I rather like that."

"He is," Charlotte proclaimed, her face flushed, "the most fascinating man I have ever encountered."

Emily saw then where things stood. Once again. She sighed, for she
sensed that most of the English words she would hear over the coming
months would be about Monsieur Heger.

❧

Charlotte and Emily received their first letters from home.

"Why is yours longer?" Charlotte wondered. "I assumed Papa
would tell me the same things he told you, and that he would write to
both of us in one letter."

"No," Emily said quickly. "My letter has a great deal about my
animals that would only bore you." She was careful to keep the pages
with their different handwriting out of Charlotte's sight.

"The difficult winter is almost past," Weightman wrote,

> and we look forward to spring. There have been too many deaths this
> season, even more than last year. But I hope spring and summer may
> soon come to the entire north of England and Wales.

Emily took this last oddly phrased sentence to refer to the continuing development of what Weightman called the Plug Plan. Weightman went on to tell Emily that Keeper was well, "although he misses you terribly. Your father says that when he rises in the morning, he finds the dog lying across the doorframe of your bedroom, waiting for your return. As for Nero, I take him out often when I walk Keeper, and he returns to the glove most reliably."

Emily had not quite believed Weightman would write. When alone, she read and reread the letter for sustenance. Each time she was done, she put it at the bottom of her trunk out of Charlotte's sight.

When a second letter arrived the next week, Weightman wrote,

> Your Monsieur Heger sounds a despot, but a kindly one, and you rise to that challenge. Emily, I am proud of you.

By then she had composed her second assigned essay, on the caterpillar. Charlotte disdained the subject. She wrote:

> The caterpillar crawls, and it eats. It crawled and ate yesterday. It will crawl and eat in the future.

Good, Charlotte thought as she paused in her writing, for I demonstrate my mastery of verb tenses.

Because she was so much less competent in French, Emily again took hours longer to write her essay. First she questioned God's creation, which "exists upon a principle of destruction. Creatures must kill others in order to live themselves." But, she continued,

> Just as the lowly caterpillar changes into the magnificent butterfly, so this world is the embryo of a new heaven and new earth. Its poorest beauty will so far exceed our mortal imagination that we will hate our blind presumption of blaming God for creating such a world as this.

She sent the essay to Weightman in its English translation. In his next letter, he wrote,

> I read your essay to the Sunday school, and when they see a butterfly this summer, I have urged them to view it as a sign of God's promise. The children long now for butterflies.
>
> *Yours, WW*

❧❧

Emily found life at the Pensionnat Heger not so difficult as the time she had tried to teach at an English school, for she had no responsibilities except to learn. The greatest trial was not the school itself, but the regular invitations to tea from families of English expatriates who had been urged by Charlotte's school chums to befriend the Brontës. Emily hated everything about the visits—the formal manners and social graces, the exquisite china and delicate finger foods, the hothouse atmosphere of the parlors with their carefully arranged flowers and expensive furniture. Emily would have felt more comfortable if she could have escaped to the scullery and engaged the maids in conversation, even scraped a pot or two. But that would not do. So she sat miserable in a corner, not attempting to engage in conversation. One family she especially disliked, the Jenkinses, sent their two sons to escort the Brontës to their house. The young men seemed put out to be seen with two such unfashionable young women, and equally unable to offer any but the most silly topics for conversation. The visits were so awkward that the Jenkins family finally stopped inviting the Brontës altogether, to the relief even of Charlotte.

The girls at the Pensionnat continued to avoid Emily. But one spring day she sat on a bench in the garden's Allée Défendue, a tree-shaded arbor, and drew a study of the tunnel of branches with their

play of light and shadow. Emily found the atmosphere claustropho-
bic; although sunlight stippled various corners of the enclosed garden,
it was filtered with dust motes and there was no breath of a breeze.
Frustrated, Emily looked up from her work to see a girl of eleven or
twelve staring at her, as though waiting to catch her eye. The girl
smiled and gave a brief curtsy. She had a gap-toothed grin, freckles,
and a pair of auburn braids that hung below her shoulders.

"*Je t'aime,*" the girl said. "*Tu es différente.*"

"*Merci,*" Emily said dryly, "*je pense.*" She asked the girl's name.

"*Je m'appelle Louise de Bassompierre.*" The girl plopped down on the
bench to look at Emily's picture. "*C'est joli,*" she said, and offered to
show Emily some of her own drawings.

They became fast friends. They shared their drawings, Emily gave
Louise piano lessons and the younger girl drilled Emily in French much
more thoroughly than did Charlotte, who spent most of her time intent
upon impressing Monsieur Heger and ignoring her sister. I can survive
with only one friend, Emily thought, and the letters I receive.

One day Louise separated herself from a group of her friends and
came running to Emily. "*Voilà!*" she cried, and indicated her skirt.

Emily saw that, unlike the skirts of the others, with their full bell
shapes, the girl's hung limp like Emily's. Louise had taken her scissors
to her petticoat, she explained, and hacked away the unnecessary cloth.
"It was quite a lot of material," she said excitedly, "and now I don't
know what to do with it."

"Perhaps you should donate it to a hospital," Emily suggested.
"They could use the strips for bandages."

Louise brightened, "There is a charity hospital nearby. And I am so
much more comfortable, Mademoiselle Émilie. It is easier to walk."

"You may even run," Emily suggested. "But have your friends
teased you?"

"*Mai oui.* I laugh at them and tell them they are jealous because they
are not so comfortable."

Emily wondered how the girl's mother would respond. But she envied Louise, who showed no sign of losing her old friends because of her unconventionality. A rare gift, Emily thought, which I do not possess.

So Emily had her friend. And to her great joy she had been to performances at the Théâtre de la Monnaie, the Brussels opera house, where she heard Mozart's Mass in C Minor and Bach's *St. Matthew Passion*.

"Mozart is heaven come to earth," she wrote Weightman. "And can you believe it? Instead of my little cottage piano, I roam the range of an Érard grand in the school drawing room. If only you could hear."

Monsieur continued a hard taskmaster. He and Emily were often at loggerheads, for if he was not critiquing her content, he pushed her to make her writing more precise, marking through a vague phrase here, a superfluous word there. On a few occasions they even engaged in shouting matches, to the great alarm of Charlotte, who continued with her infatuation and lived in terror that she would be judged badly because of her sister. But Emily throve on these sessions; she thought Monsieur Heger enjoyed them as well, for he was always in a better mood when Emily left than when she came in, rubbing his hands and smiling broadly after each clash. As for Emily, she watched her prose grow tighter, more alive, and she thought, This is what it is like to have an editor.

Emily shared all this in her letters home. And though she did not attempt to hide her general unhappiness, it seemed to those who read them that she not only endured, but grew.

❧

A letter from Brussels was cause for Patrick Brontë and William Weightman to share a pot of tea and consult. Weightman could not have been more pleased.

"I miss her a great deal," he told Patrick. "And yet you can see she is stretching."

Patrick agreed, but added, "My boy, you should be cautious. It may not be what you require, and you won't know until she is back."

"But I have been thinking," Weightman said. "When I read her descriptions of how she despises to sit in parlors and take tea, I sympathize. Emily was not meant for society, but why should that be a barrier to her happiness or mine? Who looks askance at her? Only society ladies and gentlemen. The poor certainly do not." Weightman held his cup frozen to his lips, as though so deep in thought he forgot to drink. Then he set his cup down. "And perhaps I am not so different. If I spent my entire ministry laboring among the poor, I believe I might marry Emily happily."

"But Willie," Patrick said gently, "would Emily wish to take the time required, and give up the liberty necessary, to be a wife? To have children of her own and raise them? She lives in that fantasy world of hers."

Weightman looked crestfallen. "But would it be so much loss of liberty? I would be indulgent. And freedom may be increased with some security."

Patrick smiled and shook his head, for only Emily could answer.

The six months passed quickly enough. Charity efforts throughout the district continued, the predictable round of baptisms, marriages, and funerals consumed both clergymen. Weightman was busy behind the scenes with the evolving Chartist plot to sabotage the mill boilers. Aunt Branwell demanded attention. She grew frailer, her mind muddled. Yet she thought Emily's absence forced her downstairs to supervise the housekeeping, much to Tabby's dismay.

"I mun do my own work, and Emily's, and watch out for Aunt as well," she complained to Patrick. "And then Aunt comes along behind and undoes all. Yesterday she made off with all my spoons, and I found them in the bread box."

Patrick patted the old servant on the arm. "Let us be patient," he counseled. He sympathized with Tabby, for he had several times had to search for the items from his desk after Aunt had "put them in order." He decided he must add more help in the person of Martha Brown, the fourteen-year-old daughter of John Brown. Martha, a scrawny red-haired girl, proved a willing worker, and the household settled into an uneasy routine.

Then Branwell came home in April, once again in disgrace.

He slumped with his head down on a chair in Patrick's study while his father sat behind his desk and Weightman stood leaning against the mantel.

"The railroad says I stole money," Branwell said. Then he looked up, his face stricken. "But I swear I did not. I have many faults, but do you know me to be a thief? Have you ever known me to be greedy for money?"

"I do not know you to be greedy for material gain," Patrick said, his voice heavy with disappointment. "But I wonder if the need to buy alcohol might qualify as a sort of greed?"

"I swear it's not true," Branwell protested. "Except—" He stopped, suddenly ashamed to confide in them.

"Except what?" Weightman prodded.

"I did not steal," Branwell said. "But I was feeling badly one or two days at work. Perhaps I had too much of something the night before. And I might have been rather sloppy with my figures. I might not have checked them for errors. And so the sums would not be exact."

Branwell looked from one to another, a woeful expression on his face. Then he said, "It doesn't matter to you, does it? I'm still a rotter."

No one spoke for a time. Patrick finally broke the silence. "Your youngest sister toils at a thankless position as a governess, your other sisters are abroad in a foreign land where they barely speak the language, trying to make themselves employable. And you, the only son, cannot hold a position, even for a few months. The railroad paid you a third more than Willie here earns as curate, and yet you tossed it away."

Branwell sighed. "And now your turn, Willie. You tell me what a thankless bounder I am. Then I shall slink off into my hole."

"Very well," Weightman said. "There are ten-year-olds in the mills contributing more to their families than you do now."

"Oh." Branwell blinked. "That is cruel."

"It is the truth."

Branwell stood shakily and put his hand in his pocket. "Really," he said, "I can't think what to do. And now if you'll excuse me, there is somewhere else I—"

He didn't finish for Weightman came forward, thrust one hand into Branwell's pocket, and with the other on Branwell's shoulder, forced him back onto his chair.

"What?" was all Branwell managed to say, his mouth open.

Weightman uncorked the bottle he had withdrawn, sniffed it, and then stepped to the open window and poured out the contents.

"No!" Branwell cried, and lunged for Weightman, but the curate tossed the bottle out the window and, with both hands on Branwell's shoulders, forced the smaller man back onto the chair.

Patrick, alarmed, stood and said, "Willie, do you think—"

Weightman ignored him and, with a finger in Branwell's face, said, "You. You have been spending your time with those friends of yours from Halifax and Bradford, haven't you? Those failed artists and failed poets and failed geniuses in general?"

"W-well—" Branwell stammered. "Really, you shouldn't speak of them so, Willie, they liked you well enough when we heard the Ninth together."

"Willie," Patrick interrupted again, "what was in the bottle?"

"Laudanum," Weightman said.

Branwell grew belligerent. "And what if it was?"

Denise Giardina

"Add it to the prodigious amount of alcohol you consume, and it signifies quite a lot."

"Byron took laudanum, and Shelley, and Coleridge. All the great writers. I want to be a great writer." Branwell wrestled himself free from Weightman's grasp with a burst of energy, turned to his father, and spread his arms. "My God, William Wilberforce took laudanum for a time. The family hero."

"Wilberforce took laudanum for medicinal purposes," Weightman said. "Then he had the sense to get himself off it for good." He put his hand on Branwell's arm. "And that, my friend, is what you are going to do."

Branwell shook his arm free. "How do you plan to force me?"

Weightman gripped Branwell's arm again, stood close, and leaned so that their noses were nearly touching. "Here is what I plan to do. I am going to wear you as close, sir, as a pocket watch upon a chain."

"But suppose I don't want——"

"I don't care what you want," Weightman interrupted.

"Suppose I run?"

"I can outrun you and you know it."

"And suppose—suppose I fight?"

Branwell turned suddenly and made a dash for the door. But Weightman was on him before he reached it and, with his arms around the smaller man's chest, pulled him back into the room. Their momentum caused them to crash against the desk and knock over a lamp, which shattered against the grate of the fireplace. From the kitchen Tabby called, "What on earth!" and Patrick cried out as well, "Branwell, Willie, for God's sake——"

But Weightman had already subdued Branwell, who sagged against the desk as abruptly as he had fought. "My God, Willie, have mercy. You've emptied my bottle and I was already at the edge." He leaned against Weightman and began to sob. Tabby appeared in the doorway, her apron clutched in her hands.

Weightman looked over his shoulder at Patrick and said, "Does his room have a lock?"

"No," Patrick said.

"Then I shall have to camp there for a time and guard the door. I'm afraid, sir, you must make my pastoral visits the next few days. Tabby, we shall require a good strong pot of tea from time to time. And broth at first; later something more substantial."

"Yes, sir," Tabby said with a curtsy, shocked into formality.

"I fear we've left you with a mess," Weightman added, nodding at the broken glass on the mantel.

"Sir," Tabby said again, and disappeared to send Martha Brown with a broom and dustpan.

"Now, Branwell," said Weightman, "we shall go upstairs." He marched his charge out of the room and up the stairs in the manner of a warden escorting a prisoner.

❧

Branwell remained in his room for three days, in various stages of delirium. He fell often enough into a troubled sleep to allow Weightman to snatch some rest of his own, stretched out across the doorframe with a pillow and a blanket. At other times they wrestled as Weightman sought to keep the frenzied man from escaping.

The worst of the crisis passed and calm descended upon the parsonage. Branwell was obliged to move into the spare room at Cook Gate. He went easily enough, for the ordeal had sapped his energy. Weightman kept Branwell close, as he had promised, whether working upon a sermon or walking Keeper upon the moors. He made an exception only for his parish rounds; then he deposited Branwell in the company of his father.

As the combined effects of laudanum and alcohol wore off, Branwell began to write poetry, surreptitiously at first, bending over a scrap of paper across the desk from Weightman, while the clergyman worked on a sermon. Weightman noticed, but said nothing.

A few weeks later, Weightman and Branwell arrived at the parsonage one morning to find a letter waiting.

"You have mail," Patrick said, handing over the letter to his son and peering over his spectacles. He was suspicious of letters bearing a Bradford postmark, for he wondered if his son's friends were plotting some mischief.

Branwell glanced at the handwriting and then broke the seal, saying as he did, "I don't recognize this script."

He glanced at the contents and his face flushed as crimson as his hair. He looked up, the paper trembling in his hand. "It's the *Bradford Herald*," he said. "I sent them a poem, and they're going to publish it."

"My word!" Patrick exclaimed. "Let me see that." He held the paper almost to his nose, as he was now forced to do because of his failing sight, and read, "'We are pleased to include "The Old Shepherd's Chief Mourner," in our number of Thursday next.' This is magnificent! A published author in the family!"

"It's a sonnet," Branwell said. "Inspired by the painting by Landseer."

Weightman stood leaning against the doorframe, his hand to his chin and a smile on his face. When Branwell turned to him, he thrust out his hand in congratulations.

"It's your doing, Willie," Branwell said.

"You wrote the poem," Weightman said. "All you needed was your right mind."

Branwell looked down at the sheet of paper, folding it carefully as he did so. "I must write my sisters. They will be so happy for me."

Spring passed into summer. Branwell churned out poems, and began to consider a novel. He worked in his father's study while the curate went about his parish rounds. But one night before the hearth at Cook Gate when Weightman suggested Branwell might safely move back to the parsonage, Branwell said "No, not yet. Believe it or not, I'm enjoying myself here. It's like having a brother, and do you know, I always missed that. I believe it is why I was so keen on my Bradford friends." He looked down at the cup of tea he had been drinking, "I wanted to impress them, you know. Make them think I was someone to reckon with, so they would want to be loyal to me as well." Branwell had never admitted such a thing to anyone, and only recently to himself. He added, "I don't feel I need to impress you, Willie. In fact, I assume you are singularly unimpressed, and yet you tolerate me anyway."

"I suppose I like to be impressed as well as anyone," Weightman answered. "But what hits the mark for me is a kind and generous heart and a brave soul. One does not compete for those distinctions, one simply lives as well as one can, and that is all that can be asked."

Weightman smiled as he spoke, but Branwell thought he looked tired. He knew the curate had performed a funeral earlier in the day, and sat in at several sickbeds in the afternoon. When he still seemed weary the next morning, even after a night's sleep, Branwell decided to watch him more closely. Once as they walked to a farm up Sladen Beck to visit a man who had been injured in an accident, Branwell said, "Do you know, if you grow much thinner, Charlotte and Emily may not recognize you when they return."

Weightman waved his arm. "My clothes always hang more loosely in summer. I'll plump up again in the autumn, you'll see."

At other times, as summer passed, Branwell thought Weightman grew shorter of temper. Perhaps he is tiring at last of my company, Branwell worried. Perhaps I might well move back to the parsonage and be out of his way.

One morning, on Weightman's day off, they went grouse hunting. Branwell chattered on about a report in the *Leeds Intelligencer* of growing industrial unrest in Yorkshire. Although the hardships of winter were over, the market for textiles remained depressed, work was sporadic, and food scarce. The newspaper predicted riots before the end of the summer.

"It's those damned Chartists," Branwell complained, after missing a shot with Weightman's gun. "Putting notions in people's heads. Well, let them riot. I'd be glad to volunteer with the constabulary and thrash some of the blackguards."

"Why should they fear you?" Weightman replied, his voice chilly. "They are thrashed every day of their lives."

Branwell looked at Weightman with a start. "What do you mean?"

"I mean," said Weightman, "that I would be glad to take you into Gauger's Croft with me, where you might meet a family of eight or more living in one cellar room in stifling heat because the room beside them is a wool comber's shop. But I doubt you could stand it for long."

"Well, of course there is suffering—" Branwell began to protest, but Weightman interrupted.

"Suffering! You know nothing about it." Weightman's face was so pale with anger that the natural flush of his cheeks stood out like smudges of a woman's makeup. "Let me introduce you to another family off West Lane whose twelve-year-old son has no left arm, and no hand on his right. He was pulled into a machine in the Ebor Mill. Ask your friend Hartley Merrall about that."

Branwell turned. "Of course that's horrible. But who sends those children into the mill? Their parents, of course. The Merralls are doing nothing more than producing cloth. Is that a sin?"

To Branwell's surprise, Weightman grabbed the gun out of his hand and said, "Producing cloth from the blood of others is indeed a sin."

Weightman turned and walked away. When an astonished Branwell ran to catch up, Weightman turned and said, "Leave me alone!" with such vehemence that Branwell felt he'd been slapped in the face. Nor did Weightman return to the Widow Ogden's until well after midnight, when Branwell was in bed. Branwell could not imagine where the curate might have been.

After a mostly silent breakfast the next morning, he proposed that it would be best if he returned to the parsonage.

"I suppose you are sober enough," Weightman said shortly.

Branwell took himself off without a word. Later that morning while Weightman was out, saddened by the sudden turn of their friendship, he spoke with his father at the parsonage.

Patrick said, "Willie is under a great deal of strain."

"He was out late last night."

"There was a disturbance outside the Bridgehouse Mill. He may have been tending to that."

"What does a disturbance at the mill have to do with Willie?"

Patrick considered how to answer, for he was worried himself. He had heard rumors of his curate in recent weeks, reports—or insinuations, he considered them, for they came from the mill owners in the congregation—that Weightman had been seen in the poorer districts of Haworth holding conversations of some intensity with men who were considered troublemakers. Patrick tried to ignore the rumors, nor did he wish to say much to his son, whom he considered impractical where such matters were concerned.

Finally he replied, "I believe Willie wished to calm the waters."

Branwell decided to attempt a rapprochement, for he was truly sorry to be bereft of Weightman's company. A cousin of the mill-owning Greenwoods, a charming young woman named Isabella, was visiting from York and would be honored at a tea on the coming Sunday afternoon. Because most of the Greenwoods were Baptists and Whigs, Weightman had not before been invited to their parlor, but Branwell made sure of the clergyman's welcome ahead of time. Then he convinced Weightman to come along. It was an inspired invitation, Branwell considered, for he thought Weightman enjoyed himself.

Hartley Merrall took Branwell aside and asked, "How did you get Saint Francis to attend?"

"Don't speak so sarcastically, for he's a capital fellow!" Branwell protested. "And Willie has always had an eye for the ladies."

Weightman did indeed appear pleased with the lovely golden-haired Isabella Greenwood, who bestowed an inordinate amount of attention upon the young curate. Why not, Branwell thought. Willie is handsome enough, and charming, and would possess financial substance as well if he ever decided to claim it. Weightman clearly enjoyed Isabella's attention, and ferried cups of punch and plates of biscuits to the chair where she sat. He laughed more often than Branwell had seen him do in weeks.

Then came the publication of another poem by Branwell, this time in the *Leeds Intelligencer*.

The poem, which Branwell titled "The Afghan War," was written in response to the terrible events of the spring. The British army in India had invaded Afghanistan in order to establish an outpost and provide a buffer against the Russians to the north. Upon settling in Kabul, the garrison sent for their wives and children and began to establish themselves in residence. But native tribesmen set upon the English settlers and drove them back toward India. Caught in the high passes of the Hindu Kush, some four thousand British soldiers and ten thousand women and children were massacred or carried into slavery, leaving a lone survivor, a physician, to tell the tale. Horror gripped the nation.

After he wrote, Branwell closed his eyes at night with the awful images of terror and bloodshed fixed in his mind. He suffered nightmares. At the same time, he was gratified when the poem was accepted for publication. Ironic, he realized, to have one's own pride of accomplishment connected to the tragic suffering of others. The plight of the author. He longed to placate his conscience, and did so one night by slipping out to drink with Hartley Merrall at the Black Bull, an event of which Weightman was unaware.

When the poem appeared in the newspaper, Branwell shared it

with pride in the study where Weightman met with Patrick to discuss church business.

"A fine tribute," his father said, handing the newspaper to Weightman. "One cannot begin to comprehend such barbarity."

Weightman, who continued to look thin and pale, read the poem, holding the newspaper before him for an inordinate amount of time. But Branwell soon forgot his care for his friend's health when Weightman, still staring at the poem, said, "Yes, barbarous. We do the same thing to people in England, but more slowly and with more refinement."

Branwell was appalled. "What a horrible thing to say in the face of such wholesale death!"

"Yes," Weightman murmured. "A horrible thing to say. But isn't this garrison luckier than some? At least they are memorialized. Unlike the poor sods who wove their uniforms."

Even Patrick was scandalized. "Willie," he said, "you are not yourself."

"No." Weightman stared at the hearth, empty in the heat of summer. "I am not myself." He rubbed his forehead, damp with sweat, so that the hair above his forehead stood up, and said, "I am not fit company just now. If we are done, sir?" He looked inquiringly at Patrick.

"I have nothing further," Patrick said.

"Then I am needed in Gauger's Croft."

## 14

The disturbance at the Bridgehouse Mill did not catch William Weightman by surprise. Haworth was a tinderbox ready to be set off. Weightman was aware that sometimes, when he spoke with workers from the mills, they were being watched. He had begun to suspect that a few were being paid by the mill owners to spy on their fellows, but so far his own position had given him a natural reason to be among them without raising suspicion. He wondered if that was beginning to change. Soon enough his worries would be far greater.

Patrick Brontë and William Weightman had long suspected the well water of the village was compromised, for a single privy used by a dozen families stood hard up against the water cisterns, and the cesspools beneath overflowed. The Head Well, which provided much of Gauger's Croft with its water for washing and drinking, turned green and brackish that summer. Weightman carried a pail of the scummy mess to the high street where Mr. Wheelhouse had his office. The curate called the doctor outside and set the pail beside Wheelhouse's horse, which was tethered nearby. The horse sniffed and turned his head away.

"Even a beast will not take it," Weightman said angrily. "Yet this is what our people are supposed to use."

"And what," said Wheelhouse, cross at being disturbed, "am I supposed to do about it? It has been this way since long before you arrived and will no doubt be so when you are gone."

"I will write a letter to the authorities in London," said Weightman. "Again. This time I hope to have a great number of signatures on it, and yours should be at the top. Something must be done and it is beyond our scope here."

Weightman wrote the letter and Wheelhouse agreed to sign. But when Weightman made the rounds of the more prosperous citizens of Haworth, the mill owners and shopkeepers, he was met with refusals. We have access to a private cistern at Sowden Spring, he was told, whose fresh water is piped into our houses, and we will not pay higher tax rates for the sake of some lavish new water system. It would do no good anyway, for the poor are happy to be filthy and will be naturally so, no matter what advantages they are offered.

So Weightman sent his letter, with the signatures of Patrick and Wheelhouse and a few others to London, where it, like the letters before it, disappeared.

And then, in late August, even as he waited for an answer from London that never came, even as word came down from Bradford for workers to pull the plugs in the mill boilers and step away from their looms, a different sort of call came to William Weightman. He emerged from the Sunday school where he had been preparing his sermon when young Samuel Bland came running up and tugged at his arm.

"Mr. Weightman, Mr. Weightman, come quick! Gram has collapsed and cries out something terrible, and can't get up! Mr. Wheelhouse is sent for."

"Where is she, Samuel?"

"They have carried her home," came the answer over the boy's shoulder, for Samuel had turned and run back down the hill.

Weightman went inside for his Bible and then set out for the single room in Gauger's Croft where old Mary Bland lived with only her grandson for company, and subsisted on the pittance the boy brought home from his job at the Ebor Mill. But when Weightman reached the cellar, Mr. Wheelhouse was coming out, his face white with terror.

"Don't go in, Mr. Weightman," he said in a strained voice. "There's naught you or I can do here. She's near death, and a sure and sudden death it is."

"Then she needs the benefit of clergy," Weightman said, and started to push past.

Wheelhouse continued to block the door. "You don't understand, Mr. Weightman. Cholera has come to Haworth."

Weightman stared at him and took a step back.

"Aye," added Wheelhouse, "and the farther back we stay from it, the better off we shall be."

"There's nothing you'll do for her?" Weightman managed to ask.

"There's nothing I *can* do," Wheelhouse said. "Except warn people away from Gauger's Croft. And I can try to ensure that Haworth still has a living doctor at the end of the week." Wheelhouse put on his hat and walked away down the alley and out the arched tunnel into the high street.

Weightman stood still long after Wheelhouse had disappeared. He clutched his Bible, and he prayed. He thought of Emily, soon to come home, and how he longed to see her again. Oh God, please, he prayed. At last he pushed open the door and went inside to give the last rites to Mary Bland.

※

Patrick Brontë invited William Weightman into the parsonage, but Weightman refused, upon the advice of Mr. Wheelhouse. So they talked from a distance, Patrick in his doorway with Branwell at his side, and Weightman standing at the gate to Church Lane.

"The physicians have no idea how it spreads," Weightman said, "Whether by touch, or respiration, or some other means. Except it

EMILY'S GHOST            279

comes upon a person suddenly. And yet it is capricious and some are never affected."

Patrick said, "Mr. Wheelhouse guesses it to be a miasma of some sort that attaches itself to an area. He says that poorer precincts are especially prone to cholera, and wonders if it has something to do with cleanliness. But it is indeed quick to spread. He has heard of ten cases already today, all in Gauger's Croft, but nowhere else in Haworth."

"Then I should not come in," Weightman said. "I have given Mary Bland the last rites. And I have ordered young Samuel to bed, for I fear he is infected. His stomach gives him terrible cramps."

"The Merralls are making ready to leave," Branwell said.

"Oh yes," Patrick said, his voice bitter. "I suspect good Mr. Wheelhouse is making the rounds of all the mill owners, urging them out. No doubt they will be in York or at the seashore this time tomorrow."

"Perhaps, Willie, you should go home and wait overnight," Branwell ventured. "Then if you are all right, and surely you will be, you need not fear to come to us."

"No," Weightman said. "With your father's permission, I am going to send the Widow Ogden and her servant to the parsonage. That way no one else will be at Cook Gate if I am affected."

"Willie," Branwell pleaded, "surely you don't plan to go back to Gauger's Croft?"

Weightman didn't answer, but looked at Patrick, who closed his eyes and said, "Let me go in your place. I am an old man."

"No," Weightman said. "You have dependents to consider. I have none. Besides, I doubt there shall be much sleep to be had, and you know you are not up to that at your age."

"Willie—"

"Here is what I propose," Weightman continued as if Patrick hadn't spoken. "I shall go into Gauger's Croft and return to the Widow's house, when I need to rest. I shall not attempt to go to another part of the village. That means I should not be in church this Sunday, or Sunday School."

"I think," Patrick said, "we shall close the Sunday school until the crisis is past, to keep the children from gathering."

"You must handle all the services as well," Weightman said, "the baptisms and funerals." He paused and gave a bitter smile. "I doubt there will be calls for weddings just now."

"No," Patrick said. He was having difficulty seeing Weightman's face clearly, whether because of his failing eyesight or for the tears in his eyes, he could not be certain.

"How may I help?" Branwell said in a small voice.

"You may take over one of my charges," Weightman said. "Someone must look after Keeper and Nero."

"Don't make fun of me," Branwell said. "You know I am no hero, and yet it is cruel to remind me."

"I am not making fun," Weightman said. "I take their care seriously for Emily's sake, so you should too. It would be a great kindness to her and to me." He turned away and started out the gate.

"Willie!" Patrick said sharply. "If this disease has come to Haworth, then there is no saving the people who will contract it. Will you not follow the example of those who are able, and leave? Or at least won't you ride out the storm here with us?"

Weightman turned and considered him a moment. "Are you my tempter?" he asked.

Patrick said, "I suggest it, even if I should not, as an old man who wishes the survival of a young man he has grown terribly fond of."

"And if I should leave," Weightman said, "would you?"

"No," Patrick said.

"And would you visit the sick in my place?"

Patrick took a deep breath. Then he said reluctantly, for he feared his answer sealed Weightman's fate, "Yes."

Weightman studied him a moment, an affectionate smile playing upon his face. Then he gave a slight bow and said, "The poor of

Haworth will die without a physician. But they need not die without a minister."

✄

Cholera ran like wildfire through Gauger's Croft, and by week's end over a hundred people died. The manner of their passing terrorized the living. One woke feeling well, by noonday all bodily fluid had drained, and when light was out cold dead flesh lay upon a slab. An unfortunate few lingered in agony for days.

William Weightman sat exhausted inside a weaver's hut on Sunday morning, listening to St. Michael's church bell. He expected the service would be sparsely attended. The wealthier members of the church had fled the district; most of the others cowered in their homes, afraid of contagion. Still Weightman wept to hear the tolling of the bell. It was the first Sunday in all his time in Haworth that he would not climb the steps to the chancel, prayer book in hand. In his mind's eye he followed Patrick up into the high pulpit, even as he gripped the hand of the woman beside him, whose young daughter writhed in agony upon a narrow cot.

The authorities, warned by Mr. Wheelhouse, feared the bodies of the dead might be contagious, and there were too many for conventional burial. So a lime-filled pit was readied in the pasture beyond the cemetery. The bodies were wrapped in shrouds, carried out by men careful to touch nothing but cloth, and dumped one by one. The funerals Patrick conducted were short and perfunctory. Survivors were not allowed to attend for fear of spreading disease.

Branwell brought mail and a newspaper each day to the stone gateway across from the Black Bull. These he weighted down with a large stone where someone was sure to find it and take it to Weightman. Everyone in Gauger's Croft knew where to find the curate, for no one was in greater demand. Even the sick from dissenting families sought him out, for Patrick had gone to his fellow Methodist and Baptist clergy, all of them men with families of their own to care for, and urged them to stay away, and turn their parishioners over to Weightman's spiritual care for the duration. Weightman prayed for each sufferer as requested, prayer book collects for the Church folk, extemporaneously in response to the leading of the Holy Spirit for those from the chapels. So for the first time in many years, the churches of Haworth were one.

Then Branwell sent word that he wished to meet Weightman at the arch. When the curate arrived, climbing up the steep incline, Branwell was leaning against the cool stone wall, but straightened as Weightman approached.

"My God, Willie," he said, "you look as though you could fall asleep standing up."

Weightman shrugged, rubbed the stubble of beard on his chin, and said, "I find a few hours' sleep here and there." He managed to smile and said, "I would offer you my hand, but I know you would rather I did not." He looked Branwell up and down. "So," he said, "you seem sober enough."

"How can I drink," Branwell said, "when you go through this?"

"How is your father?"

"He manages. Tabby is gone to stay with her sister. I think the sister wants some company because of the cholera. But we have your Widow Ogden and her Ruth to help now."

"How is the Widow getting on in the same house with Aunt Branwell?"

"Like a house afire," Branwell said. "The two old ladies rather like the companionship. And both of them say prayers for you every five minutes or so."

Weightman laughed. "The Lord will be forced to protect me then, to be done with the badgering."

Branwell reached inside his vest and pulled out a letter. "We have heard from my sisters. Charlotte writes Monsieur Heger has offered to let them stay until Christmas, instead of coming home. He values my sisters, apparently," Branwell said, as though he could not quite believe it. In return for their keep, he explained, Charlotte would teach English, and Emily give music lessons. "Charlotte is ecstatic, and Papa is relieved because he thinks them safe in Brussels. But Emily is furious."

"Your father has not told them of our situation?"

"No. He does not wish to worry them." Branwell handed Weightman the letter, and did not admit he had sneaked a glance. Weightman recognized Emily's handwriting; he read her anguished plea to her father that she had no wish to remain in Belgium. A second sheet was addressed to Weightman.

"'Dear Willie,'" he read,

"I have done what everyone has asked of me. But I cannot stay until Christmas. The heather will be in bloom; we said I would be home in time for it. I suffocate to be upon the moors. I can find my own way home. I don't care if traveling alone is unconventional, I don't. I miss you, and Papa, and Keeper and Nero. If Charlotte will not come with me, I will leave without her and come alone, I swear it.

*Your Emily*"

Branwell watched Weightman, a quizzical expression on his face. Weightman folded the letter. "When you go home, you must write to Emily at once. Since we don't know how cholera spreads, I do not wish to send her a letter of my own. Will you do that for me?"

"Yes," Branwell said, "but I must ask, for this letter is addressed to you, and familiarly. Have you been corresponding with my sister?"

"I have," Weightman said.

"With Emily? But why have you said nothing about—"

"It has been none of your business," Weightman interrupted, not unkindly but firmly. "Now do as I say."

"Shall I tell Emily we have cholera? To convince her to stay?"

Weightman sighed and said, "Perhaps it is wrong of me, but I am afraid for her to know. Her first reaction will be to come back. Do you understand how brave your sister is, and how stubborn?"

"I suppose so," Branwell replied.

"You must write that she should remain in Brussels with Charlotte and continue her studies. Tell her you write in my place because I am at Appleby, but I have informed you by letter that I wish her to stay." Weightman pressed his hand to his forehead. "She will be hurt, and angry. She will wonder why I do not write her myself. She may well believe I no longer care for her. But her disappointment is more likely to keep her safely away."

"Willie, you say it is none of my business. But she is my sister, and you are my good friend. May I not understand the nature of your relationship?"

Weightman swayed on his feet. He put out his arm to steady himself against the wall. "I am in love with Emily," he said.

Branwell did not know whether to be pleased, shocked, or amused. "Good Lord. Is it not like being in love with a tiger?"

"Oh yes. But by God, were it not for the danger to her, I would want her close. She fights." Weightman took a step back, as though he stood too near to Branwell for the latter's safety. Then he said, "If I don't survive, tell her that I love her and wished more than anything to see her again. As for the letter at hand, tell her to stay in Belgium. Give her no hope that might cause her to return early."

❧❦❧

Emily Brontë was angry with Charlotte and even more furious with William Weightman. When Charlotte informed her they could remain at the Pensionnat Heger until Christmas (not asking Emily's opinion, mind you, but assuming she would be pleased), Emily saw Weightman as her strongest ally. But he betrayed her.

Weightman had for a time written of various "possibilities," as he termed them.

> Although you remain unhappy in Brussels, it seems to me you have grown. I am anxious to see you again and judge how much this is so.

After several mentions of this sort, Emily grew irritated. Did Weightman believe he had sent away some sort of oddity who would return with all her eccentricities worn away by her time in society? It would not happen.

Then another letter arrived.

"Your father has been supportive of my work here," Weightman wrote.

> But if the fullness of my connection to the Chartists becomes known—and I fear that may be inevitable—the mill owners in the district will be enraged. Since they are prominent in our parish, your father will have no choice but to let me go. It may be that the only way I will be able to exercise my ministry will be abroad, in Canada or America.
>
> Dearest Emily, I know you are hesitant to marry for it might impinge upon your freedom, and you cannot see yourself in a parlor as a pastor's wife entertaining the ladies of the congregation. I know the strength of your attachment to the moors.
>
> But if you had a husband who respected your need for freedom and, yes, your singularities; if you lost your beloved moors but gained a companion who would accompany you into the larger world and one even more wild and free, would you go?
>
> I do not want an answer now. It would be unfair to both of us.

But I hope you will think about what I am suggesting. We will talk when you return.

*Yrs—Willie*

Emily did think about it. And in addition to what Weightman wrote, she could no longer ignore the physical nature of her love for him, which had only been intensified by the separation. After so long apart, she thought that if he should somehow materialize at her side, only the touch of a fingertip anywhere on her body would send her into a frenzy.

Emily took a vow. William Weightman had repeated his promise they would have something significant to talk about when she returned. Emily would hold him to that promise. And if he could offer some way for them to be together without sacrificing his ministry or her freedom, she was willing to try, even if it meant leaving Haworth.

Then in July she received a letter from Branwell. Her brother mentioned he'd taken Weightman to a party at the Greenwood mansion in honor of a visiting cousin, Isabella. "Willie enjoyed himself immensely," Branwell wrote. "You would have been amused to see him play the role of courtier to the hilt."

Emily had not been amused. A stab of jealousy made her so ill she could not eat the rest of the day. In time, her thoughts turned bitter. *He has not seen you in months, so you are forgotten. Charlotte has been right, and William Weightman is as false as the day is long. Someday he will weary of his idealism as well and return to his family and social circle. He will meet someone charming and beautiful and well connected. And conventional. He will marry her. That someone may very well be Isabella Greenwood.*

Weeks passed without a letter from either her father or Weightman, and Emily vacillated between misery and anger with herself that she was miserable. Then Charlotte further blasted her hopes. Monsieur Heger had asked the two of them to stay another term and teach. The scope of Emily's anger expanded to include Monsieur, the unwitting author of her new woes. She rebelled.

"I won't," she informed Charlotte. "Stay if you will, and I will go home by myself."

"Of course you can do no such thing. I wouldn't let you. And so, if you insist upon us leaving, you shall have ruined my life. For I must, I *must* stay longer, I tell you, and sit at his feet. He is the most amazing teacher I have ever known."

"You are in love with him. But he is a married man."

Charlotte turned red. "Of course he is married, even though that woman does not deserve him. But you know I would never act inappropriately."

"You may do nothing, but you will dream it. And you keep me here in agony to feed your dreams."

"I told you. I will go back if you insist. Only I shall be more miserable than I can say, for I shall have turned my back on all my fondest hopes."

"And I will be the one responsible," Emily said.

"You will."

Emily wrote in despair to her father ("I will not be the blame for Charlotte's unhappiness, I will not. Please, Papa, call us home"). She swallowed her pride and wrote her plea to Weightman as well.

She was devastated, then, to receive a response, a short one and looking rather hastily scribbled, from Branwell rather than Weightman. "Willie insists you stay in Brussels," Branwell wrote. "He says it will do you good. He would tell you himself but he is in Appleby. I believe he is much occupied just now."

She went cold all over. In her mind she heard Charlotte's voice taunting "fickle and faithless Miss Celia Amelia." It was enough to send her to the Parc Royale near the Pensionnat, where she found a quiet corner beneath a spreading elm tree and wept. When she returned she folded Weightman's letters and placed them beneath the volume of

Shelley, put all back in the bottom of her trunk, and vowed not to look at them again.

She hoped Patrick would rescue her, but she was mistaken there as well. Her father's letter was also brief, for he claimed to be especially busy just then. But he thought it a capital idea if his daughters remained a few months longer in Belgium.

By then Emily's heart had turned to stone. Had anyone from Haworth summoned her, she would have gone no matter what the cost. But they did not want her. She resigned herself to missing her royal season of purple heather on the moors. For solace she longed for those she knew to be loving and faithful, and fell asleep dreaming her arms were around Keeper before the fireplace, or the cat Tiger kneaded her stomach in bed, or that she ran across the moors following the graceful loops of Nero above the waves of billowing heather and bracken. As the weeks passed, she was not surprised when William Weightman did not write further. He was no doubt exchanging letters instead with Isabella Greenwood. He must have gone to Appleby to introduce her to his family. Emily trained her daydreams toward her animals and tried as ruthlessly as she could to expel William Weightman.

⚜

August bled into September. Three days later, William Weightman left the hovel of a weaver in an alley behind Ginnel. Before he reached the far side he tripped and fell. He could not get up.

Patrick received the news and sent for Mr. Wheelhouse, who declared, "If anyone goes in to him, stay as far away as possible."

"That is all you have to offer?" Patrick asked.

Wheelhouse raised his hands in supplication. "What else? We are none of us God Almighty."

The Widow Ogden, a stooped gray-haired woman who took the

news at the same time as the other residents of the parsonage, stepped forward.

"Where is he?" she asked.

"He lies in a cellar in Ginnel. In his present condition, it is as good a place as any."

The widow stood as straight as she could and looked at her servant Ruth House, a plain stout Methodist woman. Ruth nodded.

"Carry him back to my house at Cook Gate," the Widow Ogden said. "We will care for him there."

"You do so, madam, at grave risk to yourself," Mr. Wheelhouse replied.

Ruth House interrupted. "That boy has been a blessing to the missus and myself these three years. Do you think we would abandon him?"

Mr. Wheelhouse had the decency to blush. He bowed and said, "It is your decision." He thought to add, "Be sure you burn the mattress and bedclothes when he is deceased."

So William Weightman was carried around the hill to the house in Lord Lane. People stood silent as he passed, and men removed their caps. Patrick Brontë was the first to visit, but he was not certain if Weightman knew of his presence, for the curate continued in the grip of a terrible pain in his midsection. Then diarrhea began and the stench filled the room. Patrick was familiar with diarrhea from his experience with other diseases. But this was more intense, rich with blood. As Patrick had learned from his reading about cholera, William Weightman's insides were being violently flushed out of his body.

Patrick heard a knock on the door. Branwell entered, his face frightened but resolute.

"Let me sit with him now, Papa," Branwell said. "You go home and rest."

Patrick studied his son a moment. "You know the danger," he said.

"I know," Branwell said.

The older man nodded and left. Branwell sat by the door where the chair had been placed, watching Weightman struggle upon his bed, his face contorted. Branwell pressed his handkerchief to his nose for a time, but at last he removed it. He ventured to pull the chair closer to the bed.

"Willie," he said.

Weightman turned but did not respond.

"Willie," Branwell repeated.

Weightman fixed the voice and met Branwell's eyes. He opened his mouth to speak, and for a time he could not. Then he managed to say, each word an effort, "I thought you were no hero."

Branwell flushed. "Of course I am not."

"And yet here you are."

"You are my friend."

"'Greater love hath no man—'"

Weightman was interrupted by a spasm that bent him double in agony. His face was skeletal, the skin dark blue, his mouth open as though that effort would moisten it, but his lips and tongue were dry as parchment.

"Have you something to write with?" he managed to say.

Branwell looked around and saw pen, paper, and ink on Weightman's desk. He sat beside the bed and took dictation. It was a short message although its transmission took a great deal of time.

"Give it to Emily when she returns," Weightman gasped at the end.

Branwell nodded and tucked the paper in his coat pocket. Weightman fell silent except for an occasional moan. The Widow Ogden came in with a cup of tea and Ruth followed with a tub of warm water and towels.

"You may leave if you wish," the Widow Ogden said.

"No," Branwell said.

They pulled back the sheet. Weightman had been stripped naked, and his lower body was drenched with watery diarrhea flecked with white. The white bits were pieces of his intestines. Branwell looked away. The two women proceeded to wash and dry Weightman. Ruth put her arm behind his head and tried to raise him while the Widow held the cup of tea. She put it to his parched lips to help him drink. But Weightman's throat was too dry to swallow, and he began to choke.

"Branwell, help us!" the Widow cried.

Branwell helped raise Weightman into an upright position until the choking spell was over. He felt the heat from the dry skin on Weightman's back as they lowered him onto the bed.

"No-no more," Weightman gasped. "I can-not drink."

The Widow took away the cup of tea, her head down to hide her distress. Ruth bundled the soiled towels and dropped them onto the hearth where a fire was lit despite the summer heat. Weightman was shivering. "I am glad," he managed to say, "Emily cannot see me. I want her to remember me as I was. Tell her that."

"Yes," Branwell said. He settled in his chair and wondered if he and the two women attendants would soon die in their own beds. I won't consider it, he thought.

A spasm rocked Weightman so he could not speak. Then, when Branwell thought he had fallen asleep, he opened his eyes.

"You have a strong voice," he said.

"A strong voice?" Branwell was puzzled.

"I mean you sing well."

"Tolerably so."

"My hymnal is on the desk. Will you sing my—" Weightman struggled to swallow. "My favorite," he finally managed. "Four-eleven."

The last thing Branwell felt like doing was singing. But if it gave Willie comfort— He found the hymnal and page number for "How Firm a Foundation."

The two women, their task done, stood in the doorway, dabbing their eyes as Branwell sang.

*"That soul, though all Hell shall endeavor to shake,*
*I'll never, no, never, no, never forsake."*

Weightman seemed to smile. Turning his head, he said in a hoarse voice, "And you don't believe a word of that, do you?"

Branwell didn't know how to answer, but decided that even on his deathbed, Weightman would expect honesty.

"No," Branwell said. He wondered how anyone could believe in a loving and faithful God while suffering such a death.

❦

Branwell spent the night in the bedroom next door, while the Widow and Ruth took turns staying awake. When he woke at dawn, Branwell took one look at Weightman and said, "Send for my father."

Patrick was determined to track down Mr. Wheelhouse and force him to accompany him. When they arrived at the Widow Ogden's, Mr. Wheelhouse stopped at the doorway to Weightman's room, looked in, and said, "You see there is nothing I can do."

"I have ordered a coffin," Patrick said, not looking at the doctor. "He is part of my family and will lie beneath the church with us."

"I understand you want more than a winding sheet and a common pit in this case," the doctor said, "though I do not lend my recommendation to your plan. Have you notified his family, and advised them you cannot send the body home?"

"Of course. I will send his mother a lock of his hair," Patrick said. The Widow Ogden handed him a pair of scissors.

Branwell had retreated to a window where he sat on the ledge, his arms folded and his eyes wet. "Cut a second," he said to his father. "For Emily."

Patrick looked at his son. "You know, then?"

Branwell nodded. "Willie told me."

Patrick entered the room, pulled his chair close, and studied Weightman's face. Had he not known he was looking at his curate, he would not have recognized him. A spasm shook Weightman's body.

Patrick took Weightman's hand and leaned close. "Willie," he said, "can you hear me?"

Weightman squeezed his hand for response.

"Willie. Soon your suffering will be over and you will be in God's hands."

Weightman's grip tightened, then loosened and his hand dropped. He took three more rasping breaths, each more irregular than the last. With a deep sigh, he was still.

Patrick smoothed the rumpled hair back from Weightman's forehead.

"Dear God," he murmured. "Twenty-eight years old."

Branwell burst into tears.

❧❦

The Widow Ogden and Ruth House gave William Weightman a final wash and dressed him in his best black clerical garb. Four men arrived from William Wood's coffin maker's shop. When they lifted Weightman, his head fell back. Patrick placed his hand beneath Weightman's head, held it up until the men could drop him into the coffin, and folded Weightman's arms across his chest. The Widow Ogden placed a small blue pillow beneath Weightman's head. Then the men nailed the coffin shut and carried it downstairs and out of the house. The little group of two men and two women proceeded to the church, and as word spread whose coffin they followed, others added themselves to the procession.

Patrick led the pallbearers to the back of the church building where a small outside door led down into the Brontë family burial crypt. John

Brown the sexton, after noting the date of death—*6 September 1842*—in the parish register, waited to supervise.

They left the coffin of William Weightman inside the entrance to the Brontë family vault, where it waited until the next member of the family would be interred before it saw the light of day.

៛ৡৈ

A few more weeks and the cholera ended as abruptly as it began. Even as Aunt Branwell grieved for William Weightman, and the men of the family were caught up in their own cares while her nieces continued far away, the old woman grew weaker and her mind more disordered. She had a great pain in her midsection. One morning she tottered downstairs in a fog to find the house deserted. Patrick was out on the pastoral duties he was now forced to cover by himself, Branwell had escaped his despondency by going off to his friends in Halifax, Tabby had not returned from her sister's, and Martha Brown was out running errands. Aunt Branwell stood in the center of the kitchen. No food cooked on the hearth, and the cabinets appeared cluttered. Her mind filled with both cobwebs and warning bells. She went outside and the fat geese Victoria and Adelaide greeted her with a loud cacophony of honking.

Aunt Branwell snapped. She forgot Emily loved the geese; she forgot Emily existed. When Martha Brown returned from the butcher's with a leg of mutton, she was waiting.

"Those birds are taking over the yard!" she cried, her face contorted and mottled with red. The girl was startled. "And you, lazy girl, go and spend money we do not have on a stringy leg of mutton."

"Mum?"

"Go on!" Aunt Branwell flapped her apron. "Get you back to the butcher's and tell him to come for these geese. We can eat for a fortnight on what they'll fetch."

When Martha Brown hesitated, Aunt Branwell's voice raised to a screech. "Go!" she cried. "Or I'll box your ears, you naughty girl! And don't think I can't."

So Martha Brown fled, and did as she was bid. The butcher was quick enough to send his boy for the geese, for fowl that plump would assuredly find their way onto the dinner table of a mill owner newly returned from seaside exile. That is how the Queen's namesake ended a golden brown and elegantly carved by the Merrall butler, while her sister Adelaide did similar service for the Greenwoods.

But even as the butcher's boy struggled back to the shop with a squawking goose beneath each arm, Aunt Branwell had her eye on the washhouse. Something was shrieking like a banshee, and she went to look.

Nero, whose care and feeding Branwell had neglected during the ordeal of Weightman's death, ceased his screaming at Aunt Branwell's appearance and fixed her with a beady eye.

"You'll not haunt this washhouse like some imp of the devil!" Aunt Branwell declared. "Will you?"

With that she picked up the hawk's cage and carried it, swinging it so wildly the bird shrieked in protest, to the top of the back garden where the moor began. She dropped the cage with a jolt and flung open the door.

"Now," she said, giving the cage a kick. "Off with you. Shoo! Shoo!" She waved her arms and then turned and headed back to the house.

The merlin was so startled it did not move at once. But when Branwell came home the next day and went to the washhouse to feed the bird, it was nowhere to be found. Alarmed, he went outside and looked around until he saw the cage, sitting open where Aunt Branwell had left it, empty save for a single brown feather.

A few days later Aunt Branwell took to her bed and was declared by Mr. Wheelhouse, as implacably as he had pronounced doom upon William Weightman, to be dying.

❀

Patrick Brontë lay awake at night wondering how to tell his daughters of Weightman's death. He decided at last to write Charlotte as less likely to be shattered, since his oldest daughter had long treated the curate with no more than cool politeness. Patrick hoped she would deliver the news gently to Emily.

He had only just begun to anticipate that Emily would have news of Weightman's death when he was forced to take pen in hand to tell his daughters that Aunt Branwell was dying, and to beg them to return once and for all from Belgium.

15

At the opening of the new term, the Pensionnat Heger took its students to a performance of Beethoven's Ninth Symphony at the Théâtre de la Monnaie. So, Emily thought, I shall hear the Ninth after all. She supposed it might be consolation for the further time in Brussels she must endure. She longed to tell Weightman, but resisted the impulse. She had vowed she would write no more unless she heard from him.

On the night of September 8, the students, Emily among them, filed in procession into the Monnaie, that grand venue for music. Mirrors, red carpets, and the gilt-edged interior circled with tiers of boxes enclosed them inside a giant jewel box. A rococo dome, a second sky, re-created the blues and golds and oranges of the firmament, and a fake sun, a glittering chandelier, descended from the clouds. The students from the Pensionnat Heger were shepherded into a far corner of the main floor. The audience settled in amid the flutter of programs and extinguishing of wall sconces. Emily, in the back row, sat between Louise de Bassompierre and Charlotte. She leaned her head against the wall and closed her eyes.

The first movement burst upon them. Emily could imagine nothing more glorious. But the second movement, alive with energy, stirred her even beyond the first. As she listened, visions passed before her still-closed eyes of epic events, revolutionary upheavals. Then the third movement calmed her with its quiet, delicate beauty.

But when the fourth and final movement struck (for that was the only word Emily could use to describe how it broke upon her), she straightened as though an electrical current ran up her spine. The chorus, seated behind the orchestra throughout the piece, stood. Several soloists appeared and began to sing. Emily forgot time and place.

The chorus gathered itself; the orchestra tantalized with a few hesitant notes.

At that pregnant moment even as the orchestra paused, a voice said in Emily Brontë's ear, *Here is the best part.*

The chorus burst into full bloom—

> *Freude, schöner Götterfunken*
> *Tochter aus Elysium,*
> *Wir betreten feuertrunken,*
> *Himmlische, dein Heiligtum!*
> *Deine Zauber binden wieder*
> *Was die Mode streng geteilt;*
> *Alle Menschen werden Brüder,*
> *Wo dein sanfter Flügel weilt.*

The music washed over Emily in waves, an orgasm of sound and emotion. *Freude. Freudig.* Joy. Joyful. To her English ears it sounded like *Freedom.* She trembled at the final choral outburst and the frenzied orchestral finale. As the audience began to clap, she sank back in her seat, spent.

The applause died and people began at once to talk, some arguing for magnificence, others puzzled at the way, as one man said, "The thing just does not hold together." Monsieur Heger said to Charlotte, "It is odd that Beethoven waited until the very end to make use of the chorus. It puts off the balance."

This barely registered with Emily. She was stunned by the magnificence of the music and the realization that the voice she had heard, as familiar as any, was the voice of William Weightman.

≈

The letter arrived the next day. It was addressed to Charlotte, who picked it up as she and Emily headed out of their dormitory for their tutorials with Monsieur.

"Where is your letter from Papa?" Charlotte wondered to Emily.

"It has likely been delayed in the post," Emily said. "I shall receive it tomorrow." She wondered if Weightman would have written as well, but put the thought from her mind as the best way to keep from disappointment.

In Monsieur Heger's anteroom, Charlotte settled in a chair while Emily went in for her lesson, and read her letter. Her head went up and she stared at the door. She put her hand to her mouth and then thought frantically what she should do.

Though Charlotte disliked William Weightman, the news of his death shocked her. She was mystified as well by the rest of her father's letter.

"It is up to you to tell Emily," her father had written. "You do not know what has passed between your sister and my curate, but I beg you to give her this news in a sensitive way. Willie was most important to her. I cannot say more than that. But the news of his death will be a terrible blow, and I beg you to employ any means you have to protect and comfort her."

Charlotte heard, from inside Monsieur's office, the sound of Emily reading in French. She considered what to do, even as she wondered at the little her father had divulged about Emily and Weightman. Charlotte knew the two got along amicably, and she had been frustrated at her inability to rouse Emily to any contempt for the curate. But she put it down to Weightman's charm, which fooled Tabby and Aunt Branwell and, yes, Emily, into including him in the family circle. As if he had belonged. Charlotte's anger rose once more though she tried to quell it out of respect for the dead. It was sad, after all, for he was so young. Haworth must find someone else to set female hearts aflutter.

Charlotte considered. Of course Emily would mourn the loss of anyone—or anything—connected to the parsonage. Charlotte resolved to heed her father's plea and deal with her sister as gently as possible. Monsieur Heger would be her best, and most appreciated, ally.

When Emily emerged from Heger's study, Charlotte said, "Wait here. Monsieur will want to speak with you further."

Emily looked surprised but settled onto a chair in the corner. She opened her copy of Balzac's *La Fille aux yeux d'or*, bought on a street corner and of which Monsieur did not approve, and began to read.

Inside the study, Charlotte said, "Please, Monsieur, something has happened." She explained her father's letter and that Emily was a friend of the dead curate.

"I do not know how to break the news to her," Charlotte ended, hoping for Monsieur's sympathy and praise for her judgment. "It would be better if you did so, and if I stood by to support her."

Heger nodded. "A terrible situation. Cholera, my God. You must be worried about your family."

"Oh yes," Charlotte assured him. And please God, she thought, do not suggest that I go back for a long, long time.

Heger rose to the occasion, took a deep breath, and smoothed his thinning hair from his forehead. "I am not a priest, and yet I am forced now and then to deliver bad news to our pupils. Ask your sister to come in, and I shall tell her."

Charlotte opened the door to the anteroom. "Emily," she said, "Monsieur wants to speak with you."

Emily closed Balzac without a word and went back into Heger's office, where she settled herself upon a chair and looked at him.

Monsieur's clasped hands pressed upon his desk as though they held it down.

"Mademoiselle," he said, "we have had a letter from your father."

Emily looked from Heger to Charlotte, alarmed at the tone of his voice and the gravity of Charlotte's expression.

"Haworth has suffered an outbreak of cholera," he said.

Emily stiffened.

Monsieur Heger, Charlotte noted with admiration, softened his voice. "I am sorry to inform you, but an acquaintance of yours has died. Your father's assistant, *Guillaume Weight-man,* has succumbed to the cholera."

Emily sat so still Charlotte had the impression of a cracked porcelain figurine. But then before anyone could move, Emily bolted.

She ran. Across the quadrangle of the Pensionnat Heger to the main gate, which she wrenched open despite bloodying her hands. She ran across the Rue d'Isabelle, up the elegant flight of steps past the equestrian statue of General Belliard across the Rue Royale, dodging traffic into the park. She ran until the painful stitch in her side allowed her to run no more.

She did not know when Charlotte and Monsieur Heger came for her. But at last they led a dazed Emily Brontë back to the Pensionnat Heger.

❧

Emily took to her bed for days, felled by a dark melancholy. When finally she roused herself, she refused to speak to Charlotte, who was hurt and puzzled.

"Sister. Must you punish me for bearing bad news when I had no choice but to tell you?"

"It is not because you gave me the bad news. It is because you hated him. And you brought me here so I could not be with him when he needed me. I don't know if I can ever forgive you. Though I will forgive you sooner than I will forgive myself for what I have thought about him this last month."

Charlotte put her hand on her sister's arm. "I cannot bear for you to be so angry with me. I am your sister! And what was Mr. Weightman to you?"

Emily shook off Charlotte's hand and stood. "You shall *never* know what he was to me!" she declared.

Charlotte was forced to find her own explanation. She made certain Emily was occupied giving music lessons to the other pupils, a task she now performed with all the joy and energy of a corpse. While Emily was so engaged, Charlotte looked through her sister's trunk. She found the volume of Shelley and its inscription, and the letters in Weightman's hand, though she only glanced at them. It would be rude and shocking to read them, Charlotte decided. She had seen enough to know Weightman had played her younger sister for a fool just as he had every other female in West Yorkshire. And I was concerned about Anne, she thought, never dreaming that Emily— A swell of anger filled Charlotte's breast that she dispelled be reminding herself that the object of her rage was beyond feeling it.

⬥

Emily knocked upon the study door of Monsieur Heger. He stood when she entered and offered her a chair, concerned at the haggard expression on her pale face. "How may I help you, mademoiselle?" he asked.

"The other night at the Monnaie," Emily said, her voice barely above a whisper, "the program notes for the Ninth said Beethoven took his text from a poem by Schiller. Do you know it?"

"Ah yes," Heger said. "'To Joy.' I have it in the German. If you wish, you may translate this into French and English for your assignment."

"Thank you," Emily said.

Monsieur Heger searched his bookshelf for the slender volume of Schiller's poetry. He handed it to Emily. "You have a German lexicon?"

"Yes," Emily said, her head down as she clutched the book to her chest. She turned back when she reached the doorway and said, "You are kind."

Monsieur Heger bowed.

Emily carried the book to the end of the dormitory where she and Charlotte had their beds and desks. Charlotte was already there, working on a lesson. Emily grabbed up pen and ink without speaking and went out again to the Allée Défendue.

❊

Poetry was Emily's sustenance. She read the Psalms, those that comforted and those that raged, and she turned often to Shelley's "Adonais" with its mourning cry, "I weep for Adonais—he is dead!" But she could not shake the sense that Schiller, set to the music of Beethoven's Ninth, bore some special message. "The best part," Weightman had called it.

Emily listened for Weightman but heard nothing. She begged him to speak again until she wept. She gave up and sat with the volume of Schiller and a German dictionary, translating word for word, not bothering to shape the lines.

> *Joy, light divine. God we storm thy kingdom.*
> *World, do you sense the Creator? Truth enters through the*
> *cracks of burst coffins.*
> *Poverty, grief forgotten. Anger, revenge forgotten. No remorse. The*
> *dead shall live and hell shall be no more.*

Emily smeared her tears with the heel of her hand. A pair of girls strolled by and stared. Emily did not care.

*Seek him above the canopy of stars. Surely he lives above the stars.*

Emily knew she must walk upon the moors beneath those stars before she would hear his voice again. She gathered her meager belongings and slipped off into the city to find the schedule for trains to Ostend. She finished at a bank where she withdrew her share of Aunt Branwell's money.

But even as she made ready, another letter arrived from Patrick. Aunt Branwell was dying, and Charlotte and Emily must come home at once. Charlotte raged until she realized Monsieur and Madame Heger expected her to go, indeed would not have thought well of her if she insisted upon staying. So she put on a brave face and agreed to accompany Emily back to England.

Before she left Brussels for good, Emily Brontë presented Louise de Bassompierre with a drawing of a tree, its trunk split in two, one half alive and flowering, the other broken and dead.

❦

Aunt Branwell had already died and was sequestered in the family vault before Charlotte and Emily reached England. Charlotte was almost glad they had not arrived in time for the funeral. It supported her point that a precipitous return to Haworth had been a waste of time and money. She had already decided to write Monsieur Heger and ask if she and Emily might return for the term after Christmas.

Emily greeted the sight of the moors with the desperation of one starving for oxygen. She turned her face away from her sister on the journey up the brow from Keighley in the rented carriage and spoke to Charlotte only in monosyllables. Had it not been for the necessity of hauling their trunks, she would far rather have walked. When she climbed down from the carriage, she could not speak, so strong were her emotions.

Emily mourned Aunt Branwell, but the loss of Weightman was fresh and made more intense by the return to Haworth. Her last sight of him was burned into her memory, and she half expected he would come sauntering out of the Sunday school building, a smile of greeting on his face. To alight on the familiar cobblestones of Church Lane, and to know he would never more appear there, gave Emily more pain than at any moment since she had learned of his death.

But Emily was grateful to be greeted by the other creature she most longed for—Keeper. Branwell held the dog by the collar, but as soon as the beast saw Emily, he could not contain himself. He danced about in a circle and gave a series of high-pitched yips. Branwell was forced to let the dog go to save his arm being wrenched out of its socket. Keeper hit Emily in the chest and she went down to her knees, her arms around his neck. She buried her face in the dog's nape so the others could not see her face.

Anne, who knew Emily better than any, waited until her sister had time to compose herself. Then she knelt and encircled her in her arms.

"I am so sorry," Anne whispered.

"You loved him too, didn't you?" Emily said.

"Of course. How could I not? Everyone loved Mr. Weightman."

Emily wiped her eyes with the back of her hand. "Not everyone," she said, glancing at Charlotte, who was out of earshot.

Patrick approached and helped Emily to her feet. He pressed her to his chest and patted her back. Charlotte watched the reunion, her eyes narrowed. She wondered how much to share with her father about Weightman's dalliance with her sister. Meanwhile Branwell stood alone against the garden wall.

Charlotte went to her sisters and linked her arm through Anne's. Emily held back.

"It is a sad time," Charlotte said. "Yet we are all together."

"My presence comes at a price," Anne replied. "The Robinsons will not allow me home for Christmas."

"But that is terrible!" Emily cried.

"Yes," Anne said, "but it is more important to be here now. Poor Aunt, and poor Mr.—" but catching Emily's expression, Anne caught herself and bit her tongue.

"And yet Aunt was old, and had a long and full life," Charlotte said. "Let us reminisce about the old days."

Anne glanced at Emily as Charlotte led her away. Go on, Emily mouthed as she lingered. She leaned over and stroked Keeper's head. The dog licked her face.

"Dear Keeper," Emily crooned, "let us go together and see Nero."

"Emily," Patrick said rather too loudly, "it has been a long journey. Won't you have some tea?"

Emily straightened, sensing something was wrong. "May I not see the bird first?"

Patrick started to speak, and then caught himself. Emily stared at him implacably. Finally he said, "You can never be spared the truth, can you?" He took her arm in his. "Dear child, when your aunt was in her last illness, she was not in her right mind. She sold your poor geese to the butcher. And the hawk—" He hesitated. "We don't know what happened. Branwell found his cage ajar, and we could not understand from her whether he was sold or let loose."

Emily was beyond tears. "I see," she said. She continued to stroke Keeper. "Papa, do not bid me come in to tea. Nothing shall pass my lips until I have counted up all my losses. Only tell me now, where is Willie?"

Patrick said, "Willie lies beneath the church in our family vault."

"Where is the exact spot?"

Patrick hesitated at the intensity in her voice. He glanced at Branwell, who had come closer. "You know the vault is beneath the far right corner as you face the communion table. Willie is closest to the entrance at the back of the building."

Emily nodded. She said in a low voice, "Go on in the house, Papa. Leave me alone with him."

Patrick looked at Branwell, who echoed, "Go on, Papa." Patrick went on to the parsonage.

Emily began to walk toward the church. Branwell followed. Emily stopped. "Please," she said. "Leave me be."

"For God's sake, Emily," Branwell burst out, "I tended him upon his deathbed! Does that not give me some right to comfort you?"

"You tended him? I would have thought you would be off drinking with your friends."

"How could I leave him?"

"I did!" Emily said so ferociously and with such self-loathing that an alarmed Branwell thought her capable of doing some harm to herself. "I left him! And I shall never forgive myself. Never, ever!"

"Willie was glad you weren't here."

"Was he?"

She looked so stricken Branwell rushed to say, "No. No. You misunderstand. Willie's death was—" He looked at Emily's pale drawn face and knew she required honesty. "He died horribly. He did not want you to witness it. Nor did he wish to put you in danger."

"I would have been nowhere else," she said. She turned and ran, to get away from Branwell, into the church, Keeper at her heels. But she paused at the entrance to repeat her plea. "Leave me alone. Please," before slamming the door behind her.

Once her eyes adjusted to the gloom, Emily made her way to the front of the church. She stopped near the far wall where she judged Weightman to be interred beneath the floor. Then she sank slowly onto the flagstones and wailed, her voice rising to a keen, letting herself go as she could not do in Brussels. When she had cried herself out she lay still and imagined Weightman in the space below her, his body crumpled and consumed by the slow rot of death. She turned away from the appalling image and buried her face in her arms. She dreamed of digging up the floor of the church, her bare hands bloodied by the work, until she came to his coffin, tore it open, and threw herself on top of him.

Finally she drew herself up until she rested on her knees, and looked up at the wall. On a plaque she had not noticed before she made out the words WILLIAM WEIGHTMAN. She stood and began to read. *Greatly respected for his orthodox principles, active zeal, moral habits, learning, mildness, and affability: his useful labours will long be gratefully remembered, by the members of the congregation; and Sunday school teachers, and scholars.*

"I wrote it," said a voice behind her. "John Brown carved it. There is no memorial so elaborate in the entire church."

She had not heard Branwell come in and settle onto the back pew. Now he came forward.

Emily pressed the back of her hand against her mouth. Branwell put his arms around her and pressed her face to his shoulder, and she began to sob again. Then, exhausted, she slipped to the floor and sat with her back against the wall, her face turned to the ceiling. Branwell slid down beside her.

"Who else was with him?" she asked, still looking up at the ceiling.

"Papa and I, and the Widow Ogden and her Ruth."

"You wrote me and told me to stay in Brussels. You kept me away from him."

"Because Willie asked me to. He said if you knew we had cholera, you would come back at once." Branwell regarded her sideways. "Would you?"

"Of course," Emily said.

"Willie knew what he was doing then," Branwell replied. "He wanted to protect you."

"He should have known," Emily said, "I do not want protecting. That is something he never understood."

"He wanted me to tell you," Branwell said, "that he loved you."

Emily closed her eyes.

"He made me promise to tell you, even before he was taken ill. In case he didn't make it, he said. I had forgotten that I wrote you about Isabella Greenwood, and I regret it now. I didn't understand at the time that it was a holiday for him, a moment of respite. It meant nothing. The summer was so difficult. Willie was set to take his time away to visit his family in Appleby, you know, but he couldn't leave after all. I only told you he was there to explain why I was writing instead of Willie. We don't know how cholera spreads; he was afraid any paper he touched might be contagious."

Branwell took Emily's hand. She continued to stare at the ceiling. "What was his death like?"

"Emily, it was terrible and you do not want—"

"Tell me!" She was implacable.

Branwell sat for a time. Then he said, "He was skeletal, his skin turned dark, he could not close his mouth for he had no moisture, he could not breathe except to gag—"

Emily hunched up suddenly, her arms wrapped around her knees.

Branwell reached inside his coat. "He wrote this. Dictated it, rather. But he wanted you to have it." Branwell draped one arm around Emily and drew her close. He opened the sheet of paper so she could see it. "It is in my hand, but these are Willie's words."

Emily read:

*Dearest Emily,*

I do not know what the future would have held for the two of us. But I must believe there is still a future. I go on alone for a time. I am sorry to leave. If it is possible I shall stay close. I will always love you.

*Willie*

Emily turned and threw her arms around Branwell.

"I shall never forget this," she whispered. "Never."

They held one another for a long time. Keeper rose from his spot beneath a pew when they departed, and followed them down the aisle like an attendant at a wedding.

## 16

*M*adame Heger wrote that the Pensionnat would welcome the services of the Brontës as teachers for the spring term. Charlotte found Emily in the kitchen and waved the letter over her sister's head. "Is it not wonderful?" she cried.

But Emily refused to return to Brussels with her sister and turned away from Charlotte's pleas. Patrick, ever indulgent of his daughters and without Aunt Branwell to dissuade him, agreed Charlotte would make an unescorted journey to Belgium. So Charlotte returned to the Pensionnat, where she made her attentions to Monsieur obvious over the course of the year. She would realize, indeed be forced by Monsieur's growing reserve and his wife's anger, to understand that she must give up any hopes of love from that quarter.

But while Charlotte's sad drama played out on the Continent, the parsonage was quiet. Anne and Branwell were gone as well, for Anne had convinced her employers, the Robinsons, to engage her brother as a tutor for their son. The only residents of the house in Haworth now were Patrick, Emily, and Tabby, who had returned from her sister's though she was no longer able to do much work. Instead the old woman kept Emily company by the hearth, the cat Tiger asleep in her lap. Young Martha Brown came every day to help out but returned to her family's home beside the Sunday school building at night.

Emily went at night to her favorite spot on the moor above the par-sonage. She lay upon the ground in a clump of moor grass with Keeper close for warmth. She studied the stars and listened for the voice of William Weightman. She heard only wind and birdsong. Now and then, as she wrapped her cloak more tightly against the cold, she coughed.

Emily Brontë knew she was consumptive. Her time in Brussels had masked the problem, for the exertion of household chores had not been required, nor was she able to take long rambles upon the moors. But on her return to Haworth she noticed she grew short of breath while climbing the high street with her shopping basket, or blacking the kitchen hearth. Then came the invariable stitch in her side when she strode along on her walks. Nothing so severe as to prevent her from rambling. But Emily went more slowly. She wished to tell someone, but did not. Anne, she had long believed, was a fellow sufferer, but had never spoken of her situation, not even to her sister. Emily had no desire to disturb her sister's peace. Patrick had his own concerns, for his eyesight was failing. Charlotte was out of the question. One did not confide weakness to Charlotte.

One frigid morning, Emily wrapped her wool cloak about her and set out on her errands. She went first for the post. But she was forced to step back before entering the doorway of the shop, scraping her elbow against the rough stone. A burly man had forced his way out, heedless of anyone in his way. He passed by, a mustache beneath a large hat. Then he stopped and noticed Emily for the first time.

"Well," he said, looking her up and down, his eyes undressing her, "if it isn't the chit from the parsonage."

Emily stood her ground and held the gaze of Constable Massey from the Metropolitan Police. He took her directness for an invitation and sidled closer.

"Do you know," he said, "we have proof of your Mr. Weightman's involvement in the indecencies of last summer, when the mill boilers were vandalized. Some documents have come into our hands that show he deserves even more blame than we imagined. So I came to this sewer"—he gestured around at Haworth—"to place him under arrest. Only I am told he has saved me a great deal of trouble and kicked the bucket. I always was a lucky bloke. Now I've time to raise a pint in the Black Bull, and I needn't return to Bradford until tomorrow morning. If you're free tonight, I have something extra in my pocket." He winked. "And in my trousers."

Massey thrust his hand into his pants pocket to make a bulge, and a jingling sound from the change. Emily turned on her heel without a word and headed back to the parsonage. Patrick was out on his pastoral rounds. Emily ran upstairs to her father's room and flung open the drawer in the bedside table where he kept his pistol. The same pistol he had taught Emily, of all his children the only one interested, to shoot.

Emily placed a bullet in the chamber, shoved the gun in the capacious pocket of the old dress she wore for household work, and went downstairs.

She found Massey in the Black Bull. He sat quaffing a pint, his hat off, and held court before a pair of admiring bagmen who frequented the coach line between Keighley and Lancashire.

Emily wrapped her hand around the gun. Massey was so close she could see the greasy tufts of hair that lay at odd angles on the base of his skull.

A voice said, *No.*

Emily froze. He deserves to die, she thought. So I am going to kill him.

*No.*

Emily recognized the voice. She clutched the gun and squeezed her eyes shut.

*No. If you wish to hear more.*

"Please God," she murmured.

Massey swerved at the sound of Emily's voice, and his fellow travelers turned as well, their conversation interrupted. Massey leered at Emily. Bits of foam from the ale flecked his mustache.

"Well, well," he said. "Come to offer me something, have you?"

Emily hesitated for a moment. Then she said, "No. Only to tell you that you were correct. You are very, very lucky."

Massey smiled and reached out his hand, but Emily had already turned, still clutching the pistol in her pocket, and departed the Black Bull.

�❧

Emily continued to write poetry, but she also took up the novel she had long wished to write. She chose the names of her principal characters: Catherine Earnshaw, and Heathcliff. Heathcliff had no second name. Emily thought Heathcliff was her primeval self, made of moor grass and earth, the passionate outsider. She jotted down a variety of impressions to describe his character. Then she turned to Cathy. Emily's first impression of Cathy came clear when the character described a dream she'd had: "Heaven was not my home; and I broke my heart with weeping to come back to earth; and the angels were so angry that they flung me out into the middle of the moor; where I woke sobbing for joy. So I remain close." Emily thought the dreamer could have been Weightman.

And Emily had no sooner set down her pen than a voice said, *I have found Nero.*

Emily sat up straight.

*Go tomorrow morning to Ponden Kirk.*

Emily went to the parlor window and looked out. The tombstones, the church, a full moon. Silence.

The next day was Tuesday. Tuesdays had been Willie's day off, the day he and Emily had rambled the moors together.

Emily went out the next morning as soon as it was light. She but-

tered a piece of bread for her breakfast, and stuffed a cold mutton sand-
wich into her pocket for dinner, along with strips of chicken skin from
leftovers destined for the stockpot. Outside, she went to the washroom.
Nero's cage, three years empty, stood in the far corner gathering dust.
Emily opened the drawer in the old cupboard and rummaged about.
The jesses had long disappeared, and the collar and leashes and gaunt-
let. But stuck in the far back behind a box of nails she found the bell.
This went in her pocket as well. Then she set out.

The morning mist rose from the flanks of the hills like incense.
She tried to talk to Willie but heard little except *Go, Go*. The sun was
high overhead when she finally arrived at Ponden Kirk. She stopped at
the foot of the rock formation and rang the bell. Nothing.

She sat and ate the food she had brought with her, cupped her hand
and drank from the nearby beck. Now and then a raptor launched
itself from the great rock, although Emily thought that even from a
distance they appeared larger than merlins. Then Willie said *Further*.
She trudged on.

She was so far beyond Ponden Kirk it had begun to appear distant
and small again, so far past she was about to give up though she still
rang the bell, when a bird burst from a hollow and flew toward her,
then wheeled away at the last moment. She realized she had forgotten
to raise her arm. She rang the bell again. The bird came about. She
thrust her fist skyward. The hawk swooped, pulled up, and with a beating of wings, lighted.

Nero's claws cut into Emily's flesh until trickles of blood ran down
in several places. She forced herself to stand immobile despite the pain
as she grappled for the scrap of chicken in her pocket and thrust it into
the merlin's open craw.

"Oh," she said then. "Oh." She pulled Nero close. He stayed on her fist
even as she drew him to her chest, his yellow eye fixed upon her. Then he
fluffed himself and settled while she ran her fingers through his feathers.

"Oh, Nero. After all these years you have not forgot."

Nero screeched. A second bird flew close and settled on a nearby stand of gorse. Nero squawked again and was answered by a fierce scolding. The second merlin's feathers were drab brown so as to render it almost invisible against the heath. A female.

"Nero, you have a mate! Of course you do, and I suppose you have hatched chicks between you. But she is worried. I daresay she fears I will do you some harm." Emily leaned close and kissed the bird on the top of his head. "I have missed you so much. But you are free, and you have your companion. I know I will not see you again, but now I shall not mourn."

Emily flung her arm high and the merlin took off, leaving behind final punctures of Emily's fist. She barely felt the wounds. As the pair of birds disappeared into the midday sun, she gave an inchoate cry of joy and began to run back the way she had come, as she had done that long-ago day with William Weightman. She even fell as before, only this time she began to cough and could not stop for the longest time. Emily pressed the back of her hand against her mouth; she could taste the blood like a spice. She was so short of breath that she thought her heart might stop. But after a time she breathed more easily. As she lay among the heather, she turned to her left, to face someone she could not see, and said, "I'm dying, Willie."

*I know*, he said.

"We would have had small time together."

*Yes, there. But large time here.*

Emily shut her eyes and tears slipped down her cheeks. "If you had not turned your back upon me, here upon the moors—"

Of course he did not answer.

When Emily had sobbed herself out, she stood and began the long walk back to Haworth.

☙☙

John Brown had just finished digging a new grave, spade in hand, when he met Emily Brontë coming down from the moors. She strode without care for what obstacles might be in her path, her hair loose and flying about her face, which was set in an expression of ecstasy such as the sexton had never seen. Though he noted the cuts and dried blood on her left hand and arm, and the stains on the sleeve of her dress. He removed his cap and nodded but she did not see him, and went by without acknowledgment.

John Brown returned the shovel to the shed beside his house in Church Lane and went inside to get his supper. As he sat down at table, he said to Mrs. Brown, "I saw Emily Brontë coming down off the moor just now."

"And what's odd about that?" his wife asked, her voice bored.

"It was, well—she looked as though she'd seen God Almighty."

Mrs. Brown shook her head at such nonsense and shoveled a sausage from her skillet onto her husband's plate.

## 17

*O*nce more the Brontë children returned home. Charlotte, obsessed with Monsieur Heger, proceeded to write her beloved letter after adoring letter. Monsieur refused to answer. Anne and Branwell followed Charlotte back to Haworth, for Branwell had been caught in bed with the wife of his employer, silly and vain Mrs. Robinson, and Anne resigned her post out of shame. Charlotte did not empathize with her brother. Branwell had adulterously soiled the name of a married woman (although one Charlotte considered of low character) while Charlotte's love was unrequited, and so noble and chaste. Besides, Branwell, determining he could not live without his love, set out to drink himself to death in the best tradition of art and romance. Charlotte set out meanwhile to produce some of the great works of English literature and encourage the same effort in her sisters.

The arrival of Patrick's new curate caused a stir in the parsonage as well. The Reverend Arthur Bell Nicholls followed an inadequate substitute for William Weightman, the Reverend James Smith. Mr. Smith, unlike his beloved predecessor, had neglected his pastoral duties and flirted with the local ladies in a way that fit Charlotte's imagined view of Mr. Weightman. Patrick Brontë was forced upon several occasions to remonstrate with the man. Then James Smith abruptly absconded to Canada, to the puzzlement and delight of all.

So Arthur Bell Nicholls proved a relief. Had he followed immediately after Mr. Weightman, he would have been considered a disappointment. Mr. Nicholls was boring and lacking in charm; he was
dogmatic, and prone to lecture the villagers about what he considered
their bad habits and theological errors. But he discharged his duties
faithfully and carried a great deal of the burden for Patrick.

Emily Brontë hated Mr. Nicholls because he was not William
Weightman. Now she must see him every day, in his clerical garb,
going into the church or the Sunday school where he had even taken
over Weightman's desk. A presumptuous impostor. Nor could Patrick
Brontë claim to love the new man. But he was grateful to him for his
service.

Charlotte ignored Mr. Nicholls at first. He was Irish, after all, and
she was uncomfortable with her own marginal (she insisted upon its
marginality) Irishness. No need for a constant reminder, no need for
that accent which seemed to draw out an answering brogue from her
father after all these years. Still, Mr. Nicholls seemed useful and harm-
less. Charlotte was polite to him.

❧

All three sisters decided to attempt novels, where they had before
only composed poetry. Emily would say little about her work at first
except to disclose that she wrote a story of love and hate set upon
the moors. Her sisters decided that love, at least, would make a fine
subject. Anne worked on *Agnes Grey*, based upon her years as a governess and an imagined courtship with Mr. Easton. Charlotte would
produce *The Professor*, much of it set in Brussels. But that novel, though
quickly written, received no good response from publishers, to Charlotte's chagrin. She tried to be brave about her failure, to think what
she should do next.

Emily suggested, during a walk upon the moors, "Anne and I have set our love stories here in Yorkshire. Perhaps you might do the same."

Charlotte said somewhat testily, "Do you dictate what I should write?"

"No. One cannot do that." Emily was amazed at her own patience. "I suggest you might find your greatest success close to home, that is all. And," she added, "you might write about Monsieur at a greater remove."

Emily braced herself for her sister's explosion, but it did not come. Finally Charlotte said, "You do not suggest that I not write about him at all."

"Of course not," Emily said. "I think you *must* write about him."

"And you do not judge me for it?"

"Only if it harms your writing rather than helps."

They walked on while Anne lingered behind. Charlotte declared, "My new heroine shall be small and plain. It has not been done before."

"But Anne has done that," Emily pointed out. "In *Agnes Grey*."

"Oh bother," Charlotte said, careful to note that Anne was out of hearing. "Who shall notice *Agnes Grey*?"

So Charlotte turned to writing *Jane Eyre*. Though Emily did not press her sister, she thought she recognized some aspects of the principal characters. Small and plain Jane. St. John Rivers, an idealistic young clergyman who throws his life away on a quixotic missionary effort. The gruff and challenging Mr. Rochester with his raffish air of continental worldliness. And Rochester's inconvenient wife whom Charlotte condemned to confinement as a madwoman. Emily thought Charlotte took particular pleasure in slamming the attic door upon Madame Heger.

The sisters read aloud to one another in the evenings after their father had gone to bed. The readings were stimulating, but the Brontës also began to feel the strain of their shared efforts. They were sisters. They loved one another. They were also rivals, though they never admitted to it.

During these readings, Emily grew uncomfortably aware that neither of her sisters approved of *Wuthering Heights.*

"What appalling characters," Charlotte complained after one of Emily's readings. "They are none of them admirable. How shall anyone be drawn to them?"

Emily, hurt by her sister's remark, said, "*I* love them."

Charlotte continued as if Emily had not spoken. "Such lost souls! Especially that horrible Heathcliff!"

Anne said nothing upon that occasion. But Emily noticed Anne and Charlotte exchanged glances as she read aloud. After bearing several such exchanges and appearing not to notice, Emily stopped in mid-sentence.

"What?" she demanded. "Is my style unclear? Are my descriptions lacking?"

"No, no," Anne rushed to assure her.

"It is not your style," Charlotte said. "Though that is troubling enough in one way. Must you insist upon spelling out all the swear words, instead of substituting a dash in their place? Even men do not write so baldly."

"That is dishonest," Emily said. "I write the way people speak. Readers hear the words in their minds anyway, so it is hypocritical to leave them out."

"But there is more," Charlotte continued. "Your people are detestable."

Emily looked to Anne for her defense, but her sister remained silent.

"Your story gives me nightmares," Charlotte added.

"Do not be so dramatic," Emily said. "Only little children get nightmares from their reading. I thought you a grown woman."

"But much of the book is beautiful," Anne broke her silence at last, trying to calm the waters. "The descriptions. The moors. And Nelly Dean is rather sweet. Though her judgment—"

"Do not trust Nelly's judgment," Emily interrupted. "Or her sweetness." She would not look at either of her sisters but focused upon straightening the pages of her manuscript.

"Well," Charlotte said, "Nelly is sensible enough. Though it is odd she has such importance for your story when she is only an uneducated servant. But she possesses a better character than Cathy. And Heathcliff—Heathcliff is demonic."

"I would not go *so* far," Anne said. "He might be reformed if—"

Emily slammed the manuscript down on the table in front of her. "Reformed? Would you dare reform him? He would curse you for it! And do you despise Heathcliff? Then despise me! Because *I*—" She jabbed her finger against her chest as she leaned forward across the table. "*I* am Heathcliff! *I am!*"

"I don't believe it," Anne said. "Heathcliff is such a violent man, sister, and you are not."

"I am well acquainted with hate. There are times I could have killed, and gladly. I have it in me. You must not think otherwise."

Anne was shocked into silence. But Charlotte peered at her sister through narrowed eyes. "If you are Heathcliff," she said softly, "then who is Cathy?"

Emily turned away and would say nothing more.

⁂

Once, as they lay together in bed at night, Emily ventured to share with Anne that she conversed with Weightman. She had longed to tell someone, and she could say anything to Anne, could she not? But she regretted it at once. Anne was quiet for so long that Emily felt her cheeks begin to burn. At last Anne said, "Sister. I hope you will not

be hurt by this question. Is it possible that you are not talking to Mr. Weightman at all, but only to your imagination?"

Emily took her own time in answering. At last she said, "If I am not talking to Willie, then I am mad."

She did not bring up the subject again.

∂❧ઠ

The sisters hid behind masculine noms de plume—Currer, Ellis, and Acton Bell. But when *Jane Eyre* was published to great acclaim—though with some complaints about its "coarseness"—Charlotte, longing to receive the acclaim she deserved, revealed herself to her publisher. Emily chose to remain hidden as the mysterious Ellis Bell. Most reviewers had disliked *Wuthering Heights* for its violent intensity. If Mr. Bell might be criticized for his tale of passion, how much more would the author of *Wuthering Heights* be savaged if known to be a woman? But Emily told herself she did not care about the book's reception. She loved it, and that was enough.

Anne's *Agnes Grey* was largely ignored, but she was already hard at work on a new and more ambitious book, *The Tenant of Wildfell Hall*. Emily had also begun a new novel, which she called *Heaven and Earth*. She prayed she would have enough time to finish, for she felt the congestion in her lungs more acutely. The new book would be Willie's book, since her central character was a clergyman who stood up for mill workers and fell in with Chartists.

Charlotte was appalled at Emily's subject matter. *Wuthering Heights* had been bad enough, and she could have wished it had never been published. But labor unrest and sedition, dear God! Charlotte could only hope her sister's new project would be stillborn. When it continued to progress, she decided a more effective response would be to write a book on the same theme, but from a more acceptable point of view. She was now, after all, an acclaimed novelist. Perhaps Emily

would feel shamed enough to quash her outlandish work. Rebellion thrives upon resistance, Charlotte thought, whereas discouragement is a strong deterrent. If that failed, Charlotte had the satisfaction of knowing that her new book would be read widely while the public would scarcely notice a volume by the disreputable and shadowy Ellis Bell. The picture Charlotte would present, of a long-suffering mill owner persecuted by his despicable workers, would carry the day. And so she began *Shirley*.

༄

The evening readings grew ever more contentious. Charlotte named her novel after a character, Shirley Keeldar, whom she declared would be modeled after Emily. Emily was shocked when Charlotte divulged this information, and resolved to pay close attention to her literary icon. Charlotte's hero was a half-Belgian mill owner, another stand-in for Monsieur. Shirley was a rich young woman who owned a substantial share of the trade from his mill.

Emily listened as Charlotte read, biting her tongue. But she spoke out at last when Charlotte described a scene of the mill at work. "'It was eight o'clock,'" Charlotte read.

"The mill lights were all extinguished; the signal was given for break-fast; the children, released for half an hour from toil, betook themselves to the little tin cans which held their coffee, and to the small baskets which contained their allowance of bread. Let us hope they have enough to eat; it would be a pity were it otherwise."

Emily stood. "What a horrible thing to write!" she cried. She would have spoken further, but she was forced to stop and cough. She turned toward the hearth until she could regain control.

Charlotte was stung, though she should not have been surprised.

"What do you mean? Do I not describe the poor things tenderly? Do I not wish them the best?"

Emily snatched up the sheet of paper. "'Let us hope they have enough to eat; it would be a pity were it otherwise,'" Emily read in a sarcastic tone of voice. She threw the paper back across the table. "You know it is not so! You know they don't have enough to eat. Poor bairns! You make light of their cold coffee and their dram of bread, which they cannot eat until they have worked hours before dawn. Then you send your Mr. Moore home to his pleasant cottage for a breakfast of hot coffee and bread and butter and stewed pears. A character you claim is based upon me makes money from this. It is intolerable! I will not be party to it even as a fictional character."

Charlotte could not help but laugh. "What choice does a fictional character have?" she asked.

Anne could not recall Emily so angry since Charlotte had redone the portrait of their mother.

Emily said, "What do we see of the workers in this novel of yours? A few depraved idiots, a simple poor man who has no better sense than to be bought off by your Mr. Moore. And a—a drunkard who suffers delirium tremens." Even as she mentioned this last character, Emily saw the connection to Branwell. She realized others were based upon the liberal family of Charlotte's school friend Mary Taylor, and upon Patrick and his curates. Charlotte is getting her revenge upon us all, Emily thought, in one fell swoop. "And how dare you compare me to this—this monster?"

"Monster?" Charlotte was thunderstruck. "She is you, sister, if you were wealthy. That is my intent. And so she is not monstrous at all. I love her, as I love you. I give her the characteristics I most admire in you, especially your free spirit. Shirley even has a large dog like Keeper I have named Tartar."

"Oh yes, Shirley is like me," Emily said sarcastically. "Shirley is not me, she is my daemonic opposite!"

"She is you if you had wealth," Charlotte repeated stubbornly.

"If I were wealthy, I would be content to earn my living from the toil of little children? Then thank God I am not rich. I would sooner burn a mill than profit from it!"

"You defend the lower orders as rabidly as a Jacobin!" Charlotte cried, her voice rising to meet Emily's. "No wonder you were taken in by Celia Amelia and all his ridiculous—"

Before she could say more, Emily ran out the front door, slamming it behind her.

Charlotte went to the sofa and sat, the back of her hand pressed to her mouth, breathing hard. Anne remained at the table, studying her fingernails.

When Charlotte felt calmer, she said, "Emily has grown more difficult over the years since we returned from Brussels. I blame the lingering influence of Mr. Weightman. He was bad for her, truly corrosive."

"I think," Anne said, "you have presumed upon Emily in creating your character. She feels it a violation, and I believe it may be so."

Charlotte's face was set. "My characters belong to no one," she said, "except myself."

Anne said, "Yet Emily does not belong to you." She blew out the rush candle that stood beside her and went to her room. Anne undressed and washed in solitude, stopping now and then to cough, for her asthma, as she still thought of it, was worse. She was alone when she lay down, but assumed she would wake up when Emily crawled into bed beside her.

Except Emily spent the night in the church curled on her side above William Weightman's grave.

"Oh, Willie," Emily whispered as she lay, her head cradled upon a kneeling cushion from a pew and her shawl wrapped about her, "Charlotte's vision will prevail. She will be read and I will not be."

*The fear of the writer,* Willie said.

Emily found this no comfort. Still, she ignored the cold of the flag-stones, for she was happy to be where she was. At last she fell asleep.

ᴥᴥ

The end came quickly.

Branwell disappeared for several weeks, no one knew where. When finally he was deposited in West Lane, brought back to Haworth by a carter who passed him lying beside the road, he picked himself up and headed not to the parsonage, but to the Black Bull. The publican had the sense to send for John Brown.

Branwell's face was sharply etched as a skull, his mouth slack, and his hair filthy and matted. He stank. Somehow Patrick and the three young women, two of them ill with consumption, got him up the stairs and into Patrick's bed.

But if the Black Bull now refused Branwell's trade, still the local urchins could supply cheap drink, home-brewed rotgut, in exchange for coins to feed their families. One warm August morning, Anne came upon Branwell in the washhouse, happily drunk, a bottle cradled against his midsection.

Then one morning Branwell tottered the length of Church Lane where he met a lad bearing a flask in the pocket of his jacket. Bran-well could not fix upon the boy, for the lane seemed to change shape and run on forever. The surrounding graves loomed close and the steeple of the church threatened to topple over and crush him. Bran-well staggered.

The boy was glad enough to pass on the flask, and Branwell was happy to reward him. Too many coins, for the boy snatched them and ran off. Perhaps Branwell had not counted properly.

Then the world flipped, the lane crashed upon him, and the pre-cious flask smashed to bits upon the pavement, liquor running down the paving stones to contribute to the inebriation of any insects that still survived the autumn.

Branwell was past caring.

He was in bed. His father's bed? Branwell was strangely lucid. He clearly saw the people in the room. Charlotte in the far corner, staring at him with sorrow and contempt. Anne beside her, weeping, her blond hair straggling into her face. Mr. Wheelhouse, his face a mask.

A matter of hours at most, Mr. Wheelhouse said.

His father was close on one side, gripping his hand. Pray, my son. Will you not pray?

"Papa," Branwell said, "I have not prayed in so long. How can I? I don't believe."

Someone's arm was around him. Emily. She sat upon the bed and leaned close, her mouth to his ear.

"You're going on," she said. "And Willie will be waiting to greet you."

"Are you sure?" Branwell said. He seized up, gripped Emily's hand, and rose up from his pillow, his mouth open.

"Papa," Emily implored.

Patrick began to pray. "Into your hands, merciful Savior, we commend dear Branwell, a lamb of your own flock. Receive him into the arms of your mercy. Amen."

Branwell said, "Amen." His eyes turned up and the light went out of them.

⚜

Charlotte was so upset she took to her bed, leaving Emily and Anne, despite their growing weakness, to make the funeral preparations. A friend of their father's would preach the sermon, and must be fed and housed, and mourners who stopped by the parsonage to offer condolences must likewise be provided with refreshment. The funeral procession then traveled the short distance from house to church in a cold driving rain. When the service was done, Patrick, more aware than ever of his family's fragile health, sent his daughters home. Charlotte and Anne negotiated the distance to the parsonage, their bombazine garments blown about by the early east wind like blackbirds in flight.

Emily insisted upon following the coffin to the back of the church building where John Brown pried open the door to the crypt and guided Branwell's coffin inside. He and another pallbearer shoved the coffin through the low entrance into the vault that held the Brontë remains. But Emily, shivering against the cold, only had eyes for the single wood box that rested apart at the entrance, one end visible in the gray light.

She clutched her father's sleeve. "Is that Willie?"

Patrick said, "Yes. That is where we placed poor Willie."

Emily dropped the umbrella she held against the rain and moved through the doorway, where John Brown stood. The sexton was so startled he took a step back and stumbled. Emily stopped as the smell of damp decay assaulted her.

Patrick reached out and put his arm around her thin shoulders.

"Come home now, Emily," he said.

She allowed him to guide her back outside and up to the parsonage. It was the last time she would walk though the door, for she had caught the chill that would bring her consumption to a climax.

Emily spoke with William Weightman at every moment. Their thoughts flowed back and forth across the abyss as though each reached without impediment into the mind of the other. Emily continued to do her chores. On her last day, she dressed herself and made her painful way downstairs, each breath as sharp as a stabbing knife. She almost fell when carrying the dogs' food bowls to the back door. And yet she remained leaning against the wall as Keeper ate his fill. Then Emily Brontë went into the parlor and swooned upon the sofa.

John Brown and another man were summoned to carry her upstairs to her bed. Emily looked out her window. She could see the church, and the moors beyond. That was all she wanted.

Her father and sisters gathered round. Tabby sat at the foot of the bed, dabbing her eyes with her apron.

"Keeper," Emily said, "where is Keeper?"

The dog was lying across the doorway, a worried expression on his face. He raised his head and cocked it at the sound of his name.

Patrick fetched the dog and urged him up on the bed. Keeper leaped up, turned round several times, and then settled at Emily's side. He licked her face, and then he dropped his head, resting it upon her shoulder. Emily twined her fingers in his fur and looked out the window toward the church.

At a great distance, she heard Charlotte say, "Is she smiling? How can that be?"

Willie, what does she know of joy? Emily thought.

A sharp pain caused her to double over. When the spasm had passed, she managed to say, "Perhaps—perhaps I will see Mr. Wheelhouse now."

But by the time Mr. Wheelhouse arrived, the pain had lessened and Emily rested more comfortably save for the invisible hand that clamped her neck. She refused the laudanum the doctor urged upon her. She feared she might, under the drug's influence, miss her first sight of the world to come.

❦

The winter day, crisp and clear. Deep blue sky. A cloud scurries past, a shadow moves across the face of the moor.

He is waiting at the last stile.

ᴈᴉ⊱

On the bed, Keeper reared and looked around, confused. Then he began to howl.

## 18

Again a funeral. Keeper joined the procession to the church, walking with calm dignity at Patrick's side before settling into the family pew. Afterward Patrick sent his surviving daughters home to the parsonage as he had done before, because of the cold, but also because he had one more task to perform.

He turned to John Brown, about to shove the coffin back into the vault beside Branwell's.

"Is the coffin heavy?" Patrick asked.

The sexton looked surprised but said, "It is not. She wasted away terrible, you know."

Patrick said. "John, I hope you shall not think me mad. But do you have a pickax?"

John Brown looked askance, but decided Mr. Brontë's request was none of his business. No one should be surprised if the old man was a bit deranged.

When John Brown returned with the tool, Patrick took it from him and said, "Leave me, John. I will call you to close in a moment."

When John Brown hesitated, Patrick put his hand upon the younger man's shoulder and said, "Only a moment."

The sexton nodded and left. Patrick heard his boots ring against the hard pavement toward Church Lane.

He bent to his work. He leaned over Weightman's coffin and struck a sharp blow against its side. Twice more and a splintered opening appeared, large enough to stick a fist through. Then Patrick turned to Emily's coffin. He swung the pickax; the fresher wood finally gave way.

Patrick Brontë pushed the coffins together, their breaches aligned.

Outside he found John Brown leaning against the Sunday school building, smoking his pipe.

"You may close now," Patrick said, and climbed the stairs to his front door.

# EPILOGUE

nne tried to keep busy after Emily's funeral, for her dead sister had bequeathed a trust. Emily just managed to finish her novel, *Heaven and Earth*, dictating the final sentences as she lay upon the sofa in the parlor, too weak to sit up. Anne had since been recopying the manuscript, polishing it and readying it for publication.

But Anne was forced to confront her own demise, her "asthma" now certainly consumption in its last stages. She handed on the manuscript to Charlotte for safekeeping, and prepared to die.

Thus Charlotte inherited the literary legacy of her sisters. She set about the task with all diligence. First she went through her sisters' poems and rewrote them, striking lines she did not like and supplying what she considered more appropriate substitutions.

Then she considered the novels, reluctantly, for the task gave her a great deal of pain. Her publisher, Smith Elder, offered—too generously she thought—to reprint her sisters' work. They expected, she knew, a positive reply, and so she considered. *Agnes Grey* was insignificant. The tenor of the reviews for *Wuthering Heights* proved the book to be offensive, but perhaps too noticed to be repressed. If she might write a preface that would explain Emily's oddities and the narrowness of her circumstances, something of her sister's reputation might be salvaged.

But she refused to allow her publisher to reprint Anne's *The Tenant of Wildfell Hall.* Charlotte thought it out of the question that the tale of drunken depravity and wifely rebellion should be circulated further. Such an unpleasant book, she wrote, was an entire mistake that should be forgotten. And as for *Heaven and Earth*—

Charlotte lay awake at night. She prayed. At last she went to Mr. Nicholls, who would soon declare himself and ask for her hand in marriage. She said, "Dear Mr. Nicholls, I need advice which my father cannot give. If you loved someone, and yet thought they might come to great harm through information you possessed, what would you do? Might you find a way to suppress that information? Would censorship, in that case, be legitimate?"

Mr. Nicholls considered, stroking his mustache, and then said, "I suppose this is not a hypothetical situation?"

"That is correct."

"You do not wish to be specific for good reason."

Charlotte nodded in assent.

"Such a course might be justified," Mr. Nicholls said. "You possess the good judgment to decide whether or not that is the case."

Charlotte sighed and said, "Thank you, Mr. Nicholls."

Upstairs in her bedroom she added a bucket of coal to the fire in the hearth. She sat in her rocking chair, studying the flames as they leapt up. Then she stood, resolute. One tragedy could be prevented.

"Emily," she said, "I must protect you from yourself."

She rifled through Emily's chest, her drawers and portable writing desk. She set the poems aside, the rest she stacked upon the bed. The old notebooks detailing the adventures and love affairs of Alexandrina Zenobia and other denizens of Gondal. The drawing of William Weightman she found beneath Emily's old nightgowns. Weightman's letters to Emily in Brussels.

Charlotte kept the volume of Shelley's poetry, but tore out the title page with its inscription and added it to the pile. On top she laid the manuscript pages of the novel *Heaven and Earth*.

Charlotte carried the papers into her bedroom. One by one, she fed them to the fire where they turned into thin curls of gold and brown, and then into black ash.

# EMILY'S GHOST

*Denise Giardina*

# EMILY'S GHOST

## Denise Giardina

## DENISE GIARDINA ON *EMILY'S GHOST*

The story of the Brontë family has been Charlotte's story. Charlotte's story because she survived her sisters and brother. Charlotte's story because her juvenile writings were preserved where her sisters' were not, because only Charlotte's correspondence was saved.

Charlotte's story because she managed her sisters' literary inheritance. Charlotte's story because she burst the bounds of Haworth and became acquainted with London society and the literary elite of England. Charlotte's story because she was befriended by Mrs. Gaskell, soon to be her biographer.

The people around Charlotte were first seen through Charlotte's eyes as interpreted by Mrs. Gaskell. The uncivilized villagers of Haworth. (As one who grew up in the Appalachian Mountains, I am well acquainted with the way outsiders can condescend and misinterpret.) The eccentric, remote father and odd aunt. Branwell the depraved drunkard. Weak and insignificant Anne. Emily, unmanageable, solitary, and unfathomable. The fickle young curate who receives a few snide mentions in Mrs. Gaskell's account as "Mr. W." and whose death is not mentioned at all.

And Charlotte, the patient and dutiful daughter.

Both Branwell and Patrick Brontë deserve rehabilitation. We now understand alcoholism as a disease, rather than a question of willpower and moral character. Branwell deserves a second chance to be known. Charlotte's relationship with her father was often problematic as well. Patrick opposed the marriage to his curate, Arthur Bell Nichols, in part because he feared a pregnancy would kill the diminutive Charlotte. (It did.) Charlotte resented her situation in Haworth and blamed her father. The portrait of Patrick drawn by Mrs. Gaskell has endured, and yet what we know from other sources discounts much of it entirely. I have tried to portray the Patrick Brontë who raised three strong, independent, inquiring daughters and allowed them their freedom at a time when women were expected to be hothouse plants in a parlor.

And I have tried to free Emily from Charlotte's portrayal. Most of what we know of Emily comes from Charlotte. But now and then we get glimpses from elsewhere. For example, Charlotte's friend Mary Taylor wrote after trying to imagine Emily socializing with English families during her stay in Brussels, "Imagine Emily turning over prints or 'taking wine' with any stupid fop and preserving her temper and politeness." Mary Taylor also tells us that Emily "never took [Charlotte's] opinion but always had one to offer."

And Charlotte's words can be closely parsed. She wrote to her publisher of Emily that it was best "not to advocate the side you wish her to favour; if you do she is sure to lean in the opposite direction." One might notice first that Charlotte assumes Emily's positions are taken in automatic opposition to her own, rather than being assumed after serious consideration and for good reason. Then one might consider that Charlotte was a politically conservative, conventionally Victorian young woman who avidly sought to be married and escape Haworth to something like gentility.

One might then imagine Emily to be the opposite.

# DISCUSSION QUESTIONS

1. When Anne wonders why it is so difficult to meet "the right man," Emily responds, "Perhaps . . . God prefers tormented love. It is more interesting than contentment." Do you agree? What makes a good love story?

2. Young Emily rejects the Reverend William Carus Wilson's story of a young girl damned to eternal punishment because she doesn't believe the girl is "real." Later Emily thinks Mr. Wilson is also not "real." What does Emily mean and why does she respond this way?

3. Is Charlotte right when she says that William Weightman is a flirt? Discuss the ways in which his sociability is both a positive and a negative quality.

4. Emily's conception of a heaven close to earth is seen by the Reverend Dury as radical, even heretical. Why does Emily believe that the distance—far or near—between heaven and earth is significant?

5. When the sisters claim front row seats at Weightman's lecture, Giardina writes, "Charlotte wanted knowledge more than she wanted a man, as did her sisters." Do you think this is true? Why or why not?

6. From Emily's solitary walks along the moors to the lively return from Weightman's lecture, much of the drama in this novel takes place while the characters are walking somewhere. Why do you think these walks set the stage for conflict and connection between characters?

7. Why do you think Denise Giardina chose to focus on Emily Brontë? Imagine how the novel might have played out if it centered on Anne instead.

8. *Emily's Ghost* depicts a time when the British government

forbade churches to engage in charitable work. How should churches respond when their calls to mission conflict with government policy?

9. Do you think Emily and Weightman's love could have existed more easily today, considering how drastically women's roles in society have changed?

10. How did Giardina's portrayal of the Brontës compare with your previous understanding?

11. Consider the Brontë sisters' strong familial relationships. In their case and in general, do you think familial love is stronger than romantic love? Explain.

12. It is fascinating to listen in on the sisters' late-night literary discussions. How do you suppose Emily, Charlotte, and Anne both helped and hindered one another creatively?

13. Was Charlotte right to burn Emily's second novel? Is such posthumous censorship justified?

| | |
|---|---|
| Pam Houston | *Sight Hound* |
| Helen Humphreys | *Coventry* |
| | *The Lost Garden* |
| Wayne Johnston | *The Custodian of Paradise* |
| Erica Jong | *Sappho's Leap* |
| Peg Kingman | *Not Yet Drown'd* |
| Nicole Krauss | *The History of Love\** |
| Don Lee | *Country of Origin* |
| Ellen Litman | *The Last Chicken in America* |
| Vyvyane Loh | *Breaking the Tongue* |
| Benjamin Markovits | *A Quiet Adjustment* |
| Joe Meno | *The Great Perhaps* |
| Emily Mitchell | *The Last Summer of the World* |
| Honor Moore | *The Bishop's Daughter* |
| | *The White Blackbird* |
| Donna Morrissey | *Sylvanus Now\** |
| Daniyal Mueenuddin | *In Other Rooms, Other Wonders* |
| Patrick O'Brian | *The Yellow Admiral\** |
| Samantha Peale | *The American Painter Emma Dial* |
| Heidi Pitlor | *The Birthdays* |
| Jean Rhys | *Wide Sargasso Sea* |
| Mary Roach | *Bonk* |
| | *Spook\** |
| | *Stiff* |
| Gay Salisbury and | |
|   Laney Salisbury | *The Cruelest Miles* |
| Susan Fromberg Schaeffer | *The Snow Fox* |
| Laura Schenone | *The Lost Ravioli Recipes of Hoboken* |
| Jessica Shattuck | *The Hazards of Good Breeding* |
| | *Perfect Life* |
| Frances Sherwood | *The Book of Splendor* |
| Joan Silber | *Ideas of Heaven* |
| | *The Size of the World* |
| Dorothy Allred Solomon | *Daughter of the Saints* |
| Mark Strand and | |
|   Eavan Boland | *The Making of a Poem\** |
| Ellen Sussman (editor) | *Bad Girls* |

| | |
|---|---|
| Barry Unsworth | *Land of Marvels* |
| | *Sacred Hunger* |
| Brad Watson | *The Heaven of Mercury** |
| Jenny White | *The Abyssinian Proof* |

*Available only on the Norton Web site: www.wwnorton.com/guides